A CORKSCREW LIFE

A CORKSCREW LIFE

ADVENTURES OF A
TRAVELLING FINANCIER

RICHARD COULSON

iUniverse LLC
Bloomington

A CORK SCREW LIFE
ADVENTURES OF A TRAVELLING FINANCIER

Copyright © 2014 Richard Coulson.

All rights reserved. No part of this book may be used or reproduced by any means, graphic, electronic, or mechanical, including photocopying, recording, taping or by any information storage retrieval system without the written permission of the publisher except in the case of brief quotations embodied in critical articles and reviews.

iUniverse books may be ordered through booksellers or by contacting:

iUniverse LLC
1663 Liberty Drive
Bloomington, IN 47403
www.iuniverse.com
1-800-Authors (1-800-288-4677)

Because of the dynamic nature of the Internet, any web addresses or links contained in this book may have changed since publication and may no longer be valid. The views expressed in this work are solely those of the author and do not necessarily reflect the views of the publisher, and the publisher hereby disclaims any responsibility for them.

Any people depicted in stock imagery provided by Thinkstock are models, and such images are being used for illustrative purposes only. Certain stock imagery © Thinkstock.

ISBN: 978-1-4917-3476-6 (sc)
ISBN: 978-1-4917-3475-9 (e)

Library of Congress Control Number: 2014909120

Printed in the United States of America.

iUniverse rev. date: 05/28/2014

Contents

Preface vii

Chapter 1	Nassau Youth with Abby 1
Chapter 2	Roots into Branches 11
Chapter 3	Military Aberration 23
Chapter 4	Towards a Career 39
Chapter 5	Mexico? A Command Performance 55
Chapter 6	Making Friends in Mexico 81
Chapter 7	My Self-Taught Mexican History 96
Chapter 8	Business Deals, the Mexican Way 106
Chapter 9	Lunch at Sierra Nevada 122
Chapter 10	"Bill": William F. Buckley, Jr., 1924-2008 135
Chapter 11	The Fall of a Super-Star: Norbert A. Schlei, 1930-2003 168
Chapter 12	Renaissance of a Russian Prince: Nikita Lobanov, 1935- 192
Chapter 13	Sailing: Love and Obsession 216
Chapter 14	Transitions: Change in New York 241
Chapter 15	Transitions: Across the Pond to London 246
Chapter 16	Transitions: Return to Nassau 267
Chapter 17	Personalities of Tropic Life 281
Chapter 18	Bahamas Finale 302
Appendix	Sailing with Bill 307

Preface

"The unexamined life is not worth living". Aristotle's famous epigram set me to the task of examining, and that meant writing. How to begin? Photos helped. A glance at a photo can summon up a whole slab of memories, just as when Marcel Proust in *Swann's Way* tasted the famous tea-soaked *madeleine* cake and was transported to the village scenes of his childhood. Two photos have been my *madeleine*, recreating long strands of my life and serving as its bookends.

One of the photos was taken at a lunch in San Miguel de Allende, Mexico in 1996, stored in my computer. The other is a snapshot taken in 1971 near a Bahamas beach that I recently discovered in my late wife's family scrap-book. Only after looking at them time and again was I inspired to write this memoir, the high points of a passage from birth in Nassau to New York to London and back to Nassau, with frequent detours to Mexico—what I have chosen to call *A Corkscrew Life* led by myself as a lawyer, banker, and plain observer.

This is not an inspirational book. There are no clues how to achieve spiritual peace or zen-like Nirvana.

Nor is it a "how-to" book. No seven-point programs are presented to become a successful executive, investor, entrepreneur, husband, father, lover, writer, good neighbor, or plain human being.

The tales of myself and others may suggest a few lessons, but that's not their purpose. Relax: they are for enjoyment, not instruction.

Richard Coulson
Nassau, Bahamas
May, 2014

CHAPTER 1

Nassau Youth with Abby

What set me apart from other kids was not lack of a home but having too many homes. As a child in the midst of my own childhood, I never thought twice about it. Most kids, certainly me, just accept what's put on their plate, however strange the diet may be. It was only much later, with age and hindsight, that I found my early years pretty bizarre.

I was born in Nassau, Bahamas, then a British Colony, on January 8, 1931, at 11:32 a.m. weighing 8 ½ pounds, according to the Baby's Book of Events kept by my mother, listed therein as Abby Stewart Farrington. Abby was 41; I was the last of her six children by some seven years.

In the hand-written Nassau Register of Births for St. Anne's Parish my given name was recorded as Sidney, with father Sidney Farrington, holding profession "com. Agent". My race was stated simply as "E", presumably meaning "European". I was baptized as Richard Sidney, but the "Sidney" was soon dropped.

Yet the first passport that I ever received in my teens was an American one that carried the name Richard Coulson, and the application for it listed my father as Robert E. Coulson of New York City.

I never knew quite what to say when asked where I was "from." My official address for school records, passports, etc. was a street number in New York City, but in fact I spent but a fraction of my time there, until I finally settled into a Wall Street job at age 26. We moved not the way military or diplomatic families do, on to a new post every two or three years. Rather, we moved like migratory birds, following the same cycle every year between the same three nesting places. From age three to ten, my annual travel schedule was roughly as follows, with occasional variations governed by my parents' whims:

Christmas and New Year's—New York City, then a week in upstate Lake Placid.
January 15 to May 1—Nassau, Bahamas
May 1 to June 1—New York City
June 1 to September 15—Marblehead, Massachusetts
September 15 to Christmas—New York City.

How on earth was this accomplished? Why? Who made the decisions? Whose lives were torn apart and made to adjust to these seasonal rhythms? For a kid, it was no problem, a great lark, but what about for the grown-ups around me? It was only much later that I wondered.

The key to the riddle was found in the classic triangle. My mother Abby managed to keep two vigorous, strong-minded men jumping through her hoops without ever coming to blows: the bluff, outspoken, mustachioed British subject Sidney Farrington, and the bluff, outspoken, mustachioed American citizen Robert Coulson, each drawn to her as a moth to a flame, and each treating me as a son.

I later became fascinated with Abby's life. Much of her tale occurred before my birth or in my early years when I was too young or incurious to observe and query human nature. What I know of those periods depends on a few historical records and what I have been told by others.

Abby was born in 1889 in the classic mid-American town of Norwalk, Ohio, to a father she told me was a sweet but ineffective gentleman of the local Stewart family and a mother she described, when pressed, as a termagant, from the prominent Carey clan. A photograph of mother and daughter shows them as a striking lady and youth wearing the elaborate hats and gowns of that era. Apparently the Stewart household, which included two sisters, Olive and Myrna, and brother Bud, enjoyed solid middle-class comfort and respectability with no trappings of ostentatious wealth, although Abby's paternal grandfather, Gideon Taber Stewart, had earned renown as a leader of the national Prohibitionist Party. From my one trip to Norwalk probably about age six, I only have dim memories of a substantial white house with ginger-bread trimmings on an elm-shaded street, and a spacious rear garden where we played with rabbits. I was impressed mainly by passenger trolleys out front whose rails ran as far as Cleveland and Sandusky!

In this presumably peaceful milieu, Abby at about age 18 married fellow Ohioan William Jenkins, and within five years bore him the first three of her six children, my half-siblings Stewart, Patricia, and Charles. I believe they lived in Cleveland, but clearly something about life as a mid-western housewife did not suit Abby: she needed wider horizons. In the first of the cataclysmic changes in her life, she decamped to the bright lights and action of New York City about the time of World War I, doubtless scandalizing the stolid Ohio society of the day. Apparently she tried to take the children with her, but her lawyer husband brought action winning custody.

I know little about her single life in New York. I understand she may have performed on the stage. She must have been a knock-out with a vivacious personality, but all the time retaining the clean-cut image of her mid-western upbringing. During the War or shortly thereafter she met the handsome, strong (he had rowed on his college crew), and serious-minded Robert Earle Coulson, some five years older. Born in 1884 in a small town near Buffalo, New York, to parents he rarely mentioned, by dint of intelligence, hard work and forceful personality, he won scholarships to Princeton and then to Cornell Law School.

He began his legal career, but military service intervened, and he started training as an artillery officer at the Army camp in Plattsburgh, New York. He must have shown marked aptitude for the military life, as he was one of the few reserve officers promoted to the rank of lieutenant-colonel. To his life-long regret, he was never sent with the American Expeditionary Force to fight in France; his superiors put a higher value on his skill at training junior officers. But throughout his subsequent career his associates always called him "The Colonel", and he bore the commanding personality to justify the title. Even his family often used the military honorific.

After the War, he came to the attention of the higher levels of the New York legal and political establishments. A new law firm was founded in Wall Street, named Whitman, Ransom, Coulson & Goetz, known in the profession as "Governor, Judge, Colonel & Gets", since senior partner Charles Whitman was a former New York State governor, William Ransom was a retired New York judge, and Mr. Goetz collected the fees. The connections surely helped, as the firm thrived from early days, with the Colonel carrying much of the work load. Adding to the burden of his legal ambitions was his courtship of Abby, who led him a lively chase. After her death, I found a neatly tied packet of his letters to her. They painted a picture of a busy man, desperately in love, pleading with a mercurial lady to choose him and him alone. His determination succeeded, and they married, probably in 1920, as their first child, Anne, was born in 1921 followed by son Robert in 1924. The new family settled into a standard young-professional's existence in suburban Pelham, doubtless with the Colonel commuting daily to his office in Manhattan leaving Abby to supervise her second set of children.

It was too good—or too routine—to last. Sometime in the 1920s, the family met Charlie Munson, the extrovert businessman who had inherited the Munson Shipping Lines. Weekly passenger service between New York and Nassau was provided by the venerable vessel *Munargo,* which became the butt of many sun-lovers' jokes who traveled her storm-tossed voyages as the only way to reach the winter resort. Charlie and his ebullient wife Cora acquired a home in Nassau and became the community's social lions. They invited the Colonel and Abby and introduced them to everyone worth knowing, a tight-knit group of Americans, Brits, and white Bahamians who dominated local society long before the days of huge cruise ships, public casinos, and mass tourism.

The Coulsons began to make annual winter trips, and Abby fell under the seductive spell of semi-tropical Nassau, with its narrow streets smelling of jasmine, its picnics on unspoiled beaches, its elegant dinner parties with languid, amusing guests—some rich, others broke but charming. Pretty soon Abby decided that frigid winters around New York were not her style, and she began to spend the whole season in Nassau, with the Colonel making occasional visits when he could escape from the intensity of his growing Wall Street practice, not a simple process in the era before air travel.

As often happens, falling in love with a place leads to falling in love with a person, and Abby fell for Sidney Cuthbert Farrington. A never-married man's man with a booming voice, Sidney occupied as large a place in the small world of Nassau as the Colonel did in the wider scope of New York. Part of a family who generations earlier had emigrated from England, Sidney had various business and property investments and became the general manager of Pan American Airways in Nassau, one of its earliest international destinations. His brains and rectitude led to a position as chairman of the Colony's "ExCo", or executive council, the non-elective body who actually ran the local government. After the Duke of Windsor, the former King Edward VIII, became governor general in 1940, he privately called Sidney the only Bahamian leader he could fully trust.

Sidney and the Colonel, so similar in many ways, came to know all about each other. Abby did not believe in concealment of the obvious. It could have come as no surprise when she divorced the Colonel, probably in 1928, since it's recorded that she married Sidney in 1929, and I was born in early 1931. But her peregrinations in the years just before and after my birth remain mystifying.

A hint is given in a faded newspaper clipping of the *New York Herald Tribune* dated January 11, 1931, by which Mr. and Mrs. Sidney Farrington announce my birth "at their winter home" in Nassau. The article further states that Mrs. Farrington "is an American who maintains a home on East Eighty-Sixth Street, New York, and at Marblehead Neck, Mass." This must have brought a smile to her close friends, who surely knew that those American homes were in fact maintained by the Colonel, where she had lived with him during their marriage, and were now available to Abby during her northern sojourns. Her movements are confirmed by her own entries in the Baby's Book, which reports that she took me to New York in May 1931 (aged four months) and on to New England in June, and I have photographs showing me lolling on the Marblehead lawn at that age.

Those movements meant nothing to infant me. But what could have been the emotions of Abby? What were her intentions? A still beautiful 41-year-old lady, how did she foresee fitting both the Colonel and Sidney into her life? Did she expect irreconcilable conflict, and a need to choose, or was she sublimely confident that she could keep both of these vigorous men close to her heart? And simultaneously maintain the love of her children? The record of subsequent years would, amazingly, confirm her confidence. While I was still too young to know what was happening, in 1933 she obtained a divorce from Sidney (uncontested) and in 1934 re-married the Colonel, who adopted me and had my name changed to Richard Coulson, all as approved by the Supreme Court of Ohio.

Yet Nassau and Sidney remained strong strands in the fabric of her existence, as she firmly refused to winter in northern climes. Until age ten, I led the unusual tri-partite life described earlier. Winter months in Nassau were spent first in rented premises, then in a modest but elegant house named The Folly built on a waterfront lot and certainly financed by the Colonel; a bit of spring and fall in New York City, and summers in Marblehead. My first schooling was instruction by two spinster ladies, Sidney's unbending aunts, in a small stone structure down the hill from their residence, once slave quarters I was told. All I remember from the Misses Farrington Day School was learning how to sing "Onward Christian Soldiers" and how to write with chalk on hand-held slate tablets, the laptops of that day. The rest of my early education comprised private instruction by an Anglican priest, various oh-so-English schools in Nassau, and an intense Germanic tutor during my passages through New York. Somehow, I picked up enough to do well at my first structured training, a boarding school in Aiken, South Carolina, that I entered at age ten in September 1941.

In these so-called formative years, long before I knew anything of sex or the passions and jealousies it generates, in Nassau I was of course exposed to the ambiguities of Abby's romantic life, or lives. Sidney was a frequent visitor, coming down to The Folly from the breezy hill-top house where I was born, taking me on excursions in an extravagant vehicle he called the Blunderbus, or flights to the Out Islands in an early amphibian aircraft, and later sitting with Abby on the terrace through long evenings of quiet talk. Then the Colonel would arrive for a couple of weeks, and Sidney would disappear, only to return when the Colonel went back to New York. All I knew was that the Colonel and Abby slept in a big bed in the master bedroom, while Sidney never spent the night. Any implications escaped me. Both men appeared to accept their roles.

I learned subsequently that a few Bahamians, mainly female relatives of Sidney, regarded Abby as a scandalous man-eater. But neither then nor in all my later years in Nassau did I ever hear a direct word of disparagement. Uniformly, they said "what a wonderful woman" or "a real lady" or "a classic of refinement". She opened a dress-shop in downtown Nassau called Stewart's, becoming one of the "Bay Street Boys" with a successful business on the eponymous street, selling to the ultra-chic Duchess of Windsor and her fashion followers. She was no intellectual, but I often watched her at her home desk meticulously filling huge ledgers with accounting figures. I still meet elderly ladies who tell me how they enjoyed working at her shop.

When my college pals visited on holidays, they were captivated by her. One of them with a musical bent spent hours trying to teach her the piano, endlessly playing and singing a current favorite, "Mean to Me", as inspiration. Her closest friend and supporter was a rigidly precise lady named Kate Curry, who never appeared outdoors, except to swim or garden, without elbow-length white gloves and a wide-brimmed hat. Long-time chairman of the Nassau branch of the Imperial Order of the Daughters of the Empire (something like the American D.A.R.), her cut-diamond voice could slice to ribbons anyone who fell short of her high standards of ethics and etiquette.

Yet she remained an intimate friend of Abby all during the hectic years when she divorced the Colonel, married Sidney, bore me, divorced him and re-married the Colonel. As I grew older, I was privileged to sit in on their long discussions about Nassau, Kate's tight critiques alternating with Abby's more tolerant views. After Abby once had the Duke and Duchess of Windsor (loathed by the English community) to dinner at The Folly, Kate complained, "Abby, how could you invite those *dreadful* people. I cannot forgive you . . . but I suppose we shall remain friends." And they did.

What of Abby as a mother? She certainly did not fit any of the modern clichés of the breast-feeding, diaper-changing, homework-helping soccer mom. She was only found in the kitchen *in extremis*, and although she must have once changed a diaper, I can hardly imagine it. Throughout my childhood, always one or two servants were on hand to handle these chores. Doubtless Abby loved her children, but she loved them much more when they outgrew infancy and were able to carry on rational conversation. Until age six or seven, my closest companion for succor and comfort was not Abby but our resident nanny, Mary Zeh, a buxom German lady whom we called "Ma."

By current child-rearing standards, this history sounds dreadful. But as I became a teen-ager, I slowly began to appreciate Abby's qualities. She never became one of those dominant matriarchs who, in the absence of strong fathers, are said to instill ambition and shape the lives of sons like Winston Churchill, Franklin D. Roosevelt, and Bill Clinton. That was not her style. But I came to admire her relaxed, unperturbed approach to life, with impeccable manners and a sly sense of humor and never a raised voice to anyone, including Sidney and the Colonel. Clearly agnostic, her regime (to my later regret) included no words of Christian instruction. But she could quietly impose a strict code of good manners and honorable conduct, once requiring me to return to a barber to leave a forgotten tip.

Above all, I marveled how she made friendships that prevailed long after her glamorous years. The Anglican pastor in Nassau, tedious British expatriate couples, young RAF officers training in Nassau, the distraught spouse of a philandering husband, the ambitious Bahamian realtor Harold Christie lamenting how to find a wife, three garrulous Boston widowers who enjoyed a woman's touch and a good martini, a series of black factotums who kept The Folly running—all became her loyal acolytes.

Of course, her code gave me not the slightest qualms about the rigid racial segregation that prevailed in Nassau until the 1960s. I'm sure I would not have learned differently with any other white mother of that era. While Abby and Sidney and all their friends treated every black person with innate civility (Nassau had no lynchings, KKK burning crosses, or Scottsboro Boy trials), it was unthinkable that social life would be shared with blacks except at a few official receptions. That was simply the order of the day.

My siblings gave no signs of suffering from Abby's lack of attention as she wandered—a "bolter" as she would have been called in England. The three Jenkins children, much older than I, had active lives and are long deceased, as is my elder sister Anne Coulson. I exchange frequent chats with Robert Coulson, my closest sibling by six years who is pleasantly retired from a career running the American Arbitration Association. Despite our friendship, Bob has always been somewhat reticent about his personal feelings on family affairs. He may have retained a degree of coolness towards Abby and her life-style.

As I was Sidney's child and later adopted by the Colonel, I have no mystic blood feelings about my parenthood. I certainly spent more time with the Colonel and came to know his world much better than Sidney's, as I too lived in New York and became a Wall Street lawyer. They were both admirable men, and I am glad to have been raised by both of them.

And I certainly carry the blood of the amazing Abby. Long after I grew out of childhood and detached myself from its early routines, she continued her triangular existence. During my seven years at boarding schools, four at Yale College, two in the US Army, and three at Yale Law School, followed by an early legal career in New York, with only occasional Nassau holidays, she remained indissolubly wedded to the Colonel, but passed every winter at The Folly, where Sidney continued to visit until his death in 1954. She became an immaculately dressed *grande dame* of Nassau society, respected by all, whose calm dignity made it almost impossible to imagine her passionate, changeable years in the 1920s and 1930s. She never abandoned her yearly schedule of Nassau-New York-Marblehead until prevented by final illness a year before her death in 1970.

I cannot pretend to fathom her emotions during that turbulent time of dual loves so long ago, or her deepest memories about Sidney and the Colonel as her life quietly wound down. Her angular script in the Baby's Book tells me nothing but the dry facts. I never expected her to lay bare her life to me, and she never did. Every remarkable lady should remain an enigma.

CHAPTER 2

Roots into Branches

The exotic roots of my childhood must have left some mark on me. On the one hand, I have always made my closest friends and found my happiest surroundings among the different, the off-beat, the eccentric; on the other hand, I have grasped for security, been a "joiner", never ready to take the plunge into a radically different life.

Aiken Prep

I felt this conflict in the first serious school I attended. When I reached age ten, my parents decided that the casual scholastic offerings in Nassau, leavened with the occasional New York tutor, did not set the foundation for a well rounded future. A boarding school was the only answer, and they entered me in Aiken Preparatory School, in Aiken, South Carolina. APS took about 50 boys through the eighth grade before sending them off at age 13 or 14 to one of the phalanx of prep schools supporting the American establishment, from St. Paul's in New Hampshire to Lawrenceville in New Jersey.

Whatever may have been the standard junior high school experience, APS was far from it. Academic standards were high—I have never forgotten lessons of grammar and syntax from a temperamental Englishman who flung black-board erasers at dozy students, but always with a laugh. Arithmetic and algebra were effectively drilled; French and Latin were initiated; I even mastered the rudiments of mechanical drawing. The underlying style was firmly American upper-class. APS had been founded in 1916 by Mrs. Thomas Hitchcock, a member of the New York aristocracy who played polo and raised horses on Long Island. She and her friends found the mild climate and red clay of Aiken the preferred place to carry on their equestrian pursuits in winter and spring and needed a school to educate their young; they even founded a local girls' school with indicative name "Fermata", whose inmates were strictly shielded from us allegedly priapic APS males

From its beginnings APS, and the town of Aiken itself, were dominated by the wealthy northerners who enjoyed the horsey life. Right through my era in the 1940s, the school roster, and the surrounding homes, were filled with Jockey Club names like Hitchcock, Bostwick, Whitney, von Stade, Drexel, Balding, Knox, and Laughlin; the Aiken Mile Track was famed for its thoroughbred racing (I remember admiring the Triple Crown winner Whirlaway); and the Hitchcock Woods for trail riding and gymkhanas. Every APS boy was encouraged to join the equine atmosphere; a mount was provided for any of us who signed up for the bi-weekly riding lessons. I joined, and found myself loathing every session. I was permanently assigned a disagreeable beast who bit, shied, kicked, and halted abruptly and immovably, leaving me the target of our riding master's choleric temper. He was a retired army cavalry officer who, by local legend, had been blown up in the Great War and carried a steel plate in his skull that made him irascible in damp weather, which seemed most of the time.

After one term, I gave up, and did not mount another horse for 15 years, and then with the greatest caution. But I plunged into the sport of bike-polo, played flat-out on hardened clay, with official helmets, cut-down mallets, a real willow ball and contempt for the civilized rules of the real game. Riding-off and flagrant crossing and hooking were accepted tactics, resulting in mangled frames, ripped spokes and bloody shins as we collided, pedaling furiously at maybe ten mph. I became an expert bicycle mechanic, repairing my battered steed after every game.

Imported from English schools, the dress code at APS was rigid, exceptional in America even then, and unthinkable now. For our morning classes through lunch, we wore grey flannel shorts, shirt and tie, and a grey blazer with yellow piping and the school crest on the breast pocket. Above the pocket were sewn symbols of athletic prowess, each colored ribbon denoting expertise in one of the 15 official sports. Gifted jocks proudly displayed three or four rows of "colors", like our admirals and generals bearing decorations to shoulder level. Less adept lads such as myself struggled to amass even one row.

Right after lunch, we changed into sports clothes for afternoon athletics, and then at five o'clock a rush into showers and the ordeal of the evening uniform, required for another class, dinner and study hall. This included dark blue trousers and jacket, but the major snag was shirts with detachable stiff collars, affixed by inserting easy-to-drop studs fore and aft through recalcitrant button holes. Perhaps we at APS were the only boys in war-time America struggling to attach stiff collars for dinner.

`We were a pretty unusual group. We had a heavy dose of scions of leading northeast establishment families, mixed with boys from wealthy parents in the southland. In those war-time years, another group, known as "the silk-stocking refugees," gave the school an international flavor. Long before the United States entered the War in December 1941—we learned of Pearl Harbor from the scratchy common-room radio—the convulsions in Europe had dislodged not only suffering masses but also aristocratic families who refused to join the Nazi regime, forcing them to flee to Britain and even further. Their long-time social contacts in America recommended APS as the best school for lads suddenly up-rooted from traditional surroundings.

So I had as classmates Prince Ludo Rospigliosi of Italy, Count Juan de Beistegui from France, England's David Viscount Bayham, the Ramos brothers, Argentines but brought up internationally, and Jaime Ortiz y Patiño, heir to Bolivian tin mines but based in Paris and Geneva. None of these boys flaunted their titles or family position, but foreign languages were heard, and we were exposed to memories of homes far different from ours.

How did I fit into this peculiar melting-pot, who had seen nothing of the world except The Bahamas and fragments of the American east coast? Although I was undistinguished at sports, the usual path to schoolboy leadership, by acting out my innate needs for position, for stability, I gained enough popularity to achieve what passed for prominence. In my final year I was chosen as one of the school's three Monitors, entitled to wear a yellow arm-band and chivvy boys into line. I became the president of the *Semper Viridis* ("always flourishing") Club, an odd mixture of student council and snobbish coterie. We had informal subpoena power to summon troublesome students for a tongue-lashing and, in rare cases, for a gentle beating on naked buttocks, for any boy we decided was a serious "grub", APS' strongest term of opprobrium. I doubt we caused any long-lasting damage, but I look back in shame at how close we became to a little bunch of fascists claiming to know it all at age 12.

My opposite side, my search for the off-beat, was reflected in my choice of friends. The closest one, and the only one with whom I speak to the present day, was an elegant loner, a class ahead, named Mark Rudkin, respected but largely ignored. Mark was the youngest son of the family who created the famous Pepperidge Farm food brand but was already leaning toward the arts. My other pal was the Bolivian Jimmy Ortiz, with whom I had a love-hate relationship. Jimmy was a delightful buck-toothed reprobate who charmed with unending jokes and adventures. But he was an insurrectionist, an Aiken "grub" of the worst order, and I was the guy who was supposed to enforce

APS discipline and traditions. Inevitably we clashed and came to the time-honored solution: a scheduled duel (without weapons) in the dirt behind the school auditorium. We struggled mightily, but neither of us was strong or skillful enough at fisticuffs or wrestling to claim victory. We maintained an uneasy truce until the year ended and then went our separate ways. I wish I had kept in touch: I now see videos of Jimmy, plump and ultra-prosperous, as the founder of Valderrama, the best golf course in Spain, or speaking from Geneva as president of the World Bridge Federation, telling how bridge can contribute to peace. A "grub" no longer.

Pepperidge Farm

Mark Rudkin, by contrast, stayed in my life, and led to the opening of my eyes when I made the first of many visits to his Connecticut home at age twelve. It was the summer of 1943, still wartime with gas rationing that kept automobiles on a tight rein, but the darkest days were over, and on every radio we heard the joyous All-American songs from the Broadway hit *Oklahoma!* When I was driven through the Fairfield woods up the hill where stood the iconic Pepperidge tree, I was dazzled by an English-style country estate of 280 acres whose like I had only seen in *Encyclopedia Britannica* photos. In one direction lay a complex of stables, paddocks, and barns full of farm equipment; in the other, a graveled driveway led past immaculate lawns to the main house, a majestic Tudor with thick stone walls, heavy slate roof, and leaded windows. All this, I learned later, was not from the distant past, but was created in the 1920s and was now maintained thanks to that mundane comestible, bread.

Mark's parents accepted my callow self as an adult, with no pause in their wide-ranging exchanges well over my head. Tall, urbane Henry, a virtual clone of actor Walter Pidgeon complete to bushy eyebrows, usually seen wearing waistcoat with gold watch-chain, spoke sonorously through clouds of cigar smoke about new artists, galleries, auctions, plays, symphonies, singers, dancers—a world of culture totally foreign to me. His wife, the former Peg Fogarty, pert and red-haired, sat at the other end of the huge couch with feet tucked up and briskly interrupted his soliloquies with her own sharp observations, or digressed to pressing business matters. Mark frequently chimed in, while I, in those first meetings, sat silent and abashed.

In the Rudkin home, the arts were not mere idle chatter. The house itself was a grand piece of architecture and design, with flagstone or parquet flooring, beamed ceilings, *boiserie* paneling, heavy English or delicate French antiques, stained glass in the leaded windows, a barrel-vaulted library. Every table held art books—which were actually read. High fidelity speakers poured out gems of classical music—which were actually heard. I felt in a new world, far from the comfortable bourgeois style of my own parents, literate, intelligent people, but who never once took me to an art museum, a concert, or an opera and never spent a penny on a piece of fine art. With the Rudkins I did not became a true aesthete, or even a trained connoisseur, but at least the veil of ignorance began to be lifted.

I gradually learned that their patronage of the arts, though completely sincere, was based on the hard bed-rock of business success. The magnificent estate was built in the euphoria of the Roaring Twenties, when Henry thrived as a stock-broker with plenty of time for polo, and came to completion just as the Crash was demolishing Wall Street and just as Henry fell off his polo pony into a long period of immobility. With a wife and three sons to support, his hold on Pepperidge Farm with its high running costs may have become tenuous, perhaps touch-and-go. The accepted lore is that energetic Peg, the little Irish secretary whom he had married for love and not for fashion, began baking home-made bread for their asthmatic, allergic youngest son Mark. True, but the special bread with its "natural" ingredients also became the financial mainstay for the Rudkin family. As its popularity grew, Peg's baking moved out of the kitchen down into the remodeled stables (polo ponies exiled) and, by the time I arrived, into an industrial-size bakery in South Norwalk, much expanded after wartime food rationing ended.

With rigid quality control and astute marketing, Pepperidge Farm bread, even with its higher price tag, became a standard in health and taste-conscious homes, followed by cookies, pastries and other spin-offs, until eventually the business was sold to Campbell Soup for $28 million in 1961, with Peg joining the Campbell Board and running a multi-plant operation until one year before her death in 1967, a true American success story—and created by a *woman*, astounding in those all-male days.

I often wondered about any tension in the marriage, as Henry's declining brokerage business was supplanted by the bakery that clearly was Peg's creation. Perhaps, but I never saw any sign of it. Henry retired from Wall Street and supported Peg full-time by becoming chairman of Pepperidge Farm, Inc. They earnestly discussed business problems together, and once I heard that the only solution was "Call Ben!" Three hours later a black limo crunched up to the front door, depositing a small man in black suit and homburg, the renowned Ben Sonnenberg, who had escaped from Russian obscurity to become New York's publicist *extraordinaire*, using his wits, chutzpah and imagination to create the modern business of corporate public relations. He handled nothing so crass as advertising, but was a genius at getting the human-interest story of the Rudkins and Pepperidge into the *Reader's Digest, The New Yorker,* and *Time,* becoming the family *consigliere* and observing a spike in bread sales after each publication. With earnings from clients like CBS, Sam Goldwyn and Pan American Airways, Ben built and furnished a four-story townhouse in Gramercy Park that became home to New York's best private collection of fine art and furniture, where the city's elite were often entertained. In Ben's absence one day, Mark gave me a guided tour, pointing out the superb items to my uneducated eyes. I later felt that Mark's life-long devotion to the arts was generated by what he saw in those gilded rooms at 19 Gramercy Park South.

I met Mark's two older brothers, Hank and Bill, tall, hearty guys whose main pursuits appeared to be golf, sports cars, skiing, shooting, and yacht-racing, They were always affable to Mark, but clearly found him "different", a fish swimming in his own waters. When we finished Aiken in 1944, Mark and I moved on to Phillips Academy in Andover, Massachusetts. The Colonel had already firmly entered me for the Episcopalian bastion St. Paul's School, but on a recruiting trip to APS Andover's avuncular headmaster Dr. Claude Moore Fuess lured me in that direction. The Colonel was outraged by my independence. Strange, since St. Paul's was not his alma mater, religion meant nothing to him, and he was remote from the network of old-line eastern names who dominated its alumni.

Despite his many virtues, the Colonel was a social climber. Rising from obscurity in western New York to New York City prominence, he wanted his son taken into the school with the highest social cachet. He was the ultimate club-man, joining every one he could find: the proper Union Club and Down Town Association in New York; San Francisco's Pacific Union Club; both yacht clubs in Marblehead, and the same in Nassau together with the ultra snooty Porcupine Club, open only to winter visitors. He even managed to lever the family into listing in that peculiar annual publication of "acceptable society" *The Social Register*, the eastern establishment's feeble effort to emulate England's *Debrett's Peerage*—without a peerage.

Andover and Yale

Andover was a radical change from Aiken, a jump from fifty cosseted lads to 750 students from a cross-section of America and a few foreign countries. It was the closest thing to a democratic meritocracy where you were expected to find your own way and fight for your own rights. My first two years were miserable as I did not connect to any of the dominant student cliques; in the last two years I finally triumphed with literary creations and social efforts. Mark had his own life centered around the talented couple Pat and June Morgan running the school's superb Addison Gallery of American Art, and our meetings became rare, although always friendly. We gradually realized that one gulf separated us: he was, quietly and discreetly, gay (although that word was still unknown), and I was not, always seeking to break the barriers between Andover and the nearby girls' school, Abbott, and sometimes succeeding. Close as we were, we inevitably began to move in different circles.

Our friendship through Yale College continued in the same vein—warm meetings while following divergent paths. Andover's diversity showed in the three very different types who became my friends there and my room-mates through four years in New Haven: Linc, the son of a brilliant, garrulous New York ad-man who retired early to quiet Connecticut, a drink often in hand, supported by the firm Minnesota heiress he had married; Mose, whose father, blessed with all the charm of southern salesmanship, owned the General Motors dealership in Fort Smith, Arkansas; and Mac with a rigid hard-driving Dad from Dubuque, Iowa, who owned the mid-west's leading plumbing distributor. Through many laughs and noisy disputes, we somehow survived together, right into occasional post-grad reunions. All three of them were polite to Mark when he occasionally dropped in, but never understood him—chalk and cheese.

But it was with Mark that I chose to make a foreign trip. After our sophomore year, we went to Mexico City, with the excuse of taking a summer course in Spanish. When morning classes finished, we often went our separate ways. I joined a tennis club with congenial Mexican opponents, and spent many hours trying to dislodge a vacationing American college girl from her too-protective mother. Mark found a voice teacher for training to become an operatic baritone, an ambition never fulfilled; or sought meetings with Leonora Carrington, the surrealist painter who had rebelled against her aristocratic English background and escaped to Mexico. At night, we reunited and shared irreverent notes on the day's adventures, finishing our summer with an exhausting bus ride to Acapulco that Mark only survived with queasy stoicism.

The rest of my Yale career reflected the solid, safe, side of my character: studying hard enough to be on the Dean's List but not Phi Beta Kappa material, joining the right clubs, becoming an editor of the *Yale Daily News*, and getting tapped for Scroll & Key, one of the six senior societies, institutions peculiar to Yale. Since each one elected only 15 members, a total of 90 from a class of about one thousand, even in those pre-liberal days they were accused of white male elitism. But they have prevailed, and as I read every year's list of new members of Keys that now includes both sexes of all ethnic backgrounds, I am astonished at their accomplishments. Even before graduating, they have produced plays and films, written concertos, sold their paintings, organized political pressure groups. If that is elitism, it is founded on talent, not inheritance.

I graduated in 1952 with an ROTC second lieutenant's commission that took me straight into the Army. Before I went off to Camp Drum in upstate New York, I made a final visit to Pepperidge Farm, which had become a second home to me, captivated by the range of books in the quiet library with mullioned windows looking out on the formal rose garden. Mark had left me alone to walk in that garden with a vivid lady he had met in New York, Eszter Haraszty, a refugee from Hungary. She was one of those exiles who brought home to me the innocent, sheltered life led by a young Ivy Leaguer. Only ten years older, she had escaped the Nazi and Soviet regimes, losing many of her relatives and most of her inheritance, before arriving in New York to start a career as a successful textile designer. She had no restraints about plunging into intimacy.

"You love Mark, don't you?" she asked abruptly.

Not comfortable with that word, I prevaricated lamely, "Well . . ."

She seized my arm, and I still recall her penetrating look as we stopped our stroll by the box hedge, quiet but for bees buzzing in the summer sun.

"Don't worry," she said. "I love him too. He is a wonderful man. But we must know he is a homosexual. And you are not. Nor am I. We take him for what he is, no? And of course he will leave for Europe."

"Yes, he has spoken about it."

"He must," she insisted. "America is not right for him. You have too many prejudices, still. He would suffer here. In Paris he can be himself. You will soon say goodbye to him."

I could only agree with her. In those days, even sophisticated New York was not an open city for gays the way it has since become. And particularly not for Mark, with a father steeped in tradition despite his cultural interests, a mother devoted to business, and two older brothers continually displaying their *machismo*. The looming influence of Pepperidge Farm might have crushed him. He had to make a life for himself elsewhere. A few months later, he told me was planning his move to France, and soon he had left, first as a dancer with Martha Graham's traveling company, then settling in as a permanent resident.

During sixty years of almost annual visits to Paris, I have enjoyed my brief moments with him, finding no constraints despite his life veering so sharply from the direction of my own. He first leased an exquisite, multi-windowed apartment in a Paris house once occupied by Nancy Mitford and began to paint, achieving, to my inexpert eye, some of the edgy angularity of Picasso's blue period. But he was not so much a creator as a patron of the arts, meeting all the players, arranging exhibitions of new work, collecting judiciously, writing critiques, befriending classical and jazz musicians. He then bought and renovated a country house about 20 miles from Paris, where he could periodically become a recluse, designing a wild garden and sharing the seclusion for many years with his psychiatrist. With funds inherited from the sale of the Pepperidge Farm business, he created the John Mark Rudkin Charitable Foundation and began a long program of carefully chosen endowments in France and America, not least to the art galleries of Andover and Yale.

He eventually found his true *métier* in landscape architecture, perhaps inspired by his early years among the effulgent blooms of Pepperidge Farm. The French Minister of Culture Jack Lang chose him to re-design the gardens of the historic Palais Royal in the heart of Paris, which naturally led to many other commissions such as the grounds of the Monet Museum in Giverney down the Seine. In 2007 he was elected a *chevalier* of the *Legion d'Honneur*, France's recognition of achievement rarely given to a foreign citizen.

A few years ago in his long-time rural retreat in St. Denis-le Mesnil my daughter and I enjoyed a splendid dinner with Mark served by his Oriental houseman, surrounded by his eclectic, unpredictable art collection and scenting the flowers from his barely tamed garden. We had both moved far from our first meeting over the school food banged down in front of us at Aiken Prep, and I hoped it would not be our last dinner together.'

Chapter 3

Military Aberration

Yes, "aberration", because unless we choose a military career, service as a soldier is inevitably a radical detour from our normal path. It can be a tragic detour, leading to death, but it can also be a positive detour, with challenges and personalities rare in civilian life. For me, it was just that, a learning experience, paid for by Uncle Sam, that wrenched me into new awareness.

There was probably no more unlikely candidate for an Army officer than myself—perennially second-rate at running and body-building, often enjoying books more than personal confrontation, preferring a quiet dinner with a girl to a noisy booze-up with a gang of pals, totally ignorant of the "common man" American and his pursuits. I nevertheless donned the uniform without a qualm and found that I enjoyed the military life and, strangely, was pretty good at it. Like most young men in the 1950s, I was not burdened with the anti-militaristic paranoia among colleges that started with the Vietnam War and branded any soldier as little better than a bloodthirsty baby-killer. Most of us had fathers, uncles or older brothers who had served without complaint in World War II, perhaps the last truly "just" war, and we accepted as a patriotic duty that we would serve if called.

When I entered Yale in the fall of 1948, America was at peace and no major conflict appeared on the immediate horizon, despite the ever-present threat from the Soviet Union. I barely thought about war, while the Colonel, as he often did, took a longer view and urged that I enroll in ROTC, the Reserve Officers' Training Corps program that would provide exemption from any draft. I was not enthusiastic, since four years devoted to military studies would reduce the credit hours that I could devote to my chosen field of history and the liberal arts. But the Colonel's forceful views prevailed:

"Richard, the tensions are building up. Within a few years we are certain to be fighting somebody, somewhere. It's a damn sight better to go to war as a second lieutenant than a buck private."

The first two years of courses in so-called military science were soporific. We studied none of history's famous battles, Napoleon's strategies, or the German blitzkrieg; instead, our hours were filled with yawn-filling studies of mess administration and pay-roll procedures. The Pentagon regarded ROTC as a career-killing back-water and assigned as our teachers amiable officers, beyond promotion potential, who demanded little while facing retirement. Any martial spirit was limited to one afternoon per week of close-order drill.

Then, as the Colonel had predicted, we were suddenly at war as North Korea invaded the South in June 1950 and President Truman led an uncompromising United Nations resolution against aggression, with America to carry the main military burden. Abruptly, half-equipped peace-time Army divisions were thrown into the fray against the North Koreans and were often found wanting. When we returned to Yale in September, we found ROTC being taught with a new sense of urgency. We had visiting lectures from officers who had served in the Pusan Perimeter and could tell us of the bitter fighting. At last we began to study the principles of gunnery and operations of a survey team and a fire direction center. For the first time, I learned how a logarithm could have practical use, and the difference between a sine and a cosine. We were even taken to see and to touch, though not yet to fire, a 105 mm. howitzer, the mainstay of the Artillery Corps.

In the summer after junior year we had our first touch of Army life, as we were sent for six weeks to North Carolina's vast Fort Bragg, where we lived in the same wooden barracks and ate in the same mess halls as the GI's of World War II, wearing the same shapeless olive-drab fatigues and steel helmets and carrying the same M1A1 carbines (unloaded). We were not subject to the harsh discipline of basic training or Boot Camp; after all, we were not dumb recruits but cadets, who would one day be "officers and gentlemen" and entitled to some deference. Nevertheless, we had to rise with reveille at 4:45 a.m.; grind through morning calisthenics; run, run, run sweating miles through the pine woods; wrestle howitzers and spools of wire through choking clouds of the red dust that rose from every road; learn army-style rifle shooting and pull targets on the firing line; take turns at KP slopping out fetid garbage bins behind the mess hall—even spend a day with the paratroopers hearing the order "give me twenty" (push-ups) every ten minutes. We felt lean, mean and tough before returning to civilian life and a final year at Yale.

After graduation the following June, I pinned on my gold bars and reported to Camp Drum in my crisp new khaki uniform, to find—anti-climax. We were members of a Regimental Combat Team (RCT), but nobody at Drum seemed to have received orders about how I and other brand-new officers were to be put to work. After morning roll-call, we were free to practice shots on the billiard-table in the day-room, varied with occasional sallies to the motor pool to find an amiable sergeant to drive us around the base and tell us how the Army really worked.

"Listen, lieutenant, just sit back and enjoy it," was the usual advice from non-coms several years older than us. "Don't volunteer for nothing."

This serenity lasted about a month, when someone at the Pentagon decided that the RCT should become a guinea pig for a smorgasbord of varied training programs. Abruptly, we were ordered to set up a basic training course and lead a bunch of raw inductees through its ingenious obstacles, a routine that, naturally, we had to lead and that I barely survived. A few days after New Year's, when the area known as the Ice Box of the East held Camp Drum in sub-zero temperatures blanketed in snow, a lean major from the Finnish Army arrived to turn us into ski troops. Our supply rooms were suddenly stocked with cross-country skis, arctic tents, hooded white smocks, fur-lined gloves. The major taught us how to glide smoothly over frozen fields, make shelter from pine-bough lean-tos, and survive frigid nights with a tiny paraffin stove, and even, very carefully, piss on a rifle bolt to unfreeze the action. I was enjoying this Outdoor Life adventure, when I was abruptly called in, given ten days' leave and told to report to Fort Sill, Oklahoma—the end of my career as ski trooper.

Fort Sill

All artillery officers were sent to Fort Sill for four months at the Artillery School, the famed "Center of Fire". There, the earlier frivolities were left behind, and I found a highly professional operation with the end purpose of shooting large caliber guns to kill and destroy. I shared a barracks tent with two lieutenants from the Marine Corps and one from the Texas National Guard, all four of us enrolled in a class of some 100 officers learning the realities of artillery. The guts of the course was a six-weeks section called Gunnery. Every day, we either attended class-room sessions studying the special mathematics and geometry used in directing long-range weapons, or went out into the field to work with the guns, the trusty 105 mm. howitzers served by a crew of six. Loading projectiles and pulling the firing lanyard on timed commends became second nature. Usually we were taking orders about range and azimuth, sighting on aiming stakes and firing high-angle at unseen targets over the horizon, the usual role of artillery. But once the TAC officer abruptly announced, "Enemy tanks have broken through. Lower to zero. Rapid fire." And there they were, four Shermans clanking out of the scrub and aiming their turrets at us. For 20 minutes full of smoke and dust and deafening reports we banged away over open sights, seeing our shells clanging against the armor and bouncing off—they were not armor-piercing and carried no explosive charge. The TAC officer ordered "Cease fire," the tanks trundled off, and we wiped the sweat away after our successful "defense", the closest I came to combat in my Army career.

Other days we sat on bleachers and tried our hands as forward observers, giving radio instructions to a distant battery of howitzers to bring their shells down on targets a few thousand yards in front of us, derelict buildings or battered tanks sitting on a ridge line. Inhaling the crisp spring breezes of the Oklahoma plains, we enjoyed the dream of every healthy alpha-male: shoot at something. We could see through our binoculars the puffs of bursting shells near our targets, as we gradually adjusted them with commands like "left 30 clicks, up 100." This was an exercise best done in small increments, but once I cut the preliminaries and boldly directed from the initial bursts "Up 500, fire for effect." The officer running the show looked at me coldly.

"Ah, Lieutenant Coulson, and what if you are wrong?" he demanded.

"Sir, I guess it's my ass," was my candid response greeted by laughter of 20 compatriots eager for my failure.

"You are so right, lieutenant."

By good fortune, the shells landed where I had hoped; we saw a tank obliterated in smoke.

The dead-pan officer had a ready response:

"As Napoleon said, lieutenant, luck is better than brains."

Luck or brains, everything we did in six weeks of Gunnery was meticulously graded. Our TAC officers, a major and a captain, superb teachers from the Korea battle-line, were not slow to praise or criticize every day's performance. A week after the end of the course, at morning roll-call the adjutant held a brief ceremony to announce the Gunnery leader. I had the thrill of being ranked number one out of 104. My hand was shaken and back clapped in the friendly military rivalry. Number two was a Marine captain three years older than me, who had already served as a platoon leader in Korea. He had good grounds to expect the top prize over a part-timer like me, but did not hesitate to congratulate me. I never met a mean Marine.

With the strain of studying for Gunnery finished, we had a few weeks left to explore the pleasures of Fort Sill. No orders were given, but we got "command suggestions" to grace the occasional dances at the Officers' Club. The free martinis were welcome but the prevailing mood was strictly by-the-numbers. A flinty bird colonel singled me out to dance with his daughter. She was a lovely girl, but her dad was the base deputy commandant. His vigilant eye did not encourage romance. I had no chance to marry into the Army.

Korea

Just before we left Fort Sill, we received our orders for active duty. Most of us, including me, were headed for Korea, with a smaller contingent to Germany and a few, whom we suspected of wire-pulling, to staff duty at the Pentagon. Two weeks later I reported to Fort Lewis near Tacoma, Washington, and soon took an exhausting three-stage flight across the Pacific to land in Japan's late July heat wave. Assigned to several days sweating boredom in the Camp Drake replacement depot just outside Tokyo, my new pal Lt. E.C. Clarke and I found an English-speaking taxi-driver whom we enlisted to show us the night spots. He was clearly of an age to have served in World War II, but assured us repeatedly that had never fought against Americans.

"I was all time in China," he insisted. "I spend all time killing those Chinese bastards, smelly people, not like Yankees. Yankees the best. American Army the best."

Particularly with American Army officers paying his fare.

Whatever his military history, he certainly knew his way around Tokyo. He first took us to a softly-lit restaurant in an obscure back street, patronized by immaculate Japanese families with not a soldier in sight, serving all the local delicacies with full culinary ritual. We had no objection to him joining us for translation and ordering. After dinner, he introduced us to a club—"Very private, big shots only," he whispered—that featured a mahogany bar, small dance floor, discrete singer and a few tables of top-brass customers. A couple of lieutenants like us felt distinctly out of our pay-grade mingling with colonels, brigadier generals, embassy diplomats, smooth Japanese business men and a few elegant geishas. It was a remarkable escape from the gritty military compound of Camp Drake where we returned well after midnight.

An overnight train ride choking on smoke and cinders in open-window carriages took us to Sasebo, the port city on the southern tip of Japan, and after two more days of processing we boarded ship for Korea, landing shortly after dawn in Inchon, where General MacArthur had launched his daring amphibious assault in September 1950. That afternoon several hundred of us heard our final orders; I learned I was assigned to the 955th Field Artillery Battalion, not part of any division but included in IX Corps Artillery supporting elements of the Korean Army.

The next day I boarded a truck and we rolled northward. I had my first view of this war-torn country where for three years opposing armies had been battling each other as they marched up and down the peninsula. We passed quickly through Seoul, a battered shell that had changed hands four times, with hardly a building left whole, leaving nothing more than endless piles of grey rubble. The armistice had been declared and fighting ceased only about two weeks previously; in the 60-mile drive up to the DMZ (demilitarized zone, marking the final position of the truce line separating the Chinese Army from the American/South Korean forces), there was nothing to be seen of civilian life except an occasional s goateed farmer leading a donkey. The countryside was dominated by the detritus of military campaigns—artillery parks, ammunition dumps, storage warehouses, air-strips, coils of barbed wire, truck depots and tank repair centers, hastily built barracks and command centers waving a forest of radio antenna.

Our highway marked the traditional invasion route from North to South.

Beyond the once substantial city of Uijong Bu, now flattened like Seoul, Korea's ever present mountains closed in, showing nothing but bare scarred slopes from which every tree had been destroyed by shell-fire or napalm. Just as we reached a sign lettered "Warning: Approaching DMZ", the truck turned off the main route and up narrow dirt roads to find the 955th. We left behind the blasted moonscape of ravaged dirt and entered a zone of pine-clad ridges with all the beauty of Vermont's Green Mountains. We discovered the battalion headquarters tucked into a narrow ravine with a clear stream bubbling over the rocks. The truck dumped me and my duffel, to report with usual salute to the adjutant coming out of a half-complete concrete bunker. As a new junior officer, I was surveyed with languid indifference by all the old hands passing by. The adjutant presented me to the CO, a lanky lieutenant colonel named Easterday, still toweling down after a late afternoon dip in the stream. I did a double-take at his first order to me:

"Have a swim, lieutenant. Tomorrow you start to work like a son of a bitch."

So I stripped to my skivvies and plunged in.

At dinner in the officers' tent, I began the task of learning names, ranks and duties, and getting educated about the battalion. To my surprise, it was not equipped with the workhorse 105s but the much larger 155s, cumbersome pieces that I had seen but never touched. These could fire up to five miles to perform the mission of supporting the Korean infantry manning the borders of the DMZ. With the nervous truce only a couple of weeks old, every officer believed it was fragile and we would soon be shooting again. I was told about the explosive battle of the Kumsong Salient just before the Armistice, when the Chinese threw a concentration of their best troops to force the lines a few miles south and shatter the crack Korean Capital Division. The battalion, in close support of the Capital, fired its tubes to red—hot heat and had to make a fighting retreat to its present positions to avoid capture. That night I sacked out on a spare cot the adjutant found for me, my head spinning with first impressions of Korean realities.

At first light next morning a jeep arrived to give me a tour. The battalion of some 600 hundred men consisted of five separate units scattered strategically through the hills, linked by wire and radio: Headquarters Battery, where I had slept, with its fire-control center protected by a concrete roof; Firing Batteries A, B, and C, each with six massive 155s dug into earthen revetments, and Service Battery, that would become my permanent billet as officer in charge of that key asset, the ammunition dump. I met the COs of each of the units, and would gradually learn their idiosyncrasies over the coming months.

Fighting did not erupt again, so I have no tales of heroic derring-do to report in my Korean tour. As in any peacetime army, battles tended to be bureaucratic ones, enlivened by absurd territorial disputes and alliances made with congenial fellow officers. My primary task was to satisfy the three battery commanders with sufficient reserves of ammunition to meet any emergency, while keeping IX Corps from stealing our dump away from us to fill their own strategic reserve. I began to regard the inanimate dun-brown projectiles stacked in neat rows as my children whom I would protect from unlawful seizure. I had to become expert at juggling the paper work of endless reports, wrangling over scratchy telephone lines, and occasionally taking a jeep to higher headquarters to bargain or sweet-talk deals for exchanging decaying ordnance for some brand-new stuff.

I shared a cleverly built hut with a lieutenant and a warrant officer who had their own duties; we only saw each other at night, when these friendly mid-westerners taught me cribbage, which we alternated with three-handed bridge—monotony had to be survived. I learned the basic Army lesson of depending on sergeants whenever any actions had to be taken. My daily confidant was Sam Arnold, a tireless, thick-shouldered staff sergeant who inspected and nursed the projectiles, chipping rust and sniffing for any signs of powder spoilage. He could easily heft their 95-pound weight and slam them into the breech of a 155, an exercise that by the book was done by two guys holding a tray and a third one wielding a rammer staff.

Once a month I was assigned to a week-long turn on the battalion's forward observations posts. I packed a rucksack, doubled-clipped my carbine, and got my usual driver, a delightful miscreant with the unlikely name of Broadway Swim, to jeep me to the base of the ridge where our two mountain-top OPs surveyed the DMZ and the Chinese lines across the way. I slept in one but had to inspect the other, so I faced two stiff climbs every day; my legs and wind were never better. The OP itself was nothing but a bunker dug by hard work (our own) into the soft dirt, showing a slit window in the front, with heavy logs across the roof, delivered by Korean laborers sweating up the mountainside like ants carrying an out-size load. The OP team consisted of me, a corporal proficient in radios and field telephones, and a pfc. for the grunt work. But we all shared equally in any digging and in taking watches, using the field telescope to check any violations of the DMZ and any Chinese movements. The Army tradition of separating officer and enlisted men had to be delicately adjusted in this close-quarter living where we slept, ate and worked in a 12-by-12 low-ceilinged, dirt-floored space lit by a Coleman lantern. Before my first tour, the battalion CO gave me some advice:

"You'll be the boss, lieutenant; you make the decisions and take the rap for any screw-ups. Naturally you'll talk with the two guys; be friendly, but always remember, you may have to order them to do some shit, so don't get too buddy-buddy."

As the Korean winter arrived with blizzards and freezing winds, we tended to huddle around the space heater and dig our outside latrine as close as possible to our back-door. The only mental effort was hourly scoping the Chinese for any bunker construction or truck movements, plotting them on a map, and cranking the field telephone to report to headquarters. On frozen moonlit nights, I would often gaze mesmerized at snow-clad mountain ranges stretching away north to the distant Yalu River, a silent realm which only months ago had been a killing field. Even now in the uneasy peace, I could sense the hidden Chinese armies that might strike again. Shivering, I would lift my eyes from the scope and dial up the Armed Forces Radio Network, softly playing that perennial favorite requested by homesick GIs, Hoagy Carmichael's classic "The Nearness of You". To any of us, our "you" was far away.

For exercise, I would stroll down the ridge to visit a unit of the infantry we were supporting—Koreans, short, tough guys in wearing threadbare uniforms and living in little better than fox-holes, endlessly polishing their weapons or cooking *kimshi,* the standard chow any time of day or night. A grizzled noncom whom we called the Old Sarge spoke a modicum of English and quizzed us about anything American. I took him up to our bunker for a hot coffee. The weekly mail had just been delivered, including my long-forgotten subscription to *The New Yorker.* I turned the pages for the Old Sarge; he ignored the text, but stared with amazement at the slick ads for Lincoln convertibles, Chanel perfume, couturier gowns on high-fashion models, things he had never seen and probably never would. Our worlds were far apart.

My only tough exercise of leadership on the OP arrived unexpectedly in a decision about cooking. One sunny afternoon, I heard pops of a shot-gun moving up the approach trail. It was the CO, a bird-shooting enthusiast, armed with an elegant double-barrel 12-gauge and carrying a brace of pheasant.

"Look what I've brought you, lieutenant," he announced cheerily. "Wonderful dinner for your men."

Taking the birds warily, I answered with complete confidence.

"Very good, sir—make a great change from C rations."

As my two men hungrily eyed the feast and the CO disappeared down the mountain, I had not the foggiest idea how to de-feather, skin and clean the two offerings, and cook them in nothing but a space heater barrel that burned charcoal deep on a bottom grill. But an officer can never show doubt or indecision.

I took the birds down to the Old Sarge and with vigorous hand motions explained how I wanted them cleaned and ready for grilling. An hour later, they came back, pink and plucked, without guts or gizzard. By trial and error I wrapped them separately in chicken-wire and cautiously lowered them over the glowing charcoal. With satisfying crackle of fat falling on the coals, they slowly roasted and turned brown. With only a guess about proper timing, I lifted them out and carefully peeled the wire away. The three of us chewed the flesh off the bones and enjoyed a superb meal. The Army had taught me a new skill.

When off the OP, I visited the guys who ran the gun units. The tubes of the 155s were always raised and ready to fire over the mountains, zeroed-in at some unseen target plotted behind the Chinese front lines. Each battery captain had the tough task of keeping his men sharp and alert through months of inaction. The A Battery boss seemed to do it with music, always blaring from his command center. A massive, jovial Notre Dame football star, he had found a record of the Bahamian calypso song "Hold 'em Joe" that he always played in my honor, grabbing me for a brief two-man caper much appreciated by his staff.

A different personality ran C Battery. A studious intellectual, Charlie St. Clair was the battalion's certified hero, as he would diffidently recount if pressed. During the recent Kumsong Salient battle, he was a forward observer surrounded and trapped behind the rampant Chinese infantry. To avoid capture, he hid and spent a week, wounded and with little food or water, moving only at night, to rejoin the battalion, bringing invaluable notes on the enemy order of battle. He was written up for the Distinguished Service Cross, the Army's second highest award for valor. We all attended the presentation ceremony with throat-catching pomp of bands and banners. Standing stone-faced at attention, I wondered if I had arrived in Korea a month earlier, could I have filled Charlie's shoes?

Back at Service Battery, boredom would often descend. Across the road, a mountain stream flowing out of the pines provided a perfect swimming hole during warm weather. Late morning mail-call was always a welcome break, as I waited to spot the flowing green script of envelopes from my girl-friend. But after I finished my morning wrangles about ammunition supply, my duty hours could be pretty empty. I sought every chance to fill them. When the call was issued for volunteers to climb a peak to rescue air-crash survivors, I tried to leverage my limited mountain-climbing experience into joining the team; I was turned down. With the CO's tolerant amusement, to heighten security I organized a patrol party to invade and capture the fire-control center; unfortunately, my little team clad in black Korean pajamas got lost in the dark. After hearing that a nearby unit had been attacked by Chinese infiltrators, I decided to beef up our perimeter by stringing yards of barbed wire and directing that machine guns be dragged up the surrounding knolls; we never had to fire a shot.

I even played MP. The Korean Army periodically sent a truck of prostitutes up from Seoul to service its front-line troops. Our own guys could always sniff out the available sex, and we officers tried, with limited success, to block them from bedding these much-used whores. I never did find a GI *in flagrante*, only used condoms deep in the frozen grass. We were lucky—we never had a VD call. The US forces had a different policy; about once a quarter every man was granted a week's R&R in Tokyo, to spend as he saw fit, in cheap military lodgings or more exotic ones from his own wallet. I chose a couple of nights of Tokyo pub-crawling, and the rest of the week in a mountain-side spa featuring golf, massages, 40-cent Scotch, and a few wary officer nurses.

After serving 18 months I got the standard promotion to First Lieutenant and was put in charge of a team inspecting Korean artillery units. We observed Korean-style military discipline. Our word was law, and if we reported the slightest error by some hapless low-ranker, we would soon hear the "WHAP, WHAP" of an officer's swagger stick across the culprit's cheek. Strictly taboo in the US Army, but maybe that was the drill needed to resurrect the Korean nation from desolation in 1953 to today's gleaming affluence. When I misread a bubble in correcting an elevation sight, my only punishment was a chewing out from the visiting IX Corps brigadier general, my single run-in with the starred ranks.

As the departure date for my Korean tour neared, the battalion exec took me aside with gruff words.

"Even though you're a Yalie, with some crazy moves, you haven't done too bad. If you want to apply for a Regular Army commission, I might just endorse it, God help me."

Gratifying, but that wasn't my career path. I thanked him and declined. We stayed in touch. He later became a West Point football coach and years later invited me up to watch a game. I regret I never took the time.

Soon I was trucked back down through desolate Seoul to Inchon port and berthed on a troopship for the tedious five-week voyage across the Pacific, through the Panama Canal and up to New York, finally docking at the Staten Island military terminal and being greeted by the proud Colonel. Aside from nightly bridge games, I had plenty of time to reflect during that cruise, and a have often reflected since, about my military aberration. I came out of it with no wrenching experiences of war at the sharp, bloody tip. But the brief span of less than two years affected me much more than longer periods in my life. I met, and daily dealt with, people of backgrounds I had never seen before and would never see again. I learnt how to survive in a bureaucracy like most others, where many things don't make sense and you can do nothing to correct them. I earned a grudging respect for the Army, which despite its frequent bumbling ultimately got the job done. I found among its many mediocrities some extraordinary people, usually West Pointers whom we Ivy Leaguers had often disparaged. One of them stuck in my mind.

General Bob Gard.
During my duty at Camp Drum, First Lieutenant Bob Gard, just two years out of the Point, flew in for a practice drop with the elite 82nd Airborne Division and stayed for a few days of demonstrations. Right off, I spotted him as a "comer" in the Army hierarchy. Fit, handsome, decisive, quietly erudite, friendly but a bit aloof, he already had that undefinable aura of a leader. I met him once later in Korea and followed his career. After combat tours in Korea and Vietnam, he held senior slots in the Pentagon. He took a Harvard Ph.D. in political economy and was appointed President of the National Defense University, retiring with the three stars of a Lieutenant General. He might have gone all the way, but perhaps he became too intellectual, respected but a bit of a maverick.

While writing this book I found him on the Internet. I discovered that after retirement he followed a similar scholarly path, spending six years in Bologna, Italy, as head of the Johns Hopkins School of Advanced International Studies, followed by heading the Monterey (California) Institute of International Studies. Now, well into his eighties, he is the highly vocal and opinionated chairman of Washington's Center for Arms Control and Nuclear Non-Proliferation, writing and speaking frequently. After an exchange of e-mails and conversations, he sent me a couple of his pieces, one of them a long report written for NATO criticizing the Army's traditional doctrine of ignoring counter-insurgency tactics in favor of fighting traditional military set-pieces. He told me that when he served as an aide to Secretary of Defense McNamara during the Vietnam War, he suggested, to no avail, that it was a mistake for the US forces to avoid civic action in favor of killing guerillas. General Gard is not one to shy away from political controversy. His recent op-ed column clearly castigates Congressional forces, mainly Republicans "still stuck in the Cold War," for blocking rational reductions in the defense budget. In 2008, he gave outspoken and acerbic reasons why he would not vote for Senator McCain as President and found Obama the better candidate.

In 2010, he flew to the West Coast to give a talk on June 25th, the 60th anniversary of the opening of the Korea War. Instead of seeking peaceful retirement in golfing or gardening, Gen. Gard chooses to devote his time and energy to commenting on international strategy and criticizing American mistakes, often in terms that some of his former military colleagues heartily deplore.

I made an appointment to see him on a trip to Washington in 2013. I found him pink-cheeked and fit, friendly and happy to expound his views for a couple of hours. He has become an essential gad-fly, whose iconoclastic views are needed in modern America, and are all the more valuable as coming from a successful soldier rather than from a left-wing malcontent. Gen. Gard can only be regarded as one of the most unusual and distinguished of the 670 graduates of his West Point Class of 1950, many of whom were thrown directly into Korea as green second lieutenants, and 34 of whom were killed in action. Fortunately, Bob Gard survived, becoming the first in his class to win a general's star (despite, he laughed, a miserable academic career at the Point). Although I rarely saw them during my brief active duty, the military process can produce brilliant independents.

CHAPTER 4

Towards a Career

Yale Law School
After leaving the Army, I headed back to New Haven to enter Yale Law School. The Colonel was a successful lawyer and it seemed an honorable profession that could be followed for itself or lead in many directions. I had hit high marks on the law school aptitude tests. My older brother had attended the much larger Harvard Law School and spoke negatively about its grim competition for class ranking. So I settled again in the handsome Yale campus, an oasis of solidarity surrounded by the drab run-down city blocks of decaying New Haven.

All during school and college I had assumed that if I chose to work to my max, I could equal or excel in any line of study. Law School taught me different. An elite of the top scholars from a wide range of colleges, my 150-odd classmates included guys who slaved no harder than me but seemed to think quicker and sharper and write better exam papers. And girls too; we had only about seven females in the class, one of whom, the glamorous Barbara, rashly picked me as her boy-friend. I rarely saw her study, except for benzedrine binges before exams, which she zapped and I finished a couple of grades lower. She was elected to the Law Journal, and I was not, missing out on that symbol of academic success giving the best job possibilities. My only distinction was winning the annual prize for the best paper on international law, taking as my subject Egypt's seizure of the Suez Canal.

I enjoyed Law School. The intense focus on factual details and legal minutiae captivated me more than the generalities of the broad survey courses I had taken at Yale College. For me, there was nothing more stimulating than the Socratic method practiced by former Dean Wesley Sturges, as he took turns impaling one of us on his relentless questioning as a way of teaching Negotiable Instruments. "Think like a lawyer," was constantly drilled into us. "Assume nothing, question everything."

The whole institution was compressed into one neo-Gothic structure around a central courtyard, containing dormitories, class—rooms, professors' offices and the magnificent library. Pushed together, with little leisure to escape, our camaraderie was intense, and not always abstemious. Many of our professors, like the popular "Fred the Red" Rodell, clearly enjoyed hard drink, and any official occasion was celebrated with a variety of bottles paid from the School's generous entertainment fund. Fred was often opposed by the ultra-conservative J.W. Moore, expert on bankruptcy, jovially waving glasses at each other. Intellectual controversy was the accepted norm at Yale Law School.

I ended up with a reasonable ranking in the top third in our class, and I did not worry much about failing to achieve the pinnacle of the Law Journal. Although I would not be selected as a Supreme Court clerk, I could observe that high scholastic record was not essential to success as an attorney in private practice. Most of us mid-rankers found slots in respectable law firms in the major cities or in our home-towns. One classmate took a different tack by talking his way into the only firm in somnolent Burlington, Vermont, a town that hardly needed lawyers in those quiet days.

Life at Cravath

Following the stolid, safety-seeking side of my character, I went no further than New York City, and accepted an offer from Cravath, Swaine & Moore, then as now generally deemed the ultra-ultra example of the Wall Street corporate firm. I discounted its reputation as a vast grim factory that heartlessly used, chewed up, and spat out associates who did not survive to the holy grail of partnership.

Arriving in New York fresh out of law school and plunging into my first job, I was no different from thousands of other ambitious yuppies blessed with a good education and bright prospects, but minuscule income. Like them, I had to carve my own career route, learning how to maneuver with seniors and contemporaries, struggle for the good assignments and avoid the bad ones, temper the long working hours demanded of a young associates with essential escapes to entertainment and fresh air. As a senior member of the New York Bar, the Colonel was always available for advice, but my ancestry did not cut me any slack with my employers, who treated us all equally.

At first Cravath was pretty mystifying, occupying several prime office floors with about 100 partners and associates. But I soon learned that I was not dealing with a faceless monolith, but with individuals displaying widely varying personalities and peculiarities. Some of my bosses rarely showed up until 11 a.m. and enjoyed then working until midnight; others frowned if I was not present by 8 a.m. and always left for dinner. Some supervised me closely; others gave me vague directives and left me to make my own blunders. But no one ever told me exactly how many hours per day I was expected to bill, or how much vacation I could take. The Cravath rule was "do what's needed," leaving the rest to my discretion and teaching the responsibility that results from freedom. I got criticized for mistakes, but no one ever ground me down or attacked my self-esteem. We were all gentlemen working together, a far cry from what I hear about today's practice.

With its vast diversity of corporate clients, the firm always had plenty of work to assign, some tasks fascinating, others tedious, but rarely repetitive. In my first few years I had to advise on merging American Chicle Co., makers of the ubiquitous Chiclets, into a larger company; work on the legal complexities of severing the exhibitors Loew's Theatres from the Loew's film producers; represent an entrepreneur buying up companies in the prosaic business of making concrete water conduits; and freeze in mid-winter Wisconsin while helping J.C. Penney seize control of an automated warehouse from its suspicious owners. I had my share of lost weekends and "all-nighters" as complex negotiations dragged, or documents had to be proof-read in grimy printing plants to meet tight deadlines.

In my early years, I was given one semi-exotic assignment: fly down to Nicaragua and confer with the Blue brothers, Neal and Linden, adventurous young Americans with pilots' licenses who had flown all over South America in a single-engine Piper Tri-Pacer, having adventures that put them on the cover of *Life*. They were looking for a solid investment, and settled on creating a cocoa and banana plantation deep in the jungle, reachable only by air or river barge. But like any foreigner, they had to take in as partner General Anastasio Somoza, the country's long-term dictator. Inevitably, differences arose. Unfortunately, even Cravath expertise could make no headway against Nicaraguan politics. The Blues pulled out and went on to more profitable ventures, eventually becoming owners of an obscure San Diego technology company called General Atomics, and making it the highly profitable builder of predator drones sold to the US Government.

From Nicaragua, I flew across the Caribbean to Cuba. Fidel Castro had ousted the corrupt presidency of Fulgencio Batista on January 1, 1959, but for an ambiguous year he did not show his true Communist colors and tap-danced with the United States about whether he was friend or foe. Travel for American citizens was still unrestricted, and I accepted an invitation from a *New York Herald Tribune* reporter who had covered Fidel's campaign from the guerilla skirmishes in the Sierra Maestre to victory in the streets of Havana. Don Hogan became starry-eyed about the Revolution, resigned from journalism, and took a job doing PR for the nationalized sugar industry.

Tourism had fled, and my gleaming high-rise hotel, optimistically built only a year earlier, echoed with 10% occupancy. But there was no lack of festivity at Don's apartment. A stream of guys in the olive-drab uniforms adopted by their maximum leader poured in, checking their carbines and tommy-guns at the door and celebrating with rum that was dirt cheap from the nationalized Bacardi distilleries. In broken Spanglish the glories of the new regime were diligently laid forth so this Yanqui could get the picture. There was no curfew for these heroes. Long after midnight, they gave me the front-seat in a crowded jeep, and drove me home through deserted streets, cheerfully shooting out streetlights with bullets whanging past my ears.

A year later Don found that Yanquis were not so welcome in the new Cuba. His job was abolished and he returned to New York, tight-lipped about Fidel and his cronies.

New York Police Department.

Like many young lawyers thinking of a possible political career, I took a year's leave of absence for exposure to government, in my case at the New York City municipal level. I was appointed executive secretary to the police commissioner, responsible to the mayor for 25,000 of New York's Finest. Stephen P. Kennedy (no relation to *the* family), was a shrewd, incorruptible, up-from-the-ranks veteran who knew every trick that could be pulled by either cops or crooks. Operating out of a tight corner office with direct access to my boss in the ornate old headquarter at 100 Centre Street, I was exposed to a slice of New York life not visible to most "civilians", as cops call the rest of us. I had nothing to do with law enforcement, certainly not licensed to carry a fire-arm, but drafted most of the P.C.'s testy correspondence with Mayor Wagner, state politicos and high-level citizens who had a beef with the Police Department. I also had to negotiate complaints from the cops' aggressive bargaining agent, the Patrolmen's Benevolent Association (no lady cops in those days) and soothe the Civilian Complaint Review Board, ever on the lookout for alleged police brutality.

I once had the distinct pleasure of telling an arrogant White House aide that, no, he could not organize a hasty political parade in the city without police OK. He warned me "we'll go over your head," but I never felt at risk.

Once I was accepted as an insider, I heard tales and shared a few drinks with the hard-bitten men who had fought their way up to run the two police divisions: Mike, the Chief Inspector of the uniformed force, and Lefty, the Chief of Detectives. When I got married and headed off for a Paris honeymoon, they called their counterparts and arranged a warm welcome from *gendarmes* at Orly Airport and a police driver to our hotel. I spent part of every working day talking with the two lieutenants who guarded the P.C.'s door and educated me on police lore. Dispelling any prejudice that cops are dumb stooges, they were two of the smartest men I ever knew. Despite being devout Catholics they had an amused cynicism about human nature; as cops, they had collared many a phony, hoodlum, or smooth shyster.

The Department was not immune from internal politics. A certain clique of unpromoted officers had a long grudge against the P.C. They exercised their vendetta one night by ticketing my car for a parking violation, promptly advising the press that the commissioner had hired a scoff-law as secretary. When the *Daily News* called me for comment, I knew enough to stick with a terse statement "I'll pay the fine," which I saw next day quoted under my photo on page two. The P.C. just laughed, telling me I should be glad they didn't claim I was drunk.

* * *

During my career as a New York lawyer, I was shielded from the seamy side of business and financial chicanery. Cravath was the kind of firm whose blue-chip clients like IBM might have huge battles with the SEC or the Justice Department, but were never on the criminal side of cheating, stealing, or defrauding. The closest I got to a law-breaker was over-hearing senior partner Tom Halleran's end of a heated telephone conversation.

"I tell you, Sox," he insisted, "you just can't *do* it that way."

After hanging up, he shook his head in exasperation and told me, "God, what a time I have keeping that guy out of jail." He never asked me to meet Sox.

Bernie Cornfeld

It was only outside the halls of Cravath that I met the financial charlatans of the era. Bernie Cornfeld was the most notorious. Bernie's star rose as the creator of super-sized mutual funds operating under the names Fund of Funds or IOS (Investors Overseas Service) that seemed about to dominate the financial horizon by 1970 and then collapsed in utter confusion. But when I met him in 1964 he was still in the early expansion stage and was seeking a young securities lawyer from a firm like Cravath to augment his team and give him respectability. One of his staff thought I might be interested and arranged an introduction.

I found a little man with frizzy hair and boundless enthusiasm. Attractive prospects of shuttling between Geneva and New York were dangled before me, but the meeting did not go smoothly. My responsibilities were left vague. Bernie was not a man for details, very hard to pin down as he bounced energetically around the hotel suite where we met. He could sense my doubts, and they were soon reciprocated. If you did not love Bernie at first sight, that was the end of the affair. I never saw him again.

For the next few years I wondered if I had made a mistake. The Fund of Funds was constantly in the news, selling its shares to millions world-wide, making allegedly brilliant investments.

My friend Henry Buhl left his minor New York brokerage firm and joined Bernie in Geneva as a senior executive with all the trappings of the good life, including a lake-front villa and a glossy Swiss wife. On his trips to New York he stayed in a suite at the Carlyle and was besieged by every Wall Street salesman with a hot stock to flog. In 1969 a distinguished group of international investment firms gave IOS the ultimate stamp of respectability by underwriting a public offering of its shares. Bernie was the current financial genius and Henry his fortunate acolyte.

Then in March 1970 I was passing through Geneva and Henry invited me to lunch, just the two of us in the discreet dining room of Le Richemonde. It was one of those days of oppressive grey overcast typical of Geneva winters, and Henry's mood was similar. In a recent review with the IOS treasurer, he had found unexpected and widening cracks in the edifice. Next month he would call a special Board meeting and demand answers. Of course, this was ultimate insider information, and it was understood that I could not say a word.

By the end of April, the financial press was reporting steep drops in the IOS share price. The crisis deepened over the next months, with reports of chaotic all—night Board meetings and ambiguous press releases emanating from head office in Geneva. Bernie ("Cornflakes" as his office called him) was out; no, was back in. Clearly, a rescue was needed. Henry and other executives scoured their Rolodexes to find a rich, adventurous candidate. John King, a Denver mining investor, had a serious look; the immensely influential French Rothschilds were approached; a respected English diplomat, Sir Eric Wyndham-White, became a director and tried to impose order; a retired president of John Hancock Life Insurance served a brief term as CEO. Even I was called early one morning to ask whether my friends at investment bank Kuhn, Loeb could help. Without even checking, I could easily say "no" and go back to sleep.

But an obscure American businessman named Robert Vesco had been introduced in glowing terms to Henry Buhl.

Starting from scratch, Bob Vesco had leveraged a mish-mash of companies into a conglomerate that made him rich. Already known as a crude seeker of the main chance and a tireless, aggressive negotiator, Vesco spotted IOS as the route for him to spread his wings internationally. In an intricate series of transactions, he gradually gained control of IOS and looted it, leaving a trail of wiped-out investors and litigation that took years to unravel, in Switzerland, The Bahamas, Canada, New York and anywhere assets could be found. The whole unsavory story is told in the exhaustive 1987 book, *Vesco*, by the late Arthur Herzog, who grilled me about Nassau. Bernie spent a brief sentence in a Geneva prison, able to afford favored treatment in a well-tended cell. Not even his defrauded victims thought that he was a real crook, simply a genial super-salesman disdaining financial statements and similar tedious trivia. Pretty blondes were more to his taste; he flew his private jet to Acapulco to compare it with Hugh Hefner's aircraft and meet a selection of Playboy Bunnies.

Henry, jobless and divorced, left Geneva and returned to New York, unabashed as ever, forced by his reverses to become an expert professional photographer, until he finally came into his inheritance from his late mother, after a colorful legal battle with her two adopted sons—a tale worthy of a book of its own.

He had ridden the roller-coaster up with Bernie and taken the heart-stopping plunge down. I was grateful that I was never invited on the ride. I began to find drama at Cravath, where much of my time was spent on the so-called international desk. I worked with the governments of Jamaica, Malaysia and Peru, and companies in Puerto Rico and Canada, usually with unexpected twists. My unexpected assignment to Mexico started me on a long commitment to that country, described later.

Jamaica

In 1963, Jamaica had just become a sovereign nation, independent from Britain, led by its charismatic Prime Minister

Alexander Bustamante, a looming giant with beetling eyebrows and a ringing voice that inspired crowds with a mellifluous Jamaican accent. I was sent to Kingston to represent the foreign investors in a private placement of Jamaican State bonds. Despite its small size, only about $3 million, it was a landmark for the new government, establishing its international credit rating.

Bustamante's PR department organized the closing, usually a dry business of signing documents, as a full-fledged media event. The great man was posed at a conference table atop a dais, with me seated on his left and his minister of finance on his right. Flash-bulbs popped, cameras clicked and whirred, reporters scribbled. Under the strict rules of that era, American lawyers were forbidden any self-promoting publicity—even handing out business cards was discouraged. So next day I was alarmed to see the front page of the Kingston *Daily Gleaner* carry its lead story with a photo taken at a key moment, showing me passing papers across the Prime Minister's chest, with my name and Cravath neatly identified in the caption. But I never got a censure from the Bar Association; perhaps their eagle eye did not descend to Jamaica.

Malaysia

Malaysia was a more serious challenge. Investment bankers Kuhn, Loeb & Co. were retained by the Government to handle an international bond offering. As with Mexico, a detailed prospectus had to be written about this little-known nation, requiring a six-weeks mission to the capital city, Kuala Lumpur. That was no hardship. In 1965, KL, a it was universally known, was still a charming mini-city of distinctive multi-hued Oriental flavor, long before the crass modernization campaign that led to the Petronas Towers being built as, briefly, the world's tallest structures. Although the population was primarily native Malays, heavily leavened with Chinese merchants and Indian civil servants, the official language was English, and many long-time British residents remained as business owners, professionals and advisers to public ministries. The heart of town was dominated by the all—purpose social and business retreat, the Selangor Club, with shady verandahs leading to sweeping lawns doubling as cricket pitch, and the outskirts were graced by handsome tennis and golf clubs. Prominent citizens of all races were welcome in club-land, but the atmosphere still had many traces of the historic but fading British Raj. The post of British High Commissioner (equivalent to an ambassador) was held by a Viscount grandee of the Tory party, who gave us lunch at the residence, accompanied by parrots raised by his outspoken wife, who interrupted their squawks with undiplomatic comments about local personalities.

Our first task was to be educated on the unusual structure of Malaysia, a country only two years old, cobbled together by merging the original States of Malaya (each proud of its own hereditary ruler) with the adjacent State of Singapore and two remote British colonies, Sabah and Sarawak, 400 miles distant on the largely unexplored island of Borneo. Politics were dominated by citizens of Malay descent and Muslim faith, who clashed frequently with the Chinese immigrants flaunting their commercial success. Fortunately, the country was the world's largest producer of rubber and tin, and Singapore (which later seceded) enjoyed a robust maritime trade, so the country could display a stable economy and balance of payments.

We soon learned that national resources were being sapped by a low-key but drawn-out war called the "confrontation", barely publicized in the rest of the world. The large and feisty nation of Indonesia, sharing a border in Borneo with Sabah and Sarawak, objected to those two territories being included in Malaysia. Indonesian military units disputed the border with armed incursions.

Our information contact in KL was the affable governor of the Central Bank and his aides, but they shied away from telling us much about the confrontation, which we felt had to be disclosed in the prospectus. KL was bustling with the varied uniforms of the local army plus troops sent from England and other Commonwealth countries; they were clearly alerted to fight. We were shuffled off to a spokesman at army headquarters. An urbane major in green battle-dress admitted that, yes, there were "small-scale" clashes between the Indonesians and the Malaysian forces, but, no, he could not give us any details—that was top secret.

I took the advantage of a long weekend to fly over to Sabah. I never got close to the battle-lines, but a helpful British Ranger drove me up the slopes of Mt. Kinibalu so I could survey the desolate fighting zone—a vast expanse of jungle, winding rivers, swamps and mud-flats, with traces of an occasional road or village, all soaked in damp mists of pervasive humidity. I could well imagine the grim realities of warfare amid such hostile nature. A famous book had been written about previous guerilla war in Malaya, called *The Jungle Is Neutral*, but I doubt that there, as later in Vietnam, the soldiers on the ground found it that way, battling its leeches, heat, and tangled vines.

On returning to KL, I badgered the major again, telling him what I had seen. After a brief conference with his superiors, who perhaps decided on the public relations value of disclosure, he handed me some sheets, stamped "Classified", that allowed us to print in the prospectus that casualties to date for the Malaysian and Commonwealth security forces were precisely 68 killed and 63 wounded, while 127 Indonesians were captured, 78 surrendered, and an estimated 328 were killed. A local newspaper reporter told me of his amazement that we had extracted this information, which had always been refused to the press.

Before we completed our work in Malaysia, Sir Winston Churchill died. We attended the memorial service in the Anglican Cathedral, packed with mourners of all faiths, for the man who had once declared that he did not intend to "preside over the dissolution of the British Empire." Its dissolution was by then well on track, but Malaysians seemed happy to continue in the British Commonwealth of Nations, that unique, loose-knit entity that links foreign realms to the Crown and other traditions of Olde England.

Marriage

My career as a young guy in a law factory left little time for play, but after a couple of years of solitary hours, I began to think of marriage and starting a family. My income was pretty low, but others had done it at my level, so why could not I? My lady from Yale Law School and I made moves towards betrothal, but Barbara and I were not strong enough to overcome family objections. Although not devout herself, her parents were serious Reform Jews while Abby and the Colonel were nominal Protestants, vaguely Episcopalian. Doubts, ever-so delicately expressed to avoid any charges of anti-Semitism or its opposite, were made known to us. Compatibility was not helped by the fact that her family occupied an ornate Fifth Avenue co-op that dwarfed the comfortable but modest Coulson lodgings on a side-street. Perhaps in today's more liberal era, we would have prevailed, but in the narrow-minded early 1960s, the strains of subtle social disapproval were too much for our young passions. We parted, although remaining friends to the present day.

I soon met a dynamic red-haired lady, Edith de Rham, a Vassar graduate of proper background but independent spirit. She was married to a Yale classmate, but the union was unhappy and did not deter us from falling in love. Divorce was amicably arranged and our wedding soon followed. I had to start immersing myself in the details of family and social life. Where to live? How many children to plan and how to raise and educate them? How and where to take weekends and holidays for necessary escape from the daily grind? What friends to make, and how to keep, or drop, them? Which invitations to accept, and which to decline? Which charities to support, and how to avoid a totally Philistine existence by maintaining some exposure to New York's cultural offerings? And how to do all this on a tight budget?

The first decision was simple. My wife Edie, a born-and-bred New Yorker, insisted we live in Manhattan, somewhere on the upper east side. Although this was not, even then, the cheapest alternative, I readily agreed, as I could not face lengthy commutes from the outer boroughs or the suburbs, given the irregular hours of a Cravath associate. We soon had one beautiful daughter, Diana, and three years later another, Amanda; that seemed sufficient focus for our love, and affordable. Our friendships were an eclectic lot, as I did not congregate often with legal colleagues or more than a few Yale classmates. We tended to circulate with a brilliant but moody architect devoted to skiing and sailing; a Rhodes Scholar who brought foreign films to America and his choreographer wife; a former editor of *Paris Review,* now a financier with a pedantic gift for spouting obscure economic information; a brainy editor of art magazines who often struggled to work after her late nights of successful poker winnings; an intellectual dilettante who quit Wall Street after inheriting a fortune and devoted himself to composing erudite quiz books.

For many summers we shared a Hamptons house, where the family spent the week and I joined on weekends, a bargain arrangement before every hedge-fund owner escalated prices to the stratosphere. The greenery and the beaches gave my children the essential escape from New York's suffocating heat, which had to be endured by thousands of kids not so fortunate. I tried to help in a small way by contributing to the summer camp run by the Police Athletic League, which gave slum kids a break in the Adirondacks. On occasional winter weekends, we made exhausting trips to ski in usually freezing Vermont, and maybe once a year could manage a flight to Nassau.

I had to adjust to the loss of parents, first the Colonel's unexpected demise in 1962 from a botched, and probably nonessential, hospital operation. It happened just two days before I returned late from a business trip. I didn't know until I walked in our front door and Edie gave me the news. I told her to go back to sleep; I needed time to react. I sat at my desk, put my head in my hands, and found myself weeping. We had been close; I had always taken my problems, even a brief psychiatric bout, to him rather than to the charming but somehow elusive Abby. I did not object when Edie heard my sobs, dried my tears, and led me to bed.

Abby's passing was long foreseen after as her doctors struggled to control an unforgiving renal illness. With her usual spirit she declared, "I'll give a party for my 80th birthday; after that I don't give a damn." The celebration in her Marblehead house was in August 1969. One night in March 1970, she drifted peacefully away in her own apartment.

Like many wives of that era, Edie had a sharp intelligence and energy with few career opportunities. Restless, she turned to writing. She produced a book about current American women, *The Love Fraud*, and shared views with Betty Friedan, author of the trend-setting *The Feminine Mystique*. But she found Betty too obsessed with publicity about feminism and never fell under her spell. She became fascinated with female criminals. Long hours in a research library were required, as well as trips for prison interviews, resulting in another book. She also became an active supporter of the American Symphony Orchestra at Carnegie Hall, and we entertained Leopold Stokowski, its charismatic, wild-haired founder and conductor. I still regret that I was too lazy or pre-occupied to take advantage of the magnificent art available for view at New York's museums and galleries. Names from Michelangelo to Picasso barely registered. I could be called pretty square in those days, rarely venturing down to the Village for theatre or music, preferring to play squash and backgammon in the stolid surroundings of Park Avenue's Union Club, a legacy of the Colonel.

It was a busy life, with few moments for existential musings about "what does it all mean?" But, as I daily rode the jammed IRT Third Avenue subway to and from Wall Street, freezing in winter and sweating in summer, I did begin to wonder, "Will I live the rest of my years like this?" At Cravath, my career as a corporate lawyer plodded steadily forward. Then my number came up to work on another international deal. This changed the course not only of my career but of my personal life.

Chapter 5

Mexico? A Command Performance

The Mexican Prospectus

"How would you like to go to Mexico?" It was October 1962, and I had spent five years at Cravath. Tom Halleran, the senior partner to whom I was assigned, called me into his office after lunch and hit me with this startling question.

After grinding through bond indentures, Delaware articles of incorporation, mergers of struggling New England mills, I found this an exotic proposition coming from Cravath's staid halls. But, as I knew, the firm represented the powerful investment bankers Kuhn, Loeb & Co., whose ambitions and contacts spread worldwide. Brought into greatness early in the century by Jacob Schiff, leader of the New York Jewish "Our Crowd", Kuhn, Loeb continued through the 1960s to be second only to Morgan Stanley as the generator of financings both domestic and foreign. Mexico was another case of contacts long nurtured by the firm's managing partner, Nat Samuels. He did business with a bank in Mexico that was linked to the government. When Mexico's president of that day wished to re-establish the tattered reputation of the country in the world's financial markets, he turned to the bank for advice; and the bank naturally turned to the experts at Kuhn, Loeb.

But, in the competitive arena of Wall Street, it wasn't that simple. Another prominent firm, First Boston Corporation, led by an aggressive former World Bank executive named Andy Overby, also kept alert to potential deals and had its own moles in the Mexican Ministry of Finance. First Boston too had been invited to the party. After polite sparring, the two chieftains, Samuels and Overby, decided that the firms would work jointly—a common, though not popular, arrangement when the client wanted both. Each firm was convinced it could handle the job perfectly well alone, but half a loaf was better than none, so pride was swallowed and a cut of 50/50 of any commissions was agreed.

But another issue arose from the arcane style of Wall Street: who would lead and receive the crucial position "on the left" in the tombstone advertisements in the financial press? No better way to decide this than by toss of the coin: Kuhn, Loeb won. They would lead the first transaction, then alternate with First Boston on any later ones. Since Cravath served as KL's long-time counsel, we were chosen for the legal work, disappointing the eminent Sullivan & Cromwell firm historically linked to First Boston. Finally, the market experts at the two investment banks consulted their oracles and decided that the time was ripe for an international bond issue, the first by a Latin America name since World War II, and work must begin immediately so as not to miss the window of opportunity.

All these decisions had been made far above the head of a lowly legal associate such as myself, and were explained to me by Tom Halleran, the Cravath partner who served as advisor to Kuhn, Loeb's most confidential plans. What, I asked, was I supposed precisely to do on this unexpected Mexican trip?

"My boy," his ample girth stirred and he responded with his usual friendly cynicism about even the largest of clients, "you will do the *work*. We will need a prospectus to satisfy the bureaucrats at the SEC [Securities & Exchange Commission], who probably have never heard of Mexico. These bankers,

A Corkscrew Life

while nice fellows and good salesmen, can't put one word in front of another."

"But, Tom," I demurred, "I know nothing about Mexico; I have only basic Spanish [picked up during the summer-school session in Mexico City a dozen years earlier]; it's a hell of a big country, not like one of your New Bedford mills. How will I get the information we need—history, politics, industry, agriculture, finance, debt—it's like writing an encyclopedia."

"My boy," his avuncular phrase when trying to persuade, "Cravath has become great by its lawyers solving the difficult if not the impossible. I pick you to do the same. Besides," he added loftily, "we will find some Mexican lawyer to help you on the legal stuff, and doubtless Kuhn, Loeb's banker friends down there will guide you around. Fascinating place, Mexico."

Easy for you to say, I thought, from behind your desk in the 57th floor corner office at One Chase Manhattan Plaza. I had dim memories of Mexico offering weekly tummy problems, recalcitrant telephones, overloaded busses, a veneer of wealth over massive poverty.

"How long?" I asked. "You know we're expecting our first baby next June."

"Two weeks, right now. Then you'll probably have to go back for a couple of weeks later to clean up the details. Nothing. When I was your age, traveling by ship to Europe, we spent *months* away on business. We almost forgot about Jack McCloy, he was away so much. Now, I need your decision; we need someone to leave in three days."

Couched as a request, in reality it was nothing like one. I knew that I *could* decline. Nothing more would be said; reluctance to travel abroad leaving a pregnant wife would be accepted. But I also knew that if a Cravath associate turned down an assignment from a senior partner, he would henceforth be regarded as a second-class citizen in the firm, not full of the aggressive spirit to go anywhere, do anything. Partnership prospects could be forgotten. The reference to the distinguished John J. McCloy had piqued my spirit of ambition. From years investigating the infamous "Black Tom" munitions explosion that demolished Jersey City in the First World War (and effectively pinning the blame on the German Government), he went on to become Assistant Secretary of War, High Commissioner for Germany, and head of the World Bank—a recognized leader of the "establishment."

And besides, I liked Tom Halleran. Immensely experienced in both the technicalities of corporate law and the shenanigans of shady financiers, a superb draftsman, captivating raconteur, drinking companion, devoted to eccentric working hours that left his long-suffering secretary (male, like most in those days) often saying "The boss ain't in yet," he had a loyal following of "Tom's Boys" of whom I was one. I could not disappoint him.

A brief visit to Kuhn Loeb was arranged to meet the "Mexican team", men who over the next years would become my close friends: a brief welcome from the eminent Nat Samuels himself, and more time with John Winston Churchill Guest, a bespectacled English partner of impeccable breeding who combined financial scholarship with a mad spirit of adventure; John Libby, a sleek vice president being groomed for greater things; and Dick Solow, a balding top-sergeant type who I gathered would be assigned much of numbers crunching. I learned that we would be given office space at the headquarters of Banco Nacional de Mexico, the country's oldest bank, who were the essential link between Kuhn Loeb and the government—and who would be duly compensated.

Tom had made contact with the Mexican law firm Noriega & Escobedo, who would act as our local counsel and advisors on Mexican law. "Old Escobedo is probably OK," opined Tom dubiously, with his usual skepticism about any lawyer untrained by Cravath, "he's the president of the Mexican Bar Association, and I guess that must mean something. Leaves most of the work to his son Miguel . . . who rides horses a lot, I'm told. Must be gentlemen anyway. Well, you'll soon find out!"

I took an Aeronaves de Mexico flight to Mexico City that arrived after dark. Proceeding to the Hotel Alameda, Mexico's newest, I found rooms reserved at the "standard" rate of $14, with an option (unexercised) of up-grading to the "deluxe" rooms at $18. I came to know every ceiling crack of those lodgings.

The following morning, I was summoned to a team meeting—the four from Kuhn Loeb group under Nat Samuels, and the three delegates from First Boston led by the tall, white-haired Andy Overby. The leaders gave an inspiring pep-talk: how we were here to lead the Mexican nation into financial respectability by organizing a bond issue to be sold internationally, with a syndicate of English, French, German and Italian banks to assist the two American firms. We were told that since Mexico had defaulted on its debt in the revolutionary era of the 1920s and 1930s, it had been shut off from foreign capital, and now it was our job to convince the world of a "new" Mexico, stable, responsible, capitalist, willing and eager to make every interest payment on the dot. The assembled bankers would negotiate with the Ministry of Finance and write the guts of the Prospectus, while the lawyers were airily given the task of "seeing that it's all legal."

We then trooped the few blocks down to the head office of Banco Nacional de Mexico, or "Banamex" as we would come to know it, in the noisy, narrow streets of old Mexico, with the unforgettable address of No. 44 Isabel la Catolica. This structure was a traditional 18th century colonial palace, with elaborate façade, massive entrance gate, lofty vaulted ceilings on the main floor, but cleverly modernized to house all the needs of a major bank. We were ushered to the mezzanine space that would become our office: a glass-enclosed bull-pen with a long table and surrounding chairs, from where we were visible to all the bank staff criscrossing this busy level on their daily errands. Visible, but separate, keeping to ourselves since we were enjoined that our business with the Mexican Government was "confidential". The sight of these gringos working away soundlessly behind a glass barrier inevitably led to our being given a friendly nickname, *"los intocables"* (the untouchables).

This we learned much later, when we made friends with many of the staff and the confidentiality of our mission naturally disintegrated into common knowledge. Our first order of business was to meet the senior executive of Banamex, who had arranged the delicate business of introducing American investment bankers to advise the Government. All we had read and been told of Mexico underlined the still-active feelings of resentment and suspicion against the United States, starting with the invasions of the Mexican War, the annexation of Texas and the entire West, and continuing with General Pershing's ill-starred incursion on Mexican soil to capture Pancho Villa in 1916, and the "economic imperialism" of the international oil companies culminating in their nationalization in 1938, over the strenuous objections of Washington.

Although the most virulent strains of this chauvinism had died by the 1960s, as Mexico attracted earnings from northern tourism and many of the country's leaders had been educated in American universities, nevertheless the wary defense of national sovereignty was a latent factor in all negotiations. We knew we could not follow the blunt, sometimes bullying, habits of Wall Street bankers and lawyers when we dealt with Mexican Government officials, and must exercise constant tact and diplomacy We would have to practice this lesson every day.

We were brought into the office of Don Agustín Legorreta, the chairman and major shareholder of Banamex, a man who never ceased to impress me during many meetings over the years. "Don" in Mexico is an unofficial honorific given to any man of recognized prominence, and he certainly deserved it. In a country where theoretically the Spanish aristocracy had been abolished during the bloody years of the 1910-1920 Revolution, Agustín was the quintessential aristocrat. Tall, lean, voluble, hyper-active, he had been educated internationally and was as adept in English, French or German as in Spanish (much later he told me some of his happiest moments were spent at white-tie opera balls in Vienna). He had been a skilled horseman and now he (or rather his chauffeur) drove a maroon Bentley of ancient vintage, an unrivalled symbol of affluence in Mexico. He controlled Banamex almost by right of inheritance, as his ancestor Don Luis Legorreta, only recently deceased, was the founder of the bank and well-known as the savior of the Government's gold reserves. The story went that in the most anarchic days of the Revolution, Don Luis simply transferred the gold bars from the Treasury's uncertain possession to the deep vaults of Banamex, where they lay undisturbed until more peaceful times.

But Agustín was no playboy princeling. He had spent his full career at Banamex and had led it into its unquestioned position as "the" bank for major industry, wealthy investors, and foreign trade—the Mexican equivalent of J. P. Morgan. Although too lofty by now to be burdened with minor details, he had appointed skilled executives reporting to him and could devote himself to major investment decisions through his unparalleled contacts with business leaders, foreign and domestic. He gained influence in halls of the National Palace, despite the wide social gulf between him and the leaders of the Mexican Government. They were usually men of middle-class professional families who had worked their way up through loyal service to the PRI, the all-inclusive political party that dominated all elections. Doubtless Agustín's financial expertise, international contacts, and great charm (as well as major contributions to the coffers of the PRI) convinced them of his value when the country needed help from foreign wealth. Though having recovered from the depths of poverty following the Revolution, Mexico was still on all counts a "third-world" country with a vast appetite for foreign investment, and somebody like Agustín was the essential go-between.

We soon realized that our group of "untouchables" was in good hands. Agustín was on friendly first-name terms with our leaders Nat and Andy, and deftly laid out the ground-rules for us: "Tomorrow," he announced, "we will go over to the National Palace to meet the people at the Ministry of Finance with whom you will be working. You probably will never meet the President, and maybe not even the Secretary of Finance, but I assure you they know that you're here and will follow your progress. We've told them about an international bond issue, and they agree in principle, but they don't understand much about it, since there hasn't been one since the 1920s. It's up to you to explain the whole thing to them and convince them it can be done—*without*, I should add, any loss of sovereignty, which is a sacred matter to them." The lesson again.

Agustín introduced us to his colleagues who would be helping us day-to-day, including Lic. Leon Alberdi, the bank's General Counsel. The calm, pale Alberdi, of Basque heritage, eventually spent countless hours with our team and became our most trusted confidant, clarifying subtle points of Mexican law, finance and administration. His title "Lic." was the abbreviation for *licenciado,* scrupulously attached to every person licensed to practice Mexican law.

As Agustín indicated the meeting should break up, we could observe his remarkable means of departure. The chair that he occupied in the corner behind his desk began to levitate towards the fifteen-foot ceiling. The wall held vertical tracks on which he and his chair silently rose, until they vanished through a trap-door into a higher level, where, we learned, he kept his private office. His last words from on high were, "Wonderful, gentlemen, we will meet again tomorrow," as he disappeared into this sanctum—a fitting ascension for a figure somewhat larger than life.

The next morning, a procession of twelve dark-suited, briefcase-carrying men could be seen crossing the Zócalo, the vast plaza where once had stood the central Aztec pyramids and where so many events of Mexican drama had played out over 450 years of tumultuous history. Today we Americans, shepherded by Don Agustín and his Banamex lieutenants, were headed towards the long, two-story stretch of the Palacio Nacional, which bounds the entire eastern side of the Zócalo and housed the offices of the Presidency and of the Ministry of Finance, or "*Hacienda*", as we soon learned to call it. Entering through a formal gateway, we found ourselves in a museum set-piece, surrounded by the murals of Diego Rivera portraying the glories of the Revolution in stark slashes of monumental color—handsome muscular workers wielding hoes or hammers, overseen by pale sneering capitalists brandishing whips or quaffing champagne. Art as Politics, not subtle, but effective.

Pairs of ascending staircases led to the upper level, the working floor of the Palacio. Here we were ushered into the ornate offices occupied by the *Sub-Secretario de Hacienda y Credito Public*, the official who kept the Ministry ticking while the Secretary himself, a possible candidate for the presidency, was touring the country making new friends. Passed along through a series of receptionists and executives of gradually increasing rank, we eventually were presented to the *Sub-Secretario*, the stone—faced Lic. Jose Saenz Arroyo. Like many Mexican Government functionaries meeting foreigners for the first time, he was formal to the nth degree: a set-piece speech of welcome, an introduction to his juniors with whom we would be working, and that was it. Much later we were to find that, as our working relationship developed, Saenz Arroyo was a warm and friendly individual who took extraordinary steps to assist us. But first, trust had to be gained.

The stiff formalities completed, Don Agustín departed, taking Nat and Andy with him. Having set the stage, our leaders would retire to the wings and leave us to act out the drama. Lic. Hugo de Leon, the *Hacienda* functionary who was delegated to handle our team, led us back into the bowels of the building. Leaving behind the crystal chandeliers, the gold-leaf gilt and polished mahogany of the *Sub-Secretario's* ceremonial surroundings, we entered the typical substratum of government bureaucracy: rows of windowless fluorescent-lit rooms overcrowded with metal desks and filing cabinets, populated with shirt-sleeved men and bespectacled ladies poring over bulging files or typing reports in quadruplicate. Eventually we squeezed into seats around de Leon's conference table, with him presiding at its head.

For the first time, we settled down with the Mexican who would come to dominate my business hours—not for the two weeks that Tom Halleran had predicted, but, as it turned out, for nearly eight months. All stereotypes of dealing with Mexicans were soon put aside. Hugo de Leon was no bombastic Pancho Villa gunslinger, no devious bribe-seeking fraudster, but a quiet, punctilious gentleman who took pride in speaking precisely and only after careful thought, enlivened by a subtle amusement at some of our American peculiarities. Of all the officials in *Hacienda*, he was deemed the most expert in extracting from multifarious government sources the economic, financial, political, historical and legal information that we would need to explain Mexico to the world of international investors. He was familiar with English but not fluent, and our group had the same limitations in Spanish. It was decided that for all our business sessions each would speak in his own tongue, and Leon Alberdi, our bilingual lawyer from Banamex, would serve as interpreter.

John Guest of Kuhn, Loeb led off with an articulate summary of our principal task: we would have to produce a prospectus that would tell the Mexican story in a way that would sell bonds and also satisfy the rigid "full disclosure" requirement imposed by the US Securities & Exchange Commission for all public securities offerings. We would not be writing a puff piece, but a "warts and all" document that could not hide the shortcomings and needs of the economy. The political system was still emerging from the turmoil of its revolutionary period, governed by ideologies radically different from those of its capitalist, free-enterprise neighbor looming over its northern border. John had to tread the delicate diplomatic line between expressing our admiration for the country's accomplishments and pointing out its continuing level of poverty as well as controversial issues such as property confiscations, debt defaults, and the Government's direct ownership of large chunks of the economy. If fully disclosed, he explained, all the troublesome issues would pass without comment—but if *not* disclosed, would come back to haunt us.

After listening impassively to this tense prologue, de Leon leaned back and eased the strain by saying, "Well, gentleman, we have a major project here. We at *Hacienda* will do everything we can to help. Tell us what you need, and we will get it."

That meeting in October 1962 was the first of innumerable sessions around Hugo de Leon's table until June 1963. Whenever we were in Mexico, our typical schedule was: start the day at 9 a.m. with a drafting and strategy discussion at our Banamex office; 11 a.m. to 2 p.m. working session with de Leon; 2 p.m. to 5 p.m. lunch and documents review; and 5 p.m. to 8 p.m. back with de Leon—the typical late-skewed Mexican working day. Our banker/lawyer team gradually became experts on Mexico. De Leon and his staff provided us with the vast documentary arcana of the Mexican economic structure— annual Federal budgets, schedules of outstanding debt, official statements on fiscal and monetary policy, reports of the Central Bank on balance of payments and foreign exchange reserves, releases from relevant Ministries on gross national product and its components, minerals, oil and gas, steel, automobiles, glass, cement, chemicals, wheat, cattle; on railroad shipments, telephones in use, electric power consumed, toll-highways constructed, ad infinitum.

Back at our glassed-in office on the mezzanine of Banamex, we accumulated this growing mountain of paper and, sitting around a long communal table, like medieval scholars we pored over it for endless hours to extract the essential nuggets. We added a small library including the famous Constitution of 1917 establishing the "modern" Mexico, plus text-books and histories on the country's political structure and the development of the one-party system that had prevailed since the 1920's, electing every president and most congressmen and state governors (29 of them at the time).

We had no lack of raw material, backed up by helpful explanations from de Leon. Our task was to reduce it to a coherent prospectus that would satisfy the SEC and convince investors. We had to describe important social policies enshrined in the Constitution. These included the well-known Article 123 (which even has a Mexico City street bearing its name) that created workers' rights. Another was Article 27, which radically changed the structure of rural land tenure and ownership of sub-surface mineral rights.

It was well recognized, even documented, that in the post-revolutionary period after 1917, many large rural estates had been seized and broken up by government for distribution to small farmers under the *ejido* system of communal ownership. It was also known that compensation was not the norm, but rather outright confiscation, with nothing paid to the wealthy (and politically unpopular) landowners. The Mexican Government was reluctant now to mention or even suggest confiscation in an official document that would be widely circulated in the United States, the bastion of private property rights.

To the contrary, our group argued that it would be folly (and unacceptable to the SEC) to hide a notorious policy such as this, and in any event sophisticated present-day bond investors would not be overly concerned over losses suffered by land-rich country gentlemen of a previous generation. We struggled with wording to accomplish an acceptable compromise; our drafts were submitted to de Leon, from there kicked upstairs to the rarely seen Saenz Arroyo, then back down to us with regretful comments that we still had not quite got it right. Finally, we presented a masterpiece of bland language that passed muster, as follows:

> Mexico has ordinarily paid compensation to foreign nationals holding valid titles to properties affected by the agrarian reform program, although a number of unsettled claims remain outstanding... Generally, it has not been the practice to pay compensation to Mexican owners of rural properties that have been taken for rural

redistribution and most of such owners have accepted this practice.

I still wonder about the harsh reality that was covered up by this dry formulation. How many proprietors of ten-thousand acre cattle ranches or wheat fields, maintained with struggle on the dusty plains of Chihuahua, "accepted" the turn-over, except after bitter court-room wrangles, attempted bribes to the local general, and occasional last-stand gun-fights between private guards and the Federal police? They were the majority; what happened to the minority who did *not* accept? Jailed, exiled, bankrupted, shot-while-escaping under the infamous *ley fuga*? The 1920s and 1930s were hard days in a Mexico ruled by hard men. Hugo de Leon knew the history as well as we did, and approved the quoted words with his usual quiet smile. Although edited by many hands, they were put forward by me, the lawyer on the team, as a practical compromise. But I am still not proud of them.

We had our one serious skirmish with Mexican chauvinism in preparing the "choice of law" wording for the bonds—a picayune issue that we never dreamt could be grounds for a dispute. By invariable practice, US dollar bonds listed on the New York Stock Exchange carried the legend "governed by the laws of the State of New York."

When this formulation was presented to the legal department of *Hacienda,* it clearly affronted their notion of Mexican sovereignty. What connection was there with the State of New York? Were the bonds not under aegis of the Mexican Constitution, authorized by congressional legislation, and created by a presidential decree and a deed executed by the secretary of finance? Mexican law must govern! Our legal counsel Miguel Escobedo had an astute understanding of how far we could press our arguments before hitting a stone wall. In elegant Spanish he tried to defuse the issue, saying it was just a technicality accepted by other international issuers.

To no avail. The spokesman for the legal department, unlike Hugo de Leon, was a fire-eating nationalist who declaimed that Mexico had too often been exploited by foreign financiers imposing their own legal systems. He would be sacked by his masters if he agreed to this new insult to the nation! We could hardly respond. It would have been folly to state the unvarnished truth that bond investors simply did not trust Mexican law. We left a contentious meeting deeply concerned over this potential deal-breaker. Calls to the New York banks confirmed that bonds governed by Mexican law would be a non-starter. Once they read the fine print, US and European underwriting firms simply would not buy.

I called Tom Halleran to explain our impasse and ask him to exercise his ingenuity. Late that night he reported that he had discovered a precedent to satisfy both parties: the standard agreement used by the World Bank (the prestigious International Bank for Reconstruction and Development) in its many loans to sovereign governments around the world. The World Bank did not include any stipulation whatever about governing law, simply relying on the borrower's firm promise to repay. If that was good enough for the World Bank, with its billions of dollars at risk, would it not suffice for a $40 million bond issue?

The bankers agreed to this new scheme, and next morning we presented it to the choleric Mexican legal officer as a valid compromise, based on *Hacienda's* own dealings with the World Bank. The bonds would simply be silent on the legal principle; no mention would be made of New York (or Mexican) law. After brief head-scratching and consultation with a colleague, he actually smiled, shook our hands, and declared our proposal *"perfectamente confirmado."* Fortunately, there was never any call for litigation: for 15 years interest and principal on all the bonds were paid when due, with never a hint of delay or default.

By June 1963, our lengthy task was nearing completion. As my first child was nearing birth, I was replaced in Mexico by Tom Halleran, who wrapped matters up by gluing himself to the telephone, clearly enjoying his return to the trenches after many years of office-bound senior consulting. The Prospectus was boiled down to drafts that circulated between New York and Mexico City. In those days long before word-processors or e-mail, or even telefax or reliable photo-copying, all documents had to be laboriously typed and dispatched by air-mail or, if crucial, by expensive private messenger, as FedEx too was still in the future. Final revisions were agreed in hour-long phone calls, then sent off to the all-night printers, who could take reams of marked-up copy at 9 p.m. and produce a perfect document by 6 a.m. A final version of the 63-page Prospectus was printed and delivered to the SEC who gave a few desultory comments and "registered" it, so that under date of July 16, 1963, Kuhn, Loeb and First Boston offered $40 million of bonds issued by the United Mexican States.

It was not for me to know who were the actual buyers, but the issue was a sell-out, and of course profitable for the managing banks. Right on the front of the Prospectus, one read that Banamex was paid precisely $109,375 for its services. I always wondered how Don Agustín Legorreta's unique contribution was calculated in reaching this figure.

For me, a mere law-firm associate, the rewards were hardly financial. Professionally, I was proud to be part of a team that for the first time since 1917 brought private investors' capital into the coffers of the Mexican state. We each enjoyed a brief ceremonial hand-shake with Adolfo López Mateos, Mexico's President, and were given a commemorative gold medallion. The more time I spent in the country, the more I could see the poverty and the more I could hope the few million dollars inflow from our bonds would, as stated in the Prospectus, be used to improve the country's electric power system and thus trickle down to rural communities.

My enforced weeks in Mexico opened my eyes. I began to learn something of the language, and much of the history and culture, of that complex nation. Gradually I became immersed in its sights and sounds, and in the remarkable people and enduring friendships that enriched my life over the coming years.

"Due Diligence" Travels

The Mexican officials and our banker friends encouraged us to use our weekends to explore, to learn more about the nation that we were reducing to a dry-as-dust prospectus. We should venture outside the limits of Mexico City. Residents just call the City "Mexico", or use the phrase "Day Effay", the Spanish phonetic version of "D.F.". the abbreviation of *Distrito Federal,* the special juridical zone in which the City lies, just as Washington lies within D.C., the District of Columbia. (To dispel any confusion, the *Distrito* is surrounded on three sides by the State of Mexico, one of 31 states that now make up the United Mexican States, or *Estados Unidos Mexicanos*, the country's official name.)

Palenque

For our first excursion, we wanted to taste the traditional Mexico of mud and ruins, peasants and pot-holes. We found them all. John Guest had traveled in Mexico previously and had a passion for further exploration. Looking more like an inquisitive Oxford don than a Wall Streeter, his long fingers and bespectacled eyes were forever busy with obscure maps and schedules of airlines, busses and railroads. He rejected the Chichen Itza ruins as already too well-known and touristy, and on the advice of a historian friend settled on Palenque, a site in the early stages of exploration buried deep in southern state of Chiapas, with the only road connection indicated as "under construction." But John discovered an approach by air.

Saturday morning we boarded a scheduled Mexicana flight to the coastal city of Villahermosa, a DC-6 with half the seats removed for freight carriage. After landing on the windy runway, we found the single-engine Cessna that John had chartered, with barely room for the three of us and pilot, who gloomily announced, "hope we make it; nothing but rain forecast". But he avoided squalls falling from lowering grey skies as we flew low over featureless marshland. The topography abruptly changed as we saw looming up before us the first range of mountains. He banked a steep circle to give us an aerial view of the Palenque ruins. The site had been chosen for dramatic dominance, set on a ledge of the foothills backed by a steep ridge and surveying the barren plain that stretched away to the Gulf of Mexico. The ruins' pale grey towers and terraces of ancient stone-work made a vivid contrast against the dark green of surrounding rain forest.

The landing area was a rutted meadow next to a single-track railway that meandered off into the bush. Cows were grazing, but a couple of low-level passes drove them off. After a promise to pick us up at 1 p.m. the next day "if the weather holds," the pilot made a hasty turn and vanished into the clouds. We were left standing in the sudden silence of the countryside, broken only by the whirring of mosquitoes. But not for long; a battered truck pulled up—the driver said he had heard a plane land and figured we would need lodging. Seated on hard wooden benches in the truck's rear, we were driven down dirt roads past the central plaza and threadbare commercial zone, ignoring the crumbling Hotel Regional and stopping at the grandly named Hotel de la Croix, recommended but unreachable by telephone from Mexico.

Our lack of reservations posed no problem, as Palenque was hardly a boom-town.

Pedro, bright lad behind the desk, reported that the six rooms in this one-story cinder-block structure were all open, although more guests were expected when the night train might, or might not, arrive. The quoted rate was laughable, but John did the expected hard bargaining for a fractional reduction. The boxy chambers were lit by a screened but glassless window and single bulb hanging by a cord from the ceiling. The iron bed's thin mattress was encased in crackling cellophane. Expecting a communal bathroom, we happily found each one en suite, with all the proper fittings and one imaginative feature: to save space the shower-head was mounted directly above the toilet bowl.

The Croix served no meals, but we were directed to next-door restaurant El Bambu, offering dinner at the usual Mexican hour of 9 p.m., where the owner Herta was said to keep German food on the menu. With another rain squall threatening, we just had time for a beer at a nearby cantina, then a nap disturbed only by the generator that kept a flicker in the hanging bulb.

A short walk through puddles from continuing drizzle took us to El Bambu, a burlap-wrapped construction with an open patio lit by hissing acetylene lanterns. We were welcomed by Herta, a haggard but lively lady who spoke fluent English with strong German accent. Unfortunately, the previous week she had to fire the entire staff, Yucatecans from across the state border—always thieves, she told us—and the docile replacements, two boys under twelve, had only learned to make hamburgers with French fries and beans. Next week, she would teach them to make goulash and wienerschnitzel. We had no complaints about the food, and there was no lack of tequila, wine, and even whiskey, available, which she shared with us while her history unfolded.

Herta's Prussian father and Austrian mother came in 1913 to grow rubber, just the wrong time—within three years the revolutionary farmers took over, leaving parents to survive on a pittance, too broke to leave. She escaped to school in Chicago, but Mexico and her parents drew her back, and she stayed even after their death, surviving with the restaurant and by selling produce from a tiny lot whose ownership she had to prove every year in fights with distant bureaucrats. Life was not easy: the Mexicans ridiculed her as *La Gringa* and laughed when her bottled—gas cylinder exploded and demolished her kitchen, only now recovering. Becoming pensive after several Jack Daniels, she opened a cage and began stroking Marta, a lemur who she claimed shared her bed and nibbled her toes. We found him an unappealing creature, forever sticking his long tail into the food and licking one's face, but she was plainly Herta's favorite.

As it was Saturday night, and El Bambu seemed the only game in town, the bar/dining patio soon filled with Palenque's upper crust—the mayor, the school-teacher, the shop-owner and those few others who had enough cash to enjoy a night out (wives left at home). There was general astonishment at finding three gringos in darkest Chiapas, and friendly incomprehension at John's explanation of what foreign lawyers and bankers found to do in Mexico. Conversation at various levels of broken English and Spanish took a lively turn towards Panamerican brotherhood.

The good cheer was dispelled by the arrival of a man arrogantly riding a horse right up to the bar. He wore a trim khaki uniform and peaked campaign hat and was shod in polished leather boots, with a pistol belt around his waist. He was not, as first supposed, police or military, but the district surveyor, free to roam anywhere and set the metes and bounds of every property, clearly a man to be respected, and he knew it. Fortified by strong drink, with fluent English he soon engaged John in acrimonious debate about the merits of capitalism vs. communism. Castro was his hero. This encouraged his friend the school teacher, until then a quiet intellectual strumming a guitar, to declaim in favor of Marxism as embodied in the glorious Spirit of the Mexican Revolution. Bi-national warmth descended to political rancor. We decided it was good time for us to leave. After accepting Herta's invitation to return for 8 a.m. breakfast, we trudged back to the Hotel de la Croix. The generator was shut down, but we found our beds with a lantern held by the night watchman.

Awakened at 6:30 by the inevitable church bells, we saw heavy overcast suggesting more rain and threatening our flight. Dismayed at the prospect of spending another night (nights?) at the Croix, we asked Pedro about the train schedule. A shrug and a smile were his response, with the prediction, "certain never on Sunday."

Seeking breakfast chez Herta, we found all was silent at El Bambu, with dozing horse tethered to patio railing. Peering across the bar into the kitchen, we saw slovenly remains of last night's dinner, with flies thickly settled on unwashed pots and pans—so much for Herta's aura of neat Germanic precision. Our knocks on the slatted door gave no response. A quick glance through an unscreened window revealed Herta's gaunt limbs sprawled inert on a bed shared with the sleeping surveyor, fully dressed but for boots and pistol belt. Silently we crept away. Romance, however found, must not be disturbed.

We spotted another establishment of no more than two street-side tables, clean and wide-awake, that served us excellent coffee, rolls and *huevos rancheros*. Pedro commandeered the truck to take us up-hill to the Archeological Zone, free entry on Sundays. The guardian insisted we sign in at the Museum and examine its holdings, a sparse display under harsh fluorescent lighting. But the ruins themselves were unforgettable. Only partially excavated by 1962, the buildings, actually pyramids surmounted by airy pavilions and unique roof-combs, presented steep steps up which we struggled. From the top, with its sweeping view of desolate countryside, an indefinable air of majestic melancholy prevailed. A thousand years ago, the merchants and priests of a dynamic center bustled here where all was now silent but for bird-calls among overgrown paths and clinging vines. On the floor of the highest temple, the guide showed us a stone slab that had been discovered and lifted only ten years earlier, revealing a rubble-filled shaft that led 150 feet down to the resting place of the last ruling prince. Finally cleared, it now brought visitors like us to overcome our claustrophobia and view the airless burial tomb.

Rejoicing again in open air, on leaving the Zone we discovered the clear waters of a stream emerging from a tunnel under the ruins and falling into a rock-bound pool. John could not resist beating the clammy humidity by stripping down and leaping in. Not for long. The angry guardian appeared making unmistakable gestures ordering him to climb out. Our Spanish was not good enough to be sure of the reasons. I understood the mundane objection that John was polluting the town's drinking water; but he insisted he heard the more dramatic explanation that he was angering the Mayan gods by bathing in a sacred pool.

Whatever the reason, we quickly boarded Pedro's truck and avoided prosecution by heading to meet our return flight. The railroad track was as barren of traffic as the day before, and the air-strip meadow had the same muddy ruts. Peering anxiously up at the overcast, we first heard, then saw, the Cessna descending. With no cows today, the pilot merely had to keep his wheels out of the dampest patches. Soon we were aloft flying over the same dreary scrub. After one nervous (for us, not the pilot) stretch of squeezing over a ridge line and under a swirling storm cloud, we landed at Villahermosa and joined routine, every-day travel by boarding the on-time Mexicana afternoon flight back to Mexico City.

Our trip, with little comfort and certainly no luxury, could not be duplicated now 50 years later. The modern Yucatan super-highway has been completed, bringing bus loads of tourists to the cleared and gentrified Palenque ruins, with all the up-to-date advances of pathways, signs, brochures, film lectures, cafeterias and kids' areas. By Internet searching for accommodation, one can find half a dozen modern hostelries, including a Best Western and the Maya Tulipanes Eco-Lodge. There is no mention of the Hotel de la Croix, and surely El Bambu is long gone. I am glad we went in simpler days when those memorable establishments were still open.

Vera Cruz

John Guest, our Mexican history buff, insisted that for "due diligence" I must visit Vera Cruz, the port city down on the Gulf of Mexico about 180 miles east of the capital. During all the years of ship-borne travel, Vera Cruz gave European visitors their initial view of Mexico, and they universally loathed it. From far at sea they first sighted the glorious peak of Orizaba, 50 miles inland, perpetually snowy at 18,000 feet, and anticipated Mexican Swiss Alps. Vera Cruz was a sad disappointment. Sited on barren dunes near a muddy estuary, since Hernán Cortés' invasion in 1519 it was chosen as a port only because of protection offered by a string of offshore reefs and islands. The journals of every arriving traveler record the blowing sand, the muggy climate disturbed by occasional stormy "northers", a few drab buildings along the shore-line, and rows of black-winged *zopilotes* (vultures) eyeing uneaten carrion lying in the streets. The surrounding marshes were breeding grounds for mosquitoes and a fever locally called the *vómito* that felled foreigners so that of every military draft nearly one third were soon dead or in hospital.

As soon as possible after debarking, every European sought a horse, a mule, a carriage, a litter bearer, or later Mexico's first primitive railroad, to escape to the healthy highlands. But despite its malodorous reputation, Vera Cruz grew as a commercial port of entry, as docks and vast warehouses were built to hold the steady in-flow of goods that were dispatched to the interior—English woolens, French laces, and all the manufactured items demanded by the rich of Mexico City. Customs duties were collected to give the Mexican treasury its principal source of revenue, and a growing cadre of Mexicans immune to the climate, plus a small group of toughened foreign consular agents and business brokers, settled in to handle the trade and make a tidy profit. As a rich *entrepot*, Vera Cruz often became a battleground for supremacy by factions in Mexico's endless internal wars and a target for seizure by the French and later the American military forces. The story of Vera Cruz is writ large on the pages of Mexican history.

By the time of my trip, the health problem had been eradicated and a new super-highway replaced the original carriage route. I had no anxiety about renting a sturdy jeep and setting out from Mexico City. After traversing the drab eastern suburbs of the capital, I soon climbed into pine-clad mountains surrounding the Valley of Mexico and descended into the fertile plains leading to Puebla, a clean square-grid city said to be conservative, respectable, and dull. After a quick lunch and glance into the vast, typically ornate Cathedral, I hurried on across the high mesa and soon came to the stunning physical feature that defines geography in central Mexico: it's altitude not latitude that counts. Height above sea level sets the differences in temperature, climate, crops, trees, flowers, clothing—even human temperament.

The transformation was abrupt. After climbing a few hundred feet on a ridge of mesquite and cactus baked by the harsh highland sunlight of 8,000 feet, where sweat dries in seconds, the road fell off the escarpment. Pico de Orizaba briefly loomed on my left before I rounded a bend that led plunging down in sweeping curves. In a dozen miles I dropped five thousand feet from the *tierra fría* through the *tierra templada* into the *tierra caliente*—cold to mild to hot—and was surrounded by the lush greenness of banana trees, bamboo groves, and sugar cane. I zipped past the city of Cordoba, now freely perspiring in the clinging humidity, stopped for a drink on a jasmine-strewn terrace in the aptly named town Fortín de las Flores and lost another three thousand feet crossing the alluvial plain leading to *La Villa Rica de la Vera Cruz*, The Rich Town of the True Cross, as Cortés had named it.

With no monuments of architectural note, and no hint of where the True Cross might be found, the city had the tangy no-nonsense air of any commercial port in the tropic zone, with a poly-glot populace devoted to the business of stevedoring, cargo invoicing, and trade finance. After dinner in the breezy, tile-floored hotel, I strolled the quadrilateral central plaza, one side open to the sea-front *malecón*. The arcades along the other three sides, harshly lit by buzzing fluorescent strips, sheltered tables of men engrossed in dominoes, fierce games marked by slamming every piece down hard, surrounded by knots of intent, wagering spectators. Occasional marimba and guitar music was drowned out by the sharp clacking of the dominoes.

The men in this un-romantic town came to compete, not idle away hours listening to soft melodies.

Early the next day, I surveyed the scanty fleet of charter boats tied up to the docks, age-scarred but apparently seaworthy, and hired one for the morning. At the insistence of the captain, proud of his gold braided cap, and his agile mate whose knife chopped up bait with blinding speed, I tried fishing, with no luck. We motored around the oily harbor for a quick view of Fort San Juan de Ulua, built three hundred years earlier on the protecting reef. First used for defense, later as a prison, its towering stone walls and iron-barred window slots supported all the tales of shackled in-mates left to rot in dank dungeons, in a country where *habeas corpus* was unknown.

Back ashore, I enjoyed a perfect, simple lunch. Under the open-air arcades, waitresses in starched white uniforms deposited wicker baskets of shrimp freshly washed from the sea, bowls of limes, and plates of warm tacos. I and other diners bit off the shells, squeezed limes, and consumed the succulent flesh, washed down with the superb Mexican Dos XX beer.

Over the Mountains

After another night in Vera Cruz, exploring the vast crepuscular Mocambo Hotel, an icon of misguided tourism, my jeep took me climbing back up the escarpment on the super-highway. In seconds the sun vanished and I was immersed in the grey cotton wool of thick fog. All I could see was the red go-slow lights of trucks a dozen yards ahead of me and the beams of others creeping up my rear end—an hour of eye-strain and foot on the brake pedal as we all crept upwards through the interminable switchbacks. Then, another miracle of Mexican climate: cresting the summit, I burst from gloom back into the implacable sunlight of the austere plateau, blinded until I found my dark glasses.

Any sense of urgency fell away. My instinct to wander prevailed. I left the slick toll highway and checked my map to find obscure secondary roads that would lead me up towards the

Pico de Orizaba, its brilliant cone of snow and glaciers drawing me magnetically. Zig-zagging through pastures and corn-fields, I reached a village where I could go no further. After a straggle of adobe houses, a church, a miniscule general store, and a garage with a tractor hanging in chains, its main street ended in a barred gate and a rutted track. At about twelve thousand feet, the sky took on the darker blue of altitude. It was one of those crystalline days when a pine tree five miles away seemed etched on a tablet one could reach out and touch.

Knowing I would never climb higher, I got out and sat on the hood to gaze up at the forested slopes, the higher scree above the tree line, and the barrier of glittering ice around the crater. A farmer leading his horse down the track eyed me curiously and asked,

"Disculpeme, pero que pasa, señor? Tiene problema con el coche?" (Excuse me, sir, but do you have a problem with the car?)

"Nada," I answered. *"Solo mirando a la montaña."* (Nothing, just looking at the mountain.)

"Ah, es estupendo, no? Yo también miro todos los días." (Ah, it's stupendous, no? I too look at it every day.)

"Hay muchas leyendas?" (Are there many legends) I asked, thinking of Aztec and Nahuatl Indian folk tales about protective mountains.

He smiled. *"Leyendas, señor? No sé. Lo único que sé es que me hace sentir bien al puesto de sol"* (Legends, sir? I don't know. All I know is it makes me feel good at sunset).

He tipped his straw hat and continued on his way. If it made him feel good every day at sunset, it did the same for me in the brightness of noon. The remote, sun-dazzled silence, where oxygen was short, created a sensation of light-headed peace that I felt nowhere else in Mexico. I felt I might have settled down in that village forever. Of course, I snapped out of my dream and shook myself back to reality, refreshed for the long drive to my next destination

In her magnificent memoir *Life In Mexico*, the intrepid Scottish Fanny Calderon de la Barca, wife of Spain's first ambassador to Mexico, recounted her travels in 1840-1842, when every trip was fraught with bandits, sudden floods, and bridges falling into ravines. But no obstacle stopped her, and she managed to reach San Miguel Regla, the hacienda where silver ore from Real del Monte, Mexico's richest mine, was brought down to be refined. After reading her description, "the most picturesque and lovely place imaginable, but the house totally abandoned and comfortless," I had long harbored an urge to see for myself.

By the late 20th Century the estate had been acquired by a group of Mexican doctors and restored as a county retreat. I had met the Mexico City lawyer who managed the venture and encouraged my visit. I followed an intricate map he drew me, up through the bustling, charmless city of Pachuca, climbing its dominant mountain range, and weaving through a series of dusty boulder-strewn roads, until fortress-like gates appeared and I entered the manicured grounds and massive stone buildings of today's San Miguel Regla.

I was given overnight lodging in a spacious chamber still marked by iron rails for ore-wagons, where my sleep was lulled by the rippling sounds of falling water.

The river that once turned the wheels of the smelting works had been dammed, creating a series of pools and terraced gardens, where next morning I was guided by a grizzled custodian who explained the now silent works. He was a hard-bitten guy, not enthused by the peaceful scene of surrounding forest, sparkling stream, and half-submerged structures. As best I could understand his guttural Spanish, his message was, "yes, ain't it pretty now, but those poor buggers had to work their asses off for that son-of-a bitch the Count of Regla". Today's unforgettable charm of the vanished era, had, as usual in Mexico, been bought with blood, sweat and tears.

Chapter 6
Making Friends in Mexico

The Satellite Towers! On my first drive out of Mexico City on the main artery to the north, we passed through Satellite City, an early suburb just outside the *Distrito Federal* in the State of Mexico. We were taking the *Periferico*, a new divided highway optimistically intended to ease the flow of the City's already horrendous traffic. Topping a rise, I suddenly saw five closely grouped towers rising from a plaza between the lanes. Coming closer, I saw they had no windows, no decoration of any sort: simply five hard-edged concrete obelisks rising some 170 feet, each painted a different primary color, providing no service whatever to the passing motorists. Built in 1957, they seemed a continuing affront to pragmatic city planners.

How? Why? By whom?

Eventually I learned the answer. During my eight-month slog working on the first Mexican bond issue, I determined that I would not devote myself only to business, but also try to absorb Mexico's quirky social life. In a city that had already over eight million people, from the crime-ridden slum of Nezahualzcóyotl on the east (similar to the site of Oscar Lewis' classic study *The Children of Sanchez*) to the millionaires' walled mansions of Las Lomas on the west, there were innumerable sets that a transient foreigner could hardly penetrate. But there was one zesty international gang where everybody seemed to know each other, a mixed bag of Americans, Mexicans, French, Germans and Brits, some wealthy, some struggling intellectuals, but all loving a party and a chance to talk and talk. It helped to know some Spanish, but the *lingua franca* was English, in a variety of accents.

I looked up a New York entrepreneur who had moved to Mexico to run a business that I never really understood. Harold Sands was at heart a social animal. He and his wife Joanne, a charming Washington belle with a soft southern lilt, bought a narrow house on Calle Copenhague, on the edge of trendy Zona Rosa, and created in its cramped living room the closest thing to a salon, offering food, drink, conversation and unexpected meetings.

There I met an energetic young woman named Maria von Wuthenau, known to all as "Kooksie.". She was the daughter of German exile Dr. Alexander von Wuthenau, a polymath anthropologist whose studies of Olmec heads, pre-Columbian artifacts and obscure languages convinced him of direct links between Mexico's Indian civilization and African tribes. Kooksie spent her days running a ladies' dress shop on a fashionable block on Reforma, which she named Maria Catinelli in honor of her late mother's maiden name, and, as she admitted "to give it a little Italian class," which had the desired effect of attracting languid Mexican wives with little to do except shop for another gown. Many evenings Kooksie left work to organize her father's cluttered, shambolic household in arty Coyoacán. A true scholar, often with wisps of white hair tucked under a black beret, he cared little for practical affairs and preferred curating his collection and expounding his theories at length, eventually resulting in his illustrated book *Unexpected Faces in Ancient America,* a treasure for specialists.

One night Kooksie and her father brought along to a Sands buffet another German exile, a lanky younger man named Mathias Goeritz, an artist/sculptor/designer who had lived in Morocco and Spain before settling in Mexico. He was introduced as the man behind the Satellite Towers that had amazed me. He diffidently gave the credit to his partner Luis Barragán, Mexico's world-famous architect, but Kooksie insisted that Barragán was merely the expediter and Goeritz the creative genius. I asked him naively what artistic theory had been on his mind.

"Who knows?" he laughed. "We were given a big space to fill, upwards not outwards, and towers seemed the easiest. I wanted them higher, but . . ."

So much for theory, but I wondered who had paid.

"Good question," he answered. "Luis occasionally found some funds for me, and I saw him dropping wads of pesos to pay for the cement and the work—nobody had bank accounts. I guess it all came from his pal Alemán." (Miguel Alemán had been president from 1946 to 1952, making the expected pile while in office and then continuing as the country's wealthy man-behind-the-throne.) "If you knew him, you could get anything done."

Goeritz took the Towers as a light diversion from his real passion of teaching and inspiring younger people to open their eyes to their artistic potential. He was a mentor of Helen Escobedo, sister of my lawyer friend Miguel, in helping her become an acclaimed sculptress of massive abstractions and "site specific" works in her native Mexico and internationally.

But he enjoyed showing his work, and invited me to come for a look. A week later we drove out in his Volkswagen and stopped in the compressed parking area between the Towers. Nothing but rough unfinished concrete rose around us, narrow fins on diamond-shaped bases, brutal in their vertical simplicity. He opened an unmarked metal door flush with the surface of the tallest tower and waved me in. All I could see was a mesh of iron re-bars and concrete slabs vanishing up into darkness.

He slapped a wall and chuckled, "At least it's not *papier maché*. But I never knew who owns the land, and I still don't. They could blow it all up and probably get a million to sell it to Pemex for a gas station. What the hell, things change."

Not likely. Goeritz died in 1990, but his Towers have now been proposed for preservation as a UNESCO World Heritage Site.

I soon made another friend who enjoyed the Sands' hospitality, a delightful busy bee of a man named Raúl Ortiz y Ortiz always sporting a crisp bow tie. Raúl held down a teaching job at the University of Mexico, but his proficiency at languages often demanded his presence at official government conferences with foreign nations. He had the knack of appearing like The Mad Hatter at virtually every social or cultural event, with the air of being about to dash off to the next one, and so was invited everywhere, a godsend to any hostess facing a multi-lingual dinner party. His gossip about political chicanery at the highest levels was a welcome diversion, and apparently he never suffered from his indiscretions. His image as a social butterfly was contradicted by the many hours he devoted to writing the first Spanish translation of Malcolm Lowry's famous autobiographical novel *Under the Volcano*, a suicidal monologue set in Cuernavaca, opaque even in the original English and a challenge for any translator. Its publication was widely acclaimed by the Mexican intelligentsia.

Thanks to Raúl I was invited to lunch at a house whose typical blank wall dominated all one side of a cobble-stone street in colonial San Angel. Abashed at entering the sweeping entrance hall, eying the formal garden, and being led into the drawing room impeccably furnished in the finest of Mexican and European styles, I was soon put at ease by the remarkable owners, a reclusive couple with quiet influence throughout the capital. Marquis Fred de la Rozière, a gracious soft-spoken Frenchman, I learned later, had made a fortune helping Lehman Brothers find obscure Latin American investments. His half-English wife Sonya, some years younger and slimly elegant, possessed a dynamic intellect that made lunch not an occasion of casual chatter but a stimulating mental exercise. She delighted in correcting my compliments on their finding and restoring a classic mansion of the previous century.

"No, no," she explained, "we built it from the ground up just three years ago to look this way."

That was the first of many lunches and dinners over the next years, all small occasions with a quick pre-meal drink and briskly served perfect cuisine. Occasionally we dined on solid English fare over in Cuernavaca at the house of her mother Molly Vernon, a buxom lady who spoke loudly to drown out the epithets of the several parrots she kept and continually scolded. Another guest there was Nigel Davies, a former Grenadier Guardsman who abandoned England to do research on Mexican history, eventually publishing the definitive work *The Aztecs*, inscribed to Molly whose early generosity had encouraged him

Fred died a year or two later, but Sonya maintained her busy life, attending every lecture, concert or gallery opening that Raúl brought to her attention. She was no mere dilettante. She had become an experienced photographer, and set out to illustrate the images of crucified Christ that dominated Mexican places of worship, from cathedrals to the smallest chapels. She often disappeared for days travelling around the country searching for remote churches with vivid examples of this art form. I persuaded her to take me along on one of her briefer jaunts.

A different Sonya, in thick-soled shoes, jeans, wind-breaker and head scarf, led the way down the highway to Toluca and turned off on a dirt road, soon finding a church that stood alone among fields of corn. Her assistant set up special lighting (this was long before the dazzling flashes of digital cameras) and Sonya snapped away from several angles as we looked up at the larger than life-size wooden body of Christ painted a sickly yellow, nailed to the cross, with head drooping and gouts of blood streaming from his wounds. I found myself repelled by the focus on gore. Sonya, the dispassionate recorder, told me that Catholic priests, often highly educated men, simply found that depictions of agonized suffering were needed to attract the *campesinos* of Indian background who made up the bulk of any congregation. I could see our little group was clearly out of place, as the few ladies at prayer lifted their shawled heads to scowl at us as we left.

Sonya accumulated hundreds of photos showing these images by anonymous artists, each slightly different but all with the same agonized theme. She showed them to a well-known writer on Mexican art, Xavier Moyssen, and they collaborated to produce a handsome Spanish-language book named *Angustia de sus Cristos*. A few collectors' copies are still available on Amazon, for anyone wishing to spend $95.

My friend Harold Sands often entertained a man who appeared a hard-headed manufacturer during the week but consumed by a mad dream on weekends. His name was Milorad Choumenkovitch, originally from Yugoslavia. His standard outfit was the typical garb of a no-nonsense central European businessman—horn-rimmed glasses, white shirt, dark tie, black-three piece suit with gold watch chain looped into the vest pockets. His speech was slow and lugubrious, with a quick grimace and snapping of long fingers to dismiss any imbecility. I understood he owned a foolproof company making cabinets for Mexican-built TV sets, a growth industry. Somehow he had met and married Phyllis, a member of the Bostonian Brahmin Gardiner clan, a jolly lady whose braying Back Bay laughter kept everyone cheerful when Milorad looked his most somber.

They had bought a lot in the countryside an hour north of Mexico, on a barren slope near the famous archeological ruins of Teotihuacán, where I had done the obligatory exhausting climb up the Pyramid of the Sun. Of course they planned to build a weekend house, but no ordinary structure. Milorad had seen the church-then-mosque of Sancta Sophia in Istanbul with its remarkable dome as the city's landmark. His Mexican house must have a similar dome, smaller of course, but of the same unique design, supported by four corner pillars and lit by windows around the drum.

By the time of my visit, the house was nearing completion, an extraordinary sight, looming solitary amidst the low scrub. It stood gleaming white on its own platform looking down the slope, two wings with lofty French doors stretching away from the central block that did indeed support a dome—its second one, I was told, as the first had collapsed. The Mexican builders had never done a dome like this and didn't read the specs quite right. Luckily, no one was standing underneath when it crashed. The house looked more like some endowed research institute than a residence, suiting Milorad's grandiose objectives as he now greeted us as lord of the manor in leather boots and belted jacket.

We were joined for dinner by his nearest neighbor, arriving on horseback waving a lantern and clattering up the steps in the finest traditions of old Mexico. He had a perfectly good jeep, but Patrick Tritton, who will appear again, liked the dashing gesture. A beak-nosed English sportsman, he was the first to introduce pink-jacketed fox-hunting to Mexico, although a fox could never be found and his pack of beagles had to follow the trail of a scented sack dragged through the mesquite. He had a demanding wife in town, but like any English gentleman preferred country life.

Before I left the next day, Phyllis took me for a walk up a rocky ridge to view the estate and Patrick's distant stable.

"It's all mad, isn't it?" she exclaimed breezily. "The farmers and cowboys love us. The fat-cat Mexican snobs think we're nuts. They're *nouveaux riches* of course. I just call them beetles, low-down insects. Thank God I can laugh." Which she did, with full-blown Yankee self-confidence.

The mansion with its unmistakable dome lay right under the airline flight path from Mexico City to New York. Five minutes after take-off, I could look down and spot it through the haze. Later I lost track of Milorad; I heard he went bankrupt, whether from misplaced confidence in the Mexican TV business or the hubris of maintaining the dome, I do not know. I imagine Phyllis securely back in Boston, still laughing at life's absurdities.

Thanks to the Sands I met a couple who remain friends to the present day Juan Lans, a Mexican-born German, and spouse Milou de Montferrier, a French-American mixture. Juan ran the family company marketing diesel engines throughout Mexico and had starred in the country's 1952 Olympic swimming team. After an amicable divorce, Milou moved to San Miguel de Allende and created an elegant home-furnishings boutique and later founded Mexico's first hospice.

One summer, wanting a change from Mexico's cookie-cutter business hotels, I rented a house on Calle Aconcagua in the heart of the serene, hilly Las Lomas, above the worst of the smog, bringing my wife Edith and our one-year old daughter Diana. The US dollar went a long way in Mexico of the 1960s, so we had spacious rooms, with car thrown in, at a bargain rent by American standards, staffed with cook, butler/chauffeur, maid, and nurse—service that I could never have afforded, now or then, back in New York.

The Lans couple gave us many tips about living as locals: where to shop, how to deal with bill collectors, the right kind of tequila to buy, how much to pay *mariachi* musicians for a party we gave. Our mornings were spent improving our Spanish at the Mexican-American Cultural Institute down in the Zona Rosa. We were probably the only students arriving at class in a chauffeur-driven Lincoln, and of course had to absorb some friendly flak. When we took a weekend touring Taxco we simply dumped Diana in the same bedroom a with the three Lans kids. As all of them were tow-headed blondes, she made an easy fit, hard to pick out when we returned.

Through the Lans family, I saw the close master-servant relationship in Mexico—not like the United States, more akin to an extended family. The Saint's Day of their cook's grandmother was approaching, a major festivity to be held in the lady's country home. We were invited to attend, and after several fortifying shots of tequila *gran reserva*, Juan drove us far off the main highway along bumpy rural roads swirling with dust, the car laden with gifts for grandma. Her house was the typical one-floor construction of adobe brick, partly white-washed, with iron rebars rising from the roof in hopes that someday a second story would be built. As soon as the

Lans' cook leapt from the car into the miniscule front garden full of cactus and flower pots, a stream of relatives emerged to embrace her and all of us—her mother, brothers, sisters, aunts, uncles, a slew of kids hopping with excitement. Inside, grandmother was sitting in a deep chair, too aged for movement but smiling warmly on her vast family. The next few hours passed in delightful confusion, as *tacos, tortillas, quesadillas, tamales* and *carne asada* of every description were produced for lunch, together with a never-ending flow of tequila and beer.

Most of the family had clearly remained in the lower echelons of Mexican wealth, surviving by uncertain work in the "black" economy, below the eye of the tax collector. But upward mobility was possible: one handsome son of about 17, dressed like an American preppie and speaking competent English, had been accepted into a technical college and was on his way to a solid career. As the sole *gringo* present, I was urged to rise to my feet and try out my beginner's Spanish in song, which I did by creating primitive tunes for such hackneyed lyrics as *"Ay . . . mi corazon . . . sufre mucho . . . por amor . . . de ti"*, received with hilarity, whistles and cat-calls. Not until dusk fell were we allowed to escape, with endless *abrazos* of farewell, for a woozy return to the city.

Another lesson we learned from Milou Lans was to trust our staff. One day our nurse asked if she could take baby Diana to her Sunday church service. This seemed to us an awkward request, raising nervous fears of kidnapping. But when asked for her opinion, Milou told us. "Sure, don't worry." On return, the nurse was glowing with pride at showing off the blonde *niña* of the *gente amable* (nice people) who employed her. In our household there seemed none of the tension that often strains relationships between master and servant in the US.

After the Lanses separated (though with constant reunions), Juan continued to call me on my every return to Mexico. His usual invitation was "I'm very tired tonight; we'll just have an early drink". Which meant that would end up at 2 a.m. in deafening Plaza Garibaldi, hiring one of the *mariachi* bands that concentrated there. The mornings-after were dreadful for me, while he was apparently immune to dissipation.

Because I had spent much of my childhood in Nassau, Bahamas, another door was opened for me in Mexico. Nassau had been the home of Sir Harry Oakes, the busted prospector who discovered a Canadian gold mine and became a multimillionaire. His brutal murder in 1943 was world news, and despite wartime restrictions the media flocked to Nassau to cover the proceedings, made more sensational by the colony's governor, the notorious Duke of Windsor (briefly King Edward VIII), overseeing Sir Harry's racy son-in-law indicted as the culprit.

I was too young to know Sir Harry, but his five children were of my generation. The eldest, Nancy, beautiful and willful, on her eighteenth birthday had eloped with Freddy de Marigny, a French-speaking citizen of the British-owned Mauritius Islands, who settled in Nassau and could, if he wished, use the dubious title of Count. Many books have been written about the murder of Sir Harry and the subsequent prosecution of Freddy. The trial was botched and he was acquitted, but deported from The Bahamas, taking Nancy with him to Cuba. The murder remains unsolved to this day.

The marriage was not made in heaven. Nancy felt confined in Cuba and drifted off, getting a divorce and starting the life of a glamorous but rootless heiress, estranged from her mother and disdainful of her younger siblings. She was drawn to Mexico and found it suited her temperament, although with many restless trips to Hollywood, New York, London, and occasionally back to Nassau. She developed a passionate liaison with a well known English actor, and a daughter was born in Mexico out of wedlock, now a happily married lady of vigorous energy who has become my good friend.

In 1954, Nancy tried marriage again, with a German baron bearing the distinguished family name von Hoyningen Huene. A son was born, but this marriage too failed. Our paths rarely crossed, but Nancy did introduce me to a personable Mexican physician named Xavier Barbosa, then interning at Doctors' Hospital in Manhattan. Shortly before one of my early business trips to Mexico, I was instructed to pack a dinner jacket, as Nancy would be giving a ball, to celebrate her engagement to Patrick Tritton, her final husband, a delightfully eccentric English sportsman. I arrived at the gates of Marsella 44 to find her mansion, invisible from the street behind a forbidding wall. It had once been the German Embassy, with all elements copied from the ornate yet frilly fashion of late 19th century Europe. Mexico's President of that era, Porfirio Díaz, although half-Indian himself, had no use for any reflections of Mexican native culture and decreed that Europe would provide the dominant influence for the ruling classes.

I found myself caught up in a swirl of flaming torches, waiters passing champagne, diplomats in white ties, ladies proud of their diamonds, a few artists allowed in shabby jackets and head bands, an orchestra playing waltzes in the grand salon, a jazz band downstairs, and a talkative crowd of whom I knew few. Nancy swept briefly past towing a distinguished gentleman, one I did recognize from many meetings: Don Agustín Legorreta, the dominant figure of Banamex

"Dick, you know Tino, of course?" she said and hurried him on.

Tino! I would never have dared address him thus. Clearly Nancy had made her mark in Mexican society.

My one conversation before I left this glittering turmoil was with Xavier Barbosa, who sensed my lonely discomfort and affably introduced me to a few companions. He explained that while Nancy occupied the vast main floor of the house, one flight above ground in European style, he rented a tidy apartment on the lower level. Xavier had by then abandoned his medical career in favor of a more glamorous calling as assistant to a Mexican businessman named Emilio Azcárraga, known as "El Tigre" because of his forceful personality and a streak of white hair dividing his dark locks.

Emilio was the son of a tough, grass-roots entrepreneur who had cobbled together a nationwide chain of movie theaters, capitalizing on the Mexican public's appetite for the stream of cheap pot-boilers cranked out by the City's Churubusco Film Studios, leavened by a few imports from Hollywood. He had then ventured into broadcasting with a company called Televisa, which young Emilio himself took over. Emilio was already showing the ruthlessness and imagination that eventually, despite the distraction of three marriages and uncounted affairs, turned Televisa into the largest radio and TV broadcaster in Latin America and the dominant creator of Spanish-language productions in the US, with the inimitable *"telenovelas"* or soap operas. Although only in his thirties, he was already seen as a rising star, breaking his way into the close-knit cadre of old-line Mexican businessmen.

Xavier Barbosa now held a privileged position with Emilio, serving as a mixture of court jester and cultural adviser, easing the way into society and smoothing the rough edges off Emilio's blunt social graces. For this, Xavier was well paid, allowing him to indulge his talents as amateur architect/designer to develop handsome residential properties. Knowing that I was involved with a law firm and investment bank who were always on the look-out for new corporate clients, he did me the favor of organizing an introduction. He, my wife and I were invited to dinner at Emilio's walled, gated, guarded residence where we found that the three of us were the only guests. Emilio was the height of informal joviality, but the thrust of the evening was to hurry us through the meal so he could challenge me at backgammon. He was the kind of guy who could not exist without competition.

I was terrified. Although I knew the game pretty well, the prospect of facing an aggressive millionaire who would insist on high stakes raised acute fears of declaring gentlemanly bankruptcy. I escaped that fate. Although a skilled player, Emilio suffered from a flaw common to many over-achievers: pride that makes it impossible to admit a loss. I soon learned that if I doubled the stakes when his position was weak, instead of folding, he would accept, and then lose double—a classic example of misplaced *machismo*, not limited to Mexicans. After several hours of nerve-wracking play, we quit when I was up about ten dollars, which he handsomely paid with a broad smile and an *abrazo*. Maybe winning was my mistake: I never saw him again, and Televisa never became a client. But Xavier remained a good friend, and insisted that we come up to San Miguel de Allende to stay in one of his houses.

Before heading in that direction, I had to give Acapulco another chance, after my harassed weekend some dozen years earlier. It already had a down-market reputation of attracting every credulous package-tour traveler. But the incomparable bay has never changed, with its semi-circle of mountains ringing beaches and spectacular cliffs under reliable winter sunshine. In the 1960s these could be enjoyed, before the invasion of mass tourism and narco-terrorism.

As always, advice from friends was appreciated. I was told to stay at a trendy resort half-way up a mountain called the Villa Vera Racquet Club. It was run by an Acapulco character named Teddy Stauffer, a Swiss-born band leader who later circulated with Hollywood celebrities and became a virtual celebrity himself. I found a trim series of rooms and bungalows overlooking the bay far below, and had my first sight of that sybaritic invention, a bar and stools sunk into a swimming pool. Teddy himself was a handsome blond giant of a man, considerably past his prime, surrounded by a little group of fascinated acolytes. He gave a friendly nod to an unknown like me, and resumed his tales. Although he was reputed to bring a sporty gang to Villa Vera, I never saw anything remotely approaching an orgy, just a friendly group sitting waist deep around the bar getting quietly smashed. I heard many a question whether Teddy owned the place, or was just a front man backed by Sam Giancana and other Mafiosi who drifted in and out of Acapulco. I never saw them. Who cared? Teddy also ran Armando's, an excellent late-night restaurant downtown in an area that would be madness to visit now, with Acapulco renowned for turf wars between drug gangs.

The only Hollywood personality I ever met at Villa Vera was Greg Bautzer, the publicity-prone Beverly Hills lawyer with a client list that included Lana Turner, Joan Crawford (both of whom he "dated"), Kirk Kerkorian and Howard Hughes. His white hair and perpetual tan were set off by a set of flashing teeth so bright they could light up a room. Generous to a fault: if he was at the bar, nobody else could pick up a tab. He once wrapped an arm around me and whispered, "Why don't you give up that boring law at Cravath and come out to the Coast and have some fun?" Great guy, but I never pursued it. Was he really trying to recruit me for his firm? I figured my teeth were not bright enough.

I was also told to call a man with the pleasant name of Ron Lavender. A sober-sided American who had obtained full Mexican status, he worked hard to maintain his position as Acapulco's best real estate agent, fighting off the piranha who competed in this cut-throat pond. His lively blonde wife Jan handled their social life, and succeeded in making them the center of Acapulco's in-group international set, whose life revolved around the yacht club, tucked away in a quiet corner of the bay.

A weekend under the Lavenders' eyes, with an occasional quiet sail on Ron's little boat when he wanted to avoid the crowd, provided a frothy change of scene from working days in Mexico City, but had to be taken in small doses. Jan became the society editor of the local English-language rag, and was pressed to fill her columns. I began to see dreadful gossipy leads like, "Prominent NY lawyer partying down our way again on a break from his mysterious deals in Day Effay."

Back in Mexico City, I also found that my continuing visits caused puzzlement. What on earth could a Wall Street lawyer be doing all this time? For months I was not allowed to disclose the Government bond issue, supposed to be secret until launched.

A Corkscrew Life

The natural supposition: I was a CIA agent under deep cover. My vigorous denials got no response except knowing smiles. Finally I just uttered a tight-lipped "no comment", which of course added conviction to their guesses.

CHAPTER 7

My Self-Taught Mexican History

I soon found that I could not have an intelligent conversation with my Mexican friends unless I had a rudimentary understanding of the country's tumultuous history, replete with political dramas, religious conflicts, military campaigns, heroes, villains, and plenty of blood, beginning with the Conquest, when Hernán Cortés and a couple of hundred Spanish adventurers landed in 1519 and within three years vanquished the vast Aztec Empire with its millions of war-like citizens. I read how the famous *grito* (shout) of insurrection had been proclaimed in 1810 by a heroic priest at dawn on September 16, establishing that date as Mexico's official Independence Day from Spain, formally celebrated ever since. I delved into the country's brief history as an Empire, when from 1864 to 1867 the Europeans Maximilian and Carlota ruled as Emperor and Empress, with tragic consequences of death for him and madness for her.

Above all, I had to learn about the Revolution of 1910 to 1920 that radically changed Mexican society. For 34 years until 1910 Mexico was ruled by the iron hand of President Porfirio Díaz, who introduced the Industrial Revolution, with all its benefits and failings. The father of conservative pundit William F. Buckley Jr. found Mexico City more attractive than his native Texas as a place to set up a legal practice that thrived under

Díaz—until the inevitable cataclysm that ejected both Diaz and Buckley from Mexico.

For Díaz's apparently stable Mexico was a treacherous volcano of discontent that began to rumble in the early 20th century. A foreign-owned railway net work spread its links, and every capitalist lauded Díaz, but every farmer or cowboy on a hacienda worked in virtual peonage to the owner, every factory employee was denied any rights, every miner deep below ground dug and drilled until his body was broken. Any signs of dissent were put down with brutal immediacy, as when the hated *Rurales* were ordered to shoot strikers at the massive Rio Blanco textile factory in 1909, an atrocity that energized liberal leaders to consider a new regime. Díaz rashly hinted to an American journalist that he might not stand for re-election in 1910; that opened the floodgates, as an unlikely opponent announced in 1910 that he would run against Díaz's hand-picked successor. That proclamation has caused historians to call 1910 the first year of The Revolution, the whirlwind that swept Mexico.

The Revolution

Ah, *La Revolución!*—exhaustively documented, reported, analyzed, vilified by some, romanticized by others. The full name of the still dominant political party, the PRI, is *Partido Revolucionario Institucional,* and no politician makes a speech without referring to its principles, prevailing in theory although diluted in practice. Virtually every Mexican family has ancestors who were either killed, ruined or exiled by the Revolution, or raised to new eminence. Hollywood has capitalized on the drama, with frequent renderings of the colorful bandit/politico Pancho Villa, or the popular *The Professionals* showing an exhausted, wounded guerilla lying in a ditch exclaiming "How I love *La Revolución,*" and Marlon Brando became a heroic hit in *Viva Zapata.*

Its first leader gave little hint of the chaos that would ensue. Francisco Madero was a diminutive but determined aristocrat, scion of a wealthy dynasty with vast landholdings, but his education in France and the United States turned him towards liberal views anathema to Porfirio Díaz. In challenging the Díaz regime, he was not seeking a radical social and economic transformation; all he wanted was a fair election in which he could introduce his high-minded dreams of political democracy that would enfranchise the masses—including the *campesinos* who worked his own family *haciendas*.

After initial imprisonment by Díaz and escape to the US, Madero enjoyed early success with a fierce battle for Ciudad Juarez in May 1911. Together with political demonstrations in Mexico City, this battle forced the resignation and permanent exile of Díaz, and Madero became president in October. But he lacked the ruthlessness so necessary for a Mexican head of state. The very general whom he unwisely chose as his guardian betrayed him, with the shameful connivance of the American Ambassador Henry Lane Wilson. After a bitter ten-day cannonade in the streets of Mexico City in February 1913, Madero was assassinated and General Victoriano Huerta became President, joining Wilson in the boastful proclamation that Mexico had been returned to "peace, prosperity and progress."

In fact, the murder of Madero and the accession of Huerta began several years of civil war and virtual anarchy. All segments of Mexican society other than die-hard conservatives came to loathe the brutal, brandy-soaked Huerta and competed among themselves to oust him. PanchoVilla with his powerful Division of the North fought against the new "First Chief" Venustiano Carranza, with occasional forays from Zapata in the southern State of Morelos. Battles were fought in every major city in northern Mexico, as for the first time in modern warfare the opposing armies used the railways to carry trains of soldiers and camp-followers across the spread of plains and mountains—800 miles from the Texas border to Mexico City.

The violence of the conflict left uncountable destruction, of human lives, of buildings, of factories, mines, and farms, in effect the whole social and economic fabric. In formerly prosperous districts of Mexico City, residents were forced to hunt for rats to provide food, as one military gang after another swept in and out, commandeering supplies from shop-keepers and eradicating any usable currency. The only people who lived well were the self-proclaimed generals and their many leech-like dependents, clinging to every source of plunder.

To catch the flavor of those bloody years, I found invaluable the four-volume *Historia Gráfica de la Revolución Mexicana*, containing thousands of pictures, some posed, others candid, shot by an intrepid photographer who always seemed to be the man on the spot. The photos show better than any words the sharp divisions in Mexican society that underlay the Revolution. Formal portraits of newly elected cabinets, with each Minister stiff in dress uniform or white-tie and tailcoat, their faces pale as Europeans, alternate with open-air scenes of dark-skinned natives marching or stacking arms in the khaki of the *federales* or the cotton shirts and straw sombreros of the insurgent armies—or not infrequently hanging from a tree branch with a noose around the neck.

A whole section is devoted to the *soldaderas*, the intrepid females who followed their men to battle to cook, wash, and fornicate, often doing all three on the roofs of the sluggish troop trains, inspiring the enduring folk song "Adelita". We can almost feel and smell the brutish force of bombastic, mercurial Pancho Villa, and we catch the malignant leer of his murderous sidekick Rodolfo Fierro, the *pistolero* who never missed. A famous photo shows the robust, exultant Villa, seated in the National Palace during his one meeting with the fastidious Zapata, whose saturnine face suggests his distaste at sharing the limelight with the boorish northerner.

Martín Luis Guzmán was an educated young journalist, but inevitably he had to choose where to stand in the constantly shifting sands. As he wrote in his brilliant, often translated book, *The Eagle and the Serpent* in English, he was torn between the dictatorial absolutism of Carranza and the impossible alternative of Pancho Villa, "a mere brute force who was too irresponsible and instinctive even to know how to be ambitious." For generals and senior civilians, he writes: "Those were the days when each of us rode around in his private train as though it were a cab . . . our political conversations took place to the accompaniment of moving wheels and the smell of smoke and hotboxes." But even Guzman lived in constant fear of the mercurial Villa, who could smile one moment and the next pull his pistol to kill.

The once all-powerful Carranza was forced to abdicate in 1920, under pressure from his popular general Alvaro Obregón, Trying to escape to Vera Cruz, he was abandoned by his followers and ended his life shot to death in a muddy hillside bivouac. Obregón showed a knack for converting his military skills to middle-of-the-road politics, and under his leadership Mexico gradually restored its shattered structure into peace-time normality. For the next 20 years, periodic minor insurgencies had to be brutally suppressed, but the worst was over. Although Obregón was assassinated by a lone religious fanatic, his work was carried on by the tough but efficient Plutarco Calles and eventually the icon of popular democracy Lázaro Cárdenas, so that by the time his term ended in 1940 the country was achieving real stability under its tightly organized system of one political party, the PRI.

* * *

La Revolución did not leave many monuments; it was more often marked by destruction. A few years ago I was taken on a tour of a derelict mansion still standing in the heart of Mexico City. It had been the home of Antonio Rivas Mercado, renowned architect and member of the Díaz aristocracy in the early 20th century. Its history was well-known to Kathryn Blair, the aging but sprightly lady who guided our tour. Her husband is the son of Antonieta, Antonio's daughter. Kathryn has written an intriguing book called *In the Shadow of the Angel*, describing the downfall of the Rivas Mercado family during the Revolution, including daughter Antonieta's melodramatic suicide, putting a bullet through her head in Notre Dame Cathedral.

Kathryn guided us through the once elegant house, designed with all the classical elements studied by the architect-owner, that had barely escaped total ruin. Its Doric pillars and marble-floored loggia still stood, surrounded by cement mixers and wheel-barrows, as a charitable foundation tries to finance its reconstruction. Kathryn's words brought alive to us the scenes she described in her book—the rooms that had echoed to the voices of dignified, bearded Antonio, his three willful daughters, energetic son, and openly adulterous wife, a dynasty whose wealth and position were destroyed by the Revolution, leaving only these massive ruined walls.

But another monument remains gleaming and undamaged in modern Mexico City. The Angel mentioned in the title of Kathryn's book refers to the towering Angel of Independence, the lofty column topped by a golden Nike, eyed by every tourist, that rises from a traffic circle on today's Paseo de la Reforma. Commissioned by Porfirio Díaz to commemorate the pantheon of Mexican heroes, Kathryn explained that it was designed by Antonio Rivas Mercado himself and ceremonially dedicated in 1910, one of Díaz's last acts before his downfall. An edifice created by two men who were swept away by the Revolution still stands.

A Personal View

When I arrived in Mexico in 1962, the stability achieved by Lázaro Cárdenas' shrewd governance had long prevailed. My experiences gave me a few personal insights into how the country was run. The only sitting President I ever met, if just for a handshake, was Adolfo López Mateos, regarded as a mediating politician who under the slogan of "left, within the Constitution," effectively balanced the contrasting interests of the working man and the capitalist. But after his six-year term ended in 1964, he was succeeded by three of the most dreadful chief executives ever inflicted on the nation—18 years of misrule.

The first, Gustavo Díaz Ordaz shattered the country's hard-won image as a peaceful, tolerant democracy when he approved the Massacre of Tlatelolco in 1968. Suspicious and authoritarian by nature, he was unnerved by the fear that the long simmering discontent of students and labor unions would peak to interrupt Mexico's first Olympic Games scheduled for October of that year. When a massive but peaceful demonstration was held in Mexico City's Plaza of the Three Cultures, gunfire from surrounding police and military forces cut into the crowd, leaving scores dead and hundreds injured. Even my most conservative Mexican friends, some still wistful for the long-lost days of Porfirio Díaz, spoke bitterly about this atrocity, which the strongest official denials could not cover up.

Luis Echeverría was an important Minister under Diaz Ordaz, who, in the accepted Mexican style, "fingered" him as his successor to lead the PRI beginning in 1970. For six years he emitted a stream of left-wing bombast, while amassing a tidy fortune for himself and presiding over a devaluation of the local currency. Both before and after his term, he was accused of being the commander of the Tlatelolco shooting, but was always saved by legal technicalities.

The "finger" moved again in 1976, when Echeverría designated José López Portillo, his boyhood pal and Secretary of Finance, as the PRI candidate. After his nomination but before final election, I observed him at a private reception for bankers of New York City. A handsome, somewhat fleshy gentleman with the histrionic style of an actor or poet, he mouthed the usual high-sounding platitudes about Mexico's future. I could not have predicted that he would become Mexico's most reviled President in recent history, the only one to die (in 2004) without being awarded a state funeral. While the country was flush with growing revenues from new oil discoveries, he overspent the sudden wealth into virtual national bankruptcy, initiating further massive devaluation, despite his oft-quoted promise to "defend the peso like a dog." (Once out of office, he had to endure passers-by barking at him.) The country was only saved by the famous bailout by the US Government. In last-minute desperation, he abruptly nationalized the Mexican banks—a catastrophe that took years to unwind. By the end of his term, all Mexico could see the mansions he had collected while the country went broke, and the unbridled nepotism that extended to an official post for his mistress.

As the 1982 elections approached, even the Old Guard leaders of the PRI, the "Dinosaurs" as they were called, realized that a profound change of leadership style was needed, and they arranged the nomination of a non-political technocrat named Miguel de la Madrid, the first of a new breed of presidents who continue to the present day, often with higher education in US universities, English fluency, and a less parochial view of statesmanship than their predecessors.

During my work on Government bond issues in the 1960s and 1970s, I was fortunate to make many friends in the Ministry of Finance, or *Hacienda*, a breeding ground for smart bureaucrats on their way up the tortuous ladder of advancement. It was here that I met de la Madrid, age early 40s, as director of public credit, long before any dreams of becoming chief executive. As holder of a master's degree from Harvard's Kennedy School of Government, he naturally chaffed me about my Yale background. He had a calm, deliberative personality far from any political rhetoric. When I asked his view of Mexico's credit standing, he smiled and pointed to a mass of papers on his desk, saying only, "wait a few years." Once in the president's office, he reversed all previous policies by privatizing a host of state-owned enterprises and easing restrictions on foreign investments.

Another friend from *Hacienda* was the ebullient Sub-Secretary Mario Ramón Beteta, scion of a prominent family who took a degree from the University of Wisconsin and displayed the dynamic joviality of a mid-western Congressman. He had the trappings of a presidential candidate, but his career led elsewhere. He was persuaded to take the prominent but thankless post of director-general of Pemex (*Petróleos Mexicanos*), the vast government-owned oil monopoly and largest earner of foreign exchange. He was constantly torn between politicians expecting more money for their pet causes, the powerful union demanding higher wages for its 30,000 militant employees, and foreign oil buyers pressing for lower prices. Added to his woes, he had to fight off unproven, politically-inspired charges of personal corruption.

Several years after I had helped arrange a bond issue for Pemex, I called on Beteta in his office high in the Pemex tower. After a hearty welcoming *abrazo,* he turned to the window surveying the city's smog and throat-grabbing air pollution and shook his head in disappointment: "Look what we have created," was all he said. In 1987 he resigned from Pemex and was elected governor of the State of Mexico, the country's key constituency virtually surrounding Mexico City. The last time I saw him, he was making a stem-winding speech to applauding voters in the lovely lake-side town of Valle de Bravo. I always felt he would have made a first-rate president, but he died prematurely of cancer.

Another graduate of *Hacienda* with a radically different personality achieved success in the field of diplomacy. When I first saw José Juan de Olloqui, his perspiring bespectacled face was almost hidden behind towers of legal documents covering the minuscule desk he was given as a junior legal advisor. But his talents were soon recognized elsewhere and he was moved to the Ministry of Foreign Affairs, with initial responsibility for international financial negotiations, eventually rising to the pinnacle posts of Mexican ambassador to the United States and later to the Court of St. James, where he made his London Embassy home to all lovers of Mexico. With his portly frame, balding head and toothbrush moustache, he would never be mistaken for a budding politician. His interests ran elsewhere, towards art and literature. One day as he guided me around a

Mexico City art gallery and peered closely at the display, he took my arm and whispered, "If only art could have been my career . . . oh well, too late to change now." He was always a delightful companion, and I trust he died content with his high diplomatic honors.

Knowing Mexican public servants like de la Madrid, Beteta, and Olloqui gave me a better feeling about how the sprawling country was run, despite its many all-too-obvious deficiencies and the flagrant scoundrels in both the public and private sectors. Miguel de La Madrid, despite valiant efforts, was never able to fully unwind the mess created by his predecessor López Portillo.

The new millenium saw an upheaval in Mexican politics when in 2000 for the first time in 70 years the PRI presidential candidate went down to defeat, at the hands of Vicente Fox, the leader of PAN *(Partido Acción Nacional),* a more right-wing, business-oriented party. It was during his term that Mexico began to see the serious consequences of the drug wars, that were inherited his PAN successor, Felipe Calderón, elected by a bare, and contested, plurality in 2006. He faced 50,000 deaths over six years, from brutal executions by the drug gangs as well as killings by the often-corrupt army and police. In the 2012 elections, the country rejected the PAN and reverted to the PRI, although it was called the "new" PRI, under the leadership of a handsome young politician named Enrique Peña Nieto. He is immersed in fulfilling his campaign mandate of reducing the drug carnage, a patch-work plague that terrorizes parts of the country while leaving others untouched. It is too soon to judge his success.

CHAPTER 8

Business Deals, the Mexican Way

How did I support myself on my many visits to Mexico learning the country's peculiarities and meeting its personalities? How did I afford the travel and living expenses that enabled me to immerse myself in the country time and time again? I started my career with no hoard of private capital to finance a life-style of leisure and observation. I had a wife and children to support. I had to work my way.

For many years I was fortunate to be sent to Mexico by the Cravath law firm and, later, the investment bankers Kuhn, Loeb, who had Mexican clients to service, business that could not be handled by telephone or mail (snail mail; no e-mail in those days) and needed a warm body on the spot. My employers regarded me as "the guy to send to Mexico." Not that I objected. The path was up to me. I could have resisted the Mexican label and stayed in the United States, solidifying domestic contacts and probably making more money.

But in fact I sought every Mexican opportunity and looked forward to every trip. To me, a typical WASP gringo schooled in staid, rational New England, doing business in Mexico always had an exotic element, a promise of new discoveries in a different culture. where farmers in straw hats riding donkeys were found next to gleaming industrial plants. While systems in the United States were cut and dried, in Mexico one found the unexpected, the flexible solution.

And Mexicans, once the ice is broken, have a special knack for friendship.

Telephones

In 1965, long before the days of cell phones or the Internet, my first contact as a lawyer dealing with the Mexican private sector Mexico led me to the hard-working senior executives of *Telefonos de Mexico* (Telmex). With their efficiency, a $15 million international bond issue was promptly completed.

Of course my banker colleague and I had to perform the usual charade of due diligence—checking a company's tangible assets even if we had no clue how they worked. We were led down to Telmex's air-conditioned underground galleries where we observed miles of cable and rows of racks holding relay switches quietly clicking away like any electro-mechanical system, doing their stuff as total mystery to laymen like us. We could write that we had actually seen and touched the hardware: mission accomplished.

The bond issue was the first step in Telmex's transformation: nationalized in 1972 and later sold to a consortium controlled by Carlos Slim, reputed to be the world's richest man. A cell-phone division was created and spun off as a separate company, named America Movil, trading actively as AMX on the Mexican *Bolsa* and New York Stock Exchange, one of the better investments south of the border. The land lines still do their bit, but are considered a primitive technology with scant appeal to investors.

Steel

Back in the days when traditional steel making was still a solid money-spinner before being relegated to the rust belt, a company with the grand name of *Compañía Fundidora de Fierro y Acero de Monterrey* (Iron and Steel Foundry Company of Monterrey) dominated the Mexican industrial scene. *Fundidora* was the crown jewel of investments held by Don Carlos Prieto, patriarch of one of the country's "establishment" families. Tall, white haired, Don Carlos presented a formidable figure who allegedly used his influence to crush competitors and keep his work force in a state of well-paid but powerless subservience.

He needed more funds for expansion, and long-term financing was scarce in Mexico. His friends at Banamex called Washington and brought in the International Finance Corporation (IFC), the World Bank affiliate that has as its mission providing capital to private companies in the developing world. A deal was struck whereby IFC would provide $6 million for *Fundidora* debentures convertible into its common stock, inviting Kuhn, Loeb as "co-manager" for its expertise in selling Latin American securities. My task was the usual lawyer's one of drafting the papers for the debenture issuance, requiring visits to confer with IFC'S general counsel, a cheery, portly Englishman who confessed to a preference for life in London's civil courts over scrutinizing the minutia of financial terms.

I also travelled to Mexico's northern city of Monterrey, home of heavy industry and a hard-working business community that scorned the dissipated ways of Mexico City. I observed *Fundidora's* blast furnaces, channels of molten metal, rolling mills, stamping presses, slab and rod extraction machines—all the arcana of steel production and fabrication. I wore a hard hat and fire-proof smock for this rigmarole of due diligence. I was singed with a speck of molten ore that was flicked my way— accidentally, intentionally?—by a pair of goggled Mexican workers who stared impassively as a wisp of smoke rose from my smock. For them, it was an every-day risk. My company guide had a good laugh.

The debenture issue took a Mexican twist of ingenuity. The actual delivery against payment, the "closing", had to be held in Mexico City. But the engraved documents were printed in New York and then immediately "authenticated" by Irving Trust Company, *Fundidora's* appointed bank, a procedure requiring a bored assistant VP to wield an ingenious multiple pen that could affix his signature twenty time simultaneously. These debentures, in bearer form, once authenticated became fully marketable securities, that in theory could be sold by any scoundrel who seized them. How to get them to the Mexican closing without paying ruinous insurance charges? It was not my duty to serve as a Wells-Fargo delivery escort for $6 million of near-cash.

I was given a body-guard. A lean, mustachioed Mexican appeared at Irving Trust, wearing a wide-brimmed Stetson, string-tie, whip-cord jacket, and hand-tooled cowboy boots, bearing a notarized letter from Don Carlos authorizing him to help me pick up the debentures, now neatly wrapped in two 25-pound packages. He had no trouble lifting them into the waiting limousine that whisked us to JFK for the direct flight to Mexico.

Once seated in the limo, he opened his jacket to show me the six-inch barrel Colt carried in a shoulder holster. "See, no need to worry," he assured me, adding with a smile, "I know how to use it." I never asked how, or if, he got his concealed weapon licensed under New York City's tough laws. At the airport terminal in those pre-terrorist days, we boarded the DC-8 with no tedious inspection of our bodies or hand baggage. "The packages stay with us," my new friend made clear, with no argument. We had seats in the front row of the first-class section, with plenty of leg-room.

As if it were an every-day occurrence, I sat back to enjoy the food and drink with $6 million of negotiable securities at my feet and a trained *pistolero* at my side. After a few laconic words, he lapsed into silence, with a wary eye observing our fellow passengers until we landed. At the Mexico City airport, Brink's guards came right to the ramp and took the packages off in an armored truck. Don Carlos had all bases covered. With an abrupt *"hasta luego"* and a handshake, my protector turned and vanished into the crowd.

Next day, in a lawyer's conference room, papers were signed and the buyers took possession of the debentures. My task was done. They were all paid when due, but much later the famous

Fundidora was dissolved, victim of newer steel technology and unable to modernize.

Mud

A couple of years later, Monterrey gave me another example of Mexico's rough-and-ready business style. Our New York firm had as a client a so-called "oil-field service company" in San Antonio, Texas, that needed a steady supply of drilling compound, the slurry that's forced down oil-field wells between the casing of the bored hole and the drill string, to provide lubrication and prevent blow-outs. "Mud" is the common word but it's a misnomer. The slurry is usually a mixture of water, chemicals and a specialized type of clay that's ground into powder form. Northern Mexico held large deposits of this clay, and our client wanted a long-term supply contract from the Mexican owner, a firm that had the word "Barite" in its title, indicating the chemical composition.

I was dispatched to Monterrey to draft a straightforward purchase-sale contract for X tons of clay at Y Price over Z months. I found the Mexican firm in a dusty, wind-blown suburb, occupying unadorned steel and concrete buildings and run by a couple of hard-bitten miners who didn't have much time for the niceties of legal drafting. Their words poured out in fluent profane Tex-Mex style, like many northern Mexicans. As I got to work, they took a call from San Antonio. It seemed our client now wanted to buy the whole Mexican company, not just a supply of clay. "Shit, why not? Let's talk about it," was the quick answer.

Next morning a couple of executives from San Antonio landed on the dirt air-strip, guys as tough and business-like as the Mexicans. A price was quickly agreed, and I was asked to draft a corporate acquisition agreement, on the spot, the kind of job that's ordinarily done in a law firm, with forms and precedents and a research library available, resulting in a lengthy document with all the bells and whistles, subject to reviews and multiple re-drafts. But both sides were in a hurry and trusted each other. A bank was ready to transfer funds for the purchase price, the shares would be re-registered by a notary—what could be simpler? With the help of a wonderful bilingual secretary, I cudgeled my memory for few key provisions protecting my client, and we banged out overnight a basic agreement that seemed to do the job—whether enforceable under Mexican law I had no idea and nobody to ask.

By lunch time, the Texans had received oral OK from San Antonio to go ahead, and the Mexicans were their own bosses with no need to ask anybody. To my happy astonishment, execution signatures were affixed to my rough-hewn document, and the Texans and Mexicans both showed how to celebrate. Calls were made, and soon a van drew up to unload a smoking barbecue, cases of beer, and liters of tequila. Work stopped in the Barite offices, as the staff stepped out to hear a welcome speech from the new American owners. I was dragged into the festivities around an outdoor table with a view of the distant bone-dry Saddle Mountain that dominates Monterrey. Heat and implacable sunshine did not slow up the singing and dancing. Near day's end, like Shane riding alone into the sunset, I said my goodbyes to my new friends and got a lift to the airport and return flight to Mexico. I never heard whether the deal, so hurriedly given birth, turned out well. But I never heard to the contrary, and I always remembered that "mud" doesn't always mean "mud".

Sulphur

My deepest involvement in Mexican business centered around a corporate battle for sulphur, that abundant basic commodity marked only with symbol **S,** number 16 on the atomic table of elements, essential to life and found in innumerable chemical compounds.

One day in early 1966, John Guest, the Kuhn, Loeb boss of all things Mexican, barged into my cubicle office at the law firm. "Ah-ha! Another Mexican deal for you," he cheerfully alerted me, "but you have to start with hiring a guy we've found".

This Delphic utterance was fleshed out in the followings days. Once my mentor Tom Halleran approved my assignment, Guest gave me the full story. Kuhn, Loeb and Loeb, Roades, friendly (sometimes) competitors on Wall Street, had a joint client named Pan American Sulphur Company (PASCO) based In Houston, Texas, whose raw product was held through a Mexican subsidiary. The sulphur was found in salt domes along the Gulf Coast of Mexico, where it was extracted and refined by the proven Frasch process, but demand in Mexico and the US was weak so PASCO was seeking new international markets to sop up its huge sulphur reserves.

The ingenious investment bankers, always on the lookout to create a deal, came up with a scheme. A new company would be organized in Mexico that would build a processing plant on the Gulf, combining PASCO's sulphur with phosphate rock from Florida to produce phosphoric acid (P_2O_5), a popular liquid fertilizer base that could be shipped anywhere in the world. The equity of the new venture would be owned 35% by PASCO, 7% by each of the two investment banks (as usual, contributing more in ideas then in hard cash), and our old friends at Banco Nacional de Mexico were brought in for 51% to give the business the required Mexican image. By the time of my meeting with John Guest, the joint venture had already been incorporated as a Mexican company named *Fertilizantes Fosfatados Mexicanos*, a mouthful that everyone boiled down to "FFM".

My first task was to prepare an employment agreement between FFM and Jack Zerbst, an experienced American who had been recruited to serve as FFM's chief executive. I was told he had been lured away from running Union Carbide's operations in Brazil with assurances that this would be an exciting prospect where he could be his own boss in an exciting start-up. I was given a brief summary of what had been promised. All I had to do was put it on paper. Fine, but I had never written an employment agreement, which can be inflammatory documents leading to endless disputes, nor could I find anyone else at Cravath who had done so; the firm had ignored this specialized field." "Don't worry," said Tom Halleran breezily to my lament, "it's mainly common sense, and there must be few precedents lying around in our files." To still my doubts, he added the usual avuncular pep-talk: "My boy, a Cravath lawyer can rise to any challenge."

I sat in a conference room in a nervous sweat awaiting my first meeting with the highly touted Mr. Zerbst, knowing only that he would get a base salary of $75,000 (which seemed outlandish for a Mexican job in that era) plus a basket of other benefits. He strode in with all the forceful confidence of a senior manager who had been running thousands of employees in a foreign country. Six-foot-three, with girth to match, topped by a rubicund face and bristling white hair, he showed his impatience at having to negotiate his future with a junior lawyer who had obviously never met a payroll or run a plant. The first hour was pretty frigid, as he reviewed the draft that I warily presented. But over the next couple of days of intense wrangling over his perks—stock options, bonus, housing, travel and entertainment allowances, severance pay if FFM went belly-up—we gradually came to respect each other and he initialed what we had finally agreed. Formal signatures followed. It was a lesson that the most vigorous disagreements, if pursued candidly, can lead to the closest friendships, as was the case with Jack Zerbst and myself.

Jack left promptly for Mexico to take up his new career. He soon drew me into becoming the American legal counsel to FFM, privy to all the prospects and problems of a new multi-national joint venture. He insisted I fly down to meet the company's strategic business advisors, and in the Hotel Alameda bar I had my first introduction to Bob Purvin, who matched Jack's height and diameter and always erupted with a cheerful Texan laugh at any difficulties. Bob was famed throughout the petrochemical industry as a brilliant investor and technician, and was seconded in the firm of Purvin & Lee by John J. Lee, a meticulous Yale-trained chemical engineer (and basketball All-American) who had the practical experience of running a refinery in Italy. I spent many hours with these two voluble gentlemen as they tried to explain to my legal mind the potential risks and rewards of opening a new phosphate fertilizer complex in the Mexican environment. Whenever I was in New York, their office high in the Pan Am building became a favorite retreat for getting a late-day drink and hearing Bob's never-ending tales illuminating the lore of the Texas Oil Patch.

It was natural that Agustín Legorreta, the *supremo* of Banamex with 51% of the shares would be Chairman, and Marlin Sandlin, head of PASCO with 35%, would be on the Executive Committee. For what was essentially a Mexican company, Agustín was clearly its symbolic leader responsible for its success and lightning rod for any complaints, but he had innumerable other concerns on his plate, and Jack Zerbst was the one to run the every-day business and plan long-term strategy.

It was not easy. Jack rented handsome offices in a modern high-rise on Reforma, where I made many visits and observed his efforts as CEO, backed by a talented Mexican accountant as financial director and a couple of Americans as marketing officers. The grand scope and logistics of the project were breath-taking. A virgin plant, of the latest technical design for producing super-phosphoric acid, was to be built from scratch on the humid, swampy Gulf Coast, requiring major construction financing; sulphur was to delivered from PASCO's nearby deposits; phosphate rock would be bought from a couple of American companies in Florida; shipping contracts were to be negotiated to carry the rock from Tampa to Mexico; buyers of acid were to be signed up in countries like Brazil, India, Australia, and The Philippines, eager for more fertilizer in their agricultural economies; special hard-to-find vessels would be chartered to transport the corrosive acid to these distant destinations. Unexpected nit-picky problems constantly sprang up: how to get the government dredge to work faster on the deep-water channel to the plant; how to get a permit to pump gypsum waste into the Gulf.

Over the next four years of corporate struggle, my friendship with Jack and his exuberant wife Barbara was cemented. One early visit, they found a spacious house to rent in the verdant western suburb called *Desierto de Leones*, although there was no desert and no one had ever seen a lion. It was not far from San Angel, the charming colonial district of cobble-stone streets, where I introduced Jack to San Angel Inn, then as now a traditional restaurant whose beamed ceilings and tree-strewn courtyards mark the best of Mexican *ambiente*. Jack was won over by their practice of serving dry martinis in little silver buckets, just big enough for a double, embedded in a bowl of ice. For downtown celebrations near the office, I took him to the smart bistro Del Paseo, owned by American expatriate Bill Shelburne, the favorite watering hole of visiting gringos and their Mexican pals. Jack and Barbara virtually adopted the place and liked nothing better than to consume martinis while listening to Bill tinkling the piano and singing "Fly Me to the Moon" in his reedy tenor voice.

Jack had a stupendous capacity for hard spirits and late hours, but I never saw him anything but immaculate and alert at ten the next morning, the opening hour for Mexican business executives whose working days often ran to eight p.m. or later. I often helped to draft his presentations to Board meetings where he had to defend himself against tough questioning from quizzical directors, and sometimes had to attend myself and write the minutes of the long sessions, always held downtown in Agustín's familiar Banamex office at Isabel la Catolica No. 44.

Planning the plant construction consumed many hours. Bob Purvin and John Lee had recommended the San Francisco's giant Bechtel Corporation as the prime contractor, famed world-wide for their expertise in petrochemical projects. I shuttled between Mexico, California and New York to prepare the contractual jig-saw puzzle that Bechtel and its affiliates needed to document their work for FFM, reflecting production specs, payment schedules, penalties and bonuses, as well as US and Mexican tax codes and labor laws. Dealing first-hand with Bechtel's project managers, engineering specialists, cost accountants and sharp-eyed in-house lawyers was an exhausting experience that finally led to a three-inch stack of signed documents, for a plant that would cost about $52 million—if all went well.

By July 1969, the plant was virtually complete and had begun its experimental production runs. Jack asked me to fly down to the Gulf to look at it, not to perform any useless "due diligence" but to check out the American who had been hired as manager. Coatzacoalcos, an hour's flight from Mexico City, sweated in the summer heat as dampness and mosquitoes rose from the sluggish river that bisected the city, polluted with oil leaking from a giant Pemex refinery. Stripped to a T-shirt like every man I passed, I downed a couple of beers and local shrimp in a pavilion offering a view of the tepid Gulf waters, marked by off-shore wells flaring gas. After a night in the thankfully air-conditioned hotel, I took a launch across the river to land at the jumble of tanks, pipes, conduits, compressors and conveyor belts representing FFM's brand new phosphoric acid facility. After helping to create the project on reams of paper, I had the pleasure of seeing it turned into the reality of metal and concrete.

The perspiring manager who met me seemed far less firm than the construction all around him. His guided tour, explaining every valve and dial, included occasional stumbles on the steel-mesh catwalks, slurred words, and whiffs of whiskey that became an overpowering reek when we entered the closed control room. He sat down heavily and didn't try to fool me. "What the hell else can you do when you live in a shit-hole like this?" he asked. I could sympathize, having seen the ragged streets of Coatzacoalcos, but I wondered how soon he would have to be replaced by some hard-bitten character who could adjust better to a third-world cesspool sweltering in the deep tropics.

My flight back to Mexico City on July 20, 1969, landed just in time to put me in a taxi at the very moment that its radio announced Neil Armstrong's descent from Apollo 11 to plant the Stars and Stripes on the Moon. For the only time before or since, I saw all the teeming traffic on the eight-lane Viaducto come to a halt. After a moment of silence, a cacophony of horns blared out. Mexicans were not slow to celebrate America's moment of triumph.

I had to report to Jack the sad news that he had a drunk running the plant. He shook head and murmured, "Yes, I guessed, and you confirm." I never asked how he got rid of the poor guy.

My adult learning process continued. After an Ivy League education and immersion in the intense but narrowly focused concerns of a Wall Street lawyer, I was still woefully ignorant of how the rest of the world operated. The wide diversity of the men who attended the FFM Board meetings and dinners expanded my understanding of the inevitable clashes and compromises that make up ordinary business life. At these gatherings I could observe the Mexican patrician Don Agustín Legorreta, proudly bearing his ancestral reputation as successful leader of innumerable enterprises; the investment bankers John Guest and his friend Frank Weil from Loeb, Rhoades, honorable men with ingenious minds but little skin in the game, as each of their firm's investment was $500,000, a pittance by Wall Street standards; the two executives of PASCO, Chairman Marlin Sandlin and President Harry Webb, classic Texas Good Old Boys, Marlin having been polished to smooth affability by wheeling and dealing in Houston's Petroleum Club, while Harry remained a blunt boots-on-the-ground operator who thought only of how to dig more sulphur; the articulate consultants Purvin and Lee, whose brief gave them wide latitude to shoot down any fanciful proposals; and finally Jack Zerbst, the cocksure CEO armed with charts and graphs, serving at the pleasure of the Board but not too worried about being sacked, as there would always be a career for a well-connected executive. Among this collection of strong characters, I kept my mouth shut and listened.

Then in late 1969, the collegiality of the Board, and FFM's whole future, were abruptly shaken by a successful corporate raid on Pan American Sulphur Company. For many years PASCO had been a public company listed on the New York

Stock Exchange, with easily available financial statements. The sharp-eyed investment community learned that in 1968 PASCO had sold a majority interest in its Mexican sulphur subsidiary to the Mexican Government for a cash payment of about $50 million, which was still sitting in its treasury unused and uncommitted.

To any clever financier, the $50 million cash made PASCO look like low-hanging fruit, waiting for a corporate wolf to pounce. The wolf appeared in the form of Susquehanna Corporation, a conglomerate controlled by Herbert Korholz, a shrewd New Jersey wheeler-dealer who had a sharp eye for a bargain. His first friendly overtures were rebuffed by Marlin Sandlin; there was no lack of personal antipathy between two gents of such radically different backgrounds. Korholz launched an unfriendly bid for PASCO, by making an open tender offer at a price bound to be attractive to most shareholders—except, of course, Sandlin and Webb, who went to court to block the takeover that would strip them of control. They litigated all the way to the Federal Appeals Court, and lost. Korholz was suddenly the boss of PASCO, and naturally had to be elected to the FFM Board of Directors, since PASCO owned 35% of its shares.

I have kept my notes of the decidedly tense and uncomfortable Board meeting held in December 1970. Marlin Sandlin sat on the Executive Committee in deference to his expertise on sulphur, while Korholz was just a newly-minted Director made to feel like an interloper. Only frozen looks and terse words passed between the two of them, while Agustín did his diplomatic best to smooth ruffled feathers. The atmosphere was not helped by the downbeat report that Jack Zerbst, suffering from a bad cold, made to the Board. Cash-flow had been over-estimated, costs had been misallocated, unforeseen expenses were payable, and a sales contract to Australia had fallen through.

Bottom line: the company would need additional equity capital of $8 million by June 1971. Agustín looked stunned, while Korholz fired off a series of abrasive, but entirely justified, questions, then shut up. Nobody volunteered to provide the new funds, certainly not the new York investment bankers. PASCO had the money, but Korholz remained grimly silent. All eyes turned to Agustín, who could only be noncommittal after all the funding already provided by Banamex. It was a tough moment for him, who usually could make a quick call, and the strain showed on his face. The meeting broke up with no decisions and a bitter after-taste. Another meeting was scheduled for January.

As we left the building, Herb Korholz pulled me aside with an urgent request for a long talk about the company, doubtless overestimating my influence. He invited me to fly to Acapulco to spend a night at his winter home, where we would have ample leisure. I had to think carefully about this invitation—would his hospitality compromise me? I needed the opinion of John Guest; when I reached him at home, he advised, "Sure, go ahead, let's hear what he has to say. Just stay sober and don't make any promises." So for the next 24 hours I was the guest of a man I hardly knew, soaking up the sun on his bay-side terrace and listening to his machine-gun chatter while his trophy wife kept our glasses full.

As he opened up to me, I saw that many adjectives could be applied to Herb: street-smart, energetic, crude, loquacious, egotistical, but always open and frank. He had made a personal fortune from aggressive investing, at the expense of creating a somewhat unsavory business reputation—which didn't bother him at all. But for all his toughness, he was willing to admit mistakes. "I should have had my head examined to get involved with PASCO," he lamented, "I should have just shorted the damn stock." He circled endlessly around the key issue of whether PASCO would invest more equity in FFM. "Well, I might," he allowed, but only if his demands were met, some precise like firing Jack as CEO ("out of his depth") and removing Sandlin ("half asleep") from the Executive Committee, others vague and hard to define. He regarded Agustín and the New York bankers as running a private clique that excluded him.

A lone raider all his life, now he wanted to be invited to the in-group. Only that way could he dig into FFM, take the pieces apart and put them together again. Pacing up and down, he insisted, "I need to meet Agustín outside the board room, have lunch with him, find out what he really thinks. I feel he doesn't go for me." After a couple of hours of these nebulous complaints, his final message to me was simple: he wanted the prestige of Kuhn, Loeb to back his campaign for higher stature in FFM, with the unspoken threat that without the PASCO money every shareholder would be a loser. I told him I could promise nothing but would pass his views on to my senior colleagues. On these ambiguous terms we parted, and his driver took me to the Acapulco airport. I never met him again.

Before Christmas I gave my report to John Guest and the other Kuhn, Loeb partners, but in 1971 I was busy planning my transfer to London, up-rooting my wife and two young daughters, and I lost touch with FFM. Before I left, one last link was an invitation to Harry Webb's retirement party at the River Oaks Country Club in Houston. Marlin Sandlin presided, and we shared reminiscences with no mention of the unloved Herb Korholz, absent among all the Texan back-slapping. The jovial gathering introduced me to J. Howard Marshall, the astute former Yale law professor well on his way to making a fortune in the oil business, long before the press carried pictures of his aged form cuddling and then marrying the notorious floozie Anna Nicole Smith, ecstatic at capturing a near-death billionaire. We were on the same flight to New York next day, the first of several meetings full of his good business advice that preceded his sad decline into senility.

I learned later that FFM was unable to pay its debts and had been taken over by the Mexican Government, doubtless at a deep loss for its equity investors. I discovered Jack and Barbara Zerbst living prosperously in Key Biscayne, Florida, happy to be out of Mexico, with Jack having found a profitable career as an independent business broker. During a Mexico City visit I met Xavier Gonzalez, the former FFM finance director. He smiled ruefully over that experience, but said that it gave him the wits to set up an accounting consultancy firm. He invited me to his daughter's wedding reception, an affair so lavish that he must have been prospering. Life moves on.

My only regret is that I never saw Agustín Legorreta again after that December 1970 Board meeting at Banamex, looking pale and wasted as he escorted us out into the grand banking hall, perhaps a premonition of his death in 1972. To me he was an irreplaceable symbol of the best in Mexican life, a true gentleman, honorable, devoted to his nation and his career, respected by all who met him. He knew the standing of everyone in the country. Once when I privately mentioned a wealthy foreigner who was making quite a splash with his Mexican investments, Agustín laughed and said softly, "Richard, to us Mexicans he's just a little piece of shit, about so high," lifting his hand an inch above his desk. By comparison, Agustin's standing must have been at least ten feet.

Dick Coulson (center) hosting lunch at Casa Sierra
Nevada, San Miguel de Allende, Mexico, 1996.
Milou de Montferrier Lans on his right

Chapter 9

Lunch at Sierra Nevada

Years later, after I had wound up my business interests in Mexico and settled in Nassau, Bahamas, in 1980 (as described in later chapters), I continued to visit the country to enjoy its cultural flavor, and keep contact with my old friends and make new ones. The town of San Miguel de Allende became almost a second home. A photograph taken there in 1996 serves as my computer screen-saver and a stimulus to vivid memories.

There I am at the head of a table with three guests ranged down each side. For lunch during a Christmas visit to San Miguel, I chose Casa de Sierra Nevada, the town's first-ranked hotel, a linkage of several colonial buildings, giving service to match London or Paris, at Mexican prices. We are all peering at the camera held by the waiter who snapped the button. Plates and wine bottles are scattered; sunlight filters down through the arcaded dining room terrace. The photo recalled the date 34 years earlier when I had first stepped into this building.

Seated at my right was Milou de Montferrier Lans, whom I had met during my first trip to Mexico in 1962. She had told me then to escape from D.F. and take a weekend in San Miguel. At Calle Hospicio No. 42 I would be welcomed. I drove my wheezing rented Beetle over the Mexican plains and *barrancas* to find the steep cobble-stoned street and the brass number-plate. A knock on the heavy wooden door opened to the effervescent owner, plump and obviously gay. I was at "Jorge's Place", not so much a hotel as a club, with admittance only if Jorge Palomino had your name. The lofty corridors, airy patios and spacious rooms with arched *boveda* ceilings became the elegant Sierra Nevada, long after Jorge's death.

From that first day in 1962, I fell under San Miguel's indefinable spell. Ever since an educator named Stirling Dickinson began in 1945 to teach US Army veterans art and languages financed under the GI Bill, San Miguel has become a magnet for *Norteamericanos*, "gringos", seeking a renovation to shake up their spirits. They like the weather of tropics-in-the-highlands; they like the prices; they like the unspoiled colonial architecture, legally preserved in the compact *Centro Historico;* they like the food and the music; above all, they like the Mexican way of life that absolves them of the competitive strains and tensions that hound them north of the Rio Grande. Every year new books appear telling of a trial trip, rental venture, planning early or final retirement back home, finally plunging in to buy, contentment (usually) discovered!

Introductions around town by Jorge Palomino gave me an edge. An incurable socialite from an old family, every door was open to him. I met the local icons, now all deceased, like Dottie Vidargas, an ebullient American who married locally and founded the first real-estate agency; Eric Noren, the Scandinavian master builder of exotic homes; and Harold Black, laconic horseman who taught riding in corrals and mountain trails. My previous meetings with Xavier Barbosa led to astonishment at the hacienda he had created, a multi-acre spread financed with his new-found earnings from the Televisa giant. His *tienta* (trial) for young bulls turned into an all-night fiesta—one of many gatherings I enjoyed until he fell into lonely depression and final illness.

Inevitably, San Miguel changed over the years in ways that were the despair of purists but essential to a growing population. Buying food at open-air native markets was gradually replaced by shopping sprees at Walmart-like superstores; furniture, appliances and clothing were sold in modern behemoths akin to Macy's. Wisely, the municipal authorities kept all these establishments segregated on the outer ring-roads, and allowed no corruption of the colonial facades in the *Centro*. Traffic lights were first considered scandalous, but traffic still includes burros stacked with firewood navigating next to gleaming SUVs.

The gringos who settle in San Miguel are energetic types, far from downshifting to a life of drinking tequila and sniffing the jacaranda blooms. Some of them get permits to start businesses, like Dewayne Youts, owner of a workshop and salesroom for elegant hand-made furniture. Bob Thieman presides at his New Orleans Oyster Bar much as Humphrey Bogart ran Rick's in *Casablanca*. Many find satisfaction in charities and social work. I found a list of some 45 educational and cultural bodies, from the fully-staffed library to the garden club, often supported and led by Americans who cannot shake the joining habit. The hospice for those near death was founded by Milou Lans herself.

The foreigners stay aloof from Mexican politics, but a couple of years ago I wanted to look behind the scenes to find who really runs the town. At the handsome *Presidencia Municipal,* a modern structure on the outer highway, I said *buenos días* to a a pert staffer and asked for an appointment to see the Mayor. Why? I showed her an article I had written for the *New York Times* about a neighboring Mexican village Mineral de Pozos, hinting I could do something similar for San Miguel. All smiles, she checked her computer and suggested confirming a date by e-mail for the next month, when certainly Lic. Luz María Flores Nuñez would see me.

On the agreed date I arrived on time, and after no more than three minutes the lady mayor herself swept out of her office and ushered me in. Luz María was a stunner. Dressed and coiffed like a feminist's dream of executive success, with perfect English from a California education, she regaled me with San Miguel's success under her leadership, while an aide took notes and pushed sheets of statistics at me. No, she was not a politician, just a citizen who moved up from Mexico City, married locally (to the owner of the biggest TV station, I was told later), saw the need for change, and ran without the backing of any of the three parties. The people's candidate! In another year there would be elections; she could not succeed herself and would happily retire leaving a municipality free of the debt and cronyism she had wiped out. "But look," she said, "here's how you can always reach me," scribbling her personal e-mail on the back of her official card.

Tucking the card carefully away for future use, I went to lunch with two residents to tell them how dazzled I had been by their superlative mayor. There was a silence. The lady, a respected land-owner from a top family, barred her mouth with her fingers, breathed deeply, and barely uttered "That woman!" followed by a heated diatribe about property seizures and personal enrichment. Clearly, deep currents flowed beneath the sunny surface of local life. A year later, I received an item from a San Miguel news-letter. The newly elected Mayor Mauricio Trejo had found "*irregularidades*" in the municipal accounts of his predecessor and was threatening a full audit of major projects initiated by Luz María, saying that the loss of 30 million pesos was "*solamente la punta del* iceberg [sic]." A valid claim? Just Mexican politics? I have not investigated. I still have not tried that personal e-mail address.

Whatever murky vendettas unfold behind the political curtain, I have found San Miguel both unchanging and yet better on every visit. Locals and visitors still relax on hard iron benches under the manicured trees of the central *Jardín*. The narrow streets are swept clean as ever and still gleam with running water after a summer cloudburst. Entrepreneurs of the hospitality trade open new boutique hotels and restaurants, while the old chestnuts just keep going. I once celebrated that unique Mexican holiday Day of the Dead by helping organize an *ofrenda*, the gift-laden tableau built in every Mexican home to honor respected ancestors, and laying flowers on the tombs of the departed while whole families gathered to commune with prayers and hearty dining.

New ventures enrich the local menu. Over 20 years ago a textile mill, the town's major employer, owned by several generations of the Garay family, had to close when faced with lower-cost foreign competition. Paco Garay had no viable plans for the handsome building until approached by an American interior designer who suggested converting the 100,000 square feet of lofty clerestory-lit space into artists' workshops and show rooms. The idea caught on. Space in the *Centro* was tight and expensive for San Miguel's flourishing art community. Now the entire factory, white-washed and sub-divided, bustles with over 40 working artists, craftsmen, jewelers, book-stores and household boutiques. Renamed *Fabrica Aurora*, its arcades are on the "to-do" list for every visitor, a focal point of one-stop browsing and buying. Spaces are rarely vacated, and on-site landlords Paco and Rosemary Garay choose carefully among new applicants. I never visit San Miguel without stopping to see Aurora's anchor tenant, a vigorous transplanted Texan lady who creates works to match the generous wall space.

About a dozen years ago an energetic lady named Susan Page swept into town from California. She and her companion Mayer Schacter soon created a shop/museum devoted to indigenous Mexican art and handicrafts collected throughout the country, but Susan's real passion was books. A published author herself, she pulled together locals and foreigners to create the Literary Sala, a forum for frequent discussions and experimental writing. This evolved into the annual San Miguel Writers' Conference. Its ninth iteration was held in February 2014, and it now registers as a serious fixture in the world-wide pantheon of bookish events.

With a platoon of devoted volunteers, Susan organizes over 300 paying delegates to participate in five days of workshops, speeches, intensive practice sessions, even pitch meetings with literary agents. Held at a spacious bargain-price hotel, the Conference spreads out through San Miguel's restaurants and tequila bars. Some of the participants are already serious writers, while others inevitably are star-struck wannabes, but all listen to trained professionals who are recruited to give their best shot, gratis but for room and board. It's no down-market affair: last year Susan attracted Canadian Margaret Atwood as a speaker, and for 2014 she signed up Calvin Trillin) and Yann Martel *(Life of Pi)*. Prominent Mexican authors also appear, with simultaneous Spanish-English translation.

Creative emotions run high at the Conference. As I stood in line for a margarita at the 2011 fiesta, a statuesque blonde stranger rushed up, wrapped her arms around me, looked deep in my eyes, and assured me firmly, "I can see you write; you must open up and tell it all." Where was she from, this oracle? "Springfield, Illinois. But I have traveled the world!" With that, she gave me a kiss and was gone. I only saw her once again at the Conference, head down, taking notes.

The Garays and Susan Page will not survive forever, but *Fabrica Aurora* and the Writers' Conference have created their own continuing images. They will become fixtures, like the museum at the Casa de Allende. In 1962 I took my first tour of that stately structure with baroque façade occupying a full block next to the *Jardín,* built in 1760 as home of the town's leading family. It was open, but barely, dim, dusty, with an indifferent guardian. Fifty years later I toured it again, now better lit and professionally curated, retaining the ineffable aura of past centuries. Capt. Ignacio de Allende had been one of the heroes of Independence in 1810; his portrait and his coat-of-arms still loomed from the walls.

The solid things in San Miguel do not vanish.

* * *

Maddening, effervescent Mexico City, air-polluted, its glorious monuments frozen by traffic, is still the essential capital pulling all strings together. Twenty million people fight for existence, the rich thriving, the poor surviving, and all complaining but rarely leaving. Life is just too thick, too dense with challenge and opportunity. The nexus spreads out from Day Effay, the *Distrito Federal*, to cross the boundaries of neighboring States of Mexico, Morelos, Puebla and Hidalgo, linked by new highways ever failing to absorb the day and night chains of struggling vehicles.

After I wound down my Mexican business affairs, Mexico City no longer required week-long working sessions, but became a brief hiatus on visits to San Miguel de Allende. Recently, I had an urge to re-visit the places and people I had come to know during my early visits in the 1960s and 1970s, to up-date myself on the slice of Mexican life that I had then experienced. Physically, I found that little had been destroyed and much had been created. Our long-used downtown hotel the Alameda and a few others like it had been demolished after the earthquake of 1985. The central business and financial heart of the City have evolved into a "historical zone" devoted to tourism, antiquarian research, and retail shops of every variety, its narrow streets still choked with traffic. The *Palacio Nacional* remains on the immense Zócalo as the official and ceremonial seat of Government where a giant Mexican flag waves day and night, but the working offices of the president and the minions of *Hacienda* have moved to distant boulevards. The colonial structure at Isabel la Catolica No. 44 that I had entered so often as the headquarters of Banco Nacional de Mexico has been converted into a museum. Banamex together with its fellow banks, insurance companies, and industrial giants have relocated their head offices far west, along the wide, leafy Paseo de la Reforma, the trendy purlieus of Polanco, or even further where entire new commercial zones have been built on the edges of the exclusive Las Lomas residential hills. Block after block is devoted to the concrete, steel, and glass structures designed by Mexico's ingenious architects, creating more exotic versions of Houston or Dallas.

I sought the individuals I had worked with. The incomparable Agustín Legorreta, head of Banamex, was long gone, and none of his four sons stuck with the bank through its many conversions into a subsidiary of Citibank. But the first lawyer I ever met, Miguel Escobedo, who counseled us on Mexican bonds, was still at work, evolving from a slim equestrian, fluent in English and French into a portly, witty pillar of the Bar. His father Manuel Escobedo, had been an old-guard Mexican who had a hard time finding work in the heated days of the Revolution, but linked with a colleague in the 1950s and founded the two-man partnership Noriega y Escobedo. Manuel, with the visage of a tall amused owl, had attracted as his wife an irrepressible English lady who became a leader of Mexican cultural life speaking fluent Spanish with an ineradicable Oxbridge accent. Their late daughter Helen starred in a special field of sculptural art, creating large abstract "installation" pieces for display indoors and outdoors, winning awards in Mexico and abroad, sharing an international education with her brother Miguel.

When Noriega y Escobedo grew and prospered, it also moved from drab central premises to gleaming new floors in Polanco. Miguel, senior partner after his father's death, honored his sister by commissioning one of her inspirations. Entering the reception area, I was once startled by a forest of pale metal tubes and wooden slats rising from floor to ceiling. Law had joined art, while Miguel presided over a close-knit team of about 30 professionals with the cream of corporate clients. He had no ambition to become the largest firm, as newer partnerships brashly struggled for growth. I showed him a Mexican business magazine with a full-page ad extolling the expertise of several smiling attorneys. With one glance, he dismissed it contemptuously: "Publicity! Yes, that's what the law is coming to—hungry guys who just met and decide to start a firm." He sounded like a partner of New York's Cravath, Swaine & Moore deriding an ambulance chaser found in the Yellow Pages.

Yet Miguel is alert to support change in Mexico' s politics. Before the last elections in 2012, he was skeptical of the "dinosaurs" lurking in the background of the long dominant PRI, and the so-called business-friendly approach of the conservative PAN. He lunched with "AMLO", the nick-name of Andrés Manuel López Obrador, the fiery leftist leader of the Party of the Democratic Revolution, who had narrowly lost in 2006 (and would lose again). "I liked him and his platform. He means well," Miguel told me. "But he's disorganized," he sighed. "Hopeless. He could never run the country."

I also sought out Antonio Madero, whom I had first known as a lanky hyper-active engineer employed to run silver mines and set up a zinc smelter that needed investment from the US. He split with his owners to carve a route of his own, and now greeted me in the sleek headquarters of San Luis Corporación, where he had become the staid black-suited CEO, surrounded by silver plaques and framed certificates rewarding corporate success. I asked him about the comments of American journalists that the brutal drug wars were threatening Mexico with becoming a "failed state". He pierced me with his deep-set eyes, tapped my knee and responded vigorously:

"Nonsense. A colorful story for the press. We have factories all over Mexico making auto parts. We've never had a stoppage, I fact we just had our best year. Sure the narcos make trouble and it's hell along the border, but most of the country never sees a druggie and a cop shooting at each other. We already have 3% annual GDP growth. If the Government ever privatizes Pemex, it could jump to 8%."

Club de Industriales

The man with the most vivid disclosures about modern Mexico was José (Pépé) Carral, whom I had long admired as the sprightly, loquacious head of Bank of America's Mexican operations and later a multi-directional private investor. "The man who knows everybody," he was the natural choice in 2000 to become President of the *Club de Industriales,* an iconic society founded in 1956 by a tight group of Mexico's business chieftains. Now with nearly 1,000 members, this body represents a focal point of the Mexican establishment yet keeps a low profile. It's unknown to tourists and casual visitors. I have never seen it mentioned in books about the Mexico power structure, and it appears to stay under the radar of the inquisitive, out-spoken Mexican press, with its many organs of critical opinion like the periodical *Proceso*.

With justifiable pride Pépé gave me a tour of the premises where he spends part of every day—and what premises! In 1994 when the Marriott hotel chain positioned its high-end JWMarriott unit on Polanco's hotel row, the Club arranged to take two lofty floors for itself, to its own design and with its own entrance. The resulting creation puts in the shade any of the famous city clubs I have seen in New York, London or Paris. They are all mementos of a past generation, whose fading elegance dims when compared to the vigorous style and untrammeled dimensions that govern modern Mexican architecture, initiated by the famous Luis Barragán. Every item of furniture and fittings in the spacious rooms of the *Club de Industriales* illustrates the elegant simplicity of current Mexican décor, including reception areas, dining room and bar, auditorium, film theatre, conference rooms, gym and pool, together with a museum-quality collection of Mexican art that includes Rufino Tamayo's mural *Energía* spread across the entrance hall.

More than its physical size, it's the spirit of Club that supports its quiet authority. Certainly not a political entity, supporting no party or movement, it is nevertheless far more than a "social" club. As Pépé has written in the Club's elegant memorial volume, it aspires to be an intellectual center for the free (and unpublicized) exchange of ideas. Virtually every day, orchestras perform, films are analyzed (once by the well remembered Raúl Ortiz y Ortiz, the aging culture maven still sporting a bow-tie) or lectures are given covering the latest in economics, literature, world affairs, health care, or the environment. Senior government ministers often give off-the-record analyses of presidential policies. The weekly Friday breakfasts pull together men and women around a circular table who are led by a senior member into vigorous debate on key issues facing the nation. The Club never takes a "position", but the words doubtless percolate to the highest levels of government, business and the arts.

Of course, following the title of Lesley Bird Simpson's popular book, there are *Many Mexicos*, and the *Club de Industriales* is just one of them, remote from the world of the country-folk *campesinos* who still scratch out a living in the fields, or the garbage scavengers in Mexico City's giant slums. But the very existence of the Club shows that Mexico is in dynamic movement, far from collapsing into a failed state.

Fading Acapulco

Alas, stories of grim reality cannot be avoided. Friends drove me down to Acapulco for a weekend reunion with Ron Lavender, still the town's leading real-estate agent. Four years ago Ron was kidnapped and held for weeks in an 8 x 4-foot wooden crate, uninjured but confined in stifling darkness with just enough sustenance to survive—not part of the drugs war, just another typical financial grab, with ransom eventually negotiated and paid.

Ron gave up his house and now lives in the security of a gated beach-front condo. When he leaves, he is joined at the door by one of a team of slab-sided guys with careful eyes who move like NFL line-backers, keeping their hands close to a leather bag slung over a shoulder that occasionally falls open to reveal a glint of blued metal. They drive a massive SUV that tails Ron wherever he goes, and are always in the watchful background when he enters a bank, food-store or restaurant. At the yacht club, they walk him to his boat when he sets off for a sail, and are standing on the dock when he returns. Out cruising on the bay he feels secure, at least for now. That's the normal way of life for wealthy Mexicans.

Acapulco itself is a showpiece of contrasts. The yacht club piers and hoist-out cradles are full with flashy power yachts and sleek sailing raceboats of the latest design, a far grander display than what I saw 40 years ago. But casting an eye up the slopes of the surrounding mountains, one sees the shanty-towns straggling ever higher toward the summit, the home-ground of bloody battles between federal, state and local police and the warring bands of *narco-trafficantes.*

Many Mexicos indeed.

Querétaro

The most encouraging Mexico is probably the city of Querétaro, once just another sleepy state capital but now a growing metropolis in the fertile high plains known as the *Bajío*, taking advantage of its site on the main super-highway and railway between Mexico City and the US border. It manages the meticulous preservation of a historical central district of churches, museums, residences and public buildings, financed by a ring road gleaming with the brash wealth of Walmart, Sam's Club, Office Depot, Costco, and a mammoth football stadium, as well as industrial parks crammed with a manufacturing and distribution facilities of hundreds of multi-national companies from Samsung to Pfizer. Once-barren slopes now are home to two college campuses and thousands of housing units, and an international airport recently opened.

The formula works. Querétaro is often called the one true urban success story of Mexico, drawing executives with young families happy to relocate from the Capital's smog. It's not San Miguel de Allende, charming but steeped in gringo influence; it's not a replacement for the bubbling variety of Mexico City; and it doesn't share the seductive tropic appeal of Acapulco. But it may well be the best image of Mexico's future. One of its handsome colonial buildings was the home of *La Corregidora,* the alert lady who learned that the insurgent conspirators of 1810 were about to be betrayed and got a coded warning to them. But for her, the *grito* of independence would not have been proclaimed on September 16th, now the national holiday.

In Mexico, the past and the future are never far apart.

CHAPTER 10

"Bill": William F. Buckley, Jr., 1924-2008

One reason for my fascination with Mexico was that it had been the childhood home of the late William F. Buckley Jr., the ineffable "Bill", as he was called by everyone from Ronald Reagan to the lowliest staffer at *National Review*.

In September 1948 I first entered the neo-Gothic archway portal to Yale's Old Campus, where all we freshmen were herded for one year before moving to a residential college. As a typical callow newcomer, I soon looked around to learn the power structure, to find out who was who in the tiered society of America's most tradition-bound university. The name Buckley soon came to the fore. Two classes ahead of me, an Army veteran, Bill was already an editor of the *Yale Daily News* and would soon be elected its Chairman, the zenith for any ambitious undergraduate, as Yale eschewed anything so plebeian as a student council.

Once installed in the Chairman's exclusive office atop the Britton Hadden Memorial Building, he would begin writing editorials of a literary polish never seen before and rarely thereafter, expressing a coherent right-wing slant that often enraged the Yale faculty and would mark the rest of his life. He was also a leader of the Political Union and star of the debating team that vanquished its collegiate opposition around the country. To top all that, he had the wit, the looks and the casual charm of a country gentleman, easily wearing the tweed jacket and grey flannels that were *de rigueur* in those days. Of course he was tapped for senior society Skull & Bones, once deemed the highest accolade of all-round campus success. It was only natural that a credulous, untested freshman like me would regard him with silent hero worship.

Among his many would-be acolytes, I was fortunate to have special access into his rarefied world. Another classmate living near me on the Old Campus was his young brother Fergus Reid Buckley, a flamboyant character who changed plumage every season, appearing first as a Texas rancher in hand-tooled boots and a wide-brimmed Stetson, next as a Bavarian aristocrat in green loden jacket and a feather trimmed stalker's hat, then as a T.S. Eliot intellectual in a dark three-piece suit and narrow black tie. Perhaps trying to match Bill's high wattage, he nevertheless became a delightful companion with strong, and frequently reversing, opinions on any current issue.

Another entrée came via Bill's older sibling, Jim, who had finished Yale College before naval service during World War II, and was now studying at Yale Law School. Like several of his fellows, he took the avuncular role of freshman counselor, living on the Old Campus and advising us new boys how to adapt to the freedom of Yale life while curbing our over-exuberant appetites for fun and games and strong drink. In that role, he spent many hours in the suite I shared with my three room-mates, and we in his digs in down-town New Haven. Jim represented the other face of the Buckley personality—intellectual but low-key, never seeking the lime-light that focused naturally on Bill and Reid. These qualities led to his extraordinary career: lawyer, businessman running the complex family oil ventures created by his father, reluctant one-term Senator for New York under the Conservative Party banner, director of Radio Free Europe, federal appeals judge eventually taking emeritus status. He always remained a trusted mentor to Bill's more visible career, and never failed to reunite with us four room-mates when opportunity could bring us together.

I gradually learned the Buckley history: ten children, four boys and six girls, born of the *pater familias* William F. Sr., an adventurous Texan lawyer who sought his fortune in Mexico City and made it, until the revolutionary government decided a gringo capitalist had no place under the new regime and threw him out. An unbending Catholic, he married an equally devout lady from New Orleans, petite and beloved by all who knew her. Homes, and children's education, migrated wildly as the Buckley success in the oil business veered up and down. Although born in New York, Bill's first language was Spanish and at early age he became fluent in French. Often at risk with little hard capital, WF Senior always believed in presenting an impeccable front—when they lived in France in the 1930s, he rented no less than the enchanting Chateau St. Firmin in Chantilly, outside Paris, later the favorite residence of the British Ambassador Duff Cooper and his glamorous wife Diana. Eventually, stability was achieved with the acquisition of long-term homes in Sharon, Connecticut, and Camden, South Carolina.

It was not until I was invited to a weekend in Sharon that I began to absorb the atmosphere that rooted Bill's life. Great Elm, the white colonial mansion amid green lawns in one of America's most beautiful towns, was the physical setting (it still stands today). But the guiding spirit that Saturday night emanated from the formidable figure of Bill's father. As we, a variety of ages, sat around the formally-set dinner table, WFB Sr. dominated the proceedings, expecting intelligent responses to the range of topics that he set before of us, and of course we did our best to comply. Bill had been trained in this intellectual exercise from an early age, and I learned later that his father found him the most apt student among his children, and identified him as the one most likely to make a mark.

Immediately after he graduated from Yale in June 1950, Bill took two crucial steps: he found a wife, and decided to write a book. His choice of partner was made with unerring precision: a tall aquiline beauty blessed with wit and wealth (the daughter of a Canadian mining and forestry magnate). Vassar graduate Patricia Taylor was not a Catholic and had no intention of becoming one. Any sectarian difficulties with her Anglican family were resolved and a vast wedding reception held in her Vancouver home, the start of an unshakable union that lasted until their deaths over 50 years later. As to the book, its subject came easily to Bill, who had fulminated in his editorials about Yale's fall from religious grace and into the arms of moral relativism and economic socialism. After an unproductive posting as a minor CIA functionary in Mexico City, the newly married couple rented a house in quiet suburban Hamden where Bill could concentrate on writing *God and Man at Yale*. It was not an easy sell to the publishing world; only the specialized right-wing imprint Henry Regnery took it up, and then saw it become a runaway success. Bitterly critical of how Yale was run by the prevailing liberal administration, it attracted nearly apoplectic fury from "establishment" figures like Harvard's McGeorge Bundy.

When published in late 1951, it naturally became a major campus curiosity. It so happened that I was serving as a columnist for the *Yale Alumni Magazine*, writing a monthly piece called "The Undergraduate View", and was assigned to produce a a review of student reaction. Naturally I interviewed Bill to educate myself on ideological points that I, a vaguely middle-of-the-road intellectual, had never seriously considered. We became good friends, although I recall that my eventual column was a pretty jejune effort that commended his style while doubting that Yale would change. I certainly did not have the foresight to predict that *God and Man* would launch Bill on the path to leadership of the American conservative movement.

In the years after leaving Yale, I never shared Bill's all-consuming fervor for acute commentary and political influence. I never joined the staff of *National Review* or became active in Young Americans for Freedom or the fledgling Conservative

Party. Our friendship remained personal not professional. Bill had a remarkable gift for friendship, even with those like me who shared no part of his tightly-scheduled working life, as he shuttled between taping *Firing Line* for TV, writing a biweekly syndicated column, editing NR, and giving speeches (well paid) in the US and abroad.

After hours, so to speak, he became a different person. I was invited to many dinners or Sunday lunches at the home he and Pat had chosen and eccentrically decorated, on a Stamford point overlooking Long Island Sound, at which he firmly refused any talk about profound issues facing the nation or how he would resolve them. Over faultless food and wine, words were devoted to travel, books, social trivia, jokes, and high-level gossip. Usually an interesting list of guests were invited to share this heady brew. One time I found myself seated next to Richard Clurman, a grandee of *Time* magazine; at another meal, Abe Rosenthal, retired Executive Editor of the *New York Times*, whom I in ignorance did not recognize until I mentioned my frequent trips to Mexico and he quizzed me with journalistic intensity.

Sharing Bill's social life, one could not fail to see how hard he kept his nose to the grindstone. He never lingered long after meals, but firmly withdrew to his typewriter (he was self taught in touch-typing) or word-processor, lodged in the multi-car garage that he had converted into a virtual writing factory, where he presided from a central chair surrounded by computers, TV screens, telephones, file cabinets, storage disks, racks of books and periodicals.

Another obsession in Bill's life was sailing, a time-consuming, money-devouring, but deeply engaging and emotionally satisfying endeavor to which I too often succumbed. Unlike myself, Bill was never much interested in competitive racing, except in his teen-age years when he fought fiercely to win the annual Wononscopomuc Yacht Club Trophy on the tiny lake near Sharon. On his first serious yacht, unwisely named *The Panic*, he tried the famous Newport-Bermuda Race a few times, with little success and once a minor scandal when one of his crewmates broadcast unfortunate words over the ship's radio. I joined him for a race from Annapolis to Newport, with much *bonhomie*, but achieving once again only a middling finish.

Bill's real love was cruising, as long and unhurried as possible, making four trans-Atlantic passages and one trans-Pacific, always with a combination of amateur friends and a few hardy professionals, which he memorialized in several books. I declined several invitations for these long sojourns far from land, fearing I might suffer from an overdose of Bill's always brilliant rhetoric. But I was happy to sign on for shorter voyages. To give a flavor of sailing with Bill, I attach an Appendix giving an account of two of these cruises' one in the Aegean and one in Long Island Sound.

On the cruise through the Greek islands, I could observe first-hand Bill's iron concentration on work as he firmly detached himself from social chit-chat. Each morning a conference would decide the day's objective for our little convoy of the twelve-meter sailing yacht accompanied by the power boat that we all chipped in to charter as a mother ship to feed us well. Before breakfast and soon after dinner, we would hear the tapping of Bill's portable typewriter as he produced an NR article or one of his syndicated columns. One cloudless day we landed at the obscure island of Skyros to find the grave of Rupert Brooke, the English poet of the First World War made famous by his line "In some corner of a foreign field that is forever England . . ." Bill had brought with him the type-script of a column facing a dead-line, and as we trudged up a dusty road seeking the grave, he was on the lookout for a telephone. On the edge of town, he found a fly-specked glass call-box and, amazingly, was able to put through a call (collect) to an NR editor back in New York and spend nearly an hour of sweating dictation over the scratchy line. Even a holiday could not stem the flow of words.

We also observed another of Bill's long-time obsessions: his determination to play piano well enough to perform publicly a Bach concerto. His baggage on the cruise included a so-called silent keyboard, a music rack, and sheets of Bach scores. The keyboard could be unfolded to full piano width with mechanism to imitate the feel of true fingering. On late afternoons Bill could be seen on the afterdeck, scrutinizing a score, hands flying over the keys, soundless except for his own voice mouthing the notes. It was an eery sight, and inhibited pre-dinner joviality until we could pull the budding maestro away as Pat sardonically applauded the inaudible performance. He was a hard man to distract from his serious interests, which did not prevent him from shifting gears to become the life of the party—until the next bout of work loomed implacably on his horizon.

His dead-pan wit was revealed privately to his friends and publicly to his followers in the media, marked by a sudden widening of half-closed eyes to full open stare. He became famous for a TV appearance during his quixotic 1965 run as the Conservative candidate for Mayor of New York, when he was asked what would be his first action if elected: "I shall ask for a re-count."

As age approached at the end of the 20th century and start of the 21st, adjustments to life style were made. Pat had never enjoyed skiing after an accident shattered one of her long and delicate legs, so the annual winter trip to Switzerland was replaced with warmer climes, often to Nassau, where I lived and could enjoy lunches or dinners with them in the relaxed tropical air, created by the superb chef whom they always imported. Yes, that was one of the trappings of a well-endowed life that some of Bill's leftist critics despised, together with the duplex Park Avenue maisonette, the Stamford home, and the succession of owned or chartered yachts (all of them tiny compared to the mega-vessels of today's billionaires). Response to this kind of criticism was beneath Bill's contempt. Every dollar of the wealth was legitimate, either earned from Bill's unceasing labors as writer, lecturer, and TV star of *Firing Line*, or derived from Pat's doubtless substantial inheritance from the business success of her Canadian father.

Pat's contribution to Bill's life was far more than financial. She was by no means an easy person quietly supporting a more dominant personality. She had an acute social intelligence and her wit could be acerbic, unsparing of less gifted individuals. Henry Kissinger, a close friend of both of them, spoke at her memorial service. I recall his light-hearted words, "As we know, Pat did not suffer fools gladly; in fact she did not suffer them at all." One of Bill's closest Skull & Bones classmates told me that despite living nearby in Manhattan, they rarely had family get-togethers because his wife found Pat too domineering. While Bill and his older brother Jim were indissolubly close, many intimates of the Buckley family knew that Mrs. Bill rarely socialized with Mrs. Jim, a wealthy aristocrat in her own right but with quieter tastes. The mutual antipathy was carefully hidden but authentic.

Somehow, I escaped under the radar of Pat's raking sarcasm and hilarious mimicry, and we became good friends. One long evening in Nassau, after Bill had retired to write, I felt close enough to ask about their marriage. How had it worked? His life was devoted to intellectual or political causes, while she became perhaps New York's leading social figure, sharing the media lime-light with her pal the late ultra-slim Nan Kempner, perennially on the best-dressed list, invited to grace innumerable charity balls and working hard to raise funds as chairman of the annual Costume Institute Ball held gloriously in the Metropolitan Museum of Art, as well as the Sloan-Kettering Hospital fund raiser. Could the interests of an intellectual and a socialite paragon really mesh amicably? Her answer was clear: "Dickie, from the moment I met him, Bill has always been the most fascinating man in my life." Clearly, every visible aspect of their complex domestic life was immaculately organized by Pat, and below the surface one can only guess at the intelligent, loving support, spiced with abrasive humor, that she must have given him.

Pat's last months before her death in April 2007 were wracked with physical pain, and at my last ever words with Bill at her memorial ceremony, he too had the pale, hunched appearance linked with ill-health. The event was held in the magnificent space of the Metropolitan Museum's Sackler Wing housing the Temple of Dendur, with its massive north-facing window. Despite the light pouring in that sunny morning, Bill hardly had the will or energy to respond to the 300 friends offering their condolences. Her loss was indeed shattering.

Another blow fell early the following year. Evan G. Galbraith, Bill's Yale classmate and probably closest friend, died in New York in January 2008. Van, as he was known to all, was cursed with the blunt, broken-nosed face of a youthful football player but blessed with a sharp practical mind and the kind of bubbling effervescence and zany humor that raised spirits with all who knew him. Bill used his influence with Ronald Reagan to get Van, previously a lawyer and financier, appointed as ambassador to France, a choice that was not altogether a diplomatic success despite his and his cultured wife's French fluency. Van was an outspoken and unreconstructed Conservative, who felt his mission was to spread the unfettered Reagan Doctrine, whatever those lefty wimps in the State Department might advise as official policy.

When I visited Van in the Paris embassy in 1982, he was enjoying the controversy aroused by his refusal to share a *wagon lit w*ith the Soviet ambassador during an official railway junket arranged by the French Government. Secretary of State George Shultz was reportedly livid, and Van was soon eased out of government, not to return until fellow right-winger Donald Rumsfeld appointed him the Defense Department's special advisor to NATO in 2001. Bill had a good laugh over the tea-pot contretemps, and probably Reagan did too.

Depressed even further by Van's passing, within a month Bill too died. I barely could squeeze into his funeral mass where thousands of mourners over-flowed the central choir and every side-chapel of St. Patrick's Cathedral. Those nearer the front than I reported that the music, the liturgy, the prayers, and the eulogies were unsurpassed. Later, at the smaller reception for close friends held at the New York Yacht Club, I embraced Van Galbraith's delightful widow, oddly nick-named Bootsie, and we were both introduced to Sam Tanenhaus, editor of the *New York Times Book Review,* whom Bill had chosen as his authorized biographer. We knew he was a skilled writer, with a superb biography of Whittaker Chambers to his credit, but we both doubted that he had much insight into Bill's personal, unofficial life and unusual background.

The next day Bootsie and I invited Sam for a quiet drink and impressed on him our concern that the biography fully reflect not only the content of Bill's thought as found in his speeches and writings, but also his unique personality shown only to friends and family. He understood our point immediately, admitting that the Ivy League and New England surroundings that formed Bill's early cocoon were unknown territory to him. Impulsively, I volunteered to arrange some interviews with people who were my Yale contemporaries, as well as to undertake research among Bill's voluminous personal records. Sam promptly accepted my offer, and for several months I had the unexpected pleasure of unearthing bits of Bill's history that I had never known before.

One of his classmates told me that in their third year at Yale a group of them suddenly became aware of his special qualities. They asked him to write a presentation to the faculty about a delicate educational matter. In half an hour Bill conceived, drafted, and speedily typed the document, word-perfect. "We could see then he was a genius," I was told.

Another classmate recounted that about 15 years after graduation, a proposal was put forward that Yale grant Bill an honorary degree, as with other distinguished alumni or non-alumni. The proposal was shot down, one member of the Corporation (Yale's governing body) writing that a degree for Bill "would give the wrong message" and a couple of prominent professors threatening to resign, in opposition to

Bill's right-wing Christian views elucidated in *God and Man at Yale* and the pages of *National Review*. Only ten years later, after careful political maneuvering by Bill's friends, did Yale relent and present him a Doctorate in Humane Letters, with the usual pomp and ceremony.

Several of his friends told me of his exceptional moments of warmth and generosity seized from his super-busy life. He provided his Stamford house for the wedding reception of one hard-up classmate. Another was touched that after years of scanty contact, two weeks before his death, Bill dispatched his car to pick up his friend in Manhattan to visit for several hours of bed-side reminiscences—and this was a guy who had been constantly sea-sick and nearly drowned on one of Bill's cruises.

To learn more about the day-to-day life and inner tensions at *National Review*, I relied on his sister Patricia ("Pitts"), author of two vivid, entertaining memoirs who for many years served as a managing editor to keep the operation ticking while Bill thought, wrote, and traveled. We met in the apartment that has become her home, carved out from the original Great Elm mansion house in Sharon. At the vigorous age 86, she gave a colorful description, as set forth in my notes of our interview:

> She told me she was getting a little tired of her "glamorous" job with the UP wire agency in Paris when Bill invited her back home in 1956 to help with the still new and struggling NR. One of her first unusual missions was to go to Alaska to visit a sort of asylum, which right-wingers objected to because it was on federal land. The issue arose with politicians in Washington, and NR had to mediate.
>
> The original managing editor was Suzanne LaFollette, but a few years later Bill eased Pitts into the job, "the only journalist in a bunch of intellectuals fighting like cats", where she had to deal with touchy professor/writers like James Burnham, Willmoore Kendall, Frank Meyer, Russell Kirk, and many others

who came and went. Because it was a cause they believed in, and because of Bill's persuasive charm, they were all willing to contribute articles on a piecework basis, with pretty low rates, with only a few full-timers like the book editor on a measly salary.

With Bill often away from the office, it was left to Pitts to handle the endless questions and complaints from this testy crew. "The bi-weekly editorial meetings went pretty briskly, because we had a magazine to put out and there was no time for philosophizing. But three times a year we had what I called The Agony, when all the deep thinkers would get together to express their differing views of conservatism and where NR should be going. It could get pretty rancorous. Bill usually prevailed with diplomacy, but sometimes he had to take a hard line. Once he said to Frank Meyer, a very uncompromising fellow, 'you apologize or else you leave', and as I recall he left. In the long run, Bill got the magazine melded together into one philosophy."

In its early days before reaching a firm foundation of success, she said NR was often scorned and boycotted by the media and academia. "People who wrote for NR learned that the *New Yorker* would not accept their pieces. Our talented author Jeff Hart was told he would never become a full professor at Columbia if he continued to write for NR, so he left and became a long-time Dartmouth professor. In later years, we were able to pay a little more, so there was more stability, and the prejudices faded away".

I asked whether there were any problems working for a brother/boss who was four years younger. "None whatever. Bill was an excellent delegator. And, maybe because of family togetherness, our minds meshed. We both knew how to talk fast and reach decisions quickly. There was no wasted time, and no back-biting. There was always the stimulation of creating a new

> product every two weeks. And oh how we laughed at the practical jokes, including the one we played on Bill by sending him on his Swiss holiday several really dreadful phony editorial paragraphs we had concocted for the magazine. And I always insisted on a good four-week annual holiday! You know I loved skiing and bird-shooting. So it was a wonderful experience until I retired as Managing Editor in 1985 and finally left as Senior Editor in 1991. I didn't want to stay much longer after Bill retired in 1990."

Although Bill was never one who wore his religion on his sleeve and rarely spoke about it, I knew he was a devout Catholic, and I hoped to get some insights about the exercise of his faith. I arranged to meet with Father George Rutler, the principal celebrant at Bill's memorial mass. These are the notes of our friendly session one morning at the Union League Club, across the street from his pastoral church:

> Father Rutler is a delightful, pink-faced, witty cleric, of the conservative wing of the Catholic clergy, who was one of Bill's confessors and became perhaps his closest spiritual/theological adviser in his life-long search for the true Catholic faith. He plays a major role in Bill's book, *Nearer, My God,* where Bill describes how he sent a series of questions to Catholic thinkers, asking for their response. He describes Rutler's answers as "ever adamantine . . . faithful to orthodox understanding." When I reminded Rutler of this, he chuckled and said "Yes, I suppose I was steadily his most conservative influence—we both shared dismay at the distortions that arose from Vatican II, including suppression of the Latin mass. That has been relaxed now; I alternate the Latin and English mass in my church, which satisfies my parishioners by giving them a choice".

Rutler told me he had met Bill in 1978 at the introduction of Bill Rusher, NR's publisher, and got to know him better after a discussion on *Firing Line* about Liberation Theology. This was shortly after he had converted from the Episcopalian Church and left a parish in Pennsylvania. His earlier education included two sessions at Oxford, where he was a serious student of Latin. "At Bill's request, I often helped him with his Latin, which he always wanted to improve."

Bill was born and raised a Catholic and didn't need conversion. According to Rutler, Bill told him "I never lost my faith", despite a period of virtual estrangement from his son Christopher about religion and other issues—later patched up. "He was a regular and faithful receiver of the Sacraments," affirmed Rutler.

Rutler often saw Bill together with his wife Pat, and admired her greatly. "Of course she was from a high Anglican family in Vancouver, and neither Bill, and certainly not I, ever tried to convert her. She had a wonderful effect on Bill; she introduced him to certain civilizing and cultural elements that he would have missed in his intense intellectual concentration."

Rutler said that "One of the great passages in *Nearer, My God* is Bill's description of the ordination of Michael Bozell [son of late friend Brent Bozell] into a strict Benedictine Order in France. Later, Michael got an extremely rare dispensation to leave the monastery and visit America. Just the three of us joined to meet; I have never seen Bill so moved—almost wordless in admiration for the life Michael had chosen."

Rutler believes that Bill's legacy is not as a great original thinker, but one "whose mission was to make conservatism popular."

Father Rutler's final comment was particularly acute. Many of Bill's observers, and he himself, recognized that he was not a profound creator of conservative principles but a brilliant polemicist who made conservatism lively, literate, often amusing. Instead of struggling through turgid tomes or windy speeches, people could enjoy reading or hearing about a traditional philosophy brought up to date by Bill's brisk style. Sure, sometime his words were too long, "sesquipedalian", but that was part of the fun of the game. Occasionally he lamented that he never settled down to write the authoritative *magnum opus* of modern conservative thought, but probably that was never really his desire, or within his capabilities. Bill was far too much a man of the moment, reacting to events, needing immediate stimulation, to retreat into the scholarly seclusion required to produce an original thesis or a grand summation.

His essential qualities were immediately recognized by the late Whittaker Chambers, the moody ex-, then strongly anti-, Communist, often sunk in gloomy speculation that Communism would soon dominate the world. Although he had enjoyed ultimate victory over his adversary Alger Hiss with the final 1950 jury verdict of guilty of spying, his long career as an editor with the *Time-Life* empire had come to an end, despite Henry Luce's support. His own book *Witness* had been only an ambiguous success. In poor health, with little to occupy him except his unprofitable Pennsylvania farm, he felt isolated and in 1954 welcomed a visit proposed by Bill, the bright new *wunderkind* of Yankee conservatism. That first meeting was a revelation to Chambers, who immediately reported to his wife that "[Bill] is something special. He was born, not made, and not many like that are born in any time." It marked the beginning of an intense, though often argumentative, friendship of Chambers' final years. As Sam Tanenhaus wrote in his biography of Chambers, "Bill Buckley brought to the American right qualities no one could remember its ever having possessed: glamour and style, the heedless joy of privileged youth . . . Already a celebrity, Buckley had no radical past to live down. He had not been a Stalinist, Trotskyist, socialist, or even a liberal."

Chambers became intrigued with Bill's plans to launch *National Review,* as a compendium of the best of Conservative thinking, firmly set against liberal statism, but avoiding the reactionary extremism of Joe McCarthy or the John Birch Society. Although remaining cautious about NR's editorial direction, Chambers eventually committed himself to contributing to the magazine and assumed a brief editorship position before resigning over policy disagreements. But he never failed to recognize Bill as the charismatic new standard bearer for the conservative movement, a role he was too old and disillusioned to play, and he remained a friend until death in 1960, often writing plaintively to Bill, "Come to us when you can. Come down when you will and can." Bill's vigor and good cheer were constant antidotes to his mental exhaustion and moral despair.

My final research into Bill's life led to his archives stored in Yale's Sterling Memorial Library. I went up to New Haven and by pre-arrangement with the research librarian, I found about 20 boxes of documents awaiting me in the reading room. The total Buckley archive runs to several hundred boxes; I had only asked to see those with his personal correspondence over recent years, and I found each box containing files neatly tabbed with date and name of sender or recipient. Bill clearly had a meticulous secretary who logged every item that moved in or out. I found many letters that confirmed his reputation of not only making friends everywhere but also caring deeply about them and consoling them in times of trouble.

The best example was his lengthy correspondence with the English writer Alistair Horne and members of his family. He had known Alistair since during WWII he had been evacuated to the United States and enrolled in Bill's small boarding school, Millbrook. Over many years Bill gave frequent advice, encouragement, and congratulations on Alistair's growing production of history books, invited him to his ski house in Switzerland, gave imaginative gifts, and tried (unsuccessfully) to lead him to Christ. Perhaps the most touching letter comes from Alistair's teen-age daughter Camilla, written to Bill when her father was distraught by a difficult divorce. "You and Pat are his closest friends," it reads, "he needs you so much at the moment—he's lost lonely and unhappy."

Correspondence with Ron and Nancy Reagan starting in 1970, long before the presidency, shows that his attachment to the Reagan family was far closer than simply a political alliance. I read hand-written notes from Nancy thanking the Buckleys for hospitality in New York and Stamford, and a surprisingly blunt note from Bill complaining "you refuse to wrap your mind around foreign policy; it is not too early to start,"—to defeat Nelson Rockefeller. Ron often writes warmly, saying that despite disagreement about Panama, "it could not in any way affect the friendship I feel for you," and, "I am very grateful most of all for your unselfish friendship." While doubtless based on a political agenda, the feelings between the two families clearly extended to a level of intimacy.

While in New Haven, I called on people who had been involved with Bill. Professor Gaddis Smith, who served as chairman of the *Yale Daily News* some years later than Bill, told me how Bill became the first to insist that part of the publication's annual profits be used to set up a pension fund for the salaried staff instead of going 100% into the pockets of the student editors. Professor Steven Duke of the Law School, initially a Buckley detractor, described how much he came to admire Bill once he publicly joined Duke's long campaign to end the destructive, ineffective War on Drugs.

I also learned that Bill had been a close friend and supporter of the late Allard Lowenstein, a Yale Law graduate and one-term Congressman, who had been a much loved and charismatic leader of liberal causes that were ordinarily anathema to Bill. Their warmth was one of many examples that ideological differences never separated Bill from personal intimacy with those he admired for their intelligence, charm, and devotion to their principles. He shared many a skiing trip and lively verbal jousting match with John Kenneth Galbraith, the towering (both physically and intellectually) figure whose views of economic forces were 180 degrees opposed to Bill's.

I turned all of my research over to Sam Tanenhaus for use in his biography. He was not universally popular with the Buckley family, thanks to some tendentious statements in his long obituary piece in the *Yale Alumni Magazine*. One hopes that his eventual production, while not being a puff piece, will be fair to Bill's accomplishments and not brand him as mere throwback to rapacious Republican capitalism and Bourbon autocracy. Five years after Bill's death, one wonders when, or if, a publication date will be announced.

About a year after I finished my investigations, I got inspired to think about one segment of Buckley's work that has not received much critical attention: his novels, and particularly the eleven-strong series featuring Blackford Oakes. I read, or re-read, all of them, and produced a lengthy essay published online by *First Principles,* the journal of the conservative-oriented Intercollegiate Studies Institute. The next section is a revised version of that essay.

The Saga of Blackford Oakes

When Bill accepted an invitation to lunch in the fall of 1974 from Sam Vaughan, head of the Doubleday publishing house, he didn't know where the conversation would lead. Either he or Vaughan eventually raised the question, what kind of new book would Buckley like to write? By then, starting with *God and Man at Yale* in 1951, he had already produced some dozen non-fiction works, primarily about the conflict between Left and Right, interspersed with brilliantly etched tales of personal adventures. With his polemical journal *National Review* well established, and his lively TV program *Firing Line* attracting fascinated viewers, he already had a national reputation. He had particularly intrigued New Yorkers with his eccentric 1965 campaign for mayor, making both the other candidates Abe Beame and John Lindsay (the eventual winner) appear as cretinous incompetents. When asked on TV to define the difference between them, his inimitable drawl responded, "Well . . . Mr. Beame is very short . . . and Mr. Lindsay is very tall."

Bill Buckley had nothing more to prove as a public figure. Thanks to his scintillating heiress wife Patricia, his social calendar was always full and his homes in New York and Stamford immaculately maintained. Perhaps he was bored, ready for a different challenge, or disillusioned with a Republican Party that had sunk with Richard Nixon. How to usefully fill the annual two-month skiing holiday in Switzerland? He mentioned diffidently to Vaughan that he had recently read and admired Frederick Forsyth's spy thriller *Day of the Jackal.* Wouldn't it be fun to try something in the same line? Not slow to spot a publishing opportunity, Vaughan had a contract for a novel on Bill's desk the next day.

Thus began a remarkable run of fiction. In the 18 years 1976 through 1994, ten of the so-called "Blackford Oakes" novels appeared, then a hiatus, and in 2005 Oakes re-appeared and was retired with an eleventh and final work. Blackford Oakes was a hit from the beginning. And Sam Vaughan was warmly acknowledged as editor in all of them, despite changes of publishers. With publication of the initial *Saving the Queen,* Bill for the first time showed his surprising expertise at fast-moving, if somewhat improbable, tales. He had an attractive hero, a clean-cut American loyal to his CIA employer, sharp dialogue, vivid descriptions of international scenes, accurate bites of recent history, love (with pretty awkward sex), death, conflicts, suspense. The audacious premise that Oakes slept with the Queen of England (although an imaginary one) doubtless helped sales for a writer unknown as a novelist.

Buckley made a major point that all his Oakes books were designed to uphold the moral superiority of the United States over the Soviet Union and its communist satellites and intelligence agencies. In his introduction to *The Blackford Oakes Reader,* 1995, he warns us, "I would write a book where the good guys and the bad guys were actually distinguishable from each other . . . and the good guys would be—the Americans!" He quite deliberately wanted to refute the likes of authors John Le Carré, Len Deighton, and Graham Greene who he maintained described the CIA and the KGB as equivalent, each guilty of scandalous and morally insupportable practices. Not so, says Buckley, "The CIA, whatever its failings, sought, during those long years in the struggle for the world, to advance the honorable alternative." This position was of course perfectly predictable and consistent with Buckley's world view, as repeatedly stated in his writings and speeches.

The novels were written at great speed; not only the mechanical act of typing (Bill had trained himself to become a touch-typist while still a teenager) but the imaginative act of conceiving a theme and reducing it to hard words of dialogue and narrative, were completed in bursts of literary effort, mixed with skiing on slopes looming over a village near Gstaad in the Swiss Alps, a convenient two hours from Geneva airport.

Every year Bill hired an editorial assistant to help him in his labors. One of them, Peter Robinson, now a Fellow of the Hoover Institution, spent the winter of 1988 working daily with Buckley and has described the process. They shared a large studio on the ground floor of the elegant Chateau Rougemont, the Buckley annual winter rental. "Every morning I would be at my desk by 7:30," says Robinson, "and Bill would be there before me. We sat at separate tables tapping at our computers, with classical music piped in, me pulling together a compendium of *Firing Line* transcripts, him adapting *Stained Glass,* the second Oakes novel, into a stage play." (The repertory Actors Theatre of Louisville, Kentucky, opened it on Good Friday 1989, apparently to the satisfaction of the large Buckley claque who attended).

"The morning work was intense except for periodic 'phone calls to Bill, about which he complained but actually loved—Bill could not survive long without conversation. About noon we would break for a small but convivial lunch, then spend the afternoon skiing where Bill displayed his aggressive, adventurous, but distinctly inelegant style. Usually we would go back to work between 5 and 6 p.m., followed by a dinner that was the day's social event, with guests that might include Roger Moore and his wife, King Constantine of Greece, author James Clavell, the Duke and Duchess of Marlborough, Prince Romanov, and old friends Taki (Theodoracopulos) and Dick Clurman. But about 10 p.m., if guests were showing no signs of leaving, Bill played "Good Night Ladies" on the piano and we repaired downstairs for another couple of hours of work, this time accompanied by Bill's favorite jazz recordings."

After a winter season of these sessions, the manuscript was shipped off to New York, only requiring a month of clean-up editing later in the summer before being sent to the printer. In the working hours he had to find time to answer the bulky correspondence sent over daily from *National Review* by Frances Bronson, his much-more-than-secretary, and his sister Pitts (Patricia), the long-time managing editor, to say nothing of writing his bi-weekly column.

Even with his natural facility at writing, what he accomplished during these winter sojourns was pretty amazing. Each Blackford Oakes novel was not simply a theoretical construction but a *vignette* of a specific period and set of locations, built around recent events. Although Bill's wide and constant traveling gave him personal knowledge of many of the venues, certainly further research was required to get the details right. Even with a young literary assistant at hand, eager to learn from the master, it must have been a formidable task for Bill to merge the many nit-picky facts (the Russian SS-4 medium range ballistic missile stored in Cuba in 1963 was 68 feet long with a diameter of 63 inches) with the grand sweep and thrust of the current book, all within a brief and busy two months. Not many authors could have done it.

All this was hard graft. Why did he tie himself to the typewriter/computer when he could have been skiing, a pastime that we know he loved? There must have been the simple pride at unexpectedly succeeding in a new *genre*. One has a suspicion that he came to enjoy writing fiction more than his tendentious political and intellectual efforts. The record of his literary out-put shows that from 1976, when Blackford Oakes first appeared, to the end of his life he produced more novels and personal reminiscences, often about sailing, than works of right-wing ideology. Finally, there was the financial factor. In all the accounts of Bill's life, biographers have tip-toed discreetly around the question of how he and Pat afforded their glamorous and inevitably expensive life styles—a superb maisonette on Park Avenue, a shore-front estate in Connecticut, up-market winter rentals in Switzerland and later The Bahamas and Bermuda, resident cordon bleu chef Julian Booth inherited from David Niven, non-stop entertaining, long and short voyages on a series of sturdy sail-boats.

Bill's inheritance from the complex oil ventures created by his father had dwindled pretty low, drifting out of family control and divided between ten children sharing tenuous royalty income. We know that *National Review* was never a money-spinner, and had to be subsidized. Pat's inheritance certainly contributed, coming as she did from the dominant Taylor family of Vancouver, with a father amassing a fortune in timber and mining and brother Austin becoming CEO of the Canadian securities firm McLeod, Young & Weir (and one of Bill's frequent sailing mates). Doubtless she could pay the tab not only for her own lavish but tasteful wardrobe with enough left for the hefty grocery, wine and decorating bills, but Bill was too proud a man to be fully supported by a wife. He worked punishingly hard to earn his own way: fifty or more paid speeches every year at dreary motel locations across America, taping *Firing Line*, the widely syndicated column, magazine articles, well-compensated cruises lecturing to fellow (conservative) passengers, even negotiating corporate subsidies for some of his personal ocean voyages, most of which was ploughed into the magazine that underlay his fame. The novels became a welcome addition to this stream of income. The most popular book of the Blackford Oakes saga, 1985's *See*

You Later Alligator, earned him about $115,000 in hard-cover sales, considerably more than some of his "serious" efforts. The advance from another novel funded a winter trip to Russia for 20 NR staffers.

His first objective was to create a plausible and attractive Blackford Oakes, a hero who would neither bore nor annoy readers. Bill called his creation a "distillate", but that hardly seems the right word, since it suggests a mixture of qualities from varied sources. In fact, Oakes is a pretty routine product of his background—a Waspy Yalie from all-American middle-class parents, although they later split. We see nothing remotely eccentric or odd-ball about him, with no traumas or tragedies in his history; in fact he's pretty much like Bill, except that he's not a Catholic and that he's trained as an engineer, the same profession as Bill's admired Yale room-mate Richie O'Neill.

Unlike other heroes of the spy-thriller era, he boasts an image that is almost excessively perfect: "He stood there" (as described in the first novel) "tall and tanned, the straw in his hair blooming after the long winter . . . his thin, molded features without sign of age or strain, his eyes relentlessly intelligent, discerning, blue-frank, blue-cunning . . ." His long-time inamorata Sally Strawbridge, as well as various in-between girl friends, all succumb admiringly to the perfect body which Buckley fulsomely describes. Even his mother calls him, to his dismay, "my beautiful Blackie." His glamorous life begins early, when in the dying days of World War II, as an army pilot he shoots down three Kraut ME-109s, even before becoming a Yale freshman!

Recruited straight from Yale into the CIA, he takes to the spy profession seamlessly and spends the rest of his life in its grasp, having far more exotic adventures in the course of eleven books, and age 25 to 72, than any real-life agent has ever experienced, carrying him across England, Europe, Russia, Cuba, Bolivia, Viet-Nam, and of course into the Oval Office of the White House. Oakes' first episode, *Saving the Queen*, was a delightful light-weight pastiche, a finger exercise for the more serious works that followed.

His second adventure, *Stained Glass*, 1978, winner of the American Book Award for Best Mystery, enters darker waters and, presents him with the most serious moral dilemmas that he faces as a loyal Agency operative. He is assigned to befriend Count Axel von Wintergrin, a charismatic anti-Hitler German aristocrat with a heroic war record who founds a political party campaigning to re-unite post-war Germany, a campaign that Oakes personally admires but runs counter to official American policy of seeking détente with the Russians to avoid a putative nuclear holocaust. The title refers to a dominant window in the chapel of Wintergrin's ancestral schloss in rural Westphalia, where the CIA is eventually instructed to terminate Axel by means of an "accidental" electrocution. Oakes, who has come to revere the young German, is chosen to lead the execution but arranges to evade actual pushing of the button. By any standards, he is an accomplice, a role that deeply troubles his conscience, as the novel duly records in a fictional conversation years later with Allen Dulles, the first head of the CIA.

Oakes asks, "Well, Mr. Dulles, did we do the right thing back in 1952?"

Dulles responds, "The question you ask I do not permit, not under any circumstances . . . because, if you let them, the ambiguists will kill you."

"The ambiguists, as you call them, were dead right about Count Wintergrin . . . you lost the great chance."

"I believe you are right. I believe Wintergrin was right. The Russians—I believe—would not have moved . . . I *don't* believe the lesson to draw is that we *must not* act because, in acting, we *may prove* to be wrong." [emphasis in original]

Oakes absorbs this edict from the older man, and impulsively shakes his hand. He has learned the hard lesson that the US government must be deemed wise and just in acting in its best interests, even if all the facts are not, cannot, be known. The dialog between Dulles and Oakes is underlined in the 2007 book *Strictly Right*, whose authors Linda Bridges and John R. Coyne Jr., Buckley's close colleagues, quote Bill as saying, "Counterintelligence and espionage, conducted under Western auspices, weren't exercises in conventional political geometry. They were—they are—a moral art". Whatever differing view the skeptical reader may choose to take, this is the bed-rock philosophy underlying and illuminating all the Blackford Oakes novels.

Another dialog in *Stained Glass*, between Oakes and the CIA old-timer Rufus, makes the point even more forcefully about the hard practicalities of espionage work. When told of his expected role in Wintergrin's death, Oakes asks, "Are you aware that I was never told on joining this outfit that I would be expected to kill people in cold blood? Let alone the leading anti-Communist in Europe?"

Rufus, hard-bitten to the core, responds at length:

> You aren't *required* to do it even now. But I *am* required to lay it on the line. The fact is that the commander-in-chief of your government, his principal foreign affairs advisor, and the director of the intelligence agency devoted to protecting American interests—our sovereignty, our freedom—*feel that situation is critical:* that this single man's activities are about to put the lives and liberties of whole peoples on the line. They despise, as I do, the government [the Soviet Union] that has given us this ultimatum. They cannot even know whether that threat is a bluff. They agreed, finally, that responsible statesmanship forbade taking so awful a risk—*conceivably, the risk of millions of people dead* . . . . So I put it this way, Blackford. You are the front-line agent of the commander-in-chief. You have been involved in the evolution of the plan. And it was you who drew the card. [emphasis in original]

So what could the honorable Blackie do? If he had refused, he would not have been shot, unlike the probable fate for a Russian counterpart, but certainly his resignation from the CIA would have been promptly demanded. This was an action that he, like most red-blooded Americans in the more clear-cut days of 1950s, was unwilling to take.

He respected his seniors and admired his country. Shirking duty was not an option, however repulsive to personal morality that duty might seem.

The Blackford Oakes novels are not philosophical tracts weighing actions in the balance between good and evil and rendering a final judgment. But, as superb fiction, they do show in dramatic terms the intense inner struggles when humans must decide between conflicting choices. And they do, finally, express a firm point of view, that can be accepted or disparaged but certainly does not hinder the flow of action that makes for exciting suspense.

After *Stained Glass,* Bill Buckley's fictive imagination continued unabated. Blackford's adventures in service of the CIA become even more extraordinary, and the amorous dalliances thrive with lubricity, replete with "all the beautiful parts of her full body . . . that proceeded to initiate him in the arcadian mysteries, with delirious effect," while never preventing protestations of love and marriage proposals for the estimable Sally, the sexy and witty scholar of Jane Austen. He eventually weds and beds her, surrenders her to an up-market Mexican husband, recovers her after husband's dramatic murder, and finally loses her to death—freeing him for one last twilight romance shortly before his own demise. Bill perhaps created Blackie as a vicarious substitute for his own monagamous existence with the ever-fascinating Pat, free of any shadow of gossip for 57 years despite his undoubted masculine charms.

Of the next six Blackford Oakes chronicles, published from 1980 through 1987, four memorialize the Cold War as played out against Russia mainly on the European stage, while two

A Corkscrew Life

use the ever-intriguing Cuban communist regime as their foil. All of them contain marvelous set-pieces in the Washington corridors of power. In *Who's On First*, 1980, we overhear a splendid imagined conversation between the witty, acerbic former Secretary of State Dean Acheson and the devious CIA boss Allen Dulles, who seems to prefer exchanging iconoclastic views with Acheson than with the incumbent secretary, his tedious, moralizing older brother John Foster. In *Mongoose R.I.P.*, 1987, we are put inside JFK's head for a long end-of-day soliloquy about the burdens of the presidency and how to assassinate Fidel Castro because "we can't let the fucker stay around", before he's reminded that the First Lady expects him at seven for dinner.

Throughout these and other books, Bill enjoys leavening his fabricated stories with coded clues to his actual life. Clandestine meetings are held at the Chateau St. Firmin in the French countryside. This is in fact the handsome building, still standing across the decorative lake from the famous Chateau de Chantilly, that Bill's expansive father rented as a family residence in the 1930's. Bill provides the singular name Valerian Bibikoff for one of his minor characters. This is of course the unforgettable "Bibi", the ingenious Paris-based white Russian who answered the call of many Buckleys, like somehow finding two vehicles for Bill's brother Jim and Yale friends, including myself, to drive around Europe in 1949, long before rental agencies surfaced. One of them was a liberated German Army staff car, still wearing its camouflage paint, that caused not a little comment as we drove along Europe's war-torn roads. Even the sacrosanct Skull & Bones, Bill's Yale secret society, becomes fair game. When Oakes checks into a Mexico City hotel, he is given room 322, the iconic number of mysterious origin that appears in all Bones history.

Of these six books in the middle range of the series, I have two favorites: *The Story of Henry Tod*, 1984, and the dreadfully named, but best-selling, *See You Later, Alligator*, 1985. In *Tod*, Bill creates one of his most sympathetic, tragic characters in the man originally known as Heinrich Toddweiss, a Jewish lad who is abruptly torn away from his family and whisked out of pre-war Germany to escape the threatened Nazi roundups. Tod much later returns to Germany to try to block construction of the Berlin Wall, believing he has the backing of the US military. Alas, he misconceives the international climate—Jack Kennedy vetoes any help. Tod is shot by the East German forces, and Oakes narrowly escapes the same fate.

For his next Oakes adventure, Bill rapidly shifts gears from Berlin to Cuba. Blackie is dispatched to continue negotiations with Che Guevara that had been begun (in fact) in Montevideo by presidential envoy Richard Goodwin. The negotiations over nine months go nowhere, but Bill treats us to an engaging series of conversational sparring matches usually won by the highly educated Che, the recognized intellectual godfather of the Revolution. He has read Alfred North Whitehead's *Principia Mathematica*; Blackie's Yale education did not extend that far. Che lectures loftily on languages, claiming that "disappointing" has no Spanish translation. "It is a distinctively English, meiotic expression," he tells Blackie. Che speaks through Catalina, a knock-out Cuban female translator, and Oakes relies on Cecilio Velasco, a tough little Spaniard who joined the CIA. These two bit-players soon become virtually the stars of the *Alligator* drama (so titled because that reptile is a rough translation of the Spanish *caimán*, which Che uses as the name of the operation and often leaves Oakes with the valedictory "*Hasta luego, Caimán*", or, unfortunately, *See You Later, Alligator*).

Blackie's charms eventually seduce Catalina to turn against Che, and together with Velasco they discover Cuba's secret missiles and try to escape to Florida. But Che captures them. Velasco, "who wrote the book on courage," is killed in a gunfight. Oakes survives and is released at the insistence of JFK, while Catalina, though promised clemency by Che, is shot in prison.

Five years later, Oakes is in Bolivia, summoned to visit Che who has been captured and is under order of execution. The

Bolivian colonel offers Oakes the option of taking Che for the US Government. "He is your prisoner—or our corpse." Oakes is given three minutes to decide. He recalls how Che betrayed Catalina, and calmly says "He is yours, Colonel." As he walks away, he hears two shots.

So Blackford Oakes proves that in addition to being a fair-haired Yalie, he can be one tough son-of-a-bitch practicing "vengeance is mine."

The penultimate Blackford Oakes novel, *A Very Private Plot*, 1995, is staged as a lengthy flash-back. We learn that in 1985 a group of courageous young Russians calling themselves the New Narodniki, disillusioned veterans of the hopeless Afghanistan campaign and Soviet policies of repression, determine to assassinate First Secretary Gorbachev. Through his Moscow contact known as Cyclops, only Oakes in the CIA is given the full story, which he duly reports to President Reagan.

In a couple of artfully crafted one-on-one conversations between Oakes and the president, they struggle with a painful decision. Reagan rhetorically asks "Is it *our* responsibility to protect a foreign tyrant from his own people?" Pressed for his opinion, Oakes responds, "I would leave the matter alone"— in other words let the Narodniki proceed. Reagan sighs and merely says, "I'll get in touch with you tomorrow."

After Reagan's productive conference with Gorbachev in Iceland, Oakes finds the wind has changed direction in the White House. Reagan certainly does not want Gorby dead. Breaking a moment of silence, Reagan slowly says "We've got to stop this Cyclops business."

Oakes seeks clarification: "You mean you want me to call the whole thing off . . . the only sure way is for Cyclops to turn the Narodniki in to the KGB." The President says nothing, does not move his gaze up from the desk until he takes Oakes' extended hand. "Blackford saw the sadness in the eyes. It meant that he knew the full consequences of his decision."

So Oakes has been given an order never explicitly stated, and, heart-sick, immediately leaves for Moscow to make sure it is executed. He forces the unwilling Cyclops to inform the KGB about the Narodniki plot, under the threat of exposing his old sparring partner Cyclops to the KGB as a mole for the CIA. Once again Oakes proves to be a tough son-of-a-bitch, and once again he must subordinate his personal views to the iron duty of obeying his commander-in-chief.

A contrasting view of duty may be found in the 2008 book *Why Vietnam Matters* by Rufus Phillips, a Yale contemporary of Bill's who barely knew him. Phillips was also drafted into the CIA, and later the Agency for International Development, mainly in Vietnam and Laos. Phillips greatly admired his colleague the legendary Col. Edward G. Lansdale, an expert in unconventional warfare who became a confidant of the first Vietnamese Prime Minister Ngo Dinh Diem and adviser to the US Embassy in Saigon. According to a story related by Phillips, in 1963 Lansdale was ordered by Secretary of Defense McNamara to accompany him to a meeting with President Kennedy, who asked him, "If I decided that we had to get rid of Diem himself, would you be able to go along with that?" to which Lansdale replied sadly, "No, Mr. President, I couldn't do that. Diem is my friend."

Reportedly McNamara was furious with Lansdale, saying "You don't talk to the President of the United States that way. When he asks you to do something, you don't tell him you won't do it." Later that year Lansdale retired as a full Major General, before becoming the third recipient of the U.S. National Security Medal. Apparently disobedience to presidential inclinations did not trouble his conscience or destroy his career. An old friend told Phillips that "one of Ed's unique qualities was his ability to say no to anything he believed wrong, no matter who was asking it." Clearly not every public servant felt constrained to follow Blackford Oakes' code of behavior.

Bill's accomplishments lead to a beguiling question: could he who had done so much actually have done more? The publishers' blurbs for his novels print innumerable reviewers' snippets in the vein: "Tense, chilling, unflaggingly lively . . . the tales get better and better" or "stamped with hallmark of his sardonic elegance" or "An absolute delight of a book" or "almost alone in using genuine political mischief as a source of wit". But all this enthusiastic praise still restricts the Oakes chronicles to the realm of spy stories, thrillers, "entertainments" in Graham Greene's definition, without moving them across the indefinable line distinguishing "serious fiction", where literary pundits place the likes of Saul Bellow, Philip Roth, Norman Mailer, John Cheever and John Updike.

We observe Bill's superb talents and intellectual resources: knack for plotting and sharp dialog, curiosity over details, wide grasp of history and current events, feeling for the cultures of art and music, and, above all, fascination and sympathy for eccentric losers in tough spots. He had everything he needed to become a great novelist—except time. Even this he could have created. Suppose he had carved out a full year from his busy life, retreated to the green solitude of the family compound in Sharon, given up columns, speeches, witticisms with Henry Kissinger, advice to the White House.

He would never have become a recluse quietly honing his literary style. His genes, derived from a buccaneer father who cheerfully made and lost fortunes, would have prevented that fate. And he too much enjoyed being "of the world" to retreat permanently into the realm of pure thought. But we know he was a man of immense will power and discipline in his writing schedule. If he could have freed himself from his writing deadlines and his frantic schedule of other commitments, could he have stretched his abilities to give us a deeper strain of creativity, describing the modern world with the ambiguities of, say, Joseph Conrad's *Under Western Eyes* or *The Secret Agent,* or the scope of Thomas Mann's *Magic Mountain*? One of his more perceptive critics, Joseph Kanon, in a New York Times review of Bill's historical novel *Nuremberg, the Reckoning,* uncovers his basic shortcoming: "Buckley has never been drawn to character or moral irony (much less relativism) in his fiction, precisely the qualities that would be welcome here."

We can only speculate what might have been, and meanwhile enjoy the actual written record in the *genre* he chose—an output far superior to the superficial James Bond repetitions, and challenging John Le Carré's protean brilliance. Of course, Blackford Oakes never became the pop-cult figure equivalent to Bond; never was memorialized on film by the inimitable Sean Connery. Perhaps Bond's very simplicity (sex and violence served with style but no discernible political philosophy) was easier for a vast public to grasp, while Oakes remained a taste for specialists. It's interesting that Ian Fleming, Bond's creator, never became a public figure with a strong separate image, while the opposite is true of Bill, who achieved fame based on far more than Blackford Oakes.

Bill's final Oakes novel, *Last Call for Blackford Oakes*, published in 2005, shows no declining powers. Oakes, now a widower, semi-retired at age 60, is again dispatched to Moscow on secret orders from the President Reagan to defuse another possible threat to Gorbachev. However, for the first time, the story leads to tragedy for Oakes, no longer the survivor golden boy. He falls deeply in love with a Russian lady whom he impregnates and plans to marry. She dies in a Moscow hospital, apparently victim of an ectoptic pregnancy (as Pat had once suffered) but in reality medically murdered at the behest of one "Andre Fyodorich Martins" who has entertained Oakes before being revealed as the odious British traitor Kim Philby, adopted as a permanent resident by the Soviet regime. Philby and Oakes are of course bitter enemies, on opposite sides of ideology and sense of honor. The eventual grim denouement can almost be anticipated: a brief, bloody shoot-out that kills Oakes, but not before he gets off a round that seriously wounds the arch-enemy Philby.

This remarkable coda to the Oakes saga was praised by *New York Times* reviewer Charlie Rubin: "may be the best Oakes since the first . . . validates Buckley's considerable fiction skills." But sales fell short. Perhaps Oakes' eleven-year absence from the bookstores had lost him many of his fans, or tastes had simply changed. In fact, many Buckley watchers wondered why Bill had written it, long after the Cold War had ended and he himself had laid down many of his literary cudgels. He never gave his reasons. Perhaps he wanted an inflexible ending for Oakes that would discourage any impostors from resurrecting him after Bill's own passing. Perhaps the cut-off was simply part of the simplification he decreed for his own life.

At his farewell speech at the 2003 annual Bohemian Grove encampment, where he had enjoyed many summers as a Hill-Billy with the cream of the American establishment, he firmly stated this would be his final appearance. He alluded to "terminal thoughts" that led to abandonment of even the exhilaration of his beloved downhill skiing. It was about this time that he sold his sloop *Patito*, allegedly because he couldn't find crew, but more likely because the time for sailing was simply past, one of the ages of man that had come to an end. With his intensely rational mind, as his health and energy began to fail he could shuck off inessentials and retreat to his core.

Bill's lifeless body was found in February 2008, sitting before the word-processor in his renowned garage writing factory on Wallachs Point. As he suffered through his last months wheezing with emphysema and nearly immobilized in his Stanford home, no longer succored by Pat and friend Van Galbraith who both pre-deceased him, knowing that death was not far, he may have thought of the glorious career of Blackie, vigorous to the end and dying the only way a man should—from a bullet fired while battling the enemy, the quintessential Evil Empire. Bill's alter ego was fictional, but it was his own creation: the Blackford Oakes that he himself had brought to life.

CHAPTER 11

The Fall of a Super-Star: Norbert A. Schlei, 1930-2003

One thing I learned at Yale Law School: there's more to law than just the law. The black-letter statutes and regulations taught us what we could get away with in the hard world of legal practice, but Yale taught us we must go farther. We must think about what is fair, right, honorable, even moral, although we shied away from the word with its religious implications in our secular world. If we saw an injustice being done, we should correct it, even if no law required our action. And of course personal loyalty was part of the equation. It was much later that I saw an injustice, and loyalty compelled me to act. I could not be a hero, but I could at least write something.

While at Yale I hardly knew Norb Schlei, graduating in 1956, a year ahead of me, but he was visible to all, clearly a legal super-star in the making: academically brilliant, with the charisma of a tall, handsome Navy veteran and scratch golfer. The world clearly was destined to become his oyster, and for a long time it did. Over the years we became good friends, so that in April 1995 I read with shock and dismay two prominent press items, both with photos of Norb. The *New York Times* carried a three-column headline reading "Stalwart of the Kennedy

Justice Dept. Finds His World in Ashes after a Trial", and the *National Law Journal* headed its snidely slanted story with the dramatic tag "The Upending of a Camelot Knight—The Los Angeles lawyer became embroiled in a Japanese bond racket." I knew that he was a defendant in a complex criminal trial, but had not followed the details and was astonished to read that he had been found guilty, facing a possible jail term. What had gone wrong in a life of gleaming potential?

Norb was not born into the typical solid business or professional background that has spawned so many of the good and the great in the American legal fraternity. Raised in modest circumstances in Dayton, Ohio, where his father worked for 46 years in a blue-collar production job for National Cash Register, he entered the University of Ohio with the class of 1950, with the financial assistance of the Naval ROTC program and scholarship duties as a waiter. He achieved a good academic record in English literature combined with athletic prowess, earning three varsity letters in golf. Upon graduation, he immediately entered active duty during the Korean war and served as a deck officer on a heavy cruiser in the Atlantic and Mediterranean. His naval reputation and social skills can be judged by his appointment as aide and flag lieutenant to an admiral, which coincidentally allowed him enough shore time to become golf champion of the Atlantic Fleet in 1953, his final year of service.

Upon leaving the Navy, he applied for entry to Yale Law School and was promptly accepted. By this time he had married his first wife, Jane Moore, and fathered his first child, William. Added to these family responsibilities, Norb was fully pressed with the scholarly grind of legal education and during his three years was not often seen in the convivial social life of the Law School. But his legal abilities were unquestioned, as he joined the Board of the *Yale Law Journal* after his first term and went on to lead it as Editor-in-Chief, finishing first in his class of 150.

At Yale, Schlei certainly inhaled the spirit of social experimentation for which its Law School was famous, with its emphasis that lawyers should think about the broad issues of public policy as much as the technical steps for defending clients. One of his most influential professors was Nicholas Katzenbach, who later went on to become deputy attorney general under President Kennedy, and had this to say about Schlei in a character reference he later wrote to the judge who sentenced him in 1995:

> What I remember best was his final exam paper in Conflict of Laws. It was unquestionably the best exam paper I have ever received from a student . . . But, of at least equal importance, was the confidence I had in his calm judgment and moral character . . . *total* confidence in his integrity and judgment.

He also worked closely with Professor Myres McDougall, a prolific author and one of the nation's leading experts on international law. They collaborated on a major article for the *Journal* that, unlike the usual dry technical analysis, actually raised controversy. It defended the right of the United States to conduct the 1954 hydrogen bomb tests in the Pacific, a position that many of his colleagues in the liberal Law School strongly opposed. His classmate Emanuel Margolis carried on a friendly but vigorous debate with Norb long into post-graduate days.

His immaculate record at the Law School was followed by the inevitable next step—the trophy appointment to a clerkship with a Justice of the Supreme Court, John Marshall Harlan, normal precursor to a career that could go in many directions: wealthy corporate lawyer, distinguished scholar, respected judge, prominent government figure, or any combination thereof.

Norb's subsequent professional life displayed a certain restlessness, an ambition to move on to new challenges once the existing ones had been fully digested. While this may not be the mark of the usual practicing attorney who toils worthily in one furrow until retirement, it certainly is typical of any professional endowed with extreme intelligence and charisma. Few of the people who have made a mark in American life have made a virtue of "sticking to one's last", of not moving on. Often their very qualities cause them to be actively invited, almost seduced, to turn over a new leaf.

This was certainly true of Norb. In 1957, on finishing his year with the Supreme Court, many opportunities beckoned. He met Warren Christopher, later Secretary of State under Jimmy Carter and already senior partner of O'Melveny & Myers, one of the two top firms in Los Angeles. Christopher invited him to the usual associate's starting position, although doubtless hinting at a bright future, and Norb promptly accepted. But, predictably, the routine of this legal factory did not capture all his energies, and he also found the firm would not take kindly to his ambitions of campaigning for public office. After two years he left to form a new firm with two young partners, which kept him fully engaged until 1962.

In that year, there occurred one of those unexpected career switches which often strike brilliant young people who have impressed their seniors. A Supreme Court retirement saw Byron "Whizzer" White leave the Department of Justice to fill the Court vacancy, Nick Katzenbach move up to take White's place as deputy attorney general under Bobby Kennedy, and the need to fill the key position of assistant attorney general—legal counsel. Katzenbach immediately turned to his well-remembered student Norbert Schlei, who at age 33 came east from California to join the New Frontier—benefiting, it was said, from Bobby Kennedy's desire to have someone in the Department younger than he.

By all accounts, Norb's career with Justice over the next three years was capped with multiple successes. The day after moving into his office, he found himself dispatched with Katzenbach to the University of Mississippi where they survived riots to get James Meredith admitted as the first black student. Then, in October 1962, the nation was put in peril by what came to be known as the Cuban Missile Crisis. Although Norb was not one of the close-knit group of policy advisors who surrounded President John F. Kennedy during those tense days, his boss Bobby certainly was, and he needed an opinion justifying, under international law, the imposition of an American naval blockade once Russian missiles had been detected in Cuba. The task might normally have been given to the legal advisor to the State Department, but Bobby trusted Norb's abilities and assigned the task to him, resulting in his fully-researched affirmation that a the blockade, or even stronger measures, were legally justified in the face of this "threat to the peace and security of the Western Hemisphere."

Reverting to the field of civil rights, Norb served as head of a drafting committee for the Civil Rights Act of 1964, and at the instructions of President Lyndon Johnson he went to Birmingham and Montgomery, Alabama, to work with the US Army to control any violence that might arise from public-school integration enforcement. The next year he took a leading role in preparing the Immigration Act of 1965.

Early in 1966, with this record of accomplishment behind him, came the natural moment for Schlei to return to California and resume his legal practice, although with possible political forays in mind. The exciting Washington years also left him with a change in his personal life. Now the parents of two boys and a girl, he and his wife Jane divorced. I never knew what strains arose in that early marriage as Norb's career progressed, but I learned that he soon courted and then promptly married Barbara, my ex-girlfriend from Yale Law School, then working in the office of the District of Columbia federal prosecutor. She and I had remained close, and I was delighted to see the union of two such ambitious, talented professionals.

In his early years in California he retained a lively interest in the political world. With his history of public service, his vigorous appearance and command of words, he was an easy winner in the hotly-contested Democratic party primaries for California Secretary of State in 1966, collecting more than

2.7 million votes, but lost to the Republican candidate in the Reagan-dominated elections later that year.

Norb took politics seriously. I once accompanied him to a campaign dinner that he left fuming angrily, after the master of ceremonies introduced him last and then mispronounced his name (rhyming it with "see" instead of the correct "sigh"). An active and visible campaigner for Bobby Kennedy's nomination as Democratic presidential candidate in 1968, he was on the scene in Los Angeles' Ambassador Hotel where Kennedy was assassinated by the fanatical gunman Sirhan Sirhan. Like many Americans, disillusioned and discouraged by this latest display of violence in the public arena, Norb soon abandoned any further political ambitions.

He accepted the offer of a partnership with the bright young Los Angeles firm Munger, Tolles, Hills & Rickershauser. This was the same Charlie Munger who became Warren Buffet's unsung but equally successful partner in conservative investing; possibly he could have made Norb a billionaire too had he chosen to stay with the firm.

But, restless again, after a couple of years with a smaller firm, in 1972 he was approached by classmates who had become partners in the powerful Wall Street firm Hughes, Hubbard & Reed, eager to expand into the effervescent California market. They asked him to set up a Los Angeles office and become its managing partner, a dream job for an ambitious attorney. Norb soon attained a noticeable profile, defending the eccentric millionaire Howard Hughes in a high-visibility libel action. Los Angeles appeared to provide a halcyon existence for Norb and Barbara. In seven years from 1966 to 1973 they produced four children, three boys and a girl. Their separate legal incomes, plus Barbara's family wealth (aided by her brother George who became a brilliant investor) allowed them to acquire a handsome mansion in Bel Air, complete with tennis court and swimming pool, as well as a beach house in Malibu, where I was always welcome on occasional trips to the Coast.

However, tensions invisible to me developed within this high-powered couple, and in the late 1970s they separated and soon divorced, but with no apparent rancor, as I once shared a jolly Christmas Day with all parties present. Norb must have been romantically as well as professionally restless; after a two-year affair that produced a child (his eighth), he married again for the third and final time.

It was not until 1985 that Norb first met the clients who would shatter the course of his life. It would be easy to reach the simplistic conclusion that, as in a Greek tragedy, these clients harbored some form of malevolent influence that foreshadowed all his later difficulties and the tragic reversal of his brilliant career. They were certainly unusual, but there was nothing malevolent about them; the proximate cause of his nightmare entanglement with criminal prosecution was not their actions but rather the vindictive and misguided campaign of federal law enforcement agencies.

In April 1985, at the introduction of long-time Korean client Sam Han, Norb welcomed into the Hughes, Hubbard conference room in the ARCO Tower in downtown Los Angeles a group of Japanese gentlemen. They told a remarkable tale, which had to be filtered through the few of them who had reasonable English. To summarize very briefly, it was a tale of massive hidden funds in Japan, outside any control by government and managed by a small cabal of powerful, secretive individuals for the benefit of their own personal and political ambitions. These funds arose out of the rapacious seizures of foreign assets by the Japanese army during its World War II military campaigns; worse, their existence became fully known to General MacArthur's American occupying forces at war's end and were allowed to accumulate in secret with no formal accountability to either country's government, so that they could be used for selected clandestine purposes. The consolidation of these assets became known as the "M-Fund" after General Marquat, the MacArthur staff officer who allegedly took charge.

Naturally, this long, complex—and sometimes far-fetched—tale could not be absorbed in one sitting. Over a period of weeks and months the story had to be fleshed out, particularly by Toshio Takahashi, the Japanese who gradually emerged as leader of the group. It became clear that the Japanese had not come to the US purely to recount an abstract history of corruption at high levels. They had a more specific financial motive, relating to a series of unusual financial instruments that were loosely, and inaccurately, called "M-bonds", in gigantic denominations of 10 billion to 500 billion yen. Apparently these instruments represented cash, securities or other assets held in the M-Fund. As their text was entirely in Japanese, it was difficult to translate their title into relevant English financial language; the most appropriate wording was chosen as "Certificates of Balance of Redemption, Series 57". The Certificates were certainly not equivalent to the ordinary negotiable bonds well known in the financial world. But Norb's new clients were named as payees of these instruments, and the crucial legal and financial question put to Norb was, how could the payees realize any value on their holdings, even if only a fraction of the face denominations?

The very existence of the M-Fund has long been wrapped in controversy. The American and Japanese Governments have flatly denied it. But with the help of Takahashi and his associates, Norb traveled frequently to Japan to conduct basic research, resulting in his memorandum being published in 1995 by the Japan Policy Research Institute, led by University of California Professor Chalmers Johnson, a recognized expert on post-war Japanese history. Professor Johnson commented that, "The evidence of the existence of the M-Fund . . . rests on more than the statements of Schlei's clients," citing many other sources. Norb verified that his efforts were not violating any US Government policies by consulting General Counsel Stanley Sporkin, of the Central Intelligence Agency. Sporkin simply confirmed that the Government had no interests involved, and quite properly refrained from any further comment.

Although there was no doubt about the physical existence of the Series 57 Certificates, the Takahashi group ran into a stone wall when trying to cash them anywhere in Japan, as its Ministry of Finance insisted they were forgeries, a position that Norb tried to dispute, with no success. The solution was to set up a charitable organization named Japan-American Foundation headed by Takahashi that would take title to the Certificates and offer them for sale to qualified purchasers in the United States who might have more clout in applying pressure on Japan; Norb, fatefully, became legal counsel to the Foundation as well as its secretary/treasurer.

For some five years from 1986 to 1991 there ensued a tedious series of negotiations as the Foundation dealt with characters who can only be described as second-rate phonies—people with grandiose schemes that never came off. Norb bore the burden of dealing with these impecunious charlatans, spending hours in phone calls and drafting letters, faxes, and carefully worded agreements.

There was Howard Olson, a carpenter from North Dakota trying to be a financier, and Roger Hill, a wheeler-dealer who claimed important political connections in Minnesota, both of whom wanted to use the Certificates as collateral to underpin complex, unlikely schemes, and Mrs. Bravender Ah Loo, an aging American widow of a Chinese husband, suffering from cancer, operating out of a Hong Kong YMCA and later one bedroom in a friend's Los Angeles home, nearly destitute except for Social Security, who somehow collected Certificates and tried to flog them to redeem her precarious life. Olson soon dropped by the wayside with failure to come up with funds to purchase any certificates. In 1989 Norb lost all faith in the endlessly waffling Roger Hill and advised Takahashi to have no more dealings with him. He had already written off Mrs. Ah Loo as a pathetic loser of no substance and desperate for cash.

Because he continued to like and believe in Takahashi and the justice of his claim against the Japanese Government, Norb persevered, always making sure that prospective purchasers were warned that the Foundation could not warrant the genuineness or enforceability of the instruments in the face of the Japanese authorities' implacable denials. It was crucial that neither the Foundation nor himself could ever be accused of fraud from failure to disclose this essential caveat. Later, this meticulous policy of a careful, conscientious lawyer was ignored or disparaged by his accusers.

One can only wonder why Norb continued to struggle with deals that never closed and characters who seemed created by Damon Runyon, combined with exhausting trips to Japan to interview, fruitlessly, tight-lipped government officials. He certainly enjoyed no financial rewards from these efforts. From the beginning, Takahashi and his group made clear they could not afford the usual hourly fees charged by a partner of a firm like Hughes, Hubbard, so Norb agreed to a contingent fee arrangement: the firm would only be paid by the Foundation when and if a transaction was consummated by the sale of Series 57 Certificates, when a huge pay-out would be received and a fee of 5% of the proceeds would be paid to the lawyers.

Commercially, this was a disastrous decision. Norb ran up thousands of billable hours and thousands of dollars of expenses, even paying Takahashi's hotel bills when he visited Los Angeles. He eventually submitted a detailed bill of precisely $2,015,138.76 (never paid) for fees and disbursements, and had to write off $500,000 of advances to Takahashi as a personal bad debt. His partners at the firm were not overjoyed but, as later explained to me by Norb's friend and classmate, managing partner Bob Sisk, they went along because "he was very persuasive that this could be as huge jackpot . . . we didn't have much to lose, except Norb's time, and he was willing to take a hit on that . . . I was persuaded that he had a real case and that the allegations of Japanese bond dealings were true. They were certainly consistent with what I knew from personal knowledge of MacArthur and Japan in the early 50's."

What were his motivations that drove him on this quest, which many lawyers would have regarded as quixotic, a losing campaign for justice from the Japanese Government? A clue can be found in Norb's much earlier oral history interview for the Kennedy Library. He recorded his days working under Bobby Kennedy in the Department of Justice as follows: "It was great to have the Attorney General sitting there with his sleeves rolled up. It just made life more interesting, added some savor. I certainly never worked harder, or with more enjoyment, really, more feeling that we were really biting into the problems in a way that really counted, really getting something done . . . And it was just a great compliment, a great lift to the ego to be included in that bunch . . . a kind of elite corps."

Clearly, he was captured by idealism, and the thrill of working on issues of national importance. Perhaps nowhere else in his later career did he find the blood-warming challenge of fighting for a noble cause, until Mr. Takashita brought him the opportunity to use his brains, his energy, and his legal skills to expose the corruption and high-level chicanery of a powerful foreign state. In 1986, he resigned his full-time partnership in Hughes, Hubbard, becoming "of counsel", and in 1989 he severed all connections and carried the lance forward alone, virtually abandoning other affairs other than his deep commitment as sponsor of a real estate development project on one of the Hawaiian Islands.

His years of effort for the Japan-America Foundation came to an abrupt end in early 1992. Unbeknownst to Norb and without his permission, during 1991 Takahashi had retrieved several Certificate from the Foundation and given them to Roger Hill, now cooperating with Mrs. Ah Loo, broke as ever. Somehow, this transaction became known to one Craig Ivester, a bounty-hunter, who gets paid by law enforcement agents to bring them cases that look good to prosecute. Ivester knew that the Feds regarded the Certificates as phony and had been sniffing around to find a culprit on whom they could pin a charge of dealing in counterfeit securities.

What could be better than a sting directed at the broke, ailing, credulous Mrs. Ah Loo? In late 1991 they invited her to

A Corkscrew Life

a conference in Reno to hear a glorious proposition (she was so destitute they had to buy her airline ticket). At a videotaped session, the carrot was dangled in front of her, as an alleged bank officer claimed he had a buyer for Certificates in the hundreds of millions. But, even though greedy for a life-saving deal, the lady was wary. She had been told that offering these instruments in the US was illegal; she would only sell to a sophisticated securities firm who knew the full background and would assume any legal or financial risks. Fine, said the banker, we have one lined up. Satisfied, Mrs. Ah Loo returned to L.A. to get herself organized.

On normal Saturdays, brokerage offices everywhere in America are closed, and in 1992 that was certainly true for the venerable investment firm Smith Barney, Harris Upham & Co., who used the mellifluous voice and dignified phiz of actor John Houseman to announce in TV commercials "We make money the old way—we earn it."

But for the Tampa, Florida, office of Smith Barney, the chilly Saturday of January 18, 1992, was a special day, and their conference room on the 36th floor of One Tampa City Center was reserved for a very special transaction. An earlier letter from Executive Vice president A. George Saks stated that the firm would buy, for a client, three "Japanese bonds" with a face value of 70 billion yen, or about $560 million, paying a price of 25% of face. Thus Smith Barney would lay out $140 million and by the terms of the letter would take a commission of 1%. For a Saturday effort in keeping the office open, $1.4 million was an interesting example of making money "the old way."

The Smith Barney letter of January 9 was addressed to Mrs. A.J. Bravender Ah Loo, with the impressive title of Managing Director, Transfield Investments. It required her to deliver the bonds to the Tampa office, upon which a wire transfer for the purchase price would be sent to her company's bank in Hong Kong. Smith Barney would then transfer the bonds to its client Montclair Investments Inc., via Montclair's agent, the prestigious First National Bank of Chicago. The only condition was that Mrs. Ah Loo provide "supportive documents of certification of authenticity."

In a flurry of faxes and phone calls to Smith Barney, it was discovered that Mrs. Ah Loo was too ill to leave her California home, but she gave full authority to her son Bruce Hansberry and business associate Roger Hill to travel to Tampa to consummate the deal. These two hopeful gentlemen, having flown to Tampa overnight and checked into a hotel, were welcomed before noon at Smith Barney by Sean Wright, a firm executive, Jack Fox, purportedly representing First Chicago, and "Michael Montclair", apparently the principal of Montclair Investments.

After the visitors duly produced the bonds, several hours of paperwork review and casual chat ensued. Reading the recorded transcript of this session is a fascinating, grisly experience of watching two greedy, gullible guys walk blindly into a carefully planned trap. Wright, Fox, and Montclair checked out the transfer documents, with long quibbling that required phone calls to Mrs. Ah Loo to straighten things out. Montclair expansively announced airy plans to use the bonds as "cheap collateral" to buy Latin American banks, maybe even a California one. A friendly spirit prevailed, with typical male badinage about sports, holidays, travel, where to go for lunch, etc. A laugh was enjoyed over Hansberry's tale of how he had avoided making alimony payments to his ex-wife.

By 2:30 p.m. the deed was done. Signatures of Hansberry and Hill were affixed to conveyance forms, and Fox handed over to the two happy visitors a receipt for the bonds, saying: "your money is on account at Smith Barney." Since banks were closed over the weekend and on Monday, Martin Luther King Day, the wire transfer would have to wait until Tuesday, but who could worry about a Smith Barney receipt? The ceremonies ended by Fox opening the conference room door with the words "let's get out of here; I have another gentleman I'd like you guys to meet."

Surprise, surprise! The new gentleman was a Federal agent who had been eavesdropping (under court order) on the whole videotaped conference and promptly arrested the stunned Hansberry and Hill on charges of fraudulent dealing in counterfeit securities, and soon Mrs. Ah Loo in Los Angeles was also seized. It was revealed to the two naïve master criminals that their erstwhile pal Jack Fox was a special agent of the United States Secret Service and that the role of wheeler-dealer "Michael Montclair" was played by Special Agent Jack Sankey of the US Customs Service.

They soon learned that the enticing letter from Smith Barney had been concocted by the Department of Justice. The US Attorney in Tampa had written to Smith Barney requesting the "voluntary cooperation" of the "highly respected and reputable investment service company" to act "in an undercover capacity on a federal criminal investigation." Apparently Mr. Saks, counsel for the firm and a member of the New York Bar, did not hesitate to comply with the request, whatever the legal or moral implications of issuing a letter that was patently fraudulent and deceitful. Smith Barney had no obligation to join the game and could have politely declined, but Saks must have been eager to curry favor with the Feds.

All in all, it was a consummate sting that gave the Feds exactly what they wanted. After several hours of interrogation led by Assistant US Attorney Tim Jansen, Hansberry and Hill caved in with a complete confession and led the agents to their Tampa hotel safe-deposit box where a treasure of incriminating documentation was found. A man named Toshio Takahashi was named as participant in the transaction, and about 8 p.m. Hill placed a call to Mr. T at his hotel in Los Angeles to report on the successful closing of the deal.

The conversation indicated someone named Schlei would be happy to hear the news, and among Hill's papers was found a scrawled hand-written pay-out sheet to the effect that Schlei would share in the proceeds of some undefined transaction, to the extent of $2 million. He was already known to the Feds as a prominent Los Angeles attorney, and on the following Monday, January 20, a California agent informed an astonished Norbert

Schlei of the events in Tampa two days earlier, of which he was totally ignorant. Thus began the long legal dance between Norb and the federal law-enforcement machinery.

Norb was quickly advised by the US Attorney's office in Tampa of the shattering news that he was a "target" of their investigation and his indictment would be sought, together with the three victims of the sting (Takahashi was also sought, but he had fled the country). Norb dropped all other concerns while he retained Peter George, an experienced litigator in Tampa, to fight back, which he did, with many letters and conversations with the prosecutors in both Tampa and the Washington headquarters, vigorously disputing the legal and factual basis for indicting Norb, claiming that the Feds were aiming at him because they needed to catch a "big fish" to justify the massive expenses and manpower committed in setting up the sting. But the Government remained adamant. It was finally agreed that Norb would make a voluntary appearance before the Tampa grand jury on October 6, 1992. This was a rare and risky action for a Federal "target" to take, but Norb believed that the history of the case and his proven court-room skills would convince the jurors of his innocence.

He was wrong. The proceedings were orchestrated by the prosecuting US attorney, Tim Jansen, who had thoroughly researched and imbibed the Government's theory of Norb's criminal conduct—that, far more than simply acting as legal advisor, he had actually conspired with Takahashi, Hill, and Ah Loo to sell securities that were unquestionably counterfeits. The 150-page transcript of Norb's testimony to the grand jurors reveals how Jansen led them to accept this theory. His continued emphasis on Norb's friendship with Takahashi left the impression that Norb *must* have been involved in the Tampa deal despite all his evidence to the contrary.

The jurors themselves posed questions that showed their doubts about his *bona fides*. If both the Japanese and the U.S Governments disavowed the bonds' legitimacy, one juror asked, why did not Norb simply back off and refuse any involvement whatsoever? They simply did not buy Norb's explanations of why the Japanese officials might be consistently lying. Although the exact word is not quoted in the transcript, it's pretty clear that one juror commented "bullshit" (hurriedly suppressed by Jansen) when Norb described the history of the M-Fund. The end result was a formal indictment, the death knell for Norb's ability to continue his practice of law. Strangely, there was no questioning about the Tampa sting operation itself, which came perilously close to the kind of "entrapment" for which law enforcement officers are often condemned.

Years later in a telephone conversation with Jansen, he told me that he had simply been assigned a case to prosecute, which he be thought he had handled with complete fairness to Norb. He felt that Norb did not make a good witness, damaging his own cause by being "arrogant" with the grand jurors. This charge is not visible from the written transcript, but there's no doubt that his testimony often became verbose and hard to follow, even somewhat contradictory and subject to cross-examination. He may have been wiser to stay out of the proceedings and let Jansen make a more concise presentation raising fewer issues. In any event, in our conversation Jansen clearly distanced himself from the controversial actions of Mark Krum, the attorney who led the prosecution at the eventual trial.

Despite the legal requirement for a speedy trial, it took over two years, until October 1994, before the Government was prepared to proceed, initiating a months-long ordeal that compelled Norb to move to Tampa and spend every working day in the court-room. Under the supervision of hard-nosed District Judge Elisabeth Kovachevich, a host of prosecution and defense witnesses took the stand, including two Japanese Government minions brought over to dutifully testify that the subject certificates were forgeries never issued by the Ministry of Finance. Howard Olson was produced, clearly scared of being indicted himself, and aided the prosecution with fanciful stories of how years previously Norb tried to push the phony securities into his unwilling hands.

In April 1995, the jury eventually returned a puzzling and ambiguous verdict. They cleared Norb of any direct role in the Tampa events, but found him guilty of one count of securities fraud and one count of dealing in counterfeit securities, all based upon an alleged conspiracy dating from his original retainer agreement with the Japan-America Foundation back in 1985. Thus convicted of a felony, Norb immediately lost his California license to practice law. US Attorney Krum was quoted by the *New York Times* as saying "I did my job to obtain a conviction, but I'm not proud of it." Perhaps he was thinking about the motion filed by Norb's counsel claiming that he had tried to intimidate defense witnesses, a violation of due process that could get the conviction reversed and have Krum disbarred.

Norb's actual punishment had to await the formal sentencing hearing held by Judge Kovachevich on August 4, 1995. In preparation for that, Norb had filed a motion for acquittal and an *amicus curiae* brief signed, with accompanying letters, by 105 friends including prominent lawyers, judges and government officials. They uniformly requested leniency, citing Norb's character, integrity and years of public service, and their incredulity that he would be involved in a criminal enterprise. Many correspondents went further, to attack the prosecution itself. His Yale classmate Emanuel Margolis, a trial lawyer for 40 years, wrote, "This entire prosecution and unfortunate conviction are replete with injustice and the kind of abuse of power by law enforcement which is reminiscent of bygone periods . . . It is a prosecution that should have been stillborn, based on the complete implausibility of the entire theory of the Government in seeking its indictment."

But, as Norb reported in a circular letter to his friends, Judge Kovachevich refused to accept the brief and paid no attention to the letters. She interpreted the Federal sentencing guidelines in the harshest possible way and sentenced Norb to five years imprisonment, although granting bail pending appeal. In a rambling speech, she in effect indicted Norb all over again, even making the extraordinary charge that, by recommending the blockade of Cuba to President Kennedy back in 1962, he showed himself to be a reckless adventurer risking the lives of the American people. His letter also thanked his friends for their financial help in sustaining the trial expenses, which included a substantial contribution from ever loyal ex-wife Barbara, but asking for at least another $100,000 to finance his appeal, as the trial had wiped out his assets. He made the mortifying request that, having lost his license, he would still appreciate being retained as a consultant able "to do non-legal work in which legal knowledge is useful."

As he told me later, these were painful words to write.

As soon as I could break away from other commitments, I traveled west to see Norb. On a cool Sunday in February 1996, grey with mist swirling in from the Pacific, I found him, pink-cheeked and trim at 66, sitting alone in the cramped Santa Monica office that he could barely afford, drafting his own appeal, effectively bankrupt, his passport surrendered. On the walls around him hung the framed mementos of his life: *"Praeses et Sociis Universitas Yalensis . . ."* granting his 1956 LL.B. degree from Yale Law School, autographed photo of Supreme Court Justice John Marshall Harlan, for whom he had clerked, photograph of Lyndon Johnson inscribed "with appreciation of your competent approach to many complex problems," other photos of him standing with Bobby Kennedy and Governor Pat Brown, with whom he ran as Democratic candidate for California secretary of state. On the desk before him lay another more immediate memento, unframed: the sentencing document issued by Judge. Kovachevich. He showed me the unstinting letters of character support, with which his friends had bombarded the Judge, to no avail.

He was proud of his loyal friends who did not abandon him, but friendship could not re-instate his career, nor could it compensate for the millions lost in the Hawaiian property venture, rejected by the state after his conviction. And beyond any monetary loss, the loss of reputation stung bitterly: "it's completely destroyed . . . it's gone, it's gone, and I cannot hope to get it back," had been Norb's words at the sentencing hearing.

His appeal was duly filed with the 11th Circuit Court of Appeals in Atlanta, which in 1998 reversed one charge and gave the option of a new trial on the other. Unfortunately, the decision was hardly a ringing endorsement of Norb's innocence, but rather a ruling on narrow technical grounds, including Judge Kovachevich's failure to hold a hearing on the claim of Krum's witness intimidation. Norb tried to obtain a full-fledged acquittal by filing a petition for *certioriari* with the Supreme Court, which was not accepted. The unsatisfactory Court of Appeals decision remained the final word, leaving Norb in the legal limbo of being neither convicted nor fully acquitted. Totally broke from litigation expenses, he could not afford a hearing or a new trial on the issue of witness intimidation. With only a misdemeanor charge floating uncertainly over him, he was able to negotiate with the California Bar in 2001 to have his license re-instated.

That was far too late to restore his career. We kept in close touch, as I reviewed the voluminous trial transcript in his lawyer's Tampa office, showing how the government had skewed the case against him. He planned to write a book about his experience, and asked my help, which I willingly volunteered. But in 2002 he collapsed after his morning jog along the Santa Monica beach, and after a year in virtual coma died in 2003.

Although he had already given me some of his files, the bulk of them were held by his widow and principal heir, Joan, whom I had never met. I hoped that she would open them to me, but despite requests by me and by his son William, she never cooperated, apparently suspicious of my long friendship with his earlier wife Barbara, whom she refused to invite to Norb's post-funeral reception. Without these archives containing, I was told, innumerable personal records of his long career, I felt unable to proceed with a full-length account of his travails.

But I retained a keen interest in the injustice done to Norb and decided to write my own abbreviated history, dredging through papers he had given me, and speaking to his classmates, his one-time boss Nick Katzenbach, his initial prosecutor, his defense attorney, and finally to Sam Han, the amiable Korean-American businessman who had made Norb's initial introduction to the Japanese. In a quiet corner of the Los Angeles Athletic Club, he told me how he had become Norb's friend during the nearly seven years of fruitless negotiations, how he had shouted in anger at Takahashi when that gentleman continued to deal with Roger Hill against Norb's advice, how he was shattered by the news of Norb's indictment, and how US Attorney Krum had threatened to lift Han's immunity if he testified as a defense witness.

The story did not end with Norb's death. In 2003 a remarkable book was published, *Gold Warriors—America's Secret Recovery of Yamashita's Gold,* by the husband and wife team of investigative historians Sterling and Peggy Seagrave. It was the final work in their series of books about the Far East, their life-time specialty. It examines in great detail how Japan looted Asia during World War II and what happened to the plundered treasure after 1945 when, at MacArthur's behest, it was secretly used by Washington as a slush fund for favored projects and as a piggy-bank for corrupt Japanese politicians. It describes the genesis of the M-Fund and the M-Bonds as historical fact. One of the many themes of the book is that the American and Japanese governments cooperated to neutralize Norb, who was threatening to expose how the M-Bonds were actually issued to favored cronies and then converted to Series 57 Certificates that were repudiated because Japan didn't have the funds to pay them. In an e-mail to me, Seagrave wrote that there was too much "Japan bashing by Norb Schlei," which had to be stopped.

Perhaps this theme goes to extreme lengths of conjecture, but Sterling Seagrave supports it with a specific event recounted to him by an eye-witness whom he swears to be reliable.

It appears that the Government of Paraguay had trustingly acquired a $500 million Series 57 Certificate, but was getting stiffed on any attempt to cash it in. The Paraguayans then approached General Al Haig, the former US secretary of state, to be their intermediary to negotiate a deal with the Japanese. Allegedly with the approval of President Bush (the elder), who wrote a letter of introduction to former Japanese Prime Minister Takeshita, Haig visited Tokyo to get Takeshita's assurance that the Certificate would be credited against Paraguay's foreign aid debt to Japan.

After one quick look at the document, Takeshita told Haig bluntly "This paper is a forgery." But when Haig presented a policy from the Yasuda Fire Insurance Company insuring the precise Certificate against loss during transportation, Takeshita's face reportedly "turned pale and his voice became faint." After a couple of days of dancing around the issue with claims that the Certificate was not "formal" and could not be repurchased, followed by threats from Haig to go public, Takeshita's secretary conceded delicately, "We are ready to take certain measures on the certificate in question. You must treat this negotiation as strictly confidential. If a similar demand is made by another government, our administration would suffer because we are not prepared for it financially." In other words, it was a one-off deal; no other demands would be honored.

According to Seagrave and his trusted informant, this tense transaction took place in the winter of 1992. Thus, at virtually the same time that the Feds were preparing to indict Norb for offering counterfeit securities, Al Haig was able to press, successfully, for validation of an identical document. It helped to have friends in high places.

Seagrave reports another case of law enforcement selectivity, confirmed to me by Norb's lawyer Peter George. In 1992, a former Secret Service agent named James Sena became convinced of the legitimacy of the Series 57 Certificates and with several associates attempted to market several of them with a total face value of $50 billion. They were soon arrested, but in November 1995 the charges against them were abruptly dismissed "with prejudice", meaning they could not be re-filed, although, somewhat illogically, the Feds retained the securities as "contraband".

As to the essential forgery claim, Seagrave refutes this by quoting Prof. Edmond C. Lausier of the University of California, who for five years had studied the M-Fund and M-bond manipulations, collecting copies of Japanese documents going back many years. According to Lausier, "In 1982, a decision was made in the Ministry of Finance, or at an even higher level . . . to call the bonds held by certain holders and to issue Certificates [57s] in exchange for those items . . . The documents I have examined are so precisely in agreement with the official published records of the Government of Japan that, in my opinion, it is quite impossible for them, or the Certificates that resulted from them, to have been the work of any counterfeiter. No person outside the Government could possibly have had the requisite knowledge to prepare these documents . . . It is, accordingly, my unqualified opinion that the Certificates are not counterfeit."

I arranged to meet Prof. Lausier on a trip to Los Angeles in 2003, when he showed me specimen copies of the Certificates (I had to rely on his knowledge of highly technical Japanese) and repeated his firm opinions. He explained that beginning in 1982, Japan had insufficient funds to pay its genuine outstanding bonds, many of which were held by unreliable nominees, and in 1983 converted them into Series 57 Certificates. These were securities of a form unknown in the international capital markets, and thus could be repudiated and dishonored as forgeries, with only a few holders, such as the influential Al Haig, able to negotiate them for value. Long after the 1994 trial, Lausier had even provided Norb with a supporting affidavit for use at any re-trial—a course that Norb abandoned when he simply accepted the misdemeanor charge and had his license restored.

All this information confirms one clear message: the government's case against Norb should never have been brought. Its essential argument, that the securities were counterfeit, is shown to be an illusion, twisted to achieve a political result—the protection of Japan's reputation. At the very least, the history brought out by Seagrave and Lausier, and the strangely terminated prosecution in 1995, would justify any lawyer in believing he had good reason to assert the claim that the Certificates were valid and enforceable. Yet the various prosecuting attorneys did everything possible to convince the grand jurors and the trial jurors that Norb's claims were based on fictional hot air, a fanciful story created to cover up financial greed. And of course, as ambitious careerists, they were delighted to attach a former Assistant Attorney General to their prosecution rather than simply charging nobodies like Ah Loo, Hill and Hansberry.

And what final objective was achieved? Peter George estimated that 14 or 15 Federal agents worked on the sting, and that the total cost to the US Government was at least $40 million. The usual justification for such costly efforts is "protection of the public." But it was never shown that any member of the innocent public had or would lay out funds for these complex, ambiguous securities of such gigantic denominations. They could only be of interest to major investors who could investigate their background and expect to enforce a claim. The Government insisted they were fraudulent, but never disclosed an actual or potential victim of the alleged fraud.

The net result of the vastly expensive prosecution: the career of a brilliant, honorable attorney was destroyed; no innocent party was ever protected, or needed protection, from financial loss; and Japan's reputation was preserved, but only until later disclosures shattered the image. The campaign against Norb was a classic abuse of prosecutorial discretion. I not only lament the singular tragedy suffered by Norb, but more widely I wonder how many other misguided law enforcements efforts are conducted every year, at the expense of the American public.

Long after the publication of his book, Sterling Seagrave e-mailed me a final thought about Norb, whom he had met and admired. He told me he remained suspicious of the fall, called "accidental," that knocked out Norb and was reported in a call to the police by a beach bum who then vanished before the cops arrived. Homeless bums do not waste their coins on a telephone call and then disappear, Seagrave asserted, arguing that Norb was the victim of a hit man, with hi-tech means well known to professional killers. Far-fetched? Improbable? Perhaps, but perhaps no more so than the long saga of the M-Fund and the Series 57 Certificates.

As a final coda to Norb's story, in 2013 I met my Yale Law School classmate Stanley Sporkin in Washington. Long retired as general counsel of the CIA, he told me of the strange atmosphere pervading the cavernous Tampa court-room, where he had been called to testify during Norb's 1994 trial under Judge Elisabeth Kovasevich. Although Sporkin was by then himself a serving federal district judge, she offered him none of the usual civilities between members of the bench. She required all witnesses to remain standing during their testimony, and conducted the proceedings in what seemed bitter abruptness. One of her important rulings against the defense was reversed on appeal, and Sporkin wondered whether a more sympathetic judge would have brought a different jury verdict—another doubt cast, far too late, on the justice of Norb's verdict.

For the next friend of whom I write, the arc of life was the opposite, from early misery to the warmth of success.

CHAPTER 12

Renaissance of a Russian Prince: Nikita Lobanov, 1935-

Anyone who knows anything about Russia has heard of the Romanovs, the 300-year-old dynasty whose power vanished in 1918 when Tsar Nicholas II, with his wife and children, was murdered by the Bolsheviks in the early days of the Russian Revolution. But how many non-Russians are familiar with the Rurik line, which preceded the Romanovs and whose genealogy begins in the dim 9th century, when, we are told by a mixture of history and legend, a Viking warrior who called himself Prince Rurik came south and settled in Novgorod, northwest of today's Moscow, leaving a trail of progeny who fused together the lands that eventually became known as Russia?

I certainly knew nothing of the Ruriks, when in 1960 I met in New York City a slim, impeccably dressed young man called simply Nikita Lobanov, speaking meticulous English with an undefinable European accent. Years passed before I read articles naming him Prince Nikita Dmitriyevich Lobanov-Rostovsky, by then a famous art collector renowned in post-Soviet Russia for dealing directly with President Vladimir Putin and Prime Minister Medvedev He has never himself used the hereditary title and explains that the Russian word for "prince" means in effect "ruler" and is his birth-right, for his lineage can be traced through a chain of ancestors to the original Rurik.

As plain Nikita, he was introduced to me by his fiancée-then-wife Nina George-Picot. My wife Edie and I had befriended the charming, raven-haired Nina, daughter of the French Ambassador to the United Nations Guillaume Georges-Picot, and his Russian wife. We could see that Nina, circulating though new York society, would not be satisfied with a standard all-American husband, but needed to mate with a man who shared her intense intellectual interests. As she later stated, when they met at violinist Nathan Milstein's dinner, "It was love at first sight . . . Nikita immediately asked me if I was interested in ballet and opera." And of course she was. He captivated her with the tale of his life-changing epiphany, when in 1954 he had viewed a retrospective exhibition based on Serge Diaghilev's Ballets Russes. As a result, "I, a mere art lover," she told an interviewer, "was the acolyte of a true collector for 40 happy, interesting years."

When in 1962 we first visited their tiny rented apartment just up Lexington Avenue from the 92nd Street Y, both Nikita and Nina were struggling on respectable but minimal salaries. He was a very junior officer at Chemical Bank making, he later recalled, about $86 per week, and Nina, a research assistant for *Readers' Digest*, "perhaps a bit less." But whatever else was lacking, the cramped rooms glowed with art taking every inch of wall-space—art of a type that I had never seen before. They had already begun acquiring the vivid sketches of costumes used in the ballet, all designed by Russian artists before 1930; their rigid budgets could just afford works that had not yet caught the interest of the commercial art world. These privately-hung pieces were the obscure, bargain-price beginnings of the 835-piece collection that in 2008 was sold to Russia for display in St. Petersburg, now revealed in an overwhelming coffee-table book published in 2012. This assemblage was described by Professor John Bowlt, the leading American expert on

Russian art, as "unique in size, scope and composition, and among private collections is unequalled globally."

The story how the Lobanovs created this collection is a deeply personal one, and must start with the experiences of Nikita's early life, that froze into him a steely determination to excel. He was born in 1935 in Sofia, the capital of Bulgaria, a European back-water that had attracted members of the Russian nobility when forced out by the Bolshevik regime after the 1917 Revolution. Most of the noble families who had served the Romanovs fled to Paris, since they already absorbed French language and culture as second nature. But Nikita's paternal grand-parents made their way to Odessa and eventually through Romania, and a perilous, disguised passage across the Danube to Bulgaria, where a substantial exile group gathered, drawn by their devotion to the Bulgarian Orthodox Church. In 1934 they were joined in Sofia by Nikita's parents, Dmitry Lobanov-Rostovsky and Irina V. Wyrouboff, who had escaped Russia as children and met and married in Paris after their education in England. Sustained partly by assets rescued from Russia and partly from Dmitry's ability to find work as an accountant, the Lobanov-Rostovskys, with Nikita as their only child, were able to survive far from the bitter struggles that wracked Russia as Stalin carried out his brutal purges against any shadow of dissent from Soviet orthodoxy.

The exiles kept a low profile in Bulgaria, a complex Balkan state which itself suffered abrupt changes of government in the years between the two World Wars. Through age eleven Nikita had a normal close-knit family childhood, with photographs showing him wearing short pants in warm scenes with his primly dressed parents. He received the basics of a solid education both from a private school and also from the highly cultured émigré society that surrounded him. He developed his life-long ability in languages, becoming fluent in Russian, Bulgarian, French and German, to which he later added English and Spanish.

Doubtless his parents instilled in him a profound appreciation of his ancestry. His father's line included the Rurik Prince Aleksei Borisovich Lobanov-Rostovsky, the wealthy 19th century nobleman who became a diplomat and close adviser to Tsar Alexander II, and finally the Foreign Minister negotiating key treaties with adjacent nations. A true eccentric aristocrat, he became an "octogenarian *grand seigneur*, collector of Hebrew books and French mistresses, who sparkled in salons and attended church in his dressing gown." Nikita's mother's lineage ran equally deep. Her Wyrouboff father came from established land-owners near the city of Orel, and he was a nephew of Prince Lvov, a Rurik nobleman and Russia's brief first Prime Minister after the abdication of the Tsar in March 1917, preceding Kerensky before Lenin's successful October *coup d'etat*. Lvov and Wyrouboff escaped the oppressive left-wing regime and tried, in London, Washington and Paris, to find international aid for the "White" forces battling against Lenin's Bolsheviks. They failed, and never returned to their homeland, remaining rigid anti-communists.

Clearly Nikita learned "who he was", a lesson that sustained him in the hard days to come.

In World War II, the Kingdom of Bulgaria, torn between conflicting loyalties, became a half-hearted party in Germany's Axis alliance, but avoided sending troops in the campaign against Russia. When the powerful Russian armies swept westward across eastern Europe in 1944, they invaded Bulgaria and in September forced the resignation of the monarchy, replacing it with the People's Republic of Bulgaria a puppet state controlled from Moscow. At the tri-partite Yalta Conference in April 1945, Roosevelt and Churchill gave in to Stalin, accepting the Russian dominance as a *fait accompli*, and Bulgaria fell firmly into the eastern side of the Iron Curtain.

While many of the Russian émigrés had prudently abandoned Bulgaria as the Soviet forces approached, the Lobanov-Rostovsky family, perhaps naively, decided to remain, expecting a tolerant acceptance from the new regime. They were soon disabused. The "Reds" of the Bulgarian Republic shared the same suspicions as the USSR about "Whites", unrepentant descendants of the Tsar's nobility, and imposed harsh, restrictive conditions that compelled the family to seek emigration. But legal exit permits were unobtainable for the likes of the Lobanovs. There was only one solution: clandestine flight. Through friendly contacts with intelligence units in England, Dmitry made arrangements for escape over trackless mountains fringing the border with non-communist Greece, where they would be guided to safety. On a winter night in 1946, the little family of three, bearing rucksacks with a few possessions, trudged over snowy passes, and waited. And waited. Through some betrayal or failure of communication, no Greek guides appeared. Instead, the Bulgarian border guards followed their tracks and seized them on Greek territory for return to Sofia and immediate incarceration.

Nikita, at age eleven, was separated from his parents and thrown into the prison reserved for political prisoners. Most cells were windowless, but his at the end of a corridor had an opening through which he could hear screams of prisoners being beaten and occasionally shot in the courtyard. Luckily, through it he also heard the familiar whistling of "It's a Long Way to Tipperary", the only sign that his father was a fellow prisoner. After several months he was close to starvation on 150 grams of bread per day. The authorities transferred him to the central jail for common criminals, where the food was somewhat better—cheese and lime tea were offered.

Years later, he was asked in a Russian interview whether he found the prison experience essential: "Definitely," he answered (rough translations by Google system are quoted). "Inmates reassessing their values; that's one of the most crucial things jail can give. I was lucky to be imprisoned with thieves, and I learnt many useful things—how to transport currency on your body so it won't be discovered, how to steal in the crowded morning trams, how to survive as an illegal immigrant."

And a deeper effect, as stated in another interview: "It has very much influenced my mind, has created an indelible hatred of oppression, which helped in the formation of willpower. I have always tried to succeed at everything I did."

Prison even affected his personal style of dress and bearing. He was then clad "in an onion bag instead of clothes". In reaction, I have invariably seen him, in person and in many photographs, wearing immaculately tailored suits or sports jackets, with a silk square visible in the breast pocket to harmonize with a discreet tie. An interview unabashedly revealed his view: he does not adopt the "worldwide fashion of the casually dressed lowest common denominator. I try always to be elegantly dressed, walk boldly, stand tall."

After a year, he was released, alone, and ejected into Sofia as the son of an "enemy of the people," whom old family friends were scared to harbor. Only his former nurse dared to shelter him, herself trying to feed a large family with hand-to-mouth jobs. He survived by collecting cigarette butts on the street and putting them in bags to sell by the kilogram to gypsies, and stealing vegetables from the fields and coal and wood from the railway station. When his parents were eventually freed, a semblance of normal family life returned in cramped quarters arranged by friends, with Dmitry and Irina finding sketchy work as translators. But it was not to last. In 1948 Dmitry walked out one morning to buy milk and was never seen again by his wife and son. Only after *perestroika* years later did Nikita obtain a document showing simply that his father had died in government custody. Clearly, he had refused to cooperate with the Soviet-dominated authorities by giving information about other "White" refugees and had been thrown into one of the secret camps outside Sofia maintained for political dissidents—something like today's "extraordinary rendition."

Nikita, fatherless, but enrolled in a state school, was diagnosed by a friendly doctor as suffering extreme muscular and lung weakness and directed to take up swimming. This sport marked his first great success. At age 17 he became

Bulgaria's junior champion in the 100 and 200m. breast-stroke. Photographs show him receiving the school championship prize, and standing by the pool, a smoothly muscled Greek Adonis, wearing only a cod-piece bathing suit. He was ready for the first great sexual romance of his life, with an older teacher at his school, whom he often recalled emotionally. The main objective of his prowess was to escape Bulgaria by sea, swimming down the Black Sea coast to reach Turkey. He was actually preparing to do this, when another avenue towards freedom in the West opened for him and his mother.

Salvation came via Paris. His mother's brother Nicolas Wyrouboff, who had fled Russia in 1924 for education in France and England, in World War II joined General de Gaulle's Free French forces and fought through many campaigns, being wounded and decorated twice with the *Croix de Guerre* and as a *Commandeur de la Legion d'Honneur*. He became friendly with another de Gaulle war-time compatriot, the French writer Romain Gary, who in the early 1950s was posted to Sofia as Secretary of the French legation to Bulgaria. The two men planned together how to extract Irina and Nikita—safely and legally. The opportunity soon arose. Bulgaria was negotiating to buy two French-built Schneider diesel locomotives for its decrepit railway system, and a French bank would have to accept a letter of credit opened in Bulgaria. Negotiations dragged on, until finally the Bulgarians made a formal demand, "Where are our engines?" To which Gary caused the French legation to send a prompt answer: "Where are our French citizens?" Suddenly, barriers fell away. Nikita and his mother were given 48 hours to pack up and report to the Sofia station for the Orient Express to Paris. Despite farewell sobs from their Bulgarian friends on the platform, they did not hesitate in boarding. Two days later, on September 30, 1953, they arrived at Paris' Gare de Lyon, free at last from the communist yoke.

For Nikita, it was the start of his new world, although his beloved mother, already ill from years of privation, only survived until 1957. After four months with a French *abbé* tutoring him in Latin, then a requirement for acceptance by Oxford University, he set off for England. On arrival in London in 1954, one of his first sights was the dazzling retrospective exhibition created by the English ballet critic Richard Buckle, featuring works used by the impresario Sergei Diaghilev in his many productions of the Ballet Russes. Diaghilev had employed 42 painters for performances over 20 years, of whom 22 were Russian.

"I was particularly struck by the dynamism and vivid colors of the designs created by the Russian born painters as compared to their western counterparts," he later wrote. "The impression made on me was so strong that there and then I decided that one day I would have a similar collection. It took me 45 years . . ."

It is easy to understand that after a youth spent in the drab confines of Sofia, having never seen pictures hung in a museum, his eyes and his spirit were enthralled by the boisterous audacity of ballet art; what is more remarkable is that of the thousands who saw the exhibition, it was Nikita alone who had the vision and the tenacity to create an even greater one. At that point, of course, he could do nothing. He was penniless; he had to start building a career that would finance his dream.

His first step was applying for, and winning, a scholarship that Oxford offered to East European refugees. He later learned from Sir Isaiah Berlin, a long-time Oxford professor and member of the awards committee, that he was selected because he was the only applicant to request a degree in engineering and geology, rather than the "soft" subjects of classics, history or philosophy. His arrival at the historic center of learning was smoothed by his godmother Catherine Ridley, a grand-daughter of the last tsarist ambassador to London, who had married a don and opened an entrée to the best of University society. Not only was he taken into Christ Church, Oxford's largest and most eminent college known simply as "The House," he had the good fortune, unheard of for a new undergraduate, to be assigned the duplex digs of a recently deceased don, furnished with that rarity, a private bathroom. He has retained a photo of the main quadrangle with an arrow marking his lodgings next to the famous Christ Church clock-tower, and a later one of himself in cap and gown after accepting his degree in 1958.

Although he worked unremittingly hard and often struggled to find engineering libraries that stayed open late enough for his needs, his Oxford career was marked with one elegant diversion. He was elected to the Bullingdon, a social dining club favored by wealthy English "bloods," frequently old Etonians, often pilloried in the leftish wings of the English press as revelry of the "Young, Rich and Drunk," and immortalized by Evelyn Waugh as "the sound of English county families baying for broken glass." A group photograph shows Nikita with his fellow members all wearing the Club's distinctive (and expensive) uniform of dark-blue tailcoat with ivory lapels over a yellow waistcoat. An unknown European, he was already displaying the self-confident charm that led to acceptance in England's structured class system and many other future social settings. The photo includes his early friend Ian (now Sir Ian) Rankin, whose second wife he later married. Ian's mother was the exuberantly eccentric Lady Jean Rankin, long-time habitué of the Royal Household as a lady-in-waiting to Elizabeth the Queen Mother.

With his Oxford degree in hand, he sensed that the United States might better satisfy his ambitions than the still somnolent England (which had not granted him permanent visa.) With a scholarship from the National Science Foundation he entered Columbia University, which granted him an M.Sc degree in economic geology in 1960, leading to his first job. A Texas oil company sent him on exploratory trips to Patagonia and other bleak areas, far from the culture of city life. Seeking a new career, he was advised by Oxford colleague Oliver Fox-Pitt (the founder of major stock-brokerage firm): "go near the money; join a bank." His early career at New York's Chemical Bank was far from lucrative, but it allowed him to settle in New York, where he met Nina and married her in 1962. My wife Edie had become a close friend of Nina, so it was natural that we helped when Nikita sought US citizenship. I wrote a supporting letter, and Edie went down to the Federal Courthouse to lay her hand on the Bible and cheerfully perjure herself by swearing that she had known him for the required five years, instead of the actual three.

During those early New York years, his artistic dreams did not die, but he was initially so broke that he could not even afford the two dollars for a ballet costume sketch by Natalia Goncharova, the Russian painter whose paintings were auctioned by Christie's in 2007 for prices in the $10 million range. Gradually, acknowledging Nina as "very much a partner and not a mere acolyte," he was able to start buying, still at bargain prices. They both agreed that the objective was not Russian art in general but rather art specifically intended for the ballet—designs of costumes, sketches of sets, programs, publicity posters, frequently commissioned by Diaghilev. Although these artists were well known in the early 20th century when Diaghilev first produced in Paris, where he settled after the Revolution, in more recent years they had faded from memory and became virtually unknown. The Lobanovs could avoid competitive bidding and pick up items from the artists themselves or their families, at $25 for a Soudekine water-color.

A greater problem than money was lack of information. Virtually nothing was published about these artists, in any language. In the Soviet Union they were considered "non-persons," exiles originating from the despised Tsarist regime. With no Internet available, Nikita and Nina had to search out obscure books, poke through the dusty archives and store-rooms of little-known galleries, seek out-of-date programs, and track down survivors often living in obscurity—the typical pains-taking work of obsessed collectors. Fortunately their careers included travel: six months stints for Nikita at Chemical's Paris office in 1965 and 1966, where they had many discovery adventures, such as finding the studio of recently deceased Goncharova and her husband Mikhail Larionov "up four flights of rickety steps, where the chaos that reigned was indescribable, with dozens of paintings by both artists stacked against the walls or hanging on them." They became friends with the daughter of Alexandre Benois, who maintained his studio in excellent condition where they first saw his set design for the ballet *Petrouchka,* which became Nina's all-time favorite work.

They also befriended Nikolai Benois, son of Alexandre, living in Milan as chief designer of the La Scala opera house. He told Nikita that La Scala held an entire set of costumes and decorations by Alexandre for an early production of *Petrouchka* that they were about to junk. Nikita, an enthusiast of New York's Joffrey Ballet Company, quickly arranged for sale of the whole production to the Joffrey at a give-away price of $5,000,

Another serendipitous find came their way one hot summer afternoon in Athens when they chose to drink lemonade in a café named "Petrograd", as the Bolsheviks had re-named St. Petersburg. Nikita spotted the water-colors on the wall as Russian, and to his excitement identified them as costume designs by Pavel Tchelitchew. The waiter told them the owner would come for a drink at midnight, so the Lobanovs returned for negotiations with the eccentric and charming fellow Russian Nicky Iakovleff. He offered all of them for bargain price of $10,000. With only a $100 travelers' check left on the last day of their holiday, Iakovleff generously sold them one piece, and held five more of them for later purchase. Like many other owners, he preferred to make a rock-bottom sale to serious young scholars of the genre, rather than to wealthy collectors simply amassing more holdings.

With diligence and good fortune they slowly assembled the work of artists who had worked with Diaghilev: Léon Bakst, (perhaps the foremost of the costume designers with the colorful sensuality that made him Nikita's favorite), Benois, Goncharova, Larionov, Valentine Serov, Serge Soudekine, Tchelichew, and many others. A Russian publication summarized their contribution to art history as follows: "They have rescued from oblivion the art that otherwise would have vanished without a trace, in countless bazaars, flea markets, auctions, and fairs, or simply rotted in attics and basements."

By 1967, they had moved to larger premises in New York, where their findings could be displayed. One day, a friend brought John McKendry, curator of watercolors, prints and drawings at the Metropolitan Museum of Art, who took one look and said "This is wonderful; we must have an exhibition." Seeing their collection get its first public viewing at the Met, America's premier art museum, served to validate their taste and encourage further collecting. It earned them no money, but the publicity was invaluable, and was developed further when Anne Marie Pope, director of the International Exhibitions Foundation, negotiated with the Met to take the collection for guest shows around the country, eventually displaying it at some 50 museums throughout the US Alfred Barr, innovative director of the Museum of Modern Art, also saw their collection and gave them heartening motivation to continue.

Meanwhile, Nikita had to think about his career as a banker, the sole source of his funds. Not enchanted with the staid Chemical, he spotted an employment ad from California's more aggressive Wells-Fargo Bank for the head of its Europe, Middle East and Africa Division. He promptly applied, but when he learned there were 19 applicants to be processed at the rate of two per day, he decided to short-circuit the process by writing a letter describing exactly how he would market the bank's business. This earned him an invitation to San Francisco and a meeting with Ralph Crawford, the vice chairman handling international business, who liked the style of this unusual candidate and offered him a job, but at a beginner's salary that Nikita found derisory. Dramatically, he proposed to work free for six months to show he could bring in earnings five times the salary he asked. With the deal accepted, he immediately set off and got Wells-Fargo profitably engaged in trade finance in Algeria, Libya, and Turkey, capitalizing on his fluent French, his experience with authoritarian states, and his hard-won bargaining know-how from childhood days. On expiration of the six-month trial period, he joined the permanent staff, and was pleasantly surprised that New York City law required the bank to pay him for his "volunteer" time.

Wells-Fargo required that he relocate to the bank's west coast headquarters. One night before they regretfully left New York, the Lobanovs were invited to meet visiting Salvador Dali, with his exotic Russian wife Gala. They left Dali at a reception with instructions to follow to our home where we were giving them a farewell party. The eminent surrealist, with little English, got lost ending up, alone, ringing the buzzer of our neighbors' apartment, solid citizens who were staggered by the appearance of the famous pointed waxed moustache and silver-topped cane. Finally finding the right door, he seized my red-haired wife for a tempestuous kiss, grabbed a glass of champagne and then harangued Nikita for half an hour before departing. We understood he was re-negotiating the fee Nikita would pay him for painting a semi-nude portrait focusing on Nina's bosom. We never heard whether the exotic work was set to canvas.

From San Francisco, Nikita was soon traveling to Afghanistan, Pakistan, and Iran, maneuvering through their byzantine sectarian complexities and finding business through local merchants. This served him as good preparation for 1970, when the Soviet Union was actively seeking foreign finance and had to turn to western banks. Wells-Fargo fortunately had Nikita as a rare fluent Russian-speaking banker to dispatch to Moscow for opening contacts. Despite partial détente policies followed by the current leader Leonid Brezhnev, there had been no real "opening to the west." Nikita's first visit to his native country must have aroused sharp vigilance in the Kremlin and the KGB at this singular arrival—not only a representative of suspicious Western capitalism who might well be under CIA cover, but an heir of the highest levels of the despised tsarist aristocracy and a Prince no less. In this and many subsequent trips to Russia, even before the collapse of the Soviet Union,

Nikita maneuvered smoothly and suffered no indignities other than normal snafus for a foreign citizen.

Once when travelling with Wells-Fargo's President Richard Cooley, Nikita negotiated a first-class triplex apartments for the Cooley couple, only to find that he and Nina were relegated to a closet-sized hotel room. He could not budge the Intourist bureaucracy until he made it known that in Paris he had arranged for Brezhnev's daughter Galina, short of foreign currency, to purchase an admired fur coat at a big discount. Suddenly a telephone call advised him that a suite had miraculously become available—the first of many lessons that Russian red-tape could best be cut by dropping a name.

Nina found California too remote from her mother, in poor health and living in Paris. Nikita arranged a transfer to London in 1979, and soon resigned from Wells-Fargo and joined an affiliate of Bank of Montreal with roots in the mideast, specializing in project finance. They were both able to resume frequent travels to Europe searching for additions to their collection, and they renewed their contact with Russian art specialist Professor John Bowlt, who became a close friend and adviser. In November 1981 he joined Nikita in Paris for a recorded three-way luncheon conversation with Nicolay Benois, who explained to Bowlt the portrait of Nikita that he had recently finished, showing him with an enigmatic smile, dressed in a typical tailored suit and surrounded by ballet sketches.

"The collector's personality is quite fiery," said Benois, "because he's one of those people who create culture. This is a serious person. He has a deep love of Russian art. And also, he is a Prince. His family comes from the very heart of Russia . . . in some ways his attitude to life [is] somewhat demonical."

Their chat also revealed that Nikita was an iconoclast in art appreciation, often deviating from the popular line. The two friends dismiss Picasso's famous *Guernica*, celebrated for dramatizing the atrocity of bombing a Spanish town during the Civil War.

Benois: Tremendous attention is given to that painting. To me it seems a complete non-entity.

Nikita: Neither do I understand it.

Benois: It's absolute piffle. Apparently those terror-stricken eyes reveal tragic events. What terror-stricken eyes? Some sort of caricature, and quite a mediocre one at that.

Nikita: Well, Guernica was bombed. But Stalingrad was completely ruined. Berlin was destroyed.

Benois: It's a terrible thing.

Nikita: And it's terrible not because it's bad, but because it's frightening. You see horrifying human-like faces with a strong mark of erotica. But it's not humanly beautiful erotica.

Benois: No.

Nikita: It's some sort of awful sex.

Benois: Awful, degenerate.

Nikita: And I completely fail to understand the attraction. Why is there such demand?

Professor Bowlt had been working with the Lobanovs to fully document, organize, and display their collection, and in 1982 he curated an exhibition, "Russian Stage Design", for the Mississippi Museum of Art, showing some 253 selected works by 92 artists. The complete catalogue can still be found, but is of interest mainly to scholars, as it includes very few full-color plates that are needed to bring the works alive for the normal viewer.

In 1987, Nikita's career veered sharply in a new direction, that put him in much closer contact with Russia, just as the USSR was beginning to collapse. The secretive De Beers Group, privately-owned by the Oppenheimer family, that had a monopolistic grip on world diamond resources through its Central Selling Organization, needed a Russian speaker with high level contacts among the *nomennklatura* who could introduce De Beers management as reliable and trustworthy partners. After six months intense vetting by the security services of the UK and the US, he was hired by the decisive, dominant boss Sir Philip Oppenheimer, with a brief to open delicate negotiations and report only to Sir Philip and two other top executives, not to the company's Moscow representative office nor to colleague Georgy Vasilchikov, a long-time family friend. Nikita's style in his new job was shown when he took a chance by inviting the Soviet ambassador to the UK, a hard-boiled proletarian communist, to a home dinner with Sir Philip, the quintessential gentleman—capitalist. Surprisingly they got on well, and the Ambassador (a member of the Central Committee of the Communist Party) passed on key information about a new Russian diamond field on instructions from Moscow.

His ten years with De Beers was doubtless a profitable period for Nikita, as it also gave him the expertise and contacts to advise diamond investors, and his income was abetted by consultancy contracts with first Christie's and then Sotheby's auction houses. His reputation in Russia was enhanced so that in 2001 he was permitted, even encouraged, to open the Lobanov-Rostovsky Museum in Moscow's Fili Park of Culture and Leisure. After the collapse of the Soviet Union in 1991, and the rise to power of Vladimir Putin to the Presidency in 2001, Putin's policy emphasized re-glorification of Russia's imperial might during the Romanov dynasty. With the blessings of the Kremlin, Nikita stocked the new Museum building, clad in logs to look like a farmstead of "old Russia," with photographs, family portraits, maps, works of art, documents, and memorabilia of all kinds recording the life and times of himself and his ancestors. Although he had no rights of ownership, he became the unofficial curator, and an apartment was reserved for his use whenever he visits Moscow. He told a local reporter that the opening of the Museum symbolized "the return of our family after years of exile—a landmark event for me, for Moscow and Russia as a whole."

Yet he clearly remains ambivalent about present-day Russia. He has never sought Russian citizenship. After years of residing in the United States and England, he openly prefers the freedom and easy comforts he finds in London life. In a 2008 interview, he called Russia, "a country where the judiciary is subordinate to the gangsters who are referred to as businessmen and where corruption has penetrated everything from top to bottom." He shudders at the thought of maintaining any contact with billionaire post-soviet oligarchs who now control the gems of Belgravia and Knightsbridge real estate. Although he is the active deputy chairman of the International Council of Russian Compatriots, which ordinarily meets in Moscow, he can promptly return to his home in London.

His attachment to Russia seems devotion, not so much to present reality, as to an image of an historic Russia to which he is indissolubly linked through his blood-lines and to which he owes a duty. He has told interviewers, "I feel like part of Russian history . . . I hope that I serve in the restoration of certain areas of Russian culture, and in this I see my mission." Beginning in the 1970s, he and Nina had begun not only to arrange circulation of their collection for display in Russian museums, but also to make outright gifts, gradually growing in value. In 2007 he gave portraits of Alexander II and Alexander III to the Russian Embassy in Paris, and in early 2008, he donated two works of modern impressionism, by De Chirico and van Duisburg, to Moscow's Pushkin Museum, worth in experts' eyes roughly $300,000.

Inevitably, they began to consider what was the future of their collection. With over 1,000 pieces, it was far too large for any personal residence. For safe-keeping between showing, they kept it stored in an air-conditioned, climate-controlled warehouse in Germany, but that could not be a long-term solution. Overtures were received from the Library of Congress, but came to no firm offer. Instead, President Putin, in his usual decisive fashion, decreed that since the artists were Russian, the collection should be "repatriated" even though many of the works were created after 1920 when the artists, finding the Bolshevik cultural controls intolerable, had emigrated to France and Germany. Needing art to decorate the Konstantin Palace outside St. Petersburg, in late 2007 Putin directed Vladimir

Kozhin, head of the Presidential property committee and chairman of the Konstantin Charitable Fund (a front for the Kremlin itself) to open negotiations with the Lobanovs.

According to Nikita, it was smooth sailing. He quoted a price, established by Sotheby's and later by Bonham's, and without haggling Putin scribbled an immediate "do it" on Minister of Culture Sokolov's memorandum, and the deal was signed in February 2008, although not without dissent from Nina. She would have preferred to keep the works in the West, open to a wider public, and she was doubtful of the Russians' commitment to proper conservation measures for the delicate water-color designs. But her concerns that Putin might later split up the items for a huge profit were dismissed by Nikita as unrealistic, and his determination to deliver to his native country prevailed. Some 835 water-colors, drawings and gouaches were delivered to the Fund, with about 200 pieces retained for Nina's collection of personal favorites.

Publicity was delayed until June 2008, when the Russian press started a series of bubbly announcements, including a long article "Art Repatriated" in the English-language magazine *Russian Life* published in March 2009. Photos of Nikita and Nina appeared quaffing champagne among Russian hosts at the official reception in St. Petersburg's State Museum of Theatre and Music, the collection's first home pending restoration of the Konstantin Palace. It must have been Nikita's, proudest moment, as he was shown standing ram-rod straight wearing the golden Medal of Friendship on the breast of his elegantly cut blue suit, accepting the accolades of government and museum grandees, in the very heart of the city where his family had been ejected nearly 100 year earlier.

Konstantin Fund Chairman Kozhin announced that $16 million had been paid for the acquisition, The price reflected fair compensation for the many years of painstaking collecting, exhibiting and preserving by Nikita and Nina. Certainly the Russians did not feel they were overcharged, just the reverse. *Russian Life* quoted Elena Grushevitskaya, senior scholar at the

Theater Museum, as saying, "The collection could easily have been sold for much more, had the owners decided to dissemble it and sell it off piece by piece at auction in the West." At the end of the day, generosity to his fatherland must have been the dominant strand of Nikita's motivation.

Just a few blocks distant, next to the towering St. Isaac's Cathedral, Nikita could see a reminder of his family's historic prominence: a massive triangular structure of exquisite proportions and elegant detailing, built in the early 1800s and originally owned by Prince Aleksei Lobanov-Rostovsky, and known as The House with Lions after the two marble lions guarding the entrance, memorialized for all Russians in Alexander Pushkin's famous poem "The Bronze Horseman." In 1993 it had been offered to Nikita for $3.5 million, but the estimated $1 million annual maintenance was unthinkable. Now, he had to stoically accept that it had been snapped up by one of the brash new property moguls and was being renovated to become the city's leading five-star hotel under the Four Seasons banner.

The publicity of the collection's sale made Nikita into something of a celebrity in the closed world of Russian media, operating in a language barely known in the West and rarely translated. He was interviewed on subjects far removed from Russian art. He was asked, and was happy to respond, on the peculiarities of the diamond trade, problems of the Russian economy, Russia's relations with Europe, Russia's relations with Japan in the 19th century, the meaning of an ideal marriage (if any), the declining standards of present-day dress, what it meant to be a Rurik Prince, and why the title did not violate US law.

A particularly persistent lady journalist, eager to explore the "inner" Nikita, saw him frequently over several years and wrote a long article with the objective of proving that he was the incorrigible "Don Juan in search of the eternal lover"—which he could well have been, given his looks, his charm, and his disdain for the platitudes of bourgeois sexual morality. He of course down-played this image. He e-mailed me the Russian original of this piece, with his own comment (in English). "That is her idea; it does not reflect me." Nevertheless, buried in the over-heated verbiage (I have had to rely on Google's often mysterious, but free, English translation service), are nuggets of hard fact. It revealed to the Russian public what all of Nikita's friends in the West had long known: he and Nina had split in 1990, and four years later he had fallen for June, the English former wife of his Oxford friend Ian Rankin, whom he married in 2001. In Google's inimitable translation, the journalist described the events as follows:

"Our hero began to seriously think of to finally part with his wife. Untamed mustang must not keep any ties! Constant surveillance, jealousy and reluctance to release brought him to fury. In the end, took it and slipped on a separate apartment. And began to live a bachelor. His eyes shone again youthful fervor. A major obstacle to divorce was a collection that gathered together for years! How to share this priceless treasure? After all, its main advantage is in unity, a magic panorama of the amazing phenomenon of 'Russian Modernism'. But all the ordeals behind him. And the divorce was obtained, and financial problem are solved with his ex-wife. And a new marriage entered. A true English lady! Nice, educated, charming, not his prime, but with a body of eighteen young girls! [sic]."

This dramatized summary had already been confirmed to me by my late wife Edie, who lived in London until her death in 2003 and was deeply sympathetic to all parties of this classic triangle. Having enjoyed friendship with both Lobanovs since 1960, she was distressed to see the break-up, but came to accept it as inevitable between two high-strung intellectuals of such conflicting temperaments. Beginning in the late 1980s, she knew that the cool, independent Nikita was chafing at the suffocating possessiveness and over-mothering (in the absence of children) imposed by Nina. As with many men, he took to philandering, not to find a new partner but to assert his male autonomy in the only activity not governed by his wife. This predictably sterile activity came to an end when he began to court June, now divorced from Ian. Edie, who played weekly tennis with June, spotted and encouraged her as the perfect match for Nikita, a calm blonde-thatched lady with wide-set eyes from the undemonstrative ranks of the stolid English upper crust, the *gratin* as the French would put it. Each of the trio came to Edie's memorial service, held next to a tennis court, where Nikita unexpectedly gave an effusive eulogy.

Nikita's fame in Russia led to the collaboration between him and a Russian publisher to produce an autobiography. This remarkable work, bearing a three-word Russian title whose Cyrillic letters translate to *Epoch-Destiny-Collection,* appeared in 2010, a hard-cover folio-sized volume of 583 glossy pages, with innumerable black-and-white photos and a fair number of color reproductions of works of art. Its physical production must have been staggeringly expensive, and I have not heard whether sales gave any profit to author or publisher. My own copy, sent from Moscow, eventually arrived and I have retained it as a decorative icon bearing on its cover a seductive semi-nude dancer by Bakst. I have not been able to get it translated, but just riffling through its pages gives me a picture of his life. In American publishing jargon, it would probably be called a "vanity work", as we see countless pictures of Nikita greeting, being greeted, drinking, dining, signing papers, making speeches, studiously consulting, accepting awards, even standing over a mining drill-rig and holding a shotgun (better dressed than his fellow sportsmen). But it is a valuable reference work, as it provides, among many eye-catching illustrations, rare ancestral portraits and many views of the exceptional Lobanov-Rostovsky Museum in snowy Moscow, and it does not hide his marital switch, as he is shown often with Nina up to 1990, and thereafter with June, except that Nina re-appears to take part in the climactic St. Petersburg ceremony in 2008.

When I last visited Nikita in the summer of 2011, he expressed no interest in having his autobiography, or any parts of it, translated into English. I told him this seemed a pity, since it doomed his extraordinary life to be well known in Russia and hardly at all in the English-speaking world. By coincidence he was also hosting Edward Gurvich, a Russian journalist, who was taking notes for a book comparing their lives as immigrants, again to be in Russian. Nearly two years later, Nikita sent me the initial chapters of this work, in an English translation. With analytical style typical of Russian literature, Gurwich tries to bore deep into Nikita's character. He writes that he has never met such a narcissist "who loves himself so much." Yet he expresses surprise at Nikita'a abstemious, almost Spartan, habits, noting that his visits to Nikita's home were not celebrated by spreads of food and drink.

Nikita and June live in a quiet corner of northwest London, occupying a house built in 1875, typical on its lightly-trafficked street—solid, unpretentious, with a patch of lawn in front and a back garden just big enough to keep June busy weeding, clipping and trimming. The interior embraces a visitor with sedate comfort, the eye catching some under-stated antiques and plenty of family portraits and dusty-rose cushions; the over-used phrase "shabby-chic" might apply. If Nikita is narcissistic, it merely reflects his pride in the completion of his life mission and its enjoyment with a wife who utterly understands his ways. She keeps housekeeping and meals simple with no live-in staff, respecting his daily routine that includes afternoons and many evening working on correspondence with his indefatigable Russian assistant Olga Shaumyan. June can metamorphose in a flash from gardening slacks and gloves to a ball-gown to accompany Nikita in his old Bullingdon tail-coat for an Oxford reunion dance.

He can clearly afford frequent trips, often with June, to Russia or Bulgaria for the various cultural bodies he supports, or occasionally to New York to participate in his fellowship, in perpetuity, with the Metropolitan Museum of Art, and a winter trip to the Caribbean. But he loathes wasteful or conspicuous spending. Ballet aficionados, they hold tickets for the London season, but when they invited me to join them one evening for *The Firebird*, no hired car was ordered for the long trek from W12 down to Covent Garden. Instead, Nikita drove us in his sensible Volkswagen Golf to a parking lot at the nearest Underground station, where we boarded the tube for a brisk one-transfer ride, strap-hangers with many young jeans-clad opera goers who eyed Nikita's blue pin-stripes and June's Hermès scarf. "It's absurd paying for a driver just to fight the traffic," he exclaimed to me, as he led us to the opera bar to buy, naturally, champagne.

A few days later, Nina invited my family and me to lunch at the same high ceilinged L-shaped flat that the Lobanovs bought when they first arrived in London in 1979. It was a pleasure to gaze once again at the 200 vivid works covering the walls that she had kept out of the St. Petersburg sale, centered around her favorite Benois. Even the brief attention span of my two under-ten grand-daughters was captured by the brilliant colors and animated designs.

Nina's solid block of flats is under two miles from Nikita's house, but since London is divided into hundreds of small hermetic communities, there is little chance of casual meeting. Nevertheless, she told me she has no problem collaborating with Nikita on their final joint effort: a complete illustrated catalogue raisonné of their entire collection. After years of research, this was still taking many hours of communication between the two of them and their scholarly advisor, Professor John Bowlt, sometimes face-to-face, others by post or e-mail. Any animus toward the former husband was long gone, although I gathered not quite the same towards the second wife. Nina keeps her intellectual curiosity occupied with attendance at all conceivable cultural events and boundless travel: one year, after Sotheby's and Christie's Russian art auctions, she visited Portugal, Turkey, and the burial mounds of Central Siberia, before leading a group around St. Petersburg.

Nikita and Nina kept me informed of the progress of the catalogue, and in late 2012 Volume I of *Masterpieces of Russian Stage Design 1880-1930* was published by London's Antique Collectors Club, available in selected art and museum bookstores in the United States. (Volume II, the technical companion directed at scholars, followed a year later). I found my copy at Washington's National Gallery of Art, sold in conjunction with their exhibition of Sergei Diaghilev's Ballet Russes costumes. At roughly $50, it is not a best-seller, but this handsome work will not only grace any coffee table but holds unique artistic and historical value.

Its 241 immaculate color plates (from a printer in China), alphabetically covering Aizenberg through Yakulov, with natural deference to the recognized greats Bakst, Benois, Goncharova, Larionov and Roerich, now represent the only convenient way Americans, or anyone outside Russia, can see the best of these protean, brilliant artists. The items sold to Russia are still held in the inadequate show-rooms of the Museum of Theatre and Music pending the long delayed restoration of the Konstantin Palace. Even then, the continuing bureaucratic obstructions to getting Russian tourist visas are likely to deter travelers who hate signing up for large sponsored, rigidly planned excursions—the millions who can simply hop on a flight to see Paris' Louvre, Madrid's Prado, London's Tate, or Florence's Uffizi. Unless the controlling Konstantin Fund makes the commercial decision to produce and sell high-quality prints of the originals, the works are virtually lost to independent viewing.

However, one can take a tough, but practical, decision: destroy the book to make a personal gallery. First read the illuminating joint interview with Nikita and Nina and the informative historical essay that stretches through Volume I. Then select your favorite works and carefully excise the full-page reproductions, have them handsomely framed with wide borders, and hang them close together on convenient walls. With 50 or 100 examples decorating your home, you will sense how the collection had its birth and started to grow in the Lobanovs' miniscule New York apartment as I saw it in 1962, long before Nikita became known to the world as a Rurik Prince.

Chapter 13

Sailing: Love and Obsession

"Believe me, my young friend," says the Water Rat to the Mole in the famous allegorical novel *The Wind in the Willows,* "there is nothing, absolutely nothing, half so much worth doing as simply messing about in boats." I too held that view, and shared all the joys and occasional disappointments of a commitment to boats that sail, meeting some wonderful, weird, and wacky people who were victims of the same obsession. Sailing should not be confused with the sybaritic activity called "yachting". Sailing, to the contrary, suggests hauling on ropes, ducking spray, clinging to life-lines, and all the myriad discomforts of inducing a boat to move under sail—and the final satisfaction of success.

In my early years in The Bahamas, I was exposed daily to the sea and captivated by the ever-changing hues of tropical waters lapping golden beaches. But it was off the harsher shores of rock-bound New England that I was first drawn into the lore of sailing. We spent summers in Marblehead, Massachusetts, a mecca for marine activities. Marblehead Harbor lies between the Town, a network of narrow streets with well preserved historic houses wedged among shops, boatyards and marinas, and the Neck, a virtual island connected by a causeway, zoned to exclude commerce and encourage residential spaciousness.

The Harbor every summer becomes home to several hundred boats, of all sizes, dotting its waters. Four yacht clubs were open from spring until well after Labor Day, three traditional ones for mature sailors and their families, and one for junior sailors up to age 18.

It was inevitable that active young guys, and girls too, looked to sailing as the only summer sport worth their energy. In other towns it might have been baseball, or golf, or tennis, but in Marblehead these were regarded as frivolities. Sailing, or more accurately its subdivision *racing*, was the focus of every free hour. The yacht clubs scheduled regattas for all the local classes on Wednesday, Saturday and Sunday from June through Labor Day, plus special events like Race Week, when boats from all over New England gathered for nearly ten days of competition.

Bob, my older brother by six years, was first to excel at racing, becoming a local hero by twice winning the junior national championships known as the Sears Bowl, so it was natural that I try to follow his foot-steps. Now, 60 years later, I can still recall the names and faces of 30 to 40 young men and boys who taught me the special skills of competitive racing and became my friendly, but give-no-quarters, competitors out on the water. I had to start at the bottom. At about age eight, I was deposited in a craft called a Brutal Beast, a class known only in Marblehead as the first training ground for any young sailor. I slowly learned the peculiarities of these clumsy undecked cat-boats.

Five years later, I moved up to the next class in the local hierarchy. This was a new creation called a 110, designed by a brilliant, eccentric naval architect named Ray Hunt. It looked like nothing else seen before—a long, low and narrow double-ended hull, slab-sided with chopped-off bow and stern, supporting a rakish mast with a small mainsail and big foresail, and ballasted with an ultra-modern fin keel, features that made the 110 fast and fun to sail, leading to the swift establishment of fleets throughout the US. I honed my racing skills and trained my committed crew. Our band of dedicated competitors became even closer. Winning and losing shifted weekly among us, followed by long analyses of mistaken tactics on the yacht club porch. We learned the tricky waters out to Halfway Rock so well that even fog could not confound us. In my last year in the class, two of us qualified for the 110 National Championships in Lake Michigan, putting our boats on trailers for the long trek to Chicago on the two-lane black-tops of those days.

Once I went off to Yale, my commitment to Marblehead racing waned in the face of summer school, travel, and Army training. But brother Bob had acquired a larger vessel, on which I could occasionally insert myself as crew. This was a cruiser-racer, a one-design class called Owens 40. He named it after a mythical Irish giant called *Finn McCumhaill*. Following Bob's philosophy of keeping sailing simple, the *Finn* was maintained with minimum coats of paint or varnish, and total absence of brass polish,

But the sails and rigging were kept in first-class condition, and with his uncanny touch on the helm and feel for wind shifts Bob campaigned the *Finn* up and down the East Coast, often beating the gleaming yachts belonging to the haughty New York Yacht Club fleet. I learned many lessons of go-fast and endurance as Bob's acolyte, often furling sails on the foredeck doused in spray in the teeth of a gale.

My first sail in the open ocean came in 1952: the classic semi-annual race from Newport to Bermuda, some 600 miles off the east coast. As the junior crew member on a sleek, impeccably equipped sloop, I learned how different was the open Atlantic from the sheltered reaches of Long island Sound or Buzzards Bay. Spume-topped swells well over my head crashed into the narrow cockpit, keeping our booted feet steadily under water; the brief four-hour off-watch sleeping period was often interrupted by calls to overcome nausea and leap out of a damp bunk to go top-side to reef sails flogging in a sudden, soaking squall; meals were eaten while balancing precariously in a tilted cabin that never ceased its abrupt rise and fall crashing noisily into head seas—all the sensations that become second nature to any ocean sailor.

Transatlantic

On reaching Bermuda, I found another adventure. A French yacht was looking for crew to fill the roster for a race to Plymouth, England. I had a month free before my reporting date in the US Army, giving just enough time to sail over and fly back. The handsome *Janabel* was owned by a bluff Parisian metals dealer named Jacques Barbou, and the crew included his wife Eliane, a navigator from the French Navy with wife doubling as cook, a jovial Parisian advertising chieftain, and a grizzled professional. Four of us veterans from the Bermuda Race were signed, by chance all of us being Yalies. So *Janabel's* working crew had one watch of Frenchmen and another of Ivy Leaguers, each struggling to learn the other's special language of nautical terms like the *foq de gène* (genoa jib).

After the first windy night, the North Atlantic utterly failed to live up to its fearsome reputation during the 3,000-mile crossing. We never took spray aboard, and the sea often lay flat as a mill-pond, forcing us to chase cat's paws of breeze to register a measly one or two knots on the log. One hot day, slatting sails were dropped and we all swam, staring down into the sunlit blue fading into the black of impenetrable depth. We sometimes closed with our competitors similarly struggling for headway: the famous yawl *Caribbee*, skippered by author/yachtsman Carleton Mitchell, and a cutter owned by the Royal Navy with its captain standing rigidly at the wheel in winged collar, tie, and yachting cap, directing swabbies endlessly scrubbing the decks. We later discovered he was the hard-driving Commander Sam Brooks, proud of his wooden leg lost trying to explode a shark.

The Gallic style of racing sacrificed intensity to civility. At breakfast hour Madame Barbou would appear in her *peignoir* for coffee and a *brioche*, then retire to the owner's cabin before re-appearing for noon-time *aperitif*. Every lunch and dinner was a serious affair. As meal time approached, one man alone was dispatched to take the wheel while the rest of us fell below to our seats around the cabin table, enjoying three courses prepared by the navigator's *cordon bleu* wife. The deep bilges carried plenty of bottles, and *vin rouge* or *blanc* was always poured, with champagne reserved for special occasions.

After 21 days, we entered the English Channel and on a sunny summer evening I first saw the famous land-fall known as The Lizard, the sweeping downs behind it and finally Plymouth Harbour, dominated by the Hoe where Sir Francis Drake allegedly bowled before setting sail to defeat the Spanish Armada. When we landed, the crew of *Caribbee* reported beating us by only a few hours, while envying our gourmet passage.

I could only spend a night in historic Plymouth, much of it still flattened by persistent Nazi bombing of its docks during World War II, followed by a train through the rolling West Country to London's Paddington Station, a check-in at the friendly RORC (Royal Ocean Racing Cub), where I was made a member having completed a major event and bought their blue tie with its iconic white sea-horses. Too quickly I had to catch a flight back to New York, my last sight of London for eleven years.

After I completed my military service two years later, with a summer to kill before Law School started, I was eager to plunge back into sailing, in European waters if possible. I wrote to Jacques Barbou to find out what he could offer. The answer was welcome: in addition to *Janabel* for northern events, he kept a smaller cruiser, *Jalina*, in the Mediterranean, and he invited me to crew on both. The first event would be a race from San Remo, Italy, around Corsica, finishing in St. Tropez,

With my Army savings I bought the cheapest passage to Europe, which also turned out to be the slowest. I boarded a weathered Norwegian freighter in Hoboken, and found that her aging engines could not battle head winds to make the eleven-day passage to Genoa on schedule.

As soon as we landed, I rushed to catch a train to San Remo, where I found that I had missed the race by one day, but caught up with Jacques in St. Tropez and enjoyed an enchanting cruise to Marseille. A week later, the familiar *Janabel* was waiting at a dock on the Seine. With mast lashed to the deck to manage low bridges, we chugged downriver through the rich Normandy countryside to reach the harsh commercial port complex of Le Havre, another town with gaps like broken teeth left from wartime bombing. With the help of a towering marine crane, the mast was stepped, sails hoisted, and we set off into the grey dusk of the English Channel, rough, windy and cold.

Early next morning we arrived at Cowes, the town on the Isle of Wight off England's south coast that is the nerve center of English sailing. Walking down the High Street, I hardly saw a soul not sporting sea-boots, heavy sweater, and reefer, while the vista down every alley opened to marinas, shipyards, and the harbor crowded with sailing vessels.

We only stayed two nights in Cowes before hearing the starting cannon for a race to Cork, in southern Ireland. The weather remained foul. As we beat westerly down the Channel against gales and steep waves, sail was reefed to the minimum, every creeping motion on deck was doused with green water, the cabin became a slum of wet clothes, and hot meals were impossible. Madame Barbou turned green and miserable, and finally Jacques put the question to me, "This is not much fun, is it, *mon vieux*? And my office needs me." Retiring from a race is never a welcome option, but sometimes the better part of valor. We sheered off for a quick reach to the Cornwall port of Brixham, where I was put ashore, while *Janabel* sped back to France with the wind behind her.

Brixham was a picturesque coastal village whose stone quai was usually reserved for rugged trawlers and rusty colliers. But sailing yachts were gathering for a race scheduled to Belle-Île, around Cape Finisterre into the challenging Bay of Biscay. In Cowes I had met a lean, dashing adventurer of British racing who was now looking for crew. He was Major Piers Dunkley of the Royal Marines, in command of one of the sloops seized from the German Navy and turned over to the England's RNSA, Royal Naval Sailing Association. I had a look at this craft and knew that an off-shore race on her would be no picnic. Designed for day-sailing on the sheltered north German waterways, she had the low freeboard that meant shipping lots of solid water, a cabin of less than standing room, primitive winches, and sails already worn and patched.

But Piers was a tough, charismatic leader, disdainful of minor discomforts, and a genius at make-do repairs. I learned that he had been a decorated small-boats Commando hero in the War, but his career had stalled when, as aide to the Commandant of Gibraltar, he had the bad judgment to undertake an affair with the general's daughter. Both sides of his personality made him a delightful companion, together with his ability to cadge drinks by chatting up the barmaid at the harbor-side pub.

He had already signed up two gung-ho Royal Navy lieutenants straight off destroyer duty, but needed a guy with more sailing savvy. The race started late one afternoon, and soon we were thrashing in the dark towards Land's End as all my misgivings came true. The low-slung racer nearly submerged as Piers struggled on the foredeck to change jibs without being washed overboard. The two RN officers soon succumbed to the wild motion and lay inert and ashen in the scuppers. Piers came aft to take the helm, and assigned me to go below to cook dinner. By no means an expert chef, I bent over a frying pan in the claustrophobic galley, water pouring down my neck from the sieve-like deck overhead. Eventually I produced beans and sausages that made the RNs turn even greener although enjoyed by Piers and even by me, for once immune to seasickness.

With only the two of us fit enough to steer, Piers, ever ebullient in facing adversity, and me struggling to stay awake, through the night we took turns on the tiller and checking the chart as we rounded the notorious shoals off Ushant. The officers revived and became willing rope-pullers as we rounded the rocky cliffs of Belle-Île and entered the nearly land-locked harbor of Le Palais. We discovered that in a race dominated by French competitors, we had finished second on handicap thanks to Pier's hard-driving tactics. The French mayor's office arranged a formal prize-giving ceremony, or *vin d'honneur*, so we had to drag from our duffels the damp, creased blue blazers that we had stowed away The elegant French officials were followed by sonorous words from bearded Alan Paul (the "Apostle"), perennial secretary of the RORC who had flown over from London to congratulate us on upholding the honor of the British Empire, even with the aid of a Yankee impostor. Piers wasted no time in telling the Apostle that his talk was a load of balls.

The RNSA needed their boat back in England and I had to get to Paris for a cheap flight home. Piers navigated the short sail to the Brittany coast, where I said good-by to the maddest sailor I had ever known and caught an overnight train (saving a hotel bill) to the City of Light.

Entering the intense grind of law school that September 1954, I had no time to think about sailing until the next spring, when I got an unexpected phone call that led to a new chapter in my sailing career. It came from a guy called Dick Nye. He was just building an ocean-going yawl and planning a race from Newport to Sweden; he had heard my name, maybe I would be interested? I soon dropped tentative plans for low-level summer clerking in the New York district attorney's office, and rushed from New Haven down to Greenwich for a formal interview.

Racing on *Carina*

I found a bull-dog shaped man in khaki pants and sweatshirt chomping a cigar. This rough-hewn character from the mid-west had made a modest fortune on Wall Street in the tricky, demanding business of proxy solicitation for public companies. He had only discovered off-shore racing in his forties and found it suited his competitive nature. He had successfully campaigned a vessel that he had bought "off the rack", and now was seeking wider horizons by commissioning a larger boat of special design, to be named *Carina*. We sized each other up and sealed the deal with a handshake. His son Dick Jr. was present to approve me, but clearly the old man called the shots.

Thanks to Dick Nye, over the following years I sailed in two trans-Atlantic races, two Bermuda races and three of the classic Fastnet races, plus many shorter coastal events, becoming something of a fixture in the ever changing band of guys who knew how to steer and trim sails and didn't mind getting wet. Pressures of work and young family eventually put an end to these maritime idylls, but while they lasted they provided good training in teamwork and endurance. In those non-mercenary days, we were all amateurs, only getting a free bunk and grub while actually aboard, and an occasional feast ashore when the owner was feeling expansive.

Racing across the pond to Europe was still considered a rare and risky event, so my first adventure on *Carina* in 1955 got advance publicity from the yachting press. The experts' odds-on favorite was a well-tested yawl named *Circe*, a mahogany-hulled vessel from the board of renowned naval architects Sparkman & Stephens, designed with the deep, narrow, heavily keeled shape typical of that firm, and owned by an experienced Swedish-American skipper who had recruited a team of ocean-going experts. By contrast, *Carina*, from the lesser-known Philip Rhodes, was wide beamed and shallow drafted, ballasted by an adjustable center-board. Launched and completed just in time to sail from the yard at City Island, New York, to the June 15 start at Newport, she was an unknown quantity. None of the crew had sailed the full Atlantic, except myself, and that in a laughably undemanding voyage. Many grey-beards of the yachting fraternity told me I was courting a watery end in joining this rash voyage, and naturally my mother was unhappy, while the Colonel predictably said "Go for it."

Reverting to normal, that summer the North Atlantic showed its true colors, A few hours after we and our half-dozen competitors left Brenton Reef lightship behind, we separated in the windy dusk and open seas off Nantucket, not to see another vessel until the finish three weeks later. That weather condemned me to first-night heaving my guts out and trips to the leeward rail, with fortunate 24-hour recovery. We battled fog and head winds to reach the hypothetical Point Able, placed to keep us south of icebergs spawned every year from Labrador's glaciers. As soon as the navigator's figures showed that we had rounded this mid-ocean spot, strong westerly gales built up huge following seas, driving us along the Great Circle route towards the northern tip of Scotland, every day growing colder. We cautiously tested the maximum spread of sails to fly, muscling the spokes of the steering wheel to keep us tracking down the face of every wave, and calling all hands on deck when shortening canvas was needed.

By today's standards, our electronics were primitive. Loran, Satnav and GPS (Global positioning from satellites), were still in the future; our location was only fixed through celestial navigation, requiring a sextant in expert hands shooting the sun, moon or stars. Radar, invented in World War II, had not yet been downsized for yachts. Our only communication was a receiver for the precise Greenwich Observatory time ticks, essential for timing sextant observations, and a transmitter limited to sending an emergency SOS. In effect, we were flying blind, cut off from weather forecasts and news of the world or of our competitors—just like all sailors in early maritime history.

We were also woefully indifferent to safety. Even in the most extreme conditions, we never wore safety harnesses or clipped on to strong-points, a requirement now written into the rules of every offshore event, with disqualification as a penalty for non-compliance, to say nothing of civil liabilities in our litigious era. I do not recall ever holding a formal man-overboard drill, another modern must, or even testing our inflatable life-raft. But all the other boats seemed just as casual, and human loss was virtually unknown in amateur yachting, until the notorious Fastnet race of 1979 changed the rules forever. In those early days, were we more agile, or just lucky?

Our mixed-bag of a crew, who had never all sailed together before, worked like a well oiled team. Dick Nye and his talented son invited a long-time friend expert on engines, pumps, generators, anything mechanical or electrical, and rounded up others including a calmly efficient Rockefeller and the irrepressible fire-plug Buddy Bombard, who later became an intrepid bow-man in America's Cup regattas. Our skill was proven by never, in this stormy passage, suffering ripped sails or any other breakages, except the porcelain toilet bowl that shattered into a hundred cracks when one of us over-torqued a wrench to tighten the holding bolts. We all became expert at hanging over the lee rail when nature called.

When we rounded the fog-shrouded Orkney Islands off Scotland's Butt of Lewis, we celebrated with a quick strip-down under a bucket of icy water, our only wash of the trip. Crossing the North Sea towards the Swedish coast we faced a final exhausting gale, until a couple of hours after a pitch-black midnight our laconic navigator announced, "Well, we're here." As a rocky headland dimly loomed up over our bow, we heard a launch chugging out towards us in the dark, soon showing a blinding spotlight flashed on our hull and sail numbers. We heard the stunning words shouted to us, "Hey, *Carina*," pause, "you are the first."

As with any winning team, we surrendered to cheering, high-fiving and deck-stomping euphoria. The launch cast us a line and towed us into the tricky inner harbor. By 3 a.m. the dawn of high-latitude summer was already breaking, and we saw the citizens of Marstrand, as serious a sailing center as Marblehead or Cowes, pouring out to greet us; apparently our approach had been tracked by naval radar. Directed to a dock adjoining the main street, we were waved through any formalities of customs and immigration and led to a hotel whose bar had been opened for the occasion. Unshaven, still wearing our boots and heavy sweaters damp with mold, we were served champagne and lined up on a banquette to pose for a flock of photographers and newsreel cameras. Dick was interviewed by reporters from the leading dailies, delighting everybody by gruffly claiming no problems on the race except running out of cigars. We each got a turn with the press, stumbling tongue-tied at their questions. This was new to us; in America, yacht races were back-page items. Not so this time in Sweden, where we had won some sort of royal trophy. My amazement, dizzy with morning bubbly, reached its peak when a demure but buxom local lady sidled up and asked, "May I sit down with you, sir?" At age 24, I could hardly say no.

It was hard not to suffer from swelled heads, as *Circe*, the favorite, finished a few hours later and grimly congratulated us, reluctantly telling us of busted rigging and blown-out sails. For the next few days, it was impossible for any of us to pay for a meal or a drink in Marstrand. But Dick reminded us we had maintenance tasks to prepare *Carina* for her next passage. Soon we set off to sail around southern Sweden into the Baltic and a windless race of 150 boats circumnavigating the island of Gotland, finishing at Sandhamm, home of the *Kungl Svenska Segel Sällskapet* (Royal Swedish Yacht Club), where Dick was presented with his trophy and forced to douse his cigar to make a speech. After a ferry trip through the enchanting archipelago leading to Stockholm, we found ourselves feted by the Mayor at a formal dinner in the City's monumental town hall, such was our fame in sailing-mad Sweden.

Carina followed a tight schedule of leaving the Baltic for racing at Cowes, while I was dragooned to crew off Sandhamm in a regatta for six-meters, technical demanding day-sailers where agility counted for more than seamanship. Five guys in two cramped cock-pits barely had room, or time, to breathe, as we dashed around the tight courses. Any self-esteem was drummed out of me by the choleric Norwegian skipper who threatened me with a winch handle at my frequent clumsiness.

I caught a flight to England to join the crew before the start of the Fastnet race, the famous fixture that the Brits regarded as their own preserve, 608 miles from Cowes down the Channel, across the Irish Sea, around the eponymous rock, and back to finish at Plymouth. To their tight-lipped surprise, we sailed *Carina* to victory, its rounded hull proving a match for their slender vessels.

Two years later, in my gap between finishing law school and starting work, Dick Nye invited me for another summer of competition. Dick Jr. had to stay ashore with a new baby, and I was promoted to watch-captain, responsible for leading half our eight-man crew while Dick himself led the other half. Our first event was another trans-Atlantic, this time to Santander, on the northern coast of Spain. My leadership was hardly needed, as my three watch-mates all knew their stuff, including our elegant navigator who kept his cigarette lit despite wind and rain, stuck in a holder clamped between his teeth like a sea-going Franklin D. Roosevelt. We had the typical stormy North Atlantic passage, buffeted near Spain by three endless days of slamming into head seas, reefing and unreefing, never dry, chewing on biscuits, deafened and blinded by the unrelenting wind and spray. Again, we saw nothing of our seven competitors until we entered the cliff-girt Bay of Santander, where the much larger Cuban-owned *Criollo* was already moored, although we beat her on handicap and got the over-all prize against our American friends on *Figaro* and *White Mist*.

Santander was a handsome city, but offered nothing like our previous ebullient arrival in Marstrand. Aside from a few nautical types around the local yacht club, most of the hard-working Spaniards showed no interest in yachting and couldn't give a damn who had won in boats owned by rich foreigners. Santander had been caught directly in the grievous Civil War that Spain had suffered 20 years earlier, finally won by the right-wing Nationalist armies of General Franco. With Franco still alive and dominant, even we foreigners could feel the bitter political and social tensions of the War continuing to seethe under the surface.

We learned that the yacht club itself had been burned to the ground by loyalists, the anti-Franco Republicans. Our hosts there and at the ultra-snooty Royal Tennis Club and the golf course were attractive folk who showed us the utmost hospitality, but we could not avoid the impression that they represented an aristocratic clique cut off from the Spanish main stream. Several times during our week-long stay we abandoned our elegant, 19th century hotel and the rigid formality of organized social occasions in favor of Santander's seamier districts, enjoying *churros, tapas,* and brandy in bars and bistros frequented by singers, dancers, merchant seamen, off-duty cops and other night-owls curious to meet their first Americans.

Our destination was England again, and after a brisk sail across The Bay of Biscay we arrived at Cowes to discover a new event was being organized. For several years the RORC had wanted to stage a team-race against a foreign group, and that summer two British yachtsmen stepped forward to lead the effort: Captain John Illingworth, with his unlovely but highly successful self-designed cutter *Myth of Malham,* and Geoffrey Pattinson with his stately yawl *Jocasta,* soon joined by Selwyn Slater, campaigning a slippery speedster called *Uomie.* The challenge was promptly accepted by three Yanks: Dick Nye and sporty friends Bill Snaith of *Figaro* and Blunt White of *White Mist.* The RORC Commodore and the six owners and their first mates gathered in the ornate dining-room of London's Army-Navy Club to seal the deal. At the last minute, Selwyn had found a massive two-handled silver urn at a Fulham antique dealer that was christened as our trophy. A race circular was hastily scribbled and signed, setting basic rules and naming the four races for the event and how they would be weighted. The final would be the Fastnet, worth double points. This informal gentleman's agreement ultimately became the highly structured world championship of ocean racing known as the Admiral's Cup, held every two years with as many as eight national teams, until 2003, when growing complexity put an end to renewals.

As we readied for the competition, I spent hours over gin and lime with Selwyn Slater, the maverick of the English team. I asked him about the name of his boat, *Uomie,* thinking it was some obscure Greek deity; "No," he laughed, "It's a pun my customers hear every day. Get it?" A cockney with accent to prove it, Selwyn had made good in the button business, owning a factory that stamped out millions of standard items for the nation's shirts and dresses, plus special runs for the many uniforms that Englishmen love to wear. Once he discovered ocean-racing, he enjoyed it in any weather. One stormy race he took as crew a famous but elderly English yachtsman named Cutty Mason, well-known as a superb navigator who disdained parallel rulers and just rolled a rum bottle across the chart to draw position lines. When Selwyn came below one nasty night to wake Cutty for his watch on deck, he found him lying inert in his bunk. "I looked at him close up," recalled Selwyn, "and saw the truth. 'Cutty,' I says, 'you old dog, you're dead, aren't you?' And he was. Dead as a mackerel. I debated with the crew whether we should turn in right away. We decided Cutty wouldn't want us to quit a race just because he croaked. So we carried on to the finish two nights later. When we came ashore at Plymouth, of course the police gave us hell for carrying a stiff for 48 hours. But the coroner was a sailor too, so we got away with it."

The 1957 Fastnet proved to be the stormiest in memory. Only 12 of 41 starters finished. From the starting line at Cowes, we faced whitecaps and stinging spray, feeling the bow rise and plunge as we beat against westerly winds through the Needles and down the Channel, and hearing structural frames crack from the incessant pounding as we opened up multi-leaks. Pumping the bilges became as crucial as shortening sail, work made nearly intolerable by a broken tube that leaked cooking alcohol and emitted fumes reminiscent of a sinking submarine.

We had shipped two English crew over our normal eight: Sandy, a cook who never shed his felt slippers and somehow produced hot food from the heaving galley tilted on its ear, plus Buster de Guingand, a calm, collected barrister known as an expert navigator accustomed to these wild waters. With the help of these two resilient limeys, we kept *Carina* in one piece as we enjoyed a brief lull rounding the Rock, then submitted to another gale, fortunately now from astern, allowing us to set a spinnaker and blast around the Scilly Isles and up to the Plymouth finish, still pumping but first to finish. We saved our time on the few smaller boats that straggled in later, and won every trophy. Eager for a colorful story, the press quoted Dick as saying, "OK, boys, we're home, now let the damn boat sink." Maybe he did; I was too exhausted from trimming the spinnaker to hear.

Although *Uomie* did not finish, the English team had accumulated enough points to win the Admiral's Cup. But *Carina* was the individual star of that hard-earned Fastnet race, written up for years to come.

With that victory, I returned to New York and took up my job as a young lawyer. Starting a career and later a marriage, for the next dozen years I had to "swallow the anchor" and stay on shore, only spending a week on a Bermuda race and otherwise sticking to weekend events out of Oyster Bay on Long Island Sound—tight competition with sharp sailors, winning some, losing some, but always finishing in an afternoon.

Sailing in England

In 1971 when my work and family moved to England, I could not avoid the lure of racing around that sea-girt nation, but promising my wife that I would compete only on weekend afternoons and the occasional over-nighter. There can be no more challenging, yet convenient, sailing venue than the Solent, 20 miles of sheltered water lying between the south coast and the Isle of Wight, wide enough to allow fierce winds kicking up a vicious chop, and swept by tidal currents that are a factor in every tactic as yachts hug or avoid the innumerable shoals and mud banks. Marinas are scattered along the mainland shore while on the island side lies Cowes, the focal point for every major regatta and just a two-hour hop from London via express train and catamaran ferry. With these facilities, it's not surprising that most days from May through September the Solent is crowded with fleets of intense racers, weaving between innumerable sail and power cruisers and avoiding the vast liners and container ships using Southampton Port, to say nothing of Royal Navy destroyers hurrying out of Portsmouth naval headquarters, just as Admiral Nelson did under sail 200 years ago.

Friends at Cowes pointed out a trim 35-foot varnished mahogany sloop moored in the harbor and told me she might be for sale. I discovered she was the storied *Roundabout*, a Sparkman & Stephens design built in the early 1960s for the dashing yachtsman Max Aiken, RAF-decorated son of the late Lord Beaverbrook, millionaire newspaper owner and Winston Churchill's wartime confidant. She had been a consistent winner under Max, but he had many other yachting interests and sold her to a skipper who was now ready to move up to a larger scale and quoted me a bargain price. After a review on-board, I was hooked.

I put together a crew of a few regulars and many revolving hands from the pool of eager sailors circulating around the Solent. For two summers we competed almost every weekend against the cream of English boats, spiced with visitors from across the Channel. Limiting ourselves to day races, I did not mind avoiding the rigor of chilly, sleep-deprived over-night passages.

But after two years, I suffered a fit of hubris. *Roundabout* was being beaten by newer boats of more modern design. Instead of up-dating her as suggested by Olin Stephens himself, I sold her (for a small profit) and impulsively decided to build a new boat, no larger but adjusted to compete for the annual One-Ton Cup. Dick Carter, a friend from Yale, was the hot naval architect of the day, having sailed his creations to victories in the Fastnet, so I commissioned a design from him and had it built at the Lallow shipyard, the venerable firm that hand-crafted boats in Cowes.

I learned a lot about marine construction during winter inspection trips to the unheated sheds, and yard owner Clare Lallow, never seen without yachting jacket, cap and tie, was impeccably correct with his invoices. I gave her the name *Eleuthera*, after my favorite Bahamian island, and my two young daughters came down from London for a June christening so that 12-year old Diana could, barely, break a bottle of champagne over the bow. Clare handed me the final bill. It showed about 25% over the estimate earlier agreed. Without a word of debate he reduced it to the original amount, an act of a gentleman artisan that would be hard to find in today's commercial intensity. Nevertheless, the expense of construction plus outfitting with a sail wardrobe from the North lofts put a serious hole in my limited finances that took years to re-fill. My hubris cost me dearly.

Worse, when we started racing *Eleuthera* in the Solent, we found that she was fractionally slower than other boats also built for the One-Ton Cup. I got many compliments for her smooth lines and elegant varnished finish, but they were no substitute for speed. We just didn't have it, either by fault of design or our own incompetence. With official sanction to represent The Bahamas, we took her down to Torquay, for the five races of the big event, with a top crew including Hugh Bruce, a specially recruited navigator, another hard-bitten veteran of small-boat raids during World War II. We could not finish better than the second half of the fleet of 24 boats, and found *Eleuthera's* alarming instability under spinnaker in a stormy offshore event. But I did not feel too badly, since Dick Carter himself, the designer sailing a sister-ship, did little better. He ruefully admitted that his genius must have taken a holiday that season.

After another year of so-so results, in 1976 I put *Eleuthera* on the market, finally selling her at substantial loss. It was a disappointing experience, both financially and nautically, but "messing about in boats" inevitably has its ups and downs, as Rat himself learned. Sailing is a great teacher of patience and endurance, where one accepts that, like the weather, one must take life as it comes without complaint.

I did not regret the four summers of campaigning my own boats in English waters. I found there was no better antidote to stressful, office-bound dealings in the City of London than rushing down to Cowes early Saturday mornings, exchanging a business suit for foul-weather gear, and leaving the dock with eager ship-mates to battle wind and tide for a few hours in a race won or lost. The spirit of sailing in England had a special zest—a devil-may-care bravado to set sail in any conditions, with a cheery wave defying the elements. Because English summer weather is on average windier, colder, and rainier than found on the US east coast, I saw many more people, whether dedicated racers or casual family cruisers, happy to don slickers and rain gear and spend a day on the water without a trace of sun, warmed only by a mug of tea or shot of whisky.

As a foreigner, I could observe that, like so many things in England, even sailing was governed by social stratification. Out at sea or racing around the buoys, everyone was equal, with no snobbish merits or downgrades, but once ashore each sailor repaired to his own club, or pub if he had no club. The geography of Cowes offered a visible example. At one end of the bustling High Street loomed the Castle, built as a fortress in 1521 and now, much modified, the home of the Royal Yacht Squadron, often called the world's most exclusive club. Membership allows owners to fly the distinctive White Ensign on their yachts, a right otherwise reserved to ships of the Royal Navy, while the other thousands of registered British yachts are limited to the Blue Ensign, or even the less exclusive Red—the well-known "Red Duster" of merchant vessels.

Even as a class-exempt American, I could not just stroll into the Castle; I would be stopped by a guardian uniformed like a Chief Petty Officer and politely asked what was my business. I could never figure out what were the qualifications for membership in the Squadron—of course you didn't apply, you were invited. For starters, one had to show an interest in sailing. The Duke of Edinburgh was an active member; the Queen liked horses and corgis, but he preferred boats. Wealth seemed irrelevant, but an Oxford or Cambridge degree was useful, as was a peerage or baronetcy, or a judgeship on the High Court, or a commission in the Brigade of Guards or the Royal Navy, but beyond that were subtleties that only an Englishman could unravel. Max Aiken was most definitely a member, but the genial millionaire property developer who to whom he sold *Roundabout* was not; the young Lloyds broker who arranged my marine insurance was elected, but the man who built *Eleuthera*, long a pillar of Cowes society, was never taken in, nor was the ebullient Admiral's Cup skipper Selwyn Slater.

The strait-laced upper crust of English yachting could abruptly switch from formality to manic gaiety. My wife Edie and I saw a bit of Max Aiken and his perennial girl-friend (his wife preferred hunting to hounds), who moved in higher social levels than us and often entertained Prime Minister Ted Heath, a keen sailor, in his Cowes home. He had simply converted a 200-foot sail loft into a dining hall decorated with historic naval guns and other memorabilia. We were invited to a black-tie dinner there that started with utmost decorum—greetings to "My Lords, Ladies and Gentlemen", toasts to the Queen, tedious speech by General the Lord Cathcart, Commodore of the Squadron, discomfited to find himself seated across from that strange creature, an *American! Female!* in the shape of impertinent Edie.

Somehow talk turned to the Battle of Trafalgar, with Max moving chairs around to demonstrate Nelson's tactics. The long dining table was pushed aside, cannon were trundled up, and their shot, twelve-pound iron balls, were tested for weight. It became irresistible to start rolling the balls down the length of the room, and soon a full-fledged bowling match was under way. Dinner jackets and ties were shed, shoes removed and gowns hiked up, so that ladies and gentlemen, probably strangers to any public bowling alley, could become cut-throat competitors chucking heavy iron down the hall to an improvised target of a sofa backed up against a wall. Amid cries of encouragement at expert bowls and derision at wild ones, Max's wooden floor rumbled ominously but was held up by the sturdy beams beneath. Of course a male and female winner had to be declared, and a bottle of champagne awarded to each. By the end of the evening, even Lord Cathcart, now in shirt-sleeves, clapped Edie on the back with a hearty "Jolly good show!"

I discovered that even the august Squadron itself had a sense of humor. All regattas were started from a line across the Solent extending north from the Castle flagstaff, with the experienced Squadron Race Committee handling the procedure. With up to a hundred sailing craft in half a dozen classes starting at five-minute intervals, following pre-printed race circulars, the system had to be tightly run with clockwork precision. The inner end of the line was marked with a buoy, anchored close under the Castle walls, to keep aggressive skippers from skirting too close to the rocks. I knew the routine, and would keep *Eleuthera* slowly circling under power while we waited for the warning gun, when engines had to be shut off. That day I was careless. I steered too close to the buoy and the spinning propeller cut the rope between buoy and anchor. Horrors! A five-knot tidal current briskly swept the marker floating away down the Solent. With no buoy in place, the starting sequence was disrupted until a Squadron launch rushed out to plant a replacement. For nearly half an hour, the fleet milled about in confusion while the Race Committee struggled with postponement guns and flags and hurried new wireless instructions. Eventually we all got started, with me behind the wheel pretty red-faced as the culprit.

One of my crew was a Squadron member, burly, mustachioed Hugh Lawson, a hard-working newspaper executive who would become Lord Burnham on the death of his father. After the race finished, he suggested that we should apologize for our *faux pas*. I promptly agreed and we soon found ourselves standing uneasily on the Squadron's so-called Platform, the Race Committee's domain viewing the starting area, equipped with telescopes, radios, and brass signaling cannon. We faced five solemn Committee members in blue blazers and white shirts, all amateur gentleman but committed to the highest professional standards of managing regattas. The Chairman heard my regrets without comment and stepped forward unsmiling to hand me a carefully typed document itemizing a bill for new anchor and chain, plus launch fuel consumed, saying coldly "Of course, your personal cheque will be accepted."

I was reaching for my pen when they all burst into laughter. "Just pin the damn thing on your wall," cracked the Chairman, "and let's go have a drink. We had a lively time handling your little fuck-up." We all trooped into the Squadron bar. I made many new friends—but nobody offered me membership.

After selling *Eleuthera,* I limited myself to crewing with friends, struggling to leap on deck like a youngster but avoiding the stress (and expense) of ownership. In the summer of 1979 I declined an invitation to sail in the Fastnet, and woke one morning to hear the disastrous news of that year's race. Successive gales had racked the course, and confused reports poured in of damage and perilous rescues.

I drove down to Plymouth to see old friends and examine boats limping in to the Millbay Docks with shattered cabins and stumps of mast. The grim results were soon known: 90% of the starters had retired and sought shelter, but nearly 30 boats had sunk or been abandoned, and worst, 16 yachtsman had perished, either drowning or succumbing to hypothermia. The populist press, always happy to pillory an "aristocratic" sport, lost no time in querying the whole yachting scene, blasting the race organizers and criticizing the Admiralty for spending public funds to dispatch Navy ships and helicopters to save irresponsible yachtsmen from their folly.

That was hardly the spirit I met in Plymouth. At a subdued prize-giving ceremony, the Commodore of the RORC promised an enquiry and new rules to enhance safety at sea, but emphasized "we cannot eliminate danger from ocean racing," to vigorous applause. After a memorial service for the victims of the storm, many crews returned to their boats, eager to leave port with the next tide. As I wrote in a contemporary article, "Whatever committees met, whatever reports were drafted, out beyond Plymouth Sound a passage cruise lay ahead, and then, of course, other races." Nothing would kill the British taste for marine adventure: for the 2013 Fastnet race, the entry list had to be capped at 300 applicants.

When I later changed my home from London to Nassau, I found that among the many charms of The Bahamas, ocean-racing was not one of them. Understandably, most Bahamians prefer to own power vessels, suited for quick runs to the teeming fishing grounds and pristine beaches found in our archipelago of barely-populated Family Islands. But I often observed at the crowded marinas of Nassau or anywhere in Florida that even on the best days only a tiny fraction of the thousands of comfortable cruisers could actually be seen out on the water. Did most people really have time to use their expensive marine toys? I was doubtful.

I kept sailing in the simplest possible way, on a Windsurfer. I struggled to learn on a friend's primitive board, not so easy at age 50, and then bought a more advanced model and kept updating the rig. I never became a high-wind expert leaping over waves, but for nearly 20 years the frequent spur-of-the moment outings, rarely needing a wet-suit, were a great way to keep fit. A Windsurfer gives you the closest possible contact with the sea, as you often find yourself in it.

* * *

After a life-time of sailing, sometimes I am asked whether the sea has any mystic, transcendental message for me, encouraging deep meditations about the meaning of life, achieving perfect karma, etc. Like any kid growing up near boats, I had committed to memory John Masefield's oft-quoted ballad "Sea Fever", with its seductive opening lines:

> I must go down to the sea again,
> To the lonely sea and the sky,
> And all I ask is a tall ship
> And a star to steer her by,
> And the wheel's kick and the wind's song
> And the white sail's shaking . . .

But whenever I went down to the sea I was usually absorbed in mundane matters like paying yard bills, out-witting competitors, keeping dry, and heating coffee for the watch on deck. The mast often seemed too tall, the stars were hidden by clouds, the wind was a gale and the sail needed reefing. I had little time to enjoy Masefield's rhapsodic odes to seaborne life and ponder the hidden allegories.

There were nevertheless moments when the sea offered flashes of unforgettable beauty. I was captivated by *Islands to Windward*, Carleton Mitchell's first book, written in 1949 before post-war prosperity led to every palm-fringed cove in the Caribbean being filled with marinas, boutiques and resort hotels. Its text and pictures told of un-spoiled native villages and secluded anchorages throughout the Lesser Antilles which I was determined to see. I managed to escape New York a few times to join friends or arrange charters to explore these almost-forgotten English, French and Dutch islands steeped in history.

Sailing east into the warm trade winds at dawn and watching the mountainous peaks of Guadeloupe or St. Lucia or Dominica slowly rise over the horizon in the growing light of sun-rise seemed like entering a fresh world, gradually taking shape as the vague blue outlines became green rain forests climbing sheer cliffs above breaking surf. Often without another sail in sight, we felt the thrill of Columbus making his land-fall in what he named the Indies.

I once became so mesmerized by this tropic scene that I nearly joined forces with an eccentric seaborne nomad. He was Humphrey Barton, a scholarly English odd-ball well known for his books about solo ocean passages. I had read them, and was intrigued to find his famous but clapped-out little vessel anchored near us. Burnt brown as a nut, clad only in baggy shorts and frayed singlet, his educated voice quoting the Iliad, Humphrey was searching for a companion to help him on a month's cruise down to Trinidad and Venezuela. He turned his hypnotic eye on me and I nearly accepted. Fortunately my realistic wife snapped me out of this mad dream. We heard later that he terrified two adventurous young ladies who rashly signed on, by keeping them on iron rations and interminably repeating the "Rhyme of the Ancient Mariner".

Much as I loved sailing, I always knew that every voyage must end, that I would have to come ashore. Even the Water Rat finally settled on *terra firma*. For myself, I was glad to have ended with windsurfing.

Chapter 14
Transitions: Change in New York

In 1967, my unrest, my growing need for a change, led me to resign from Cravath, a surprise to those who thought I could win the much sought golden ring of partnership. But despite the many friends and useful lessons I would leave behind, I felt that corporate law, even at its pinnacle, was a matter of solving problems created by others. I wanted to get closer to the creative process myself. In this spirit, I was recruited to join Kuhn, Loeb & Co., whose business and people I already knew well.

Investment banking with Kuhn, Loeb

If I had been shrewder or more experienced, I might have foreseen that the firm was destined to become a fading star in the Wall Street firmament. Brought to prominence with a world-wide client list by the dynamic Jacob Schiff, it was now governed and largely owned by his descendant John Schiff. A tall, austere figure esteemed by all who met him, John unfortunately did not share the aggressive instincts of his ancestor. Perhaps more consumed by the gentlemanly pursuit of breeding racehorses, he did not exercise the tough discipline and unrelenting salesmanship of his competitors like André Meyer of Lazard Frères, Billy Salomon and John Gutfreund of Salomon Brothers, Sidney Weinberg and Gus Levy of Goldman

Sachs, or the upstarts Donaldson, Lufkin & Jenrette. All of them understood that in the changing financial scene, earnings had to be ploughed back into building up capital, or new money must be raised by the unprecedented measure of issuing shares to the public. Kuhn, Loeb ignored these trends and followed the *laissez-faire* policy of letting partners annually draw out their share of the pot.

At the time, however, the firm's track record and roster of brilliant individuals covered up the structural defects to someone like me, and I confidently signed on, with indications of a partnership to come. I had no immediate regrets: I was sent to Argentina twice to handle international bond issues, to Washington to help re-structure the Rural Electrification Administration, and to the Philippines to introduce the new Asian Development Bank to the US capital markets.

Then, fatefully, I had to spend most of the summer of 1968 commuting to England to work on a complex financing for a British oil company. It was my first business experience in London, and I found the atmosphere exhilarating.

The City was still a financial center of low buildings and narrow lanes, busy with top-hatted bill-brokers making their rounds. Although the working hours were as long as in New York, its bankers, lawyers, and business executives acted with a lightness of touch, an *insouciance*, unknown in more solemn Wall Street. Because secrecy had to be maintained until our bond issue was launched, all the draft documents had to bear fictitious names. The senior executives of the oil company made a great game of thinking up code words based on fish varieties. I learned that it was unpardonably bad form ever to admit to making intense effort; a gentleman must appear to accomplish all with casual ease. As a New York-trained lawyer, I had to adjust to historic peculiarities of the English legal system. After working for a couple of weeks planning the $70 million deal in the modern premises of a leading firm of City solicitors, we all had to troop up to the Inns of Court for a session in the Dickensian chambers of a barrister. Only a barrister, I was told, could give a taxation opinion that the scheme would pass muster with the suspicious Inland Revenue Office. He listened, muttered through his pipe, "Hmm, that looks OK," and we all trooped out again. His bill came later.

The country was in the midst of the swinging sixties. and evenings offered many diversions. London's restaurants were just beginning to be recognized by "foodies", and the King's Road scene of trendy guys and dolly-birds vibrated cheerfully. Old and new friends gave me dinner and took me to the night spot Annabel's, recently opened as a home for civilized entertainment that excluded hip-hop ravers. Dancing to a new Burt Bachrach melody was doubtless frivolous, but hardly sinful, and I seemed to need less sleep in the short summer nights. On Sundays, two tennis clubs offered play on grass courts. I re-established contact with Geoffrey Rippon, (later Lord Rippon of Hexham), an ebullient Tory Member of Parliament who took me around the historic buildings and invited me to a conference in the mountains of tiny Lichtenstein for the leaders of Europe's conservative political parties. Conservative or not, they gave even the subdued Duchy a lively weekend.`

By the end of summer, I began to think about England as a good place to live. Prices were low, people friendly, schools excellent, and I could probably find a career. The next year, unforeseen events pushed me in that direction. New York City violence grew, and a good friend was shot in the face while walking with his wife on a "safe" street, leaving him permanently brain-damaged. The drug culture was invading even the careful schools that our daughters were attending.

Then the unthinkable happened, one Friday night at the Hamptons cottage where Edie and our daughters spent summer months and I came for weekends. On Saturday morning I found her waiting for me on the railway platform, soon collapsing in tears and struggling to utter fragments of her all-to-true nightmare. A man had crept into her room, said he had been watching her for days, couldn't resist her beautiful body, "let me have you . . . I won't hurt you, just be quiet . . . your kids will never know . . . if you scream I'll shut them up." To succumb was inevitable.

What man can ever really know the reality of rape, the physical and mental agony of invasion of the very self, that any woman suffers? I sought to say the right words of grief, of understanding, but how could they give solace? I wanted to demonstrate the anger and passion I felt against the violation of the woman I loved. Unstrung, I conceived a plan of revenge. The rapist, a gardener on a nearby estate, was arrested, identified in a line-up, indicted, and set for trial. I would get a pistol, enter the court-room and shoot dead this foul villain. Of course I would plead guilty and serve time, but as a heroic martyr, defending some chivalric ideal of man's duty to avenge his wife's honor.

Fortunately, I broached this insane plan to my college classmate Norman Roy Grutman, a hard-boiled litigation lawyer whose practice veered towards flamboyant cases that often put him in the public eye. He was known for bombastic oratory that made colorful editorial copy. But with me he was brief and direct: "Dick, are you absolutely nuts? Most people will think you are a crack-brained fanatic. Because the guy is black, you will be called a racist. You will lose your job and your license to practice law. How will you support your family? The publicity will be huge, and will pull Edie back into a tragedy she wants to forget. Drop it, move on. The guy will get a stiff sentence. Edie will survive."

His cool advice prevailed. My brief fit of insanity flared out. Even the most passionate impulse must be tamed by rational thought. Edie's strong psyche saved her, never forgetting the night of horror, but never overwhelmed by it. The rape had one clear consequence. It was the final catalyst for our move to London. If it could happen in the leafy lanes of the Hamptons, why not in the gritty streets of New York, where our two daughters would soon reach their teens?

And then Kuhn, Loeb invited me to transfer to their expanding office in London. We did not take long to consider. In June 1971, we pulled up many roots, wished good-bye to many friends, sold our co-op, packed our furniture and boarded a flight to Heathrow.

CHAPTER 15

Transitions: Across the Pond to London

We had already found a house in a popular square in Knightsbridge, a typical narrow structure of four floors plus basement. The property boom had not yet exploded, and I was ecstatic to pay much less than for similar digs in Manhattan. The moving van arrived on time, and a frantic weekend found us fully installed. As with any building from the 19th century, a survey was required, and for the first time I learned what a "Bessemer beam" was, and how to strengthen it. A new kitchen and other modest improvements were made, and soon we were enjoying the sight and sound of leafy tree branches tapping on our windows. Our daughters no longer had to navigate New York's hectic traffic grid of cross-streets, but simply un-latched a gate opposite our front-door to play in the residents' park-like square. When their schools opened in September, they fell in place like round pegs in round holes, the younger one enjoying the uniform of blazer and floppy tie topped by a straw boater.

We bought a car and cautiously explored London's serpentine road net-work, stretching over a dozen square miles with names constantly shifting from "road" to "street" to "lane" to "mews" to "gate" to "circle" to "oval" to "close" to "square" to "place" to "terrace" to "walk"—and more. For quick business or shopping tips, it was essential to fathom the spidery Underground map with its dozen intersecting lines and stations from central "Bank" to remote "Ealing Broadway".

We made these routine adjustments pretty quickly. The more subtle, intangible differences were another matter. It has become a truism that foreigners, even long-time residents, can rarely penetrate the inner bindings of English society, the unspoken habits and assumptions that keep its people functioning together, or sometimes drive them apart.

Where could we meet them on their home ground? At one end of the spectrum, pubs of course were open to anybody, but we found that despite their democratic reputation, they were intensely cliquey. If a foreigner walked in, or even a stranger from a distant borough, the local gang would give him a "hi, mate," and offer a seat, and then ignore him. At the other end of the scale, we could hardly expect to pierce the aristocratic nexus who served the Royal Family and moved within its orbit—lords and ladies in waiting, chamberlains, equerries, secretaries, advisors, all intensely proud of their status. Nor could I become more than an occasional guest in the discrete old-boy clubs like White's and Boodle's lining St. James and Pall Mall.

Playing a sport is a good route to new friends, and my commitment to sailing gave me a slight edge in opening English doorways. But my wife and I never joined the "huntin', shootin', fishin'" set that assured entry into country house-parties where, I was often told, "You will see the *real* England." Polite and friendly as they always were, our English friends seldom showed their inner selves. Intimacy and emotions appeared only in rare moments of intense joy or bitter despair. Edie was better than I at drawing them out. She often shared the laments of an establishment gentleman whose wife "does not understand me" and made his life a living hell. He was not looking for an affair, just tea and sympathy, which she gave in abundance. Though never a believer in Christian solace, and dismissive of psychiatric help, Edie had a deep fund of personal kindness for anyone who needed an emotional crutch.

I was often struck by the profound split in English society between the conventional majority and the vivid eccentrics, few but visible. On the one hand, I could see thousands of dark-suited wage earners scurrying daily between train stations and City offices, content to return home at evening to cultivate a patch of garden and watch the Telly. On the other hand, I met and read about dissenters, men and women who found that routine life a stultifying prison and could only tolerate brief spells "at home", eternally seeking the freedom of foreign adventures. I thought of T.E. Lawrence, the licensed surveyor who later donned Bedouin robes and became Lawrence of Arabia in a war of independence against the Turks; Freya Stark, who spent a lifetime crossing and writing about the Near East; Gertrude Bell, the intellectual spinster who virtually ran Iraq as a protectorate of Great Britain; Paddy Leigh Fermor who at age 18 walked for five months across Europe, later becoming a Commando hero in Crete and settling in Greece, producing classic travel books.

I briefly met gruff Wilfrid Thesiger, the Eton and Oxford classics scholar who became an explorer never happier than on a camel treading the desert of the Empty Quarter or living with the Marsh Arabs of Iraq, and I heard many a tale from Hugh Millais, the six-foot-six great-grandson of the famous pre-Raphaelite painter. Proud of never once holding a salaried job, he had, among other careers, been a free-lance journalist, semi-professional guitar player, Caribbean yacht captain, Hollywood star discovered in a bar by a famous director, cook to the famous, and promoter/owner of Spanish resort property. My former sailing friend, Major Piers Dunkley of the Royal Marines, was a similar breed, right to his death, when I heard he shot himself over rejection by a lady he sought.

These kind of Brits were always in my mind when I felt the suffocating tedium of dinner parties given by respectable middle-class Pillars of Society. After our first visits to experience

Wimbledon, Royal Ascot, and Henley, we found these fixtures in the English social calendar too traditional for us and did not repeat. In England, the contrast between boring and fascinating seemed much sharper than in America. We could not always find the fascinating ones, but fortunately London, then as now, bubbled with an eclectic mix of foreigners, resident or transient, who were not bound by local customs. Yanks, French, Germans, Scandinavians, innumerable Italians, Latin Americans, even a few suave Iranians, simmered cheerfully in the melting pot. The genial Mexican Ambassador often offered his Embassy to host multi-national festivities, where even solemn guests from the Foreign Office unwound with tequila and *mariachi* music.

My arrival at Kuhn, Loeb's small City office was welcomed by the under-staffed managing partner, an immaculate English gentleman with world-wide contacts who was extremely kind in guiding my untutored exposure to European financial centers. He immediately led me to Madrid, made a round of introductions, and left me there to see if I could rope in new clients. Having some familiarity with the language, over many trips I found Madrid a gracious city, with a kind of restrained dignity that suited the dour, hard-boiled Spanish personality. But because the country was still dominated by the ultra-rightists under the steely leadership of General Franco, a Fascist pariah, the capital markets were doubtful about accepting Spanish credit.

Back in London I teamed up with John Craven (later Sir John), a bright young director of S.G. Warburg, the ingenious English merchant bank that had close links with Kuhn, Loeb, and together we approached *INI-Instituto Nacional de Industria*, the Government holding company that owned most of the county's steel mills, coal mines and electricity companies. When we were allowed a look at the financial statements, we could see that *INI*, not being run like a private enterprise, was far from profitable but had solid assets that would support an issue of Eurobonds. We wrote up a prospectus and circulated it for interest to potential investors, including a major Swiss bank who agreed to underwrite a large chunk of the issue. With the hard work of "road shows" calling on banks and investment funds around Europe, our firms succeeded in getting the $25 million issue oversubscribed—the first major fund-raising for Spain since their Civil War.

Those first trips to Madrid in 1971 were followed by many more over future years, with similar business-development approaches to Paris, Frankfurt, Amsterdam, Brussels, Luxembourg, Lisbon, Milan, Athens, Zurich and Geneva. I found that my transfer to London not only opened my eyes to England but to the whole panorama of continental Europe. For the first time, I became immersed in European culture. My revelations started with a tour of the Prado, Madrid's formidable repository of European paintings, still gloomy and poorly-lit, but startling my senses with Goya's work, ranging from dark nightmares and war-time atrocities to brilliant portraits, leading to galleries of the other renowned Spaniards Velazquez and El Greco. On every hasty business visit, I tried to find a few hours or an extra day to explore the museums, churches and architectural monuments, even haunted ruins, that are strewn with such profligacy across the Old World, from city centers to remote hill-tops.

My tours of course came to include the Louvre and Picasso Museum in Paris, the Rijksmuseum and Van Gogh Center in Brussels, London's Tate and National Gallery, My interest in art had been virtually dormant while living in New York. Many works of the same quality and historic periods were easily available at the Metropolitan Museum and similar well-endowed displays in Boston, Chicago, Philadelphia and Washington, but somehow my eyes never focused there; I was too steeped in the pervasive go-ahead spirit of success-oriented modern America to seek out those oases of past culture. In London and across the Channel, I soon sensed a different atmosphere, subtle but distinct. Many more people were actually discussing the arts and expressing opinions, not simply curators and art professionals, but hard-headed accountants, attorneys, gentleman farmers, and corporate executives.

For myself, I simply felt my life enriched by exposure to the Old World, the foundation of our Western Civilization. Although my roots remain Bahamian/American, they were watered from European springs.

Edie and I planned that our two daughters would enjoy similar exposure. After they finished their years in London day-schools of the highest standards, first Diana and three years later Amanda opted for the American College in Paris, with our complete approval. A two-year junior college, it attracted youths of all nationalities, whose parents were often expatriates from their home countries and wanted a standard liberal-arts experience for their kids, given in English but with a strong dose of French language and environment.

I do not disparage American education; our daughters could have enjoyed an equal or better curriculum in any number of US institutions. But outside the class-room they would not have been immersed in a different culture and day-to-day practice of a foreign language. Their minds were always challenged at ACP, one teacher so effectively drew Amanda into art appreciation that she spent an extra term specializing in this field, the foundation of her life's career. Both daughters made friends who keep re-appearing over three decades.

I also wanted to find an off-beat spot where we could pass Europe's August doldrums, when many businesses close or operate on skeleton staff. The first year we rented from Italian friends a tiny cottage on the coast near Pisa. We often escaped from its claustrophobia to a welcoming trattoria where Edie enchanted the owner and his customers by strumming on a guitar and singing French and English tunes in her clear, untrained contralto. We took our daughters up to Siena to see the wild medieval horse race called the Palio. That was the very day that Nixon took the US off the gold standard. In the financial confusion, our dollar travelers' checks could not be cashed, and we Americans had to beg sympathetic Italians for a few lire to buy lunch.

I was told about El Cuartón, a Spanish village on the Mediterranean but far from the ruined Costa del Sol, where package-tour flights from England turn once quiet towns like Torremolinos into enclaves of Brits with fish-and-chips and lager more visible than *paellas* and *vino*. Driving from Seville, I followed directions to the coastal highway leading to a remote cluster of buildings in the compact form of a typical whitewashed Andalusian community, high on a slope overlooking the Straits of Gibraltar separating Europe from the tawny Moroccan mountains. I soon found the bar. An in-group of multi-national types stopped talking, looked me over, decided I was OK, and introduced me to a towering figure who I learned was Hugh Millais, the adventurer I have mentioned earlier.

Within a day his charm and salesmanship led me to buy a two-room apartment with a breathtaking view over the Straits. Unlike most rash decisions, taken without wifely in-put, this one turned out brilliantly. We spent six years visiting in August and over Easter week, meeting a quirky gang of characters owning apartments or houses spread through the surrounding oak forests. We made English friends who would have been outside our scope back in London, including Elisabeh Luard, an indomitable lady who painted meticulous flower pictures, bore four children, nursed her brilliant but wayward husband until his death from drink, and then became an authority on European cooking, noted for books, newspaper columns and TV specials.

The untrammeled countryside allowed our daughters to run wild like untamed rabbits with a pack of other kids. We planned picnic expeditions down to the wide, wind-swept beaches, and dined on giant crabs, *cangrejos,* bought in the fish market of Tarifa, the town of Moorish walls that is the southernmost community in Europe. Once a year, a replica of the Virgin is brought down to Tarifa from its sanctuary in the hills. The procession is led by local cowboys, one of whom once seized Amanda up onto his saddle and gave her a delighted canter through the town's arches and alleys.

Iran

My investment banking ambitions kept me busy. Traveling in Europe continued, and Iran suddenly came into focus as a credit-worthy country, apparently stable under Shah Reza Pahlavi who had ruled since 1941 as a Moslem but a very westernized one. On my several trips to Tehran with a team of Japanese bankers, we painfully negotiated deals with nit-picking Iranian engineers, advised by an even more difficult American, a retired army officer who had become a crony of the Shah. I had no premonition of the regime's overthrow by the Islamic Revolution only few years later, but I could see the tensions of an unbalanced society. The city of Tehran itself was a geographic template of class divisions, stretching between the lofty Elburz mountain range to the north and the dry plains to the south. Millions of workers and minor artisans lived in the smog and pollution of slums, bazaars and smoke-stack industries stretching across the flats; up the slope one found the commercial district of modern office buildings and hotels; and further up, the Royal Palace and gated residences of the rich. The higher one climbed, the thicker the shrubbery, the more expansive the gardens, the more ornate the houses themselves. The denizens were rarely visible, hidden behind dark glass of chauffeured limousines

I had an introduction to one of these oligarchs, the owner of coal mines who I understood wanted to talk business. No, Ghoshti (not his real name) had a personal matter to discuss. Alone in his vast drawing room except for servants silently bringing glasses of tea, he told me of his infatuation with Anna, a red-headed beauty whom he had met in London married to a hard-working English executive. Ghosti must have this extraordinary lady; in all Iran she had no equal. As I happened to know the couple, he asked my advice: simply, how could he buy her?

He had offered the husband one million pounds for the transfer—a divorce unnecessary, just separate and dispatch the lady to Tehran, where she would be given full respect and every luxury. He was astonished that the offer was declined.

"After all, I am not a savage," Ghosti complained. "I offer a clear proposition that is good for everybody. The husband becomes rich; Anna can live like a queen here. What is the objection?"

Apparently this type of transaction was well-known among Iran's aristocracy.

"I have no wife. Without a woman I cannot sleep; I am a nobody," he lamented, wringing his hands in frustration. Could I help, he asked—have a word with the husband on my return to London? Stunned at this unique mission, I had to decline, and said my farewell to the unhappy gentleman, sunk in gloom amid his wealth.

Ghosti and his cohorts were destroyed by the Revolution; his house and business assets seized in nationalization, himself either executed as an enemy of the state or forced into permanent exile. I never learned his fate. I later met members of the ubiquitous Farmanfarmaian family, power brokers under the Shah, who were adept enough to thrive in New York, London, or Paris, but they were the lucky few.

Before leaving Iran I took a detour to Persepolis, whose ruins near modern Shiraz mark the city built by Darius the Great about 500 years before Christ. The archaeologic site is vast, but the most visible remains were 15 slender columns over 65 feet high, top-heavy with double-bull capitals. They are the only ones still standing on a terraced platform of grey polished marble that once held magnificent palaces ruling the Persian Empire. These solitary shafts, etched against the background of a stark mountain range, gave the site an ineffable air of desolation.

The English poet Shelley described other ruins in words that could well apply to Persepolis, ending his poem "Ozymandias" with the haunting lines:

> And on the pedestal these words appear:

> "My name is Ozymandias, king of kings:
> Look on my works, ye Mighty, and despair!"
> Nothing beside remains. Round the decay
> Of that colossal wreck, boundless and bare
> The lone and level sands stretch far away.

In 1971 the Shah organized a reception for foreign dignitaries at Persepolis to celebrate his reign, so extravagant and egotistic that it offended many Persians and was a factor leading to his own overthrow in 1979. The proud Pahlavi dynasty fell far more abruptly than Persepolis

Bruce Rappaport.

Soon after I moved to London, one of Kuhn, Loeb's senior New York partners called me; a one-time client named Bruce Rappaport now had a new project. Could I take the time to fly down to Geneva to investigate? The request was more like an order, so two days later I made the trip.

I was directed to a trim, modern structure bearing the name Inter-Maritime Bank, on the lakeside boulevard Quai de Mont Blanc. I was taken to the top floor, where Bruce was presiding in his executive office, equipped with a brass telescope to survey the lake through full-length windows sweeping across the front of the building. I found a stocky middle-aged ball of energy with a big nose and a big smile, in shirt-sleeves rolled to the elbow, shuffling papers around a spacious desk-top while talking in three languages on telephones or to his hovering secretary. He waved me to a seat until he could give me his full attention.

"Richard," he cried, leaping up and shaking my hand with both of his, "you have arrived at just the right moment. I have secured this amazing project, probably the biggest being handled out of Switzerland, and I need smart financial thinking. I know Kuhn, Loeb are the smartest, and they have sent me a great guy like you!"

"That's very interesting," I answered warily, "and where is this project?"

"*Republique de Guinée,* Republic of Guinea. Wonderful country. Unspoiled. Loaded with natural resources. Run by crooks you can do business with. Ha-ha. You've heard of it?"

Indeed I had. Guinea, on Africa's west coast, had been a French colony until 1958, and since independence had been run with an iron fist by Sekou Touré, one of Africa's most corrupt and dictatorial autocrats. The country held huge deposits of bauxite, the raw ore for making aluminum. It so happened that I had played a small part in one of Cravath's most challenging deals, preparing the complex documentation for a consortium of foreign companies to mine the bauxite, build an alumina smelter and improve decaying highways for transport to the coast, providing all the financing and allowing President-for-Life Touré to take an acceptable cut. My heart sank as I foresaw all the difficulties that Bruce would face.

But his enthusiasm was boundless. He bustled me into a conference room with a table covered by maps of Guinea, and jabbed his finger deep into the country.

"Look," he said, "here's where the iron ore is, biggest undeveloped deposits in the world; here's where we dig the open-pit mine; here's the conveyor to the crusher; here's where we build the workers' town; here's the route for the railway to the port; here's the harbor for the new docks."

The country is shaped something like a boomerang, and I saw the iron deposits were at the far end of the curve, deep in the jungle and remote from the sea. But Bruce had everything planned. He called in his accountants, who gave me sheets of figures—engineering studies, construction cost estimates, revenue projections, profit margins, right down to fuel bills and truck drivers' wages, and the inevitable allowance for "honorariums". The numbers were huge, but on paper it looked unbeatable. Paper was a lot different from reality.

"And you have all the permits? The agreements with the government?" I asked.

"Well on the way. Should be a piece of cake. The key guy is the Minister of Mines, and we know what he likes." Bruce grinned and slapped me on the back.

"Anyway, look all this stuff over tonight and tell me what you think tomorrow. I've got my own capital in this, but we'll need some outside financing. Think we can do a Eurobond issue?"

I told him that would be a long shot; I was too diplomatic to say impossible. I could not see the usual investment community of Swiss pension funds and Belgian doctors getting overjoyed about Guinea. I spoke vaguely about approaching the World Bank, but I was reaching for straws.

The next day Bruce produced a surprise. He brought in a plausible guy who claimed to represent a major Indian steel producer that would firmly commit to buy X million tons per year of high grade ore, about half the mine's total production. That put a new light on the financing, and left Bruce more ebullient than ever.

That night Bruce took me to his home for a lively dinner, a rare invitation for the clannish, in-bred Genevois. But Bruce was not Swiss. He had been born in Haifa, the Mediterranean port of what was then Palestine, and had served in the British army when England held a mandate for the area, later becoming a lawyer and judge. But he only stayed briefly after the State of Israel was created, finding that being a Jew in a tight Zionist society cramped his scope for doing business internationally, and in the 1950s he, his wife Ruth, and four daughters moved to Geneva.

I found Bruce's family fascinating, certainly Jewish but with no dietary constraints. Bruce, intelligent and cosmopolitan, was an uncut diamond in the rough, while Ruth was a lady of high culture, contributing unexpected bits of Christian, Muslim, Jewish and Druze history and theology, and the daughters were being educated to the same high intellectual standards. The eldest, Irith, was a tall lady with captivating features too strong for actual beauty. Then and at a few later meetings, I felt that she liked me but found me a hopelessly innocent American who could never grasp the subtleties of European and Mid-Eastern civilizations. She used to tease me with dead-pan questions like, "Did you get enough Wheaties this morning, Richard?" or "Are you a Republican today, Richard? Or a Democrat?"

I also learned how Bruce had built up his fortune, to allow him to take risks like Guinea. When he arrived in land-locked Geneva he set up a maritime supply business, ship chandlers that did not have to be right on the docks. This led to ship management, then arranging construction contracts for owners who chartered the ships to him. "Operating is better than owning," he told me. Eventually he was operating some 74 tankers for Pertamina, the Indonesia Government oil monopoly run by the corrupt strongman General Sutowo. When a new regime ejected Sutowo, all Bruce's contracts were cancelled, and that gave him his first real coup. He won a huge arbitration claim for breach of contract and walked away with about $150 million. "I didn't have to run those damn ships any more," he laughed, "and got a big pot of cash to play with."

Despite Bruce's tough cynicism about business, I knew that he and Ruth remained loyal to their original home in Haifa and became major contributors to charitable ventures, particularly in the field of medicine, creating the Rappaport Institute for Medical Research, and also founding the Haifa Center for Culture and Art. Ruth must have had a civilizing influence on Bruce. Although not constructed to be an expert golfer himself, he played vigorously and sponsored an annual pro-am event in Evian that drew high visibility names and raised millions for children's charities.

After we agreed on general terms of strategy I returned to London, bearing Bruce's letter appointing Kuhn, Loeb as financial advisor to the Guinea project, although with many "out" clauses about fee payment. Bruce never stopped being a tough negotiator. A week later I got an urgent call. I must drop everything and meet him in Brussels. Two essential officials from Guinea, the Ministers of Mining and of Finance, were coming there to advance the negotiations.

"Of course they're just stooges for the President", Bruce told me, "and black as baboons, but we've got to meet them." There was no political correctness about Bruce, when speaking in private.

The sessions were set to begin with a dinner, so I met with Bruce and his team in their hotel suite in mid-afternoon for advance planning. Suddenly Bruce smacked his forehead and exclaimed.

"My God! We've forgotten something. Iggy, get on it."

Iggy, his harassed aide, was mystified.

"Girls! Broads! Those bongos won't come all this way without getting laid. At our expense. Call that guy we know in Paris, Iggy, and have him send over two of his best. Blondes, mind you, no niggers! But hurry, they'll have to catch the next flight. Don't haggle his terms."

Three hours later, two six-foot bomb-shells in full working rig strode into the suite. Blonde hair was piled up in artful whirls, pancake make-up gave them tropical tans, pouting lips were bright with lipstick, and plenty of cleavage hinted at busts like torpedoes. I could not help staring, but Bruce wagged his finger at me and warned, "They're not for you, Richard." I heard him give French instructions to the ladies about tonight's requirements. At first they were not happy about servicing *noirs*, but a bonus solved that problem. Business was business. The gentlemen from Guinea soon arrived, and broke into smiles at the appetizing scene of champagne, caviar, and females.

After the warm-up drinks, dinner plans were announced. I had hoped it would be in the suite's private dining room, but Bruce had booked a table at Villa Lorraine, Brussel's most high-visibility restaurant, patronized by rich tourists and bankers on expense accounts. We were seated right under the center of the domed glass ceiling, visible to all curious eyes. I was placed next to one of the statuesque blondes and tried to remain inconspicuous without shrinking under the table-cloth. I could not avoid the eye of a banker I knew from London who waved with a knowing smile. I was learning a new lesson in how to succeed in international finance.

After dinner, the overnight linkages at the hotel were arranged without any input from me, but I assumed were satisfactory. At next morning's business meeting, the two Ministers cheerfully read papers pushed at them by Bruce and made voluble comments. Before I saw anything signed I had to fly back to London at noon. Over the next few months Bruce kept assuring me that everything was on track, and he and Ruth were very generous, inviting Edie and me to an elaborate dinner during a visit to England. Bruce could be a charmer when he wished. Whether he was also a crook was a matter of opinion. Guinean iron ore seemed to fade away. I periodically kept in touch even when I returned to Nassau, which he promised to visit but never did.

I could frequently find him in the business press, usually with a question mark over his head. He achieved close links with the family dynasty of Vere Bird, the scandal-tainted prime minister of Antigua and his questionable descendants, using their favor to set up a bank and build a refinery on the island. When an opposing political party ejected the Birds, Bruce was sued by the new government for some $25 million of damages to the country, but the case was dismissed when he settled for $10 million. He became the largest single shareholder of the respected Bank of New York, which incidentally acquired his Inter-Maritime Bank and then was convicted of laundering money for the Russian mafia. Bruce, with his Russian contacts, was called the conduit for this money, but was never indicted. He was often mentioned for playing a role in the Iran-Contra scandal by moving Israeli weapons, and being protected by the devious CIA boss William Casey, a fellow golfer. Again, nothing went further than media speculation.

His obituary in 2010 gave fulsome praise to his charitable contributions in Israel, telling of his trip to Stockholm, with two Rappaport-backed scientists receiving the Nobel Prize. The good works, it was reported were being continued by his wife and daughters, the heirs of this controversial, contradictory man.

Shivers at Kuhn, Loeb

After three years of enjoyable work in Kuhn, Loeb's London office, I began to sense financial tremors. Rumors came from New York that the firm's shaky capital base had been eroded by one unfortunate underwriting gone wrong. Here in London I could see that the burgeoning Euromarkets were presenting a new financial paradigm. Kuhn, Loeb had always prided itself on "relationship banking", the cultivation of old friends in government and the private sector who could be relied on to provide deals. The firm would structure and "lead" any required finance, but then turn to other, less distinguished, players to make the loans or place the bonds. But now competitors were brashly changing the rules of the game. They set up trading desks and sales departments, willing and able to buy blocs of bonds or shares and later unload them. This was what clients were now demanding: an immediate commitment to provide funds and maintain an active secondary market.

Trading and sales were foreign to the Kuhn, Loeb tradition, and upstart firms with these capabilities were now rising to the top of the much hyped "league tables" ranking Euromarket players. The City became a center for financial personalities. I had many lively sessions with bright guys of every nationality each eager to carve a place for himself in the changing systems. Americans and Swiss formed flexible, fast-moving alliances; Italians contributed manic energy; a Greek rose to prominence as a fearless innovator. All were memorialized in *Euromoney*, the new monthly magazine well read for its mixture of hard facts and gossipy commentary. No one wanted to rub its influential editor, Sir Patrick Sergeant, the wrong way, even by beating him at tennis.

I sensed the time had come to move on, before Kuhn, Loeb was swallowed up by a bigger, smarter fish. I was right: within a few years the firm was merged into Lehman Brothers (which suffered its own famous collapse years later), retaining its name briefly, then vanishing forever—a sad end for the partnership that had once been second only to the House of Morgan. The London office was closed, and its staff scattered. Perhaps if I had been based in New York, I could have survived in the tough in-fighting at Lehman, but I had no wish to return to the Wall Street rat-race.

World Banking Corporation.

I was recruited by a senior officer of Bank of America to join their affiliate World Banking Corporation, based in Nassau with units in Luxembourg and the Channel Islands, and now eager to open a new operation in London. WBC was a "consortium bank", the trendy invention of that era, majority owned by Bank of America but with lesser stakes held by leading banks in Canada and Europe. Of course I had to be vetted at BofA's glass and stone tower in San Francisco. I was led to the sacrosanct fortieth floor, where underlings tip-toed across deep carpets into the seignorial offices of the most lofty executives. My presence was explained to President Tom Clausen, who could spare me a smile and five harassed minutes, and then I was sure he completely forgot me.

I must have passed muster. Back in London I was shown an empty floor and told to fill it with smart people who would bring in business, for a new unit named Wobaco Investments Limited. Starting with an American who knew Spain, another who knew Germany and its language, and a multi-lingual Italian who could surface anywhere, for over four years we arranged loan syndicates, participated in bond issues, and negotiated a few business deals, often with the help of our affiliate in Nassau achieved after long telephonic debates or telex messages (still no fax or e-mail). My European travels continued, but with detours to New York, the Caribbean and once again my beloved Mexico, where I soon linked with Bank of America's hyper-active representative Pépé Carral, the guy who was said to report direct to the President—either of the Bank or of the country.

Amid terse chats with visitors interrupted by ringing of multiple phones and calls to his harassed secretary, he led me to the cream of Mexican business.

Iraq

After several fruitless rounds of visits to Saudi Arabia and the Gulf States, with an alleged contact man whose contacts were useless, I enjoyed one productive trip to an unusual destination: Iraq. In 1975, the country was already governed by the Ba'ath Party with Saddam Hussein one of its rising stars. An odd mixture of Socialism and Islamic Nationalism, it was seldom visited by western bankers; more linked to the Soviet Union than to the US, it rarely welcomed Americans. But Greeks were warmly accepted as neutral players in the Cold War. We were asked to join a syndicate lending to a Greek construction company named Scapaneus ("Pioneer") which had successfully bid for a major irrigation project south of Baghdad. Clearly, the loan would only be repaid if the Iraqi Government duly made the scheduled progress payments to Scapaneus. Was the whole scheme feasible? Simply reading the documents was not enough. I had to investigate on the ground.

Only through introduction by the Greeks was I able to get a visa from the suspicious Iraq Embassy in London. I first stopped in Athens to review the Scapaneus track record. After a night of dining and frenetic dancing, the energetic president of the company picked me up at 6 a.m. for a mountainous drive to visit Delphi, home of the mythic oracle, and then on to a vast construction site swarming with workers and earth-moving equipment building the Mornos Dam, to be the largest in Greece. Through chilly drizzle I hiked muddy paths and examined sheets of blue-prints while Scapaneus managers explained that Mornos would provide water essential for the growing Athens population. Exhausted but impressed, the next day I flew to Baghdad, via stopovers in Beirut and Kuwait.

Despite the anti-American banners hanging in the airport, I found every local citizen friendly and endlessly talkative. A leftist economic policy and Muslim theology did not prevent Baghdad's teeming streets from being choked with clamorous commercial enterprises. Businessmen in dark suits did not eschew the pleasures of capitalism. One of them took me to the members-only Jockey Club, where we dined on steaks, sipped martinis, and placed bets on horses running on the track just outside the windows, while he explained the property development scheme on which he hoped to make a killing. Still, all was not a bed of roses; a friend had abruptly vanished into the hands of Saddam's secret police. My host shrugged—"He just didn't pay off the right guy."

A Scapaneus Range-Rover drove me down the dusty highway to their base camp in the Hilla-Diwaniyah district, names that would become briefly famous in 2003 as the center of the toughest battles during the US Army's drive to capture Baghdad. That night I dined with the Greek engineers in the mess hall lit from a sputtering generator. Over plates of souvlaki and many shots of ouzo, enlivened by guitar and songs, the project boss, a genial veteran of international ventures, told me the objective: restoration of the irrigation system between the Tigris and Euphrates Rivers that in antiquity had made Iraq an agricultural center, the granary of the Mid-East. During the long Ottoman regime it had been allowed to degenerate into useless swamps, and now the aggressive new government had assigned the task to Scapaneus.

By dawn the next morning engines were being cranked up and flood-lights switched on. Soon I saw thousands of Iraqi workers donning hard-hats, and a fleet of vehicles rolling to their missions—bulldozers, scrapers, front-loaders, drill-rigs, trucks of every variety. I was driven for miles over canals, drainage ditches, berms and dikes being scoured out of the rich earth. Deafened and sunburnt by lunch time, I caught up with the boss and asked if he was confident of success.

"Why not?" he answered. "I know this business backwards and forwards. A guy from the Central Bank comes out once a week and pays my invoices on the dot. I meet the payroll, and indent for a few million barrels of cheap fuel, courtesy of Iraq Petroleum Co. We'll be finished in another year, with a nice profit."

When I returned to London, I made my report and we made the loan. We too were repaid on the dot. All the irrigation improvements were wiped out in the 2003 fighting and later civic collapse. Now I read that another restoration project has been authorized. The last, or only until the next war sweeps the Middle East?

Divorce—Personal and Professional

While investment banking kept me busy, my personal life began to run over rocky ground. Edie had seemed fully preoccupied writing another book, a biography of film director Joseph Losey. Then one day as we sat on the beach near Tarifa she told me, tearfully but firmly, that she needed her independence, that we must separate. Not to re-marry, she insisted, although I knew Edie was too beautiful not to be sought by other men. She simply felt constrained while tied to me and needed breathing space. Of course I was stunned. I thought that I had given her total freedom; indeed, that I had spent far too much away from the marital home while off on business trips.

But when we returned to London and she left my bed, I knew that parting was best for both of us. She did not ask for much more than support for our daughters. There was no wrangling about visitation rights. She encouraged me to come for meals, and take them out as often as I wished; some outings we actually undertook together, even a ski holiday to the French Alps. "After all," she often said, somewhat illogically, "we are still a family."

Although a severed one. I rented an airy house belonging to a friend whose bank had dispatched him to Tehran, moved my clothes, and began to pick up the pieces of a new jig-saw puzzle, with regrets but no paralyzing lamentations. With Edie no longer at my side, briefly I succumbed to the romantic adventures common to any spun-off husband. A brilliant, eccentric lady entered my life but proved too abrasive for permanence. Liaisons with no future held little lustre for me and I began to embrace celibacy, with rare lapses.

Adjusting to London life as an ambivalent bachelor, I then faced another change. The appeal of consortium banking had run its course. Bank of America asked itself, why should we share our international earnings with other banks?—we are now big and savvy enough to take on the world alone. All the international affiliations and co-investments were politely unwound. Our close-knit group in London was disbanded with severance pay, and each of us chose a different path. I was offered a position in the Bank's growing London office covering Europe and the Middle East, but I did not pursue it, as I was sure I would not fit in that highly structured system. Several other opportunities in financial services were available for the asking, but I found none as interesting as what I had been doing.

Frankly, I was angry at London, or disappointed. Perhaps irrationally, I felt that the tides had turned against me, no longer in the house I had bought, or the office I had founded. Maybe I should turn my back on England and make a radical change. Maybe I could re-build my bridges in New York, but it would be costly both in money and self-esteem. I started thinking of The Bahamas, and confirmed with a lawyer in Nassau that I could return as a Bahamian citizen, having been born there although always using an American passport. I would not need a work permit and could not be thrown out for offending some powerful politician. Nassau was known as an offshore financial center where my experience could be useful.

CHAPTER 16

Transitions: Return to Nassau

I had good friends in Nassau who owned a complex of commercial and financial businesses and for several years had hinted that I should join them and play a role. A partner of a Geneva private bank suggested that I become an adviser to their Nassau subsidiary. The omens seemed favorable. The fantasy of leaving a congested, fume-choked city for sunshine and fresh breezes became ever more appealing. The spirit of adventure in my restless self urged change. My daughters had spent a couple of holidays in the islands and had warm memories. Edie agreed they would pass summers with me; she herself might visit.

A crisp Bahamian passport arrived by registered mail from my Nassau lawyer. As often after long weighing of pros and cons, the decision virtually made itself. I booked a flight to Nassau just before Christmas 1979, Diana and Amanda to follow for their holidays. My spirits rose as the unknown future beckoned.

Until the final dawn before departure. Leaving England in the grey of winter suddenly seemed a sorry retreat from the sunlit family arrival in June nearly nine years ago. Had I taken a wrong path? I could not repress tears as Edie drove me to Heathrow, until she kissed me and said, "We love you. You'll have a wonderful time." On the strength of that, I strode to the

British Airways counter and upgraded to first class. It was time for confidence, not economy.

Returning to Nassau was like coming back to a country that I knew but didn't know. Since my childhood in the 1930s and 1940s, profound changes had taken place that I had read about but had hardly registered during brief holiday visits. British colonies throughout the world had felt "the wind of change" announced by British Prime Minister Harold Macmillan in his epochal 1960 speech, and The Bahamas were no exception.

The country whose population is 80% to 90% black was no longer a British Colony governed, and largely owned, by a tiny white minority. In the post-war years, London had insisted on opening up the race-dominated suffrage restrictions, and by the time internal self-rule was granted in 1964, the country already had a vigorous political scene with an active party dominated by blacks. This party won a close majority in the parliamentary elections of 1967 and installed the first black Prime Minister, Lynden O. Pindling, who served until 1992 and was knighted as Sir Lynden. Under his leadership, against token resistance from some white elements, the country moved towards complete independence and negotiated its separation from Great Britain. On July 10, 1973, the Union Jack was hauled down, to tears from the Old Guard, and the new green, yellow and black Bahamian standard hoisted for the first time as the freshly composed national anthem, "Bahama Land" was sung enthusiastically, still strange to ears accustomed to "God Save the Queen". The Bahamas were now a sovereign member of the British Commonwealth of Nations, as much on their own feet as Australia or Canada.

Yes, it was a revolution, but a velvet revolution. Virtually every elected politician and civil servant was now black, and the country had entered the modern world by abolishing, without dissent, all forms of public racial segregation. The cabal of "Bay Street Boys" had been broken up, but no assets had been confiscated, no encouragement given to land-less blacks to seize white properties, and only a rare demagogue would rant against "oppression by the white man" and would be immediately silenced by his political colleagues. One of my childhood comrades, son of a next-door neighbor who was a consummate Bay Street Boy, had established a successful wholesale distribution business, another was expanding the family-owned hardware store, and others had become leading members of the Bar.

On the other side of the equation, many more blacks had achieved good jobs, as the result of an aggressive campaign to extend education to all, and perhaps the psychological boost of working in a new nation. Initially, a few unreconstructed whites murmured to me, "Well, the black man is very nice, I love him, but he can't run anything." If ever true, that soon became an untenable position, as every enterprise in The Bahamas relies on black staffing, often to the level of manager or CEO. When I arrived in 1980, blacks were not stealing the white man's companies, they were starting their own, By now, over 30 years later, they control major firms, becoming millionaire entrepreneurs and supplementing whites as partners of law firms and accountancies.

We have two political parties that fight like screeching cats, but they are both led by blacks who have fought their way up the political ladder.

I often feel that The Bahamas could give a salutary lesson to the United States. We display little of the tension about race that permeates the US, the constant anxiety about achieving the correct racial balance. Fortunately, we have nothing like the intransigent bloc of southern whites who still fight to resist black equality, or at the other extreme the northern liberal establishment that agonizes over any action or media statement that might appear "racist." We are more relaxed about these things. Maybe it's better to be a black country with a white minority than a white country with a black minority.

My first exposure to local business showed that sunny Nassau could present issues of company management just as knotty as in New York or London, I was elected a director of a company owned by an old friend, Shirley Oakes Butler, younger daughter of the late Sir Harry Oakes, the Canadian mining millionaire whose 1943 murder in his Nassau mansion attracted world-wide publicity.

Oakes Tragedy

I had known and admired Shirley since childhood. We built beach sandcastles together and she won a scavenger prize at my eighth birthday party. I watched her career progress to Vassar, Yale Law School, the Inns of Court for an English legal degree, and to a promising start with a specialized New York bank. She took a post-graduate course in international relations at Columbia University. She was determined to be more than just a rich man's daughter. She had the looks, brains and warm vivacity to attract a host of suitors, including my college roommate. I remained simply a comrade, to whom she would laughingly complain, "Dickie, I've got to clean the deadwood out of my life. Who goes first?"

In 1961 Shirley finally married, choosing Allan Churchill Butler, a suave Bostonian banker who had divorced his heiress wife to pursue Shirley, his second heiress. At the wedding dinner I was placed between his two sisters, who effused about his good qualities, and I too was impressed. He had a lean, chiseled face and all the social graces, expert at skiing, tennis and wearing double-breasted blue blazers. On serious matters, he would speak quietly with few words. Ah-ha! I decided: still waters run deep. Over several meetings I came to like him, and looked forward to productive harmony.

It was not to be. Shirley had originally preferred to stay in New York, but Allan persuaded her that it would be fun and profitable to set up a merchant bank in Nassau that would make both local and foreign investments, and incidentally help the Bahamian economy, to which Shirley felt a family obligation. So Butlers Bank Ltd. was incorporated, using his name and her money. Its offices were in a handsome little building adjacent to Jacaranda, the Oakes' colonial mansion that became their home.

Long before my arrival, Butlers Bank had been liquidated, thanks to a dazzlingly complex series of transactions with the notorious financial crook Robert Vesco before he was forced out of Nassau to eventual exile and death in Cuba.

A year before I made my move to Nassau, I took a brief trip to discuss a possible brewery for The Bahamas. I could sense tension between the couple. Shirley could sometimes be a difficult partner, and I heard rumors that Allan was having an affair. I dismissed them, only to have dramatic confirmation. Shirley had flown to a meeting in New York, and I came to Jacaranda for dinner with Allan. I was baffled to hear the click of female heels descending the stairs from the bedroom floor. A trim American lady appeared and calmly introduced herself as Sue, the very subject of the rumors. I was staggered, speechless with rage at having been deceived. Those were *Shirley's* stairs, not hers. I walked out and left Nassau next day in a whirl of confusion. Over the next few months, Allan assured me that he and Shirley had patched things up and that Sue was out of the picture. Hoping this was true, I naively believed him and accepted Shirley's suggestion that I settle in Nassau and work with them.

I immersed myself in the books and records of their venture called General Bahamian Companies and investigated its holdings: a wholesale/ retail liquor chain, an auto dealership, a potential shopping mall, and a beach-front hotel. Within three months I reached an unhappy conclusion. Allan, as chairman drawing a nice salary and all the perks of being Shirley's husband, was making disastrous business decisions for GBC. Worse, I saw his slippery ethics. When I found an attractive corporate opportunity for GBC, he proposed that I show it strictly to him as a personal investment, for which he would "take care of me." Shirley's capital was being steadily eroded. The hotel in particular was a loser from day one, and its construction infuriated local golfers since it required the demolition of the Bahamas Country Club, a traditional fixture on land originally owned by Sir Harry. As a loyal wife, Shirley had let her husband be the boss and gave him a free hand.

I faced a painful decision: how to tell her of the unfolding debacle being created by Allan. I consulted Ivy, the brisk, no-nonsense lady who was the company secretary and Shirley's intimate, privy to her closest fears. "You've got to do it," she advised me. I arranged to have lunch alone with Shirley. As we sat on Jacaranda's breezy dining terrace, I took a deep breath and bluntly expressed my views, saying that I could not continue as a director under Allan's leadership. I feared her reaction: would she tell me coldly that I was meddling between husband and wife and that my resignation would be promptly accepted? But after a brief silence, she looked me in the eye and calmly announced: "You're right. He'll have to go."

Shirley could be a forthright lady. It was her company; she had the votes. With the help of Ivy and a lawyer, papers were drafted, the other directors summoned for a meeting, resolutions passed, and in three days Allan was handed a document formally dismissing him as chairman and director. He said nothing and walked out of the office. Soon, as might be expected, he walked out of Jacaranda too, with no forwarding address. We heard that he rented somewhere, and commuted to Florida, joined by Sue. She was a champion on the tennis courts.

Although the marriage was already doomed, I felt the blame, or the credit, for being the catalyst of its destruction. A few locals thought I was scheming for Shirley's hand myself, but I kept a business-like distance. She soon decided that she had no interest in running a commercial conglomerate, and we negotiated the sale of her company to an aspiring black businessman. He offered a fair price, in cash. I went with him to his bank to check that the funds were real. They were. The deal closed and he invited me to join his Board. Shirley could relax, and I learned that negotiations for a separation from Allan had begun.

About a year later, on April Fool's Day, Shirley and I were invited to a birthday party for Billy Salomon, the retired head of Salomon Brothers who took his holidays here. She seemed distracted during the festivities, and after dinner I learned why, as we talked for over an hour on a bench under the palms. Three days earlier as she was checking into a Boston hotel, a process-server had tapped on her arm and handed her a divorce summons from Allan. Her words poured out.

"Betrayal! I am reasonable about separating and look what I get! A divorce! Court fights and gossip dragging me through the press! Does he want my money? He won't get it—that woman's got plenty of her own!"

She paced up and down, nearly incoherent with frustration. There was little I could say to calm her. I wanted to drive her home, but we had come in separate cars, and she insisted on taking hers. As she climbed in, she pounded the wheel and gave me one more distraught lament, "How could he do this to me?" They were the last words I ever heard from her.

She shot off, far too fast for me to chase. But we were on the same highway passing the airport, and as I rounded a bend minutes later my headlights picked out her Datsun against the trunk of a palm tree, broadside to the road, the driver's door wide open. I saw her body lying face-down on the central asphalt. I leapt from my car and it took but a moment to find that she was breathing but unconscious, unmarked by any blood. I did not try to move her. Although it was well after midnight, a car soon passed whom I directed to the police station just back along the highway. Within minutes we had a full accident scene: two police cars and a van with officers querying me and already checking skid marks and taking measurements, a flashing ambulance wailing to a stop, three tow-trucks brashly competing for the removal job. Silent with shock, I watched the paramedics' meticulous routine of keeping Shirley horizontal while they placed her on a stretcher and slid her into the ambulance, which I followed to Princess Margaret Hospital. They vanished through the emergency doors while I was left in the lobby to wait for news. I grilled the duty nurse fruitlessly with questions until a doctor eventually appeared. Through his medical jargon, all I took in was: concussion, pressure on the brain, coma, too early to predict. In a daze of exhaustion at 3 a.m., I telephoned Ivy, desperate for relief.

Fresh from sleep but crisp as ever, she took charge. Shirley's younger brother Harry arranged a Medevac air-lift to Miami, where she was delivered to the specialists at Jackson Memorial Hospital. Shirley spent about a month there, stable, but with no return to normal, and was then transferred to her mother's ample house in Palm Beach.

Naturally, the accident was major news in Nassau, with different rumors floating every day. She had been drinking; no, the car had been sabotaged; no, she had a lover driving who ran away; no, there was a voodoo curse on the Oakes as her older brother had died in a car smash almost the same spot. Nonsense, I told anyone who asked, she had simply been driving much too fast (as she was known to do) and was blinded by headlights on a bend.

Shirley survived five years in Palm Beach before she died in 1986. Perhaps coma is not the correct technical word, but she passed most of the day in bed, immobile except for occasional wheel-chair garden jaunts, unresponsive to speech or other stimulus, spoon-fed or via tubes with 24-hour nursing. I was urged to visit her; she would recognize me, I was told, and be cheered up. I only did it twice. I saw no flicker of recognition, and I could not bear the staring but vacant eyes, the expressionless face, the open but wordless mouth, her hand limp in mine. Her guardians considered euthanasia, but nothing could be done. She was not in pain and retained her vital functions—and the money would not run out. But to those of us who recalled her laughing, vivid years, it seemed a living death.

A few years later, as I entered a crowded party in a country barn outside New York, I spotted Allan and Sue, whom he had married, his third and final heiress. The hostess rushed over and said,

"I must introduce you to Allan Butler. He knows Nassau too!"

"Don't bother," I answered, "I know him already."

When he saw me, he turned away. I did the same. He died in 2007.

Private Banking; Honorable with Exceptions

With Shirley's friendship and stimulation gone from Nassau, I had to find other pursuits. I turned to private banking. This was not a matter of making loans and analyzing credit, but of managing the funds of foreign clients who used Nassau because of The Bahamas' absence of taxation and strict client confidentiality. Banks with an international reach, particularly the Swiss, had a long tradition of specializing in this business and established many subsidiaries in Nassau.

Although government watch-dogs in Washington and Europe continually denounce off-shore financial centers for catering primarily to fraudsters, cocaine lords, money launderers, terrorists and tax evaders, that was not my observation. Nassau banks sought clients with honest accumulations of wealth who had legitimate, legally defensible, reasons to sequester their funds away from prying eyes.

Dennis Levine

Unfortunately, there were exceptions. One whom I came to know was the notorious Dennis Levine, a New Yorker who brought his business to Bank Leu International, the Nassau subsidiary of an old-line Swiss bank. I had been invited to become a director by the energetic French CEO in Nassau, Jean-Pierre Fraysse; I had known him in Wall Street and London as an aggressive, business-hungry adventurer. I accepted, but only after travelling to Zurich for vetting by the chairman, the Swiss-German Hans Knöpfli, steeped in old-world dignity and quiet warmth. The austere, stone-floored headquarters building reflected the conservative nature of Bank Leu.

As a non-executive director, I was not expected to get involved in the day-to-day business of the Nassau bank or to second-guess the decisions of its executives, who in addition to Frayse included two experienced Swiss and a few dozen well-qualified Bahamians. I did not even know the clients' names, except those whom I had personally introduced. My task was simply to attract new business, formulate broad policy objectives, help resolve any continuing legal issues, and exercise high-level vigilance. As Bank Leu had always been a smooth-running operation that made its money by managing clients' portfolios and did not put its own funds at risk, there seemed little likelihood of facing any serious problems.

Then one day Fraysse told me that he had received a letter from the US Securities & Exchange Commission (SEC) requesting information on a series of profitable stock trades executed for the Bank by brokers on the New York Stock Exchange—in order to retain strict confidentiality, all trading was carried out in the name of the Bank and not the individual clients. Fraysse and his Swiss colleagues initially dismissed this request as a minor annoyance that occurred as a matter of course to any bank. Yes, these trades were made for clients, but they had no inside information and the trades were based purely on the decisions of our shrewd investment analysts relying on public information.

The SEC persisted with ever more forceful demands. Finally, on a trip to New York, our Swiss trader Bernie Meier was served with a subpoena for detailed information. This could not be ignored. It looked like another battle was brewing between US enforcement of the securities laws and Bahamian legislation criminalizing any disclosure of client identities, with serious penalties for any offender. The bearded, rotund Harvey Pitt, a leading American securities lawyer, was summoned from Washington, as well as the Bank's Swiss general counsel from Zurich. These two gentlemen with a team of para-legals fine-toothed all our trading records and called a group meeting to announce their results.

I was stunned. First, I learned that all our trades were actually for one person—Dennis Levine, a Wall Street investment banker who was in the thick of corporate mergers and take-overs. The timing showed clearly that he had used his advance knowledge to make profitable trades in over a dozen companies that were "in play", amassing about $10.6 million insider profits. He had made every decision himself, not our brilliant analysts.

Second, and far worse, my pal Fraysse and the two Swiss executives had known exactly what Levine was doing and had actually "piggybacked" on his trades, making tidy gains for themselves and relying on the justification that there were no Bahamian laws against insider trading.

I felt like a fool. I had never sensed what was happening virtually under my nose. I had never exercised healthy suspicion and investigated, as a director should, any whiff of off-beat behavior. I might even be accused of negligence. I was bitterly amused that my three colleagues had never invited me to join the party. Why would they want to spread the wealth around?

Bank Leu was in a tight spot. Not only had it serviced an insider (earning handsome commissions on his trading), but its three top executives became insiders too. Although the Bank was incorporated in The Bahamas, the US authorities had many ways to squeeze. They could close or discipline the affiliated branch in New York City. The SEC could prevent any dealing in American stocks or bonds. They could threaten any staff traveling to the US with civil subpoenas, and the Department of Justice could bring criminal charges. On the other hand, compliance with SEC demands would risk prosecution under the Bahamas Bank Secrecy Act.

Harvey Pitt did a masterful job of navigating between the rocks and shoals He had once been an SEC staffer (later becoming its Chairman) and knew the right strings to pull. In negotiations lasting several months, he assured Washington that a big fish, a whale, was on the line and could be caught with patience and with a grant of immunity to the Bank. Our client, still unnamed, became known to the SEC as "Moby Dick". At the same time, the Bahamas Attorney General was approached and finally issued a decision that made good sense but bad law. He decreed that secrecy only covered "banking business" not "securities business" so Bank Leu was suddenly free to release the name of Dennis Levine.

Meanwhile, the Bank was suffering internal convulsions. Fraysse announced that he would shortly be resigning to take a better job, based in New York which his cosmopolitan wife much preferred to Nassau; soon the problems of Leu could be left behind—or so he thought.

Bernie Meier felt the heat and vanished into Switzerland, never to be heard from again; he took theoretical risk of extradition to the United States, but that was unlikely under Swiss law. The other Swiss officer fully cooperated by giving a meticulous affidavit about Levine's trading and was given immediate amnesty.

I did not take kindly to the SEC sniffing around me without ever saying precisely what they were after. I could not count on Harvey Pitt to protect my best interests while his main client was the Bank, so I called on my old friends at Cravath, Swaine & Moore. Never was there a better example of loyalty. Two senior partners, Ben Crane and Allen Maulsby, took a couple of hours from their busy schedules to hear my problem, smiled and calmly said, "we'll take care of it." I guess the weight of Cravath was felt, for I heard nothing further from the SEC. The firm offered to treat me as a *pro bono* client, but I insisted they send a standard bill to Bank Leu, which was promptly paid.

Our agreement with the SEC required that we keep Levine in the dark about the investigation. Of course he knew that he was a target, but we were instructed to say that the Commission was making no progress and would probably drop the matter. As I was the only senior person who had never traded with him, I was given the unpleasant task of answering his phone calls and greeting his occasional visits. During the very days that we were scheming how to throw him to the wolves, I had to say, "Don't worry, Dennis, nothing is happening." Flat-out lying is no fun, even if ordered by the US government. I think most of us are hard-wired to tell the truth. I even consulted my pastor, who assured me that Christian ethics accept lies when used to combat crime.

Nevertheless, I was relieved when the charade ended. Soon after we provided the Levine name and masses of back-up information, the Department of Justice pounced. One morning in early May 1986, two men from the New York US Attorney's office arrived without warning at Levine's employer, the well-known Drexel Burnham investment bank, and asked for him. Panicked, he avoided the elevator and ran down the stairwell to evade them. But he was tracked down and by late evening he found himself in custody, arrested for obstruction of justice and securities fraud, and forced to spend the night in a jail-house lock-up. Next day he retained Arthur Liman, my Yale Law classmate, as his defense attorney, who quickly got him released on bail and began to plan his strategy, which was simply: plead guilty. The evidence was overwhelming. His account at Bank Leu was frozen and he was later sentenced to two years in federal prison.

His arrest was front page news. It did not take long for enterprising reporters to discover Bank Leu and photograph its premises. Feature articles in the *New York Times* and *Wall Street Journal* named Fraysse and Meier and laid bare their links to Levine. Meier had disappeared and was subject to prosecution *in absentia*. The unfortunate Fraysse was sacked from his new job as soon as the reports appeared. He died a few years later, leaving a deeply embittered wife who had obtained a divorce and accused him of losing her modest fortune managed by Bank Leu.

I was asked to stay on at the bank to help revive its battered reputation, but after a year I had a falling out with new CEO and either quit or was fired; it was hard to say which. Harvey Pitt had succeeded in gaining Bank Leu total immunity from civil or criminal charges but failed abysmally to warn against the deluge of bad publicity. I was amazed to read magazine articles where he extolled the brilliance of his own defense work and down-played the competence of Bank Leu executives. It seemed a strange twist of legal ethics to denigrate a former client, but he had already been paid a handsome fee, and Harvey was never known as a guy to avoid publicity.

After his release from prison, Levine wrote his personal story *Inside Out*, published in 1991, as a measure to recoup his reputation and a portion of his wealth. After a scathing TV interview with the late Mike Wallace, it never became a best seller. But of course I bought it. He does not deny his own guilt, but I was entertained by his inflation of me into a major villain, virtually a co-conspirator of the cover-up who then turns on him and serves him up to the government "on a silver platter." Since, he complains, I wrongly came off "clean as whistle", he brands me "the Teflon banker—nothing sticks to him."

I was quite content to have Dennis Levine as my enemy, and I wished him well in his stated intent to reform, to start over. "This time I will do it right," he writes in the book's penultimate paragraph. A Christian must always be hopeful for a sinner's redemption.

Chapter 17

Personalities of Tropic Life

Fortunately, I had clients other than Dennis Levine. I visited a colony of Germans who had emigrated to southern Brazil and made shoe manufacturing the dominant industry of the area. I met bankers in Rio de Janeiro backed by the country's major commercial groups. I drove around Guatemala in an armored car with the *supremo* of the chicken business, from breeding, to slaughtering, to selling, to retail dining. (I can attest it's not easy to lunch on fried chicken after seeing the birds being gutted earlier in the day.) I saw owners of banks in peaceful Costa Rica and violence-wracked El Salvador transform their holdings into major financial entities. I dined at the Nassau home of an English baronet to set up a trust resolving disputes between his heirs.

All these parties used The Bahamas as a jurisdiction to protect or re-structure their international assets. As a private banker, my efforts were devoted to solving their problems. Although intellectually challenging, it was an activity remote from the interests of most Bahamians. I felt shut off from the ebb and flow of local endeavor, from the efforts of fellow citizens to survive and make a buck or two.

I withdrew from private banking and turned to advising local companies and entrepreneurs how to raise funds in our infant capital markets using our new stock exchange, or sometimes by private placements or mergers with other companies. By New York or London standards, the deals were peanut-size, but gave the satisfaction of personal contact with a whole class of Bahamians, both black and white, whom I had hardly known before. Behind the tourists' vision of Nassau as a center for lolling in the sun, I met the hard-working people who sold insurance, generated electricity, managed garbage trucks, and ran pension funds. I got to know and advise the shareholders of a retail chain who lost their investment thanks to management incompetence. I began a monthly newspaper column on business and politics that made me a household figure, often button-holed by strangers. At last I was considered a true Bahamian despite not bearing one of the traditional family names like Pinder, Albury, Kemp or Bowe, shared by both races.

Miami, just an hour's flight across the Gulf Stream, attracted me for many visits because of its Latinization, which started in 1960 when Cubans began to escape the country in the face of Fidel Castro's embracing communism, confiscating private property, and locking up any dissenters. The out-flow has continued to the present day, reaching its peak in 1980, when Fidel raised the bar for 125,000 refugees in the famous Mariel Boat Lift. Miami's Southwest Eighth Street became *Calle Ocho*. Spanish signs often replaced English, and Spanish became the common language among shop-girls and even senior executives, to the dismay of rock-solid Americans who accepted Miami as a sleepy monoglot backwater.

The Cuban diaspora was split by bitter factions, between those who sought the immediate downfall of Fidel and those who simply accepted his rule as an unfortunate *fait accompli*. I had a personal view of this rancorous difference when I came to know a determined lady named Maria Luisa Ryan, first in London and then at her condo on Miami's Key Biscayne. She was the Cuban-born daughter of Julio Lobo, the prime oligarch of the Cuban sugar industry. His vast complex of cane plantations and industrial refineries were promptly seized by Fidel, but he retained an off-shore fortune from his international trading activities, allowing his children to live in modest affluence. Maria Luisa had an intense intellectual streak devoted to photography and architectural studies. She was determined to return to Cuba to record the baroque mansions of Havana and the country plantation houses that had inspired her childhood, now suffering decay under state ownership. Despite her father's controversy with Fidel, she was able to negotiate with the *jefe maximo* for the crucial permits to enter Cuba and take her pictures.

For this she was vilified by the ultra conservative wing of the Miami Cuban community. In their view, anyone who dealt with Fidel and spent as little as $10 in his nation was a supporter of his regime and a traitor to the true Cuba. At one of her open-house Sunday lunches, a well-dressed guest was admitted, walked quietly to the buffet table, seized a glass of red wine and heaved it in her face, shouting *"puta de Fidel"* (Fidel's whore) before being thrown out. That did not stop her. A few months later, she showed me the haunting photos that she later used to illustrate her magnificent book *Havana—History and Architecture of a Romantic City*, published by her collaborators in 2009, long after she died of cancer in 1998.

The Latin arrivals were not only from Cuba. They poured in from Argentina, Brazil. Colombia, Costa Rica, Venezuala— not simply penniless refugees but people of substance investing in property, starting new businesses, patronizing up-market boutiques, bringing a new wave of prosperity to Miami. Nicaragua's leading families kept a base there, and I came to know well Hope Somoza, wife of Anastasio ("Tachito") Somoza, son of the founder of the Somoza dynasty that dominated the country for 50 years from the capital city of Managua.

Hope was in born in Tampa, Florida, to the wealthy and cosmopolitan Portocarrero family, who like the Somozas divided their time between Nicaragua and the US. Hope and Tachito, cousins, were childhood playmates, and they married in

1950, the union of the country's two leading families celebrated with high pomp for 4,000 guests in Managua's cathedral.

After his father's death, Tachito eventually became President in 1967, and Hope slid easily into the role of First Lady, hosting international contacts from President Nixon to Emperor Hirohito, with an immaculate regal style that put her on the Best Dressed List, exercising her multi-lingual abilities derived from education at Barnard and in Paris. It seemed a perfect partnership, but Tachito, displaying manly *machismo*, naturally had to take a mistress. Defying all normal rules of protocol, he did not keep her locked in a gilded cage but openly adored and flaunted the considerable charms of Dinorah Sampson.

Hope could not tolerate this. A vigorous lady of independent means with friends everywhere, she was not deterred by ties to their five children. In 1975 she divorced Tachito and moved to London, where I met her briefly, an enigmatic figure who spoke little of her past but moved gracefully into London society, showing a perfectly coiffed helmet of dark hair, and keeping possible suitors at bay with a sharp wit that proved she was any man's intellectual equal, or better.

We met again in Miami, where she bought a house and created a tropical greenery of plants lit by sunlight through wooden shutters, more at home in the Latin atmosphere. I was a frequent guest from Nassau, fascinated as I learned about her life and her shrewd grasp of foreign affairs. In 1979 Tachito fled from Nicaragua, driven from the Presidency by the Sandinista forces. Denied asylum by the US, he settled in Paraguay, under the protection of his pal the iron-fisted dictator/president General. Alfredo Stroessner. But safety was illusory. His enemies, possibly backed by Fidel Castro, tracked him down and assassinated him in September 1980. Family and political cronies decided he should be buried in Florida with a funeral memorializing his life, and advised Hope.

Far from lamenting as a grief-stricken widow, Hope sought a low profile in the obsequies. To keep some degree of family cordiality, she agreed to attend a semi-private viewing of Tachito's body, and asked me to escort her. Driving to a funeral home in the heart of Coral Gables, we found the building guarded by a few local cops, uneasily surveying platoons of beefy dark-suited Somoza bodyguards, hardly bothering to conceal the heavy metal under their jackets. When we entered the modest chapel hall, I stayed at the rear, while Hope, dressed in black with a veil hiding her face, stepped forward to look down at the body displayed by the mortuary experts in the open coffin. I saw her bend her head, whisper a few words, then come back up the aisle, recognized by only a few of the mourners.

After a brief exchange with her estranged sons and relatives-by-marriage, we drove away and she flung off her veil. I could sense that by saying a final farewell to Tachito she had also flung off a 30-year stage of her life and was ready to move forward.

I never asked whether she was lonely, but I knew a man who certainly was. Archie Baldocchi was a sweet-tempered American, living on Key Biscayne, whom I had met many years earlier on a trip to El Salvador where he had married into the business hierarchy and became famous for flying a restored P-51 Mustang fighter (he had wedged me behind the pilot's seat for a brief terrifying spin). Now retired and devoting his time to tennis, experimental motorboats, and supporting his son's campaign to become the leading banker of El Salvador, his quiet charm seemed right for Hope. With considerable trepidation, I arranged a casual meeting. Though he was some 15 years older, it was a match. They married and enjoyed a modest but elegant house facing the quiet waters of Biscayne Bay, giving candle-lit dinners for a few guests.

After she died in 1993, Archie, surviving until 2010 into his nineties, would often go silent at the memory of his dynamic wife, murmuring, "Dick, I have lost Hope," smiling ruefully at the pun that so well summarized his emotions.

Richard Coulson

* * *

One of the spices of Nassau is the rare mix of international characters who choose to live here. A few of them are raffish mountebanks, who create massive financial grief for many victims, both the shrewd and the credulous. One of them was the infamous Robert Vesco, who came and left before my days here, after entangling my friend Shirley Oakes Butler. The press labeled a later one "The Pirate of Prague", a charming scoundrel (vigorously denied by him) convicted *in absentia* by many courts, but never for a Bahamian crime.

The Pirate of Prague.
One autumn evening in 1994 I was seated at a dinner party next to a large, affable young man with a reddish crew-cut. In perfect English with just a trace of European accent, he introduced himself as Kozeny, Viktor. From where?

"Well, I have just arrived to live here. I am from Prague, but . . . I prefer to be away for a while."

When I told him I was planning a business/holiday trip to that fascinating capital of the Czech Republic, he immediately insisted, "I'll arrange for my office to look after you." Office? It seemed that he ran some sort of mutual funds in Prague. He called me a few days later to get my arrival details, saying, "OK, they will take care of everything."

As I came through customs at Prague airport, a solid bullet-headed guy in a black suit was holding a sign reading "WELCOME MR. COULSON". He gave me a crushing handshake with firm words "I Bruno. Viktor say I with you". And indeed he was, for most of the next five days. He whisked me out to a long black Mercedes with tinted windows and rushed me to one of Prague's few high-rise office towers. I was escorted to a suite filling the two top floors, with stunning views and all the accoutrements of a modern brokerage office—trading screens, stock quote board, and scurrying staffers. Trim Petra Wendelova, the economist who was the investment boss, politely explained that, yes, although an office bore Viktor's name as President, no, the only contact was by daily telephone calls with Nassau. I later saw a headline in the *Economist* saying Viktor suffered from "The Loneliness of the Long-Distance Fund Manager."

Manna from heaven! Millions of Czech shop-keepers, farmers, and mechanics bought vouchers and over 700,000 of them exchanged for the Harvard shares. The Harvard Funds in turn used the proceeds to acquire up to 20% of the equity in the Czech Republic's top 50 companies, with a book value in the billions. The Funds were managed, for hefty fees, by Harvard Capital and Consulting (HC&C), Viktor's private vehicle. Virtually overnight, Viktor, at age 30, controlled a large chunk of the Czech economy.

Petra invited me to the annual shareholders' meeting of the Funds, scheduled for the very next morning. Over 2,000 Czechs filled every seat in the gleaming auditorium of Prague's Palace of Culture, facing a huge banner reading:

HF Harvardske Fondy, Harvard Funds.

The typography and the crimson font were identical to what Harvard University uses for all its announcements. Harvard had of course protested this unauthorized free-riding, but to no avail. Viktor held a legitimate economics B.A.

On a raised dais in front of the banner six corporate executives conducted the usual corporate rigmarole. I got the drift, even in Czech: Annual report (with handsome photo of Viktor) read, questions asked, ballots marked, directors elected, resolutions proposed, approvals by unanimous voice vote, followed by vigorous applause. The Harvard shareholders were enjoying their first taste of western-style corporate democracy. About 20% of them had earlier cashed in for the promised profit, which Viktor was able to deliver since the stock market had risen. He had guessed right that the original valuations were absurdly low. The celebrants at the annual meeting were loyal investors waiting for the even greater pay-off—that never came.

I was puzzled why Viktor stayed absent from the festivities. I discovered persistent rumors that the Government was investigating his alleged bribing of a public official to provide inside information about the privatization program, although no charges had been brought. Local lawyers and bankers downplayed these rumors, attributing them to former communist officials venting left-wing envy of a young man who had struck it rich. However, a research report about the Harvard Funds by Wood & Co., Prague's leading stockbroker, carried this caveat:

> A legal investigation into the conduct of HC&C Chairman Viktor Kozeny raises questions about the integrity of the management company and the ramifications for the funds if he is found guilty of criminal activity.

Little noticed at the time, those words rang an ominous note for the future.

Every morning for the rest of my stay, Bruno appeared at my hotel, a cheerful guide prepared to drive me wherever I wished, and usually insisted on buying my lunch. One day I sent him home, as I wanted to walk through the City's historic sites, including the exotic Charles Bridge and across to the overwhelming heights of Prague Castle. But his expert driving was delightful for visits to palaces in a couple of outlying towns that had been restored to the aristocratic old-line Lobkowicz family after years of communist control.

When Bruno arrived on my last day to drive me to the airport, I found to my shock that my hotel bill had already been paid. With friendly smiles from the desk clerk and Bruno, there was no way to reverse the transaction. Not wanting to be a complete free-loader, I insisted that we rush by the Harvard office, where I filled out a subscription form (in Czech, hurriedly translated for me) and deposited a $1,000 check to buy Harvard Growth Fund shares. Alas, together with thousands of Czechs, I never saw a penny back on my investment.

On my return to Nassau, I worried that Viktor would expect some *quid pro quo* for his favors to me. Not at all. He invited me to his modest house in Lyford Cay for breakfast with his ex-wife Kendall and their young daughter Victoria, making a quick visit from Massachusetts. Kendall, nee Callahan, was a handsome lady of wealthy Bostonian vintage, who had financed his years of struggling towards a Harvard degree. Though firmly split, they revealed not a hint of acrimony. He asked me to explain how I could create a Bahamas trust to hold the financial assets settled on her by Viktor, a task that I politely declined.

Initially, Viktor took remarkable strides in the Nassau community, only leaving for occasional trips to Zurich, London and New York—never Prague. Clearly, earnings from the Harvard funds were flowing heavily his way. He befriended a long-time Lyford Cay resident, David McGrath, genial golfing partner of Sean Connery and perennial host of the Cay's liveliest New Year's Eve party. David introduced him widely among the leaders of the gated Lyford Cay compound, always happy to meet an interesting newcomer. One of his early contacts was the illustrious late Sir John Templeton, the expatriate American renowned for creating the Templeton Funds (now part of the Franklin-Templeton Group). A self-made man of strict rectitude, donor of the annual Templeton Prize for Religion, Sir John took a liking to Viktor's youthful chutzpah and sponsored him for membership in the Lyford Cay Club.

He soon bought one of the Cay's grandest residences, perched on a promontory ridge overlooking the untamed sea to the north and the calm Clifton Bay to the south. It was already breath-taking, but Viktor immediately undertook to add a sports complex of olympic swimming pool and tennis courts. He insisted that I be an early arrival at his house-warming party, an event that proved as awkward as *The Great Gatsby* reception described in F. Scott Fitzgerald's novel. Standing at the head of the grassy entrance slope, impeccably clad in double-breasted blue blazer, the six-foot-plus, pink cheeked Viktor stiffly greeted a reception line of guests, few of whom he had ever met, invited from a list created with David McGrath's advice.

For the next few years, his meteor continued to rise, despite rumblings from the Czech Government and the arrest and conviction of the state officer whom he allegedly bribed. I and the other Harvard shareholders gradually realized that our investment was hardly blue-chip as the quoted price on the Prague Exchange steadily dropped. "A shame," said Viktor, shaking his head sadly, "The Government is following policies that are ruining the country, and I can't stop them.".

But he was able to buy another hill-top house in Lyford Cay, not quite as grand as his own, for his mother, the formidable Dr. Jitka Chvatik, a retired psychiatrist who dominated his childhood. He also acquired Andrew Lloyd Weber's house in London's Eaton Place for a reputed £10 million, and The Peak, a mountain lodge on Aspen's slopes for $22 million.

One of his personal conquests at Lyford Cay was Michael Dingman, the semi-retired American investor (like Sir John Templeton, he gave up his US citizenship), well-known to the financial press for fast-moving corporate turn-arounds that always worked out well for himself. Still alert to an interesting deal, Dingman joined Viktor in setting up joint ventures and scouting out new prospects in the Czech Republic, Eastern Europe and Russia. A photograph in *Fortune* showed them smiling at each other aboard Dingman's unusual yacht, a 115-foot maxi-sloop, in Lyford Cay Marina.

My employer Coutts Bank encouraged me quietly to explore whether we could snare Viktor as a client. I visited his principal lawyer, Hans Bodmer, at his discreet offices in the heart of Zurich. Dr. Bodmer, speaking with usual Swiss precision, assured me about the propriety of multi-tiered financial structures centered on Cyprus. However, several meetings held in the Coutts Nassau board-room with Dr. Bodmer and other counsel, convinced us that Viktor's affairs were too complex to be a happy fit at ultra-conservative Coutts. I continued to see Viktor often across the net at the Club tennis courts. His large, somewhat ungainly frame did not prevent him from playing a high-quality game, vigorous and aggressive, but between points he was unfailingly smiling and courteous, never forgetting to shake hands with partner and opponents after every match and usually offering to buy a round of drinks. I saw no clouds of worry cross his face.

Then in 1997 he made his first trip to Azerbaijan, that tiny off-shoot of the shattered Soviet Union on the land-locked Caspian Sea that was blessed with one natural resource—oil, first discovered thousands of years ago. After independence, the country became a bidding ground for world petroleum interests, and its capital, Baku, became notorious as home of a corrupt regime where anything was feasible with a bribe and nothing without one. Azerbaijan evolved for Viktor into his "Bridge Too Far", where his overpowering financial ambitions led to his downfall. Once again, he started buying up government-issued vouchers. He claimed he had an ironclad agreement with Azerbaijan's devious President Haidar Aliev that the vouchers could be used to acquire SOCAR, the government oil company and the crown-jewel of the national economy. Back in the United States, he raised over $400 million to sink into this superb investment, hard cash, not just promises—and not from widows and orphans but from the smartest of the smart, like Leon Cooperman of Omega Advisors, Columbia University, the insurance giant AIG, and Senator George Mitchell, often using his palatial Aspen lodge for lavish parties to seduce potential investors who fell for his personal charm and a prospect of oil riches. Michael Dingman, however, was too shrewd to play this game.

The house of cards collapsed in stages. Despite frantic efforts by Viktor and minions he dispatched to Baku, the promised conversion of vouchers into hard assets was interminably delayed. Investors grew restless, demanding news and threatening legal action. In 2000 *Fortune* and the other media starting dubbing him "The Pirate of Prague". When the hard truth dawned that Azerbaijan had no intention of selling its oil riches, the law suits began. In 2003 Viktor was indicted in the New York courts for a variety of fraud and related charges, and naturally civil suits followed to recoup the invested millions. Even the Feds got into the act, with the Justice Department charging that he had violated the Foreign Corrupt Practices Act (FCPA) by bribing Azerbaijan officials. Several of his American compatriots, and even Swiss lawyer Hans Bodmer, soon pleaded guilty rather than fight the multiple charges of conspiring with Viktor.

Viktor was converted from a golden boy into a business pariah. Although not actually broke, as he had tucked away his Nassau, London and Aspen realty into trusts controlled by his mother Dr. Jvatik, his wings were severely clipped. He could travel nowhere outside The Bahamas for fear of immediate seizure in the United States. Even his local life was shattered: he lost his membership in Lyford Cay Club, and Sir John Templeton privately regretted his original sponsorship.

Then the hardest blow fell. The US government formally requested the Bahamian authorities to extradite Viktor, and to lock him up during the extradition proceedings. One morning in 2005 Nassau constables, armed with the proper warrant, arrived at his mansion by the sea and led him away to Her Majesty's Fox Hill Prison, deep in the scrublands near the other end of the island. Fox Hill is not a brutal hell-hole, but, overcrowded and underfunded, still is "no hotel" as confirmed by its own Superintendent, and surely a traumatic descent from Lyford Cay.

I called on his formidable mother Dr. Chvatik to find out how Viktor was faring. I found her holding forth in his home, now sadly run down; hedges un-trimmed, pool scummy, sofas stained and damp with mold. Like any mom, she supported her wayward son, proclaiming his innocence and making weekly care-package prison calls. She arranged my inclusion in the tightly restricted visitor list. Viktor had never done anything to hurt me (forget the lost $1,000), so I made the trip.

I was led to the maximum security block and saw he was not held in the communal ward where I had once visited a young murderer pleading insanity, racked with others in the sweaty, malodorous gloom. Viktor had been assigned a private cell upstairs. There was no formal visitors' area. For our meeting in the guard-room, only a moveable screen was placed between us. The duty sergeant took no interest except to check the snacks I had brought. Clad in shorts and a tee shirt, Viktor glowed with health and self-righteousness. Glad to have so much time for reading, he proclaimed that his innocence would soon be recognized.

"Listen," he said, "those guys who are suing me for millions? We were in it together. They knew the risks. I lost big bucks myself. We were all screwed by those crooks who run Azerbaijan. And the US government? Let me tell you, they *wanted* me to bribe Aliev, so they could pin something on him. And now they indict me!"

He encouraged me to see the lawyers who were defending him. I met with two blue-chip QCs who had come from London to support his local counsel. They were careful to express no opinion about his guilt or innocence. Their sole task was to argue that the US-Bahamas extradition treaty did not apply and he should not be locked up. After 19 months of incarceration, the Bahamas Attorney General let him out, although still holding his passport. I have only seen him twice since then; he has gone to ground, location unknown, occasionally answering voice mail but refusing more contact.

It was only in 2012 that his counsel got a no-appeals ruling from the British Privy Council that he could not be extradited because the US FCPA has no equivalent in the Bahamas. The Czech Republic, suing him for $400 million for bilking the Harvard Fund investors, has no extradition treaty with the Bahamas, so it seems his life can continue with no risk of being dragged away from Nassau.

But what a life! Nearing 50, wary of any travel, social life at zero, business opportunities dead, his obvious charm and intelligence are stymied. I wonder, but cannot discuss with him, whether defending himself in the United States courts and suffering the inevitable penalties would not finally free him to start life over?

Henryk de K.—The Man Who Never Lost

Another man in Nassau, also from eastern Europe, made his pile from nothing—and kept it. Henryk de Kwiatkowski, as I knew him in the last 20 years of his life, was the most cocksure person I ever met. Everything was done with cheerful certainty; doubts and hesitation were unknown, expense be damned. Some called it conceit, arrogance; I simply enjoyed his style.

By the 1980s he was a non-resident Canadian citizen with his base residence in Nassau. I was a director of the local offshore bank that channeled his multi-million-dollar currency deals. I had no training as a FOREX dealer, but when our trader took his two-week holiday, I was the guy to fill in. I was simply an order-taker, the middle-man between Henryk and the dealers. But, in those primitive days before Bloomberg market screens at every desk, my task had its goodly share of stress.

I had Henryk on one line demanding the latest price of dollar-sterling futures, the trading room at Deutsche Bank or JPMorgan in New York on another line giving me their current quotes, back to Henryk to report, take his buy or sell order and give it to Deutsche or Morgan, report back to Henryk with the execution price, up-date his account on the bank's records, then repeat the whole process with dollar-yen futures or dollar-swissy futures. As prices were changing every second, and Henryk never dealt in positions of less than a million dollars and was always barking for the best price, there was no time to relax. Only when trading closed at 2:30 p.m. did the tension unwind so I could slump back from the phones and look out at the sunny vista of Nassau's Bay Street.

Henryk lived in a beach-front mansion called Serendip Cove deep in the gated enclave of the Lyford Cay Club, where

I also was a member (without a mansion), and at week's end I delivered the trading sheets for his review. He spent five minutes of intense silent study, threw them aside, smiled, and said, "OK, let's have a martini." He had all the trappings of any successful New York socialite lounging in the tropics: Gucci loafers without socks, pink slacks, double-breasted navy blazer, blue cuff-linked shirt with white collar, striped tie of the tight-knit club called The Brook, rooms enriched with the unmistakable touch of society's favorite decorator Sister Parish. But clearly the back-story was very different. His deeply tanned face showed the Slavic/Mongol features of high cheek-bones and slanted eyes, topped by a sheaf of coarse black hair that fell down to his thick brows. The gleaming white teeth seen in his frequent smiles suggested humor but also avarice, an urge to seize and consume.

He often chose me as a favored listener when he fell into his raconteur mood. Whether or not I was being told the hard truth, the audacity of his tales never failed to captivate me. I learned, and it seems a matter of record, that he was born in Poznan, Poland, in 1924. Of his childhood years, I was told virtually nothing, and doubt remains whether he was entitled to the "de" prefix that implies descent from nobility. Of his trials beginning in World War II, when Poland became a punching bag for first the Third Reich and then the Soviet Union, I heard many dramatic accounts, often varying in the details and of course impossible to verify. I gathered that he was taken from his parents by the Germans, later captured by the Russians, nearly starved on a diet of potatoes, was held in Siberia, sheltered and befriended by an elderly lady who helped him escape to Persia, where he boarded ship to England, surviving a sinking by torpedo. He often mentioned flying lessons and service in some branch of the RAF, although researchers have not unearthed any military records.

There's no doubt that he arrived in Canada in the 1950s and found work as an aircraft mechanic. A friend from Montreal told me that Henryk used a few introductions to charm his way into formal dinner parties, laughing about the work-day grime that he couldn't clean from his under his fingernails. He himself told me of a girl who wanted to marry him, and how he declined to her father because he was still broke and had a future to build. He was no ordinary grease-monkey. He managed to get Canadian citizenship, and earned a degree in aeronautical engineering, moving to the United States to take a job with Sikorsky, the early developer of helicopters.

Then began the most productive period of his life, when he settled in New York City in the 1960s and set up his own operation, De Kwiatkowski Aircraft. I wish I had known him at this time, when starting from zero he began to earn serious money, and then moved his residence to The Bahamas to avoid US income tax. New York was clearly the base to make contacts with banks who financed him, lawyers who structured his complex deals, and aircraft brokers who put him in touch with the builders of planes and the governments and companies who flew them. His career must have been helped by his marriage to the comely Lynne from the New York establishment, step-daughter of popular lawyer and judge Paul Williams, later a denizen of Palm Beach.

I never got an exact account how he made his fortune. His most frequent tale involved Iran. Boeing had many new and used 707s for sale, but did not want the political stigma of dealing directly with the Shah's repressive regime. Henryk put his company in the middle, buying from Boeing and selling to the Iranian generals; whether he had befriended the Shah over a backgammon table remained pure myth. He took a very generous dealer's cut, as it was by no means a risk-free business. He told me of spending tense hours at Nassau airport waiting for the 707s to land, so that title could pass under Bahamian law, not subject to American taxes. He had already borrowed heavily to finance the purchase, and he was never certain that he would be paid by the devious Iranians until he got a wire from Chase Bank confirming receipt of funds. His nerves were so high-strung that he nearly fired a young lawyer who rushed in to report a glitch: the airport's Coke machine had run out.

Similar deals were set up to sell aircraft to the Argentine government, and doubtless many others. By the time I met him, he had made his pile; it was now time to spend it. And spend he did—lavishly, flamboyantly. First there were the homes (and the staff for round-the clock service): Serendip Cove, with its main house of five bedrooms and a beach cottage of four more; the duplex in Manhattan's river-view Beekman Place, with a ration of Degas and Renoir originals; the forty-acre estate in Greenwich's Conyers Farm including a cut-stone manor house and dozen-stall stable; an apartment and stables at Wellington, the polo center inland from Palm Beach. He travelled restlessly between them, although he was meticulous about not spending more than 90 tax-free days annually in the United Sates. When he once gave me a lift on his private jet (owned or leased, I never asked), the pilot logged our Florida touch-down just after midnight in order to save a day.

And we all heard about his fascination with thorough-bred racing, with advice from famous trainer Woody Stephens. He owned the Belmont Stakes winner Conquistador Cielo, and the non-starter Danzig Connection, who nevertheless made Henryk a small fortune in record-breaking stud fees and syndication. When Kentucky's famous breeding base Calumet Farms fell on hard times and had to be sold at auction in 1992, Henryk was the mystery buyer who flew in from Nassau and picked it up for a bargain $17 million. The event was covered by half a dozen TV stations. Henryk bought all their tapes and stitched them together into a program always on display at his giant screen in Nassau. Every visitor was given a drink and dragooned into watching. It was a celebration of hubris that I saw more than once.

Flat-racing led to polo, "The Sport of Kings", a ruinously expensive undertaking at the levels to which Henryk aspired. For the summer matches in England, November's Argentine

Open in Buenos Aires, and the winter season championships at Wellington, every team of four riders usually had a ranking of at least six goals, under the international system that gives each registered player a ranking from minus2 to the rarely achieved plus10. Except for a few wealthy amateurs, these players were paid professionals, lean young Argentines who had been mounted since age six on the grassy *estancias* forming the world's leading incubator of polo expertise. And every player at this level must have four to six top ponies on hand to rotate between the eight seven-minute chukkas of each game.

Henryk hired a revolving group of these Argentine pros, ranked plus5 to plus8, to play three positions on his Kennelot team, while he, at a lowly minus1, took the fourth. This skewed arrangement led to few victories, but Henryk always wanted to be on the field, willing to take the risks of his own feeble efforts among the high-paced play of the dashing Argentines. He became a popular figure in the polo world. Once at Wellington I saw him almost by accident strike a ball between the goalposts, winning a point for his team. The spectators rose to applaud this singular success, and Henryk, as surprised as anyone, doffed his helmet to the crowd.

He loved the whole macho polo routine of donning leather boots and knee pads, buckling on helmet, grasping mallet and crop, mounting a chosen pony, and trotting onto the field with his Argentine teammates. At the Guards Polo Club, just outside Windsor Castle, he was in his element, hob-nobbing with Prince Charles, another devoted player, and occasionally invited to bow and shake hands with the Queen. His summer pilgrimages to England were handled in typical fashion, by renting a suite, or sometimes the entire penthouse, of Claridge's in London. There was no snobbery in his style; I once joined him in a country pub to celebrate with a mixed band of English blue-bloods, Argentine cavaliers, and tough stable lads and girls.

Henryk was never one to keep his exuberant expenditures quiet. That did not lead to universal popularity within the closed world of the Lyford Cay Club community. A conservative Old Guard group regarded him as a boastful vulgarian with a shady past. At one dinner party an elderly heiress excoriated him for creating fiction about his exploits with the RAF: "He's a liar; I know he never served." After several tedious repetitions, I had to say, "Madam, he has done much more with his life than you have." A silence fell over the table, until the hostess cheerfully agreed with me.

By the time we met, he and Lynne had divorced, amicably it appeared, leaving him with six children, two boys and four girls, just entering maturity and being educated abroad. He had begun a long and enduring romance with a glamorous lady named Barbara Allen. The name meant nothing to me, but I later learned that she had been an active player in the New York scene surrounding Andy Warhol, a knock-out beauty who had inspired Mick Jagger to leap through a bedroom window (the wrong one) to seek her affections. By her own account she was swept off her feet by Henryk's dynamic charm when he landed by helicopter on a friend's lawn.

As soon as they married (after having given birth to a son, Nicholas), Henryk faced the Lyford Cay rule that a new wife had to pass the same membership scrutiny as her husband. He asked me to write the required sponsor's letter. By then, I had seen them often—at Nicholas' christening party, at polo events, at quiet dinners for just the three of us, where Barbara listened while Henryk elaborated on the state of the world. I wrote a letter confirming that they were a devoted, home-loving couple; the membership committee soon approved her.

One winter morning in 1996, Henryk settled me in a corner overlooking the sunlit snow of Conyers Farm and quietly handed me a long document. I was astounded. It was a legal brief claiming some $250 million from the high-powered investment bankers Bear Stearns & Co. They had, it alleged, lost this amount by unauthorized trading in currency futures for his account. He would say nothing until, he confidently predicted, he would win the legal battle. He was right, initially.

The New York Supreme Court found in his favor, awarding him some $164 million in damages, a victory widely publicized by Henryk to the consternation of the Wall Street brokerage community. Happiness was short. Within six months, the Court of Appeals reversed. Henryk had to swallow the debacle, but he never spoke about it. He was the Man Who Never Lost.

In fact, I saw no change in his life style, except abandonment of polo at Barbara's insistence after he cracked a rib in a collision with an Argentine. The fortune was large enough to lose a couple of hundred million without anguish. Risk was part of his life. Intense high-stakes black-jack continued at Nassau's Atlantis casino, usually playing four hands simultaneously at a reserved table. One night he quietly confirmed winning $250,000, although there must have been losing nights, never mentioned. After an initial trip to his birth place, Poznan, where he returned as the Prodigal Son and was given the symbolic keys to the city, he made substantial contributions to Lech Walesa's Solidarity party that led Poland out of the communist grip.

His energy seemed unabated until he asked me to drop by one afternoon at Serendip Cove early in 2003. For the first time I saw him waxen-faced and exhausted, in a blue blazer as always, but breathing hard to give orders to the Calumet manager who had flown in from Kentucky. There was no offer of the usual martini. A few days later I had to leave on a business trip. When I returned he was dead, the funeral already held. Barbara, tear-streaked, embraced me at Serendip's front-door. She told me she had arranged his burial in the cemetery of St. Augustine's Monastery, on a Nassau hill-top where a few monks still served.

Serendip, owned by a trust for her and the children, is still immaculate, but she rarely visits. Conyers Farm is gone, sold for $50 million. She lives in the Beekman Place duplex, alone but for visits from son Nicholas, now stunningly handsome at age 25. One recent night she invited me for dinner and we played backgammon. We had a lively match, dredging up a few memories with tears and laughter, but I was no substitute for Henryk.

Dick's Granddaughters, Emily and Daisy, Bahamas, 2012

Time to Go Home! Dick's daughters Diana and Amanda, Bahamas, 1971

Chapter 18

Bahamas Finale

I was blessed with unexpected good fortune just two years after my Nassau return. I accepted a dinner invitation from a banker friend, and there met Rosemary, a Bahamian lady with whom I am still talking almost daily, sharing our deepest thoughts for over 30 years. Having lived in England for a decade, she remains an inveterate traveler, always happy to explore with me. After finding her own spiritual life in Christianity, Rosemary never preached to me about religion, but one night, like any other, I woke to find myself standing at bedside giving an oration, a full-blooded sermon about the nature of the Trinity, using words and concepts that until then were foreign to me. Next morning I was able to recall and write down my words. I have kept the manuscript, to prove that I was not simply dreaming,

Epiphany

I have no rational explanation for this epiphany. It reflected nothing in my past. I had always called myself nominally a Christian, but it was a meaningless term as Christian doctrine was of little interest to me and I was not a church-goer. I could not have even named the four synoptic gospels of the New Testament. St. John—who was he?

And yet from that day forward, I believed. At first, I didn't know exactly *what* I believed, so I began to educate myself, reading not only the Bible but seeking books of theology, apologetics, and church history. I never called myself a "Born-Again" Evangelical Christian, and still do not. Nevertheless, I became firm enough in my views so that when asked by agnostic or atheistic friends, "Dick, do you *really* believe in God?", I am able to say simply, "Yes, I do." I no longer try to provide non-believers with rational arguments why they should adopt Christianity. Belief derives from faith, not from rational analysis, and faith seems to descend without rhyme or reason, just as it did on me that night, or on Paul on the road to Damascus in the first Christian century.

Or on the Emperor Constantine three centuries later. His own epiphany came in 312 AD, as he was leading an army to conquer Rome. He looked to the sky and saw the Chi-Ro symbol, with a message that he should affix it to his army's shields to achieve victory. He did so and won the decisive battle of the Milvian Bridge. Suddenly a believer, he called a conclave of bishops in 325 AD, in the town of Nicaea, renamed Iznik by the Turks. A forceful leader, he was determined to end the interminable bickering on picayune points of doctrine, and kept the 300 prelates hard at work until they adopted the formula known as our famous Nicene Creed.

On a business trip to Istanbul, I discovered that Iznik was just a three-hour drive across the Bosporus. I rented a car with guide and found the peaceful little town, surrounded by golden wheat fields, a grid of streets on the edge of a sunlit blue lake. The guide pointed down to stone pillars visible under the surface, which, he claimed, were the foundations of the very palace where the conclave was held, later destroyed by fire. Who was I to doubt? By Constantine's edict, Christianity had abruptly become the one true faith of the Empire, adhering to the formula: "I believe in one God, the Father Almighty . . ."

Constantine's epiphany changed the western world; mine might at least change me.

Family Shifts

I arranged for my daughters to become Bahamian citizens so that they could sink deeper roots if they wished. On my trips to Europe I always took time to observe their evolving lives. Diana remained single, becoming a senior advertising director in London and Paris, then a free-lance marketing consultant making a dizzying round of world-wide travels. Amanda, after a couple of false starts, married a superlative German, owner of a Frankfurt art gallery, and followed her instincts to become an arts entrepreneur.

And of course I stopped in London for dinners with Edie, who never remarried. I was glad to see that she continued an active existence, always at work on a book when not playing with an energetic group of ladies who loved tennis. It was painful to see cancer eventually take its toll and curtail her energy. We all made hospital visits to express good cheer while knowing that, despite periods of remission, the end was certain. One March evening in 2003 I got a call from Amanda with the choked message. "I spoke to the doctor. This time she won't recover. It's weeks, not months; you need to come over."

I took the next flight and found Edie sitting on the sunny terrace of her flat, alert as ever, but with the sunken-eyed pallor common to cancer victims and her glorious tawny locks shorn and replaced with a turban. That night she was her usual practical self, chiding me for using the fancy guest dinner plates rather than the kitchen ones. She was able to hold her first grandchild, Amanda's daughter born only weeks earlier, but then the decline was rapid. She had already contributed to a hospice, and the transfer was easily arranged. It was a beautiful place to spend one's final days, facing a park with trees just in their spring budding, decorated in soothing pastel colors with music softly playing. But that did not ease the anguish of seeing her lying pale and almost wordless, whispering for a speedy end.

Visiting hours over, a nurse gently ushered us out into the gardens. Diana and I could not help clinging to each other as she wept, "Isn't it awful to see Mummy like that?" It was indeed. I feel sure the hospice staff quietly took measures to advance Edie's demise, as she wished. A week later I attended her private cremation, and a month after that my daughters arranged a glorious celebration of her life, with friends and family sitting on the courts of her tennis club. Edie had always been a committed atheist, leaving instructions that religion should play no part in her obsequies.

I later re-read a letter she had sent me a few years before her death. She had written; "I only wish I had been able to deny or conquer my stubborn passion for independence that dominated my young life. It doesn't seem all that alluring now." I could not avoid speculating "what if?" What if she had wanted to continue our marriage? What if family unity had kept me in London? What if I had continued my career there? Would I now be richer or poorer, happier or gloomier, wiser or denser? What if I had never left my cocooned lawyer's life in New York

Life is full of "what ifs", and it's fruitless to speculate too long. The untaken fork in the road will always remain a mystery. One can only accept and enjoy the cards that have been dealt. I came to Nassau in 1980, and years later in 2011 Amanda followed my footsteps to leave Germany and start a new life here. She and her husband found a sea-front town house near our best school, and brought their two daughters Emily and Daisy, who plunged cheerfully into a new gang of kids.

She also brought family scrap-books that had been meticulously up-dated by Edie until her final illness, Thumbing through the crackling pages, I stopped at a snap of Diana and Amanda, taken in 1971 when they were aged eight and five. We were on holiday from New York, and the photo showed our daughters trudging up a sandy path at end-of-day retreat from a Bahamas beach. Edie had written a caption for the photo: "Time to go home." The simple words hit me with a moment of intense nostalgia over long-dead memories. But then it came to me how lucky I was to have two granddaughters of virtually the same ages, whom I can now see frolicking on a Nassau beach at their front door, throwing a tennis ball to be caught by Bunny, the family Labrador.

Amanda was chosen as the Director of our National Art Gallery, a handsomely restored colonial building where she toils every day, and many nights. I hear on all sides that her efforts have sparked a renaissance of the Gallery and of our Bahamian cultural scene. That was not the initial objective of my move to Nassau, but the unforeseen result is gratifying. In my semi-retired state, I am happy to be identified now merely as "Oh, he's Amanda's Dad!"

Appendix

Sailing with Bill

One Friday in 1994, the New York Times weather forecast did not waffle. No uncertainties of "Possible showers—sunny patches." This time, uncompromising gloom: "Temperature mid-50s, cooler near the shore, rain this afternoon, turning heavy tonight, with thunderstorms. Winds southeast, 20-30 knots; seas Long Island Sound, five to seven feet.—small craft warnings." In mid-morning I peered out from a Manhattan tower; windy grey clouds were already gathering.

I had been invited by Bill Buckley to join a Friday night cruise on his 36-foot sloop *Patito*, an event graven in stone on his weekly schedule; meeting time 6:30 p.m. at his Stamford home; prompt departure from marina, course then set for one of two harbors on the Long Island shore; when reached, dinner was served, early retirement decreed; and the mooring dropped at 7:00 a.m. sharp on Saturday for the return passage.

Knowing many sailing faint-hearts I called his ever vigilant assistant Frances Bronson. Was there, I enquired hopefully, a chance that tonight's cruise would be cancelled? A pause ensued; I sensed shock and disapproval over the silent line. Came the response, "Bill *never* cancels a sail merely because of *weather*. I suggest you be there."

I was. Driving up to Stamford through strengthening rain-squalls, I realized that my call had been misconceived. Bill loved to sail; it's as simple as that. More: while not courting trouble (that would be unseamanlike), at its prospect a wild light flashed in Bill's eyes with an excitement akin to skewering a muddled liberal on *Firing Line*. His four books about sea-borne adventures attest to his zest in adversity. Possibly his readers do not take him at face value—as a dedicated intellectual, in the teeth of marine crises did he perhaps become like Hamlet "sicklied o'er with the pale cast of thought" and descend to his cabin leaving hard decisions to horny-handed crewmembers?

Not at all. I had my own memories of Bill's resilience. Some years earlier, we were both aboard an elegant pre-war sailing yacht that began to disintegrate on the Aegean's wine-dark seas. Bill, though not quite Ulysses' age as idealized by Tennyson, nevertheless showed his zeal to "smite the sounding furrows." We were sailing past the southern shore of Mykonos in a late afternoon of brilliant sun and a gradually increasing wind from the south. Our graceful vessel, a twelve-meter Camper & Nicholson design, all teak and mahogany, had been lent to us by Bill's friend Taki. Although beautiful, she had suffered a decadent life of long periods tied up at a Piraeus marina with occasional cocktail outings around the Saronic Gulf.

This afternoon, traveling at an impressive nine knots, her starboard rail began to bury itself and unhappy creaks and groans were heard, then suddenly a ripping sound like clawing open a wooden crate. The bronze track, holding the jib-sheet to the deck, pulled its bolts up through the timbers and became a threatening flail. We dropped the jib and set a small staysail in its place. The speed and angle of heel became more sedate, but the full mainsail seemed excessive in the rising wind. We exchanged words about taking a reef; at that moment our work was done for us. The entire sail and heavy boom crashed to the deck, trailing three feet of wire halyard showing where it had neatly frayed through at the masthead sheave.

No matter: start the engine, a massive diesel that emitted clouds of smoke on firing, an event that could only be invoked by the Greek seaman of little English assigned to us as Taki's "expert". The engine was his secret and his few explanations were fittingly Delphic in their obscurity. This time his magic failed him. A few coughing revolutions were followed by silence. Our Greek retired to the farthest point of the stern and appeared to become lost in prayer.

So we had only a staysail which barely gave us headway, and thirty knots of breeze pushing us inexorably to leeward towards an unforgiving rocky cliff fringed with breaking surf. A promontory ahead and another astern put us in the classic position of being "embayed." Literary memories came to mind of Captain Horatio Hornblower maneuvering his unhandy ship-of-the-line in Mediterranean gales. He had always wriggled out; would we?

A quick scan of the horizon spotted potential rescue approaching from seawards. The hefty powerboat that had been chartered as our tender, for carrying Mrs. WFB Jr. and the other wives of the cruise, pulled abeam two hundred yards to windward. We lined the rail and waved our arms in the overhead wig-wagging style of sailors in distress. The ladies lined *their* rail and cheerfully waved back. Wine glasses and smiles of encouragement were just visible, but the tender continued its dignified course into the sunset and around the promontory towards Mykonos Port. Some un-spouselike words were heard aboard our vessel. Naturally a classic twelve-meter carried no radio.

No other craft of any type could be seen along this desolate coast. We had drifted further to leeward, towards the line of surf. With ten feet of keel beneath us, grounding was not far off. Even Bill's two long-time crew and stalwart fellow Skull & Bonesmen, Van Galbraith and Bill Draper, looked, shall we say, bemused.

This was the moment for the Buckley manic smile to appear. Pulling his cap with tarnished braid down over his ears, his shorts as usual low over his knees, he left the helm to Draper and came forward for consultation. The staysail, we decided, was not going to save us. The main was a dead issue: nobody was climbing to the masthead to reeve a new halyard. We needed the jib. From our combined years of experience coping with ill-found yachts, rusted bolts, shredded rigging, jammed fairleads—all the gamut of marine incompetence—we created from spare lines, blocks and shackles a jury-rig that just *might* serve to hold the tension of a jib-sheet. The jib was cautiously hoisted, strain was slowly taken on the sheet winch. Cautious not to trim too hard, we left half the jib luffing; the half that drew was just enough to get us underway, and miraculously let us set a course slightly to windward, about what Captain Hornblower's square-rigger could have achieved. Bill took the wheel again and for nearly an hour practiced the delicate art of sailing to windward without mainsail, carefully tacking to avoid being caught in irons and driven astern. The surf-line slowly receded. We rounded the point and reached off to Mykonos Port, where a rapacious Greek trawler skipper took us in tow (for a "salvage" fee that required two days of bargaining by Bill and legal advisor Van). Bill vented a few harsh thoughts to wives and the captain of the tender about abandonment at sea, but his consumption of wine and cigarillos that night revealed a figure once again mellowed by adventure.

At least it had been warm in the Aegean in 1978. As I left my car in the Buckley shore-front compound that Friday afternoon years later, chill damp air blew in from Long Island Sound, barely visible through the grey murk. Inside the house I joined Bill and our two other shipmates, Tony and Danny, fit men young in years but old in knowledge of Bill's nautical pursuits, changing from shore clothes into foul-weather gear. Pat Buckley surveyed us all with sardonic eye, serving us, as condemned men's last meal, a marvelous claret with toasted cheese brioches. Sunk into the library's softest chair, I stared at the mist flowing against the picture windows and thought how civilized would be a dinner party right here amidst polished walnut and candle-light, created by the resident and excellent chef.

The reverie passed as we set out for the marina. An omen this Friday evening—*Patito* was the only vessel preparing to go to sea. We cast off and motored through the narrow channel into Stamford Harbor, towards the breakwaters sheltering it from the open Sound. No other yacht stirred. I wondered what might be the questions of the harbor patrol observing this solitary disappearance into the windy, drizzling, darkening fog.

As we cleared the breakwaters, the mainsail was hoisted, the roller-jib unwound, we took a heel to starboard in the southeast breeze, and soon Connecticut vanished into the gloom astern. With five-foot seas making even the narrow Sound a bouncy ride, with chill, with damp from fog and spray, with all shore lights blotted out, one felt more attuned to the North Sea than to the busy streets of Manhattan only thirty miles away.

I had never before relied on electronics in a routine six-mile crossing of the Sound, but they were Bill's hobby, and soon we had two radar screens displaying their flickering patterns, with Satnav and Loran on standby. I tried to master the buttons and dials that adjusted range, bearing and focus, following staccato instructions from the hooded figure at the helm. Eventually I turned the job over to Tony, Bill's trusted acolyte on all electronic subjects, and took the passive role of watching the screen guide us flawlessly into Oyster Bay, where the bulk of Lloyds Neck and Cove Neck loomed up just where expected.

As we reached into the anchorage off Centre Island, the weather took one further turn from bad to dreadful. The wind rose to vicious gusts of 35 knots, and the misty drizzle became a solid downpour with raindrop pellets driven horizontally into any face foolish enough to look to windward. Three of the four of us wore glasses, and were more or less blinded; I suffered another sensory loss as the rain penetrated my hood and shorted out my hearing aid, leaving me deaf to all but the most desperately shouted commands.

Bill managed to turn *Patito* into the wind amidst the clatter of flogging sails, the main was dropped, the jib furled, and— barely missing several anchored yachts in the feeble beam of a spotlight—we picked up a guest mooring off the Seawanhaka Corinthian Yacht Club, whose glowing dining room could be glimpsed dimly through the frigid rainfall. Abandoning topside to the elements, we fell below to shed soaking gear and create a gently steaming mass of sodden clothes: the joy of cozy cabins on small sailing yachts! Bill's first action was a radio-telephone call to check in at home: "Pat? Yes, we had a marvelous sail . . . What? Would you have liked it? No, dear, you wouldn't have liked it at all . . . but we had a wonderful time,"—eyeing the three of us, who nodded dutifully as we got deep into our first whiskey gripped with thawing fingers.

From the confines of the small galley Danny produced a pre-planned dinner of haute cuisine standards accompanied by a smooth claret from the Buckley cellars. Conversation revolved around other sailing exploits, but it wasn't long before fatigue set in. The owner retreated to his stateroom port-side aft, while we three crew disposed ourselves on the main cabin's berths, reserving choice positions for our slowly drying clothes.

After waking at first light on Saturday, I climbed to the cockpit and found the prospect mixed. The wind had dropped away to a whisper, but a solid grey fog and fine drizzle persisted. Even Bill's hardy constitution rebelled at the usual morning swim. On schedule at seven, the mooring was cast off, and we motored out of Oyster Bay, sails barely drawing, radar guiding us once again. Breakfast was produced, but, being only a minor chord in the symphony of Bill's diet, the production was modest—to call it "continental" would be stretching the word. Instant coffee was fortified with several rounds of crackers coated with peanut-butter, but not just *any* peanut-butter. The label showed we were consuming private brand "William F. Buckley" peanut-butter, produced by an obscure firm in the Catskills owned by one of Bill's entrepreneurial friends. Despite the name, I have been unable to find it in supermarkets even in conservative constituencies; too bad, since it was a tasty durable spread, impervious to drops of moisture dripping off the main-boom that morning. I speculated that the peanut butter label may endure even longer than Bill's books.

As we left the invisible Lloyd's Neck to starboard and entered the open Sound, the radar paid its way by warning us of a tug with a long tow of barges heading down-Sound. We veered to port, and passed close under the stern of the final barge leaving a turbulent wake behind its square, ungainly sections. By the time we reached mid-Sound, the fog lifted under a warming sun, and a sailing breeze sprang up to raise our dampened spirits. When we closed the Stamford breakwaters at the end of our little cruise, the whole Sound gave a clear and sparkling invitation to fair-weather Saturday yachtsmen. Well, more joy to them; *we* had braved the elements, and were making port as crusty old salts who could spare a superior smile and wave to the day-sailors.

Bill wasted not a minute in leading us off the dock to enjoy a soufflé and Riesling lunch in the Buckleys' sunlit, dry and spacious dining room. Land could be tolerated too. And Bill had an afternoon of writing ahead of him, as usual.

Made in the USA
Middletown, DE
12 March 2020